To Michelle
may you have
many years of satisfying
writing!
Gail

The Button Field

A Novel

Gail Husch

Gail Husch

Barley Mill Press

To Michael

Barley Mill Press
ISBN: 0615965008
ISBN 13: 9780615965000

www.gailhusch.com

BERTHA LANE MELLISH.

Preface

Excellent novelist that she is, Gail Husch is also an art historian, and *The Button Field* begins with her contemplation of an image, albeit an uncertain, cloudy one: a portrait of Bertha Mellish, who vanished from Mount Holyoke College at the end of the nineteenth century.

From a scanty historical record, Husch has reconstructed the world of Bertha Mellish; a project something like a paleontologist's rebuilding a whole dinosaur from inferences about a handful of scattered bones. Husch breathes new life into Bertha's mother and father, her sister Florence, her teachers and friends at Mount Holyoke and elsewhere—and finally into the girl herself. She brings Bertha back to us.

In this meticulous recreation of the turn of the century society where Bertha Mellish tried to find her path, Husch unveils the opportunities Bertha would have found open to her, as well as the limitations and frustrations that a young woman of her gifts and character would inevitably have faced. Most so-called historical fiction does little more than place modern personalities in period costume. Combining impeccable research with unusual insight, Husch has achieved something better than that, endowing her characters and her heroine with sensibilities true to their time. She shows us what a challenge it must have been for an intelligent, feeling young woman like Bertha to win self-realization in the world she was given to inhabit.

Still, *The Button Field* is more than a vivid and accurate representation of another time and place. Bertha's vanished world reflects our own; she reappears to tell us something about the way our lives are lived, by comparison to hers. In the end, the author's inquiring eye is twinned with the eye of the reader. We see that the mystery of Bertha Mellish's disappearance cannot be solved, unless it will yield to the imagination.

–Madison Smartt Bell

I imagined her about five feet eight inches tall. I had two newspaper engravings of her. One gives her a piggy, upturned nose, but in the other she has a pleasant face with full cheeks and a slight smile. She was going to have curly hair, probably because I like the way mine spirals now that I've let it grow. She had a lot of coiled up energy—her thick hair ready to explode out of its bun.

When I finally do find a photograph, I decide that I will give up the curly hair. Bertha's is straight and pulled taut against her head. Her lower lip is pouty and her exposed ear curls over in a strange, elfin way.

And she wasn't going to kill herself. That seemed too dramatic, reaching for effect. No dark urges driving her towards death. Just a healthy, adventurous girl of the late nineteenth century, out walking too late on a wet and cold November afternoon. Nobody in the story would be sure that it was an accident, or even that she was in the river. Rumors would fly around the campus, some people would whisper about suicide, her poor family would be baffled and hope that she had simply run away.

Thirty years ago, I worked as curator of a small art collection in the Holyoke Public Library, legacy of the city's glory years when it still made cloth and paper. Sometimes during breaks I would look through dusty volumes of articles clipped from a patchwork of local newspapers—the *Holyoke Transcript*, the *Northampton Daily Herald*, the *Bellows Falls Times*, the *Hampshire Gazette*, the *Springfield Republican*. Many of the articles were about notable local people and ordinary things like weddings and anniversaries. But a large number—maybe the majority—had to do with odd, macabre and often grisly events.

A case of slander brought by one young lady against another. A wife accused of palming off a foundling as a legitimate child. A doctor charged with performing criminal operations on women. A young boy choked to death on a peanut. A well-known businessman struck down and killed by a speeding bicycle. A young woman dead of a self-inflicted bullet wound from a .22-caliber Smith & Wesson revolver. An entire family hacked to death by their ax-wielding hired man. Miss Bertha Lane Mellish, missing from Mount Holyoke College.

It was Bertha's mystery that intrigued me. I know that Bertha had a sister, Florence. I know that her father, John Hyrancus Mellish, was a Congregationalist minister. I learn that Florence was twenty years older than Bertha, their parents old enough to be Bertha's grandparents. I can find no mention of children born between the two sisters, but many infants died young then.

Bertha was 5' 5" tall and of medium build. Rather petite, with an attractive face, read one description. She had dark auburn hair, which she wore pulled straight back or parted in the middle, a pale complexion, brown eyes, round cheeks and full lips. She had some freckles on her face and a small, faint scar on her forehead.

The newspapers called her a fine scholar with a studious disposition, well-liked by fellow students and faculty, a particularly venturesome girl who liked to take long walks in the fields and woods. But she was also "somewhat reticent in disposition" and "accustomed to eat alone." She was "a recluse." The mother of this "strange girl now missing," it was said, had been subject to fits of insanity before the girl was born. And, somehow, the paper was able to report that Bertha—a minister's daughter studying at the most evangelical of women's colleges–was recognized as an agnostic.

On a fine day, probably in late September 1895, the freshmen who made up Mount Holyoke's Class of 1899 assembled on the stairs of Williston Hall for their class portrait. In the photograph, the taller ones stand in the rear, in the dark entranceway under the building's central arch, or off to the sides. Some of the smaller girls sit directly on the grass or on the path in front of the building, their skirts tucked and folded around their bent legs. Here and there among the young faces are some past their first bloom, older seminary-trained women come back to earn a college degree.

The photograph has a strangely disjointed look. No one was told to watch the birdie or say cheese. Few of the girls face forward and even fewer look directly into the camera. In no discernable pattern, some turn to the left and look off in that direction, others do the same to the right. Each person has a slightly different focus of attention somewhere beyond the frame of the picture. Two or three look up at the sky. Some mouths are curved as if caught in the act of smiling. One large, pleasant-looking girl is almost laughing; her face is tilted towards her neighbor and her broad cheeks bulge. But most have more serious expressions. They seem conscious of the situation and want to convey a certain dignity, which some pull off better than others. A young lady with heavy eyebrows sits stolid as an Egyptian statue; behind her, a skinny girl in a necktie looks pinched and worried.

Bertha should be in there somewhere, and I am anxious to find her. I search from face to face. Most of the girls and women in the photograph look nothing like Bertha's images. Their faces are the wrong shape, their hair is clearly different, they're too young or too old, too fat, thin or too strikingly pretty.

And then I am sure I have found her. She is on the right in the second to last row at the outer edge of the building's open doorway, leaning against the straight line of its jamb. She is hidden except for her face and neck and one shoulder of a plaid shirtwaist. I see the round cheeks and squarish jaw of the newspaper photograph, as well as the full lower lip that pushes slightly forward and the fleshy chin. It's hard to discern the nose in either image, but both seem to be short, slightly snubbed and rounded at the tip. The hair could be Bertha's dark auburn.

But it is the girl's expression that convinces me. She is one of the few who look directly at me, and she is the only one who presents a challenge with that look. I try to be careful and not read too much into this intense and stony gaze, not exactly angry and not exactly contemptuous.

I will look at you as long as you can bear to look at me, she says, and I will continue to look after you have turned away.

Mount Holyoke College Archives

Part One

Summer and Freshman Year, June - October 1895

Chapter 1

Commencement

When Hattie Darling's mouth went dry, Bertha didn't smile. Nothing in her face, she vowed, would betray her satisfaction. Any other time she might have felt sorry for Hattie, but not today. Her own performance would be–had to be–the best of any delivered by the twelve graduates of Killingly High School's Class of 1895, and she was pleased but not surprised that Hattie posed no threat.

Besides, Hattie Darling didn't need her sympathy. Everyone adored Hattie, sweet and confiding as a child with her plump little mouth and artless smile. Bertha observed Hattie's effect on other people with amused superiority. How foolish they were, to be taken in by such simple-minded charm.

The auditorium was stifling, even with all its windows open. Hattie, after a timid sip of water, spoke clearly now but very low, and her words lost their shape and melted in the heavy air. The audience drowsed or fidgeted in their upholstered seats and some used their programs as fans. Bertha would have done the same, but she was conscious of her place on the stage and kept her hands folded in her lap.

At last, Hattie was done. The audience, Bertha noticed with irritation, roused itself to clap enthusiastically, and several young men whistled their appreciation.

When Charlotte Cogswell rose to take her place at the podium, Bertha felt a knot tighten in her stomach. Charlotte was smart and self-assured, taller than two of the boys in the class, and she spoke and moved with an unaffected ease that Bertha tried to emulate but couldn't. Charlotte sang well, in a strong contralto that some people said was good enough for the concert hall. Sometimes Charlotte laughed with her mouth open, and sometimes when she sat, Bertha could tell that her knees were not together beneath her skirt. Bertha tried that too, a few years ago, sitting in a chair with her feet wide apart, until her mother noticed and frowned a silent reprimand.

She might have grown closer to Charlotte and Hattie, Bertha admitted with a twinge of regret, if she had tried harder. Three years earlier, when she was new to Dayville, the two girls had done everything they could to make her welcome. They walked with her to the high school in Danielson, invited her to picnics and skating parties, complimented the color of her hair. They even called her Bertie.

At first, she believed it might be possible to join them as their equal. She hadn't felt that way with any of the other girls in any of the other places her family lived, a year or two here and there as they followed her father's call from pulpit to pulpit. Yet, kind as they were, Charlotte and Hattie laughed at private jokes. They mentioned absent friends unknown to Bertha, reminded each other of adventures from years ago that Bertha couldn't share. Patient and polite, they slowed their pace for her but the effort to overtake them was exhausting and, over time, Bertha gave it up.

The fashionably inflated sleeves of Charlotte's white dress added volume to her solid figure. The audience leaned forward when she cleared her throat.

"The American girl of today," Charlotte began in a clear and confident voice, "leads in all things, and is self-reliant to a degree that was unknown by her grandmothers."

A simple enough argument, Bertha thought, and released the breath she unconsciously held. The knot in her stomach loosened. She could speak in public as well as Charlotte–she'd done it before, in church and at school– and the subject of her essay was more impressive. Bertha unclasped her hands and pressed them against the reassuring surface of the pages that rested in her lap. She knew every word on them by heart.

Bertha shifted her gaze from the back of Charlotte's head to the audience, avoiding the place, five or six rows back, where she knew her family sat. Below her were the people she called—that her father and sister called— friends and neighbors, all of them come to watch the exercises out of curiosity or obligation and to inspect and pass judgment on the graduates and on each other. Most had no more education than a few terms in a one-room schoolhouse, most had no thought in their heads but their next meal, or how many eggs their hens would lay, or how many yards of woolen cassimire the mills would produce next week, or which girl was marrying which boy, or who was sick and who had died.

A few short weeks and none of them would matter.

The realization, so obvious once it struck, came to her without warning and when it did, Bertha had to bite her lip to keep from laughing. How absurd, that she had ever cared what they thought of her, these ignorant people with their blinkered lives and their small concerns. In a few short weeks, a new life would begin, in a place where everything was possible. No disappointments would follow her there; she would be reborn, a butterfly released from its chrysalis, a winged creature ready to fly.

Although the graduates were not her students, Florence listened closely to every speaker and clapped appreciatively when each was done. As a teacher, it was Florence's duty to encourage all young people without favoritism or prejudice. But it was hard not to look at Bertha, seated on the far left of the stage between Charlotte Cogswell's now-empty chair and a large potted fern.

She seemed so serious and self-assured, brilliant in her new white dress with her shiny hair pulled back, but still so young, too young to go off by herself to live among strangers. Florence glanced at her sister and felt a lump of pride and regret catch in her throat.

When she was a girl, before and then after Bertha was born, Florence watched those around her—no better, often worse—reap rewards that, for reasons she could not understand, were denied her. The mirror told her she wasn't beautiful, but neither was she ugly and other girls, plainer girls, had young men courting them. Still, when Bertha was a baby, Florence sat with her in a rocking chair and imagined the day when she would have a child she could call her own.

She'd tried picturing a husband, but could form no clear image in her mind. Sometimes the man resembled a young minister who had twice filled her father's pulpit, sometimes he looked like the visiting brother of a friend, met in passing one summer afternoon. When she reached twenty-five, she stopped imagining. She already had Bertha; that would be enough.

Now Florence remembered the first time she held her sister, on the night that she was born. While their mother slept pale as death in the lamplight, the midwife placed the swaddled infant in the cradle of Florence's arms. She'd stared at the strange little creature with its eyes squeezed tight as a newborn kitten's, and realized what a treacherous place the world truly was.

Over the years, there had been so many dangers to anticipate and avoid. The little objects that a baby, crawling on the floor, poking into receptacles and under chairs, could find and put into her mouth, bits and scraps of things, pebbles, buttons, then, as Bertha got older, foods that could choke her, chunks of bread and meat, fishbones, peppermints. Fire, of course, from candles, lamps, fireplaces, stoves, and also high places—chairs, tabletops, second story windows–and water, in tubs, in wells, in ponds, in rivers, and always, of course, fevers, coughs, agues, poxes, fluxes, diseases too many to name. There was whooping cough and measles, and that terrible day when Bertha was two and fell and hit her head against the stove. With God's help, though, Florence managed to deliver her sister out of childhood.

Florence pursed her lips and blinked hard. It would be weeks before Bertha was to leave, she reminded herself, and she must not let that approaching shadow darken the day. She sighed, too softly for either her mother on one side or her father on the other to hear, and turned her attention once again to Charlotte, who was ending her speech with a stirring call to the young women of America.

With the audience still applauding, Principal Hibbard motioned Bertha, the last speaker on the program, to come forward. Florence thought Bertha might glance in her direction, to take courage from her familiar face, but she stared straight ahead. Florence worried that some of those watching might see arrogance in Bertha's raised chin. Her eyebrows were dark against her pale skin, and made her seem severe. Florence was proud of Bertha's determination, but wished, for her own sake, that she looked a little more endearingly awkward, a little softer.

By the time Bertha reached the podium and laid the pages of her speech on its sloping surface, the audience had grown quiet. Except for a stifled cough here and there, the tiny squeak of a hinged seat, and the whisper of a program fanning the air, the room was still.

"The bust outlasts the throne," she began. "Art and poetry are eternal; earthly power fades."

Bertha believed in those words, borrowed from a well-known poet and practiced for weeks in the woods behind her house. The walls of the tiny Mellish home were hung with framed prints of well-known paintings and monuments; volumes of Greek and Latin poetry sat in its shelves and on its parlor table. Bertha had grown up with those books; long before she could decipher them herself, her father or her sister read them aloud, and they explained what the strange people in those pictures were doing, and described who had built those monuments so long ago and why.

Bertha never doubted that, someday, she would go to Athens and to Rome to touch the weathered marble of the Parthenon and the Colosseum and experience the electric spark of genius they surely must contain. And someday she hoped to leave some small thing– not like Virgil, of course, or Michelangelo or Phidias—but something, a poem, perhaps, or a story, to mark her own place in history, like a stone, a pebble even, immovable in the rushing current of time.

Soon Bertha was pleased how smoothly her voice flowed. She looked up from the podium and let the faces of the audience come into focus. Here and there she saw a head fall forward before snapping sharply up. She saw her father leaning towards her in rapt attention, lips parted. Florence was next to him, smiling and nodding. Then her mother, dabbing a handkerchief to her forehead.

Bertha felt a bead of sweat trickle towards her own eye. She was conscious of herself alone on the stage. The easy rhythm of her words broke. She stumbled over the next few sentences and let the audience blur.

Behind her, Bertha heard Mr. Hibbard cough. Aware of the low murmur of impatient rustles and sighs, she tried to measure her words. She knew she was a trial to be endured, the last obstacle before fresh air and supper.

Bertha walked back to her seat in confusion, forgetting to acknowledge the applause. She could tell, however, that it was not as loud as it had been for Charlotte, or even for Hattie, and that it ended long before Mr. Hibbard thanked the ladies and gentlemen in attendance and the chorus of schoolchildren began a farewell hymn.

Chapter 2

Departure

Sarah Mellish slept in an easy chair in the darkened bedroom, her head lolling to one side. A book lay open on her lap and a small hand mirror rested glass-side down on a table to her left. At sixty-six, Sarah bore traces of her former beauty but now considered examining her reflection a stern duty. With bitter pleasure she tabulated every fold and wrinkle, allowing herself such voluptuous self-loathing only in the strictest privacy. She had finished the task some time ago, before turning first to her book and then to sleep.

Sarah was not bedridden, but over the years various digestive and other, vaguer symptoms kept her at home and, most of the time, in her room. She refused to leave the house without corseting, which only aggravated the headaches, irregular heartbeats, and spells of dizziness that came upon her suddenly. She dreaded the thought of an episode in public. Bertha's graduation, more than two months past, was the last time she'd endured such an ordeal. Driven by the significance of the event, she changed her wrapper for her black silk and made Florence lace up her stays as tightly as she could bear. Through force of will, she did not collapse until safely home and Dr. Hammond could be summoned.

The tremor of footsteps on the stairs woke her and for some seconds all she heard was the startled beating of her own heart. Sarah closed her eyes again and waited. The flutter in her chest disturbed her, and she placed a hand above it, as if to calm its rhythm. She had a vision then, a vivid picture of her heart, small as a chicken's, brown as dried blood, bitter as wormwood. She dropped her hand and opened her eyes, anxious for the visitor to arrive and drive the picture away.

The footsteps could not belong to Florence—she must still be on her rounds, making polite calls on silly women——or to her husband—tiresome Dr. Hill was visiting and the murmur of men's voices was audible from the parlor below. They must be Bertha's, then, and Sarah prepared for a visit from her younger daughter. She had determined weeks ago not to spoil Bertha's leave-taking with sentiment. This was an occasion for pride, not tears. Besides, she still had Florence. One to keep at home, one to send into the world. It was, she had come to believe, a natural balance, however precarious, and a sacrifice God always intended her to make.

In the twenty barren years between her first and second daughters, Sarah often considered which of her sins required such punishment. Pride, she finally decided. She thought too much of her looks. She was ashamed of her pinched upbringing in a raw Massachusetts hamlet. Her marriage to John Mellish saved her from the purgatory of school-teaching but bound her to a life of shabby gentility and frequent moves. Sarah was often irritable with her good-natured husband, arrogant with his parishioners and too severe with Florence. She dreamed of life in Boston or Providence. She tried, but could not become a model minister's wife. At last, Sarah decided if God didn't think she deserved more children, so be it. She was who she was.

When, at the age of forty-eight, she found herself pregnant, she could not bear the smirks she imagined would follow her and so did not leave the house. She was sure the process would come to a premature and bloody end.

Then God gave her Bertha, perfect and plump. The child's safe arrival was a greater and more frightening mystery to Sarah than all the years of disappointment. When John solemnly reminded his wife that her biblical namesake bore Isaac at the age of ninety, Sarah stared at him in horror. She could barely bring herself to touch the precious infant and left almost every aspect of her care to Florence, who resigned her teaching position to come home. At the time, Sarah saw the raised eyebrows and knew there was speculation, although no rumor ever took hold. She realized that the young men of the area, rarely seeing Florence without the child, ceased to think of her as a potential bride. But their indifference did not seem to concern her daughter, and Sarah knew that Florence would be with her always.

And now, she had to admit, it would be something of a relief to have Bertha gone. In these last few weeks her moody presence filled the house like a cloud. Florence would be less distracted, John would stop acting so forlorn, once Bertha was settled at the college.

She picked up the book from her lap and held it as if she were reading, anticipating Bertha's arrival at her door. She made out the faint sound of breathing and the rustle of fabric.

"Bertha!" she called. There was silence, then a reluctant shuffle.

"Come in, Bertha," Sarah said. Her voice was firm. She wanted Bertha to know her little game of hide-and-seek had been found out. But there was a plaintive note in her command; Sarah heard it and she was sure Bertha did too.

The doorknob turned and, reluctantly, the door swung open. An oblique triangle of light preceded Bertha into the room. She had a sullen look on her face, a dark-browed hardness that Sarah could not abide.

"Have you come to brighten my day, then?" Sarah asked, shielding her eyes with the back of her hand.

Bertha pursed her lips and sighed, as if it were all too much to bear. She ignored the question and her mother, staring instead at the canopied four-poster that filled the space like a docked ship.

"Dr. Hill is here," Bertha finally said. "Do you want to visit with him?"

She spoke softly. The parlor was directly under the front bedroom and sound carried easily down the short flight of stairs.

Dr. Hill was not Sarah's physician; she relied on the younger and more sympathetic Dr. Henry Hammond.

"I realize that he's here," she said, "I am not yet deaf." Sarah absently touched the lobe of her left ear, as if to prove the point. "And I have no desire to waste my time with him. He's an old bore."

She made no attempt to lower her voice; she didn't care if he heard. In fact, she hoped he would. Bertha's concern for Dr. Hill's feelings annoyed Sarah, given how thoughtless her daughter was with hers.

She closed her book and set it on the table. The perfect silhouette of a small pair of scissors was visible on its surface. The table had belonged to Sarah's grandmother, who sat by it every evening of her married life, working her needle while her husband read by flickering lamplight. One night, feeling suddenly ill, she left her scattered things, went to bed and never left it. After she died, her husband would not touch the abandoned work. Her needle and thread, a half-sewn shirt, a thimble and the scissors lay for years on the mahogany table. Over time, iron interacted with moisture and the scissors left their mark. When the table came to Sarah as a young bride, she tried to hide the ugly tattoo but John wanted it exposed, evidence of indelible love.

Sarah traced the shape of the scissors with her finger, then looked up at Bertha, still standing just inside the doorway.

"I hope you appreciate all the gifts you've been given," Sarah said, unsure if it was envy or regret that impelled her.

Although the day was warm, more August than September, Bertha felt a breeze as soon as she stepped outside the kitchen door. It had rained almost every afternoon for a week, but now the sky was clear. She could breath again, away from the desiccated air of her mother's room.

She turned to the right, towards the barn whose roof sagged like the back of an old mare. It would be cool in there, but damp. On a level plot beside the barn grew a rain-bedraggled mess of corn stalks, pea vines, and staked tomatoes. If she were a good girl, Bertha knew, there would be a bowl of freshly shucked peas and a pile of plump tomatoes waiting on the kitchen table when Florence came home from her calls, ready to start supper.

The moist ground, sodden as a sponge, yielded under her feet. The narrow ruffle at the bottom of her skirt picked up small clots of mud and grass, and she unbuttoned the cuffs of her shirtwaist and rolled each sleeve as she walked. She stopped at the edge of the plot, picked a tomato from the nearest vine and wiped its flesh against the gray fabric of her skirt. She bit into the tomato like an apple and ate it, not wiping the juice from her chin until she was done.

Bertha left the garden and headed down the sloping yard, past a tall oak tree whose roots raised welts in the surrounding earth. A thick screen of brambles and trees, oaks and birches and evergreen pines, marked the boundaries of the Mellish property, with a low stone wall guarding the southern border. When she reached that wall, Bertha found the place where, three years before with tools borrowed from the barn, she had cleared an opening and a path into the woods.

The ground was not as wet under the shelter of the trees as in the yard, and its moisture did not penetrate Bertha's thick-soled shoes. She walked purposefully, as if hurrying towards an appointment, although there was no one she was scheduled to meet. Another day, she might have stopped to examine a curious fungus, striated and lobed like a cup made of agate, attached to the side of a fallen branch, or to run her finger along the edge of a perfect birch leaf, serrated like a knife blade but softer, but now all she wanted was to put the house behind her.

By the time she reached the clearing where the train tracks ran, her breath had quickened and her hair and face and the exposed skin of her forearms were slick with sweat and drops of leftover rain, shaken loose from jostled branches. She had often watched from the safety of the brush as the trains that rode those tracks rumbled by, hissing steam, carrying passengers up from the Long Island Sound to Worcester and back again, or headed to the Dayville depot to deposit bales of unspun wool and pick up loads of finished fabric. And, after listening carefully for the sound of an approaching locomotive, she had often scrambled across the railbed on her way to the river that ran parallel to the tracks but deeper in the woods.

Yet she had never stopped in the middle of those tracks to measure how far ahead of her or how far behind they might extend. Whenever she was tempted, she remembered those terrible stories she had heard since childhood, the warning examples held up by her sister of fool-hardy young men, shiftless drifters, drunkards who walked on train tracks as if they were country roads or village streets, crushed in one horrific moment by an unseen monster, breathing fire at their backs before they heard it coming.

Now, there was no sound but the hum of hidden insects and the soft rustle of leaves. Bertha closed her eyes and listened. It seemed impossible, she thought, that a train had ever broken such stillness. She opened her eyes and walked towards the tracks, the gravel that covered the rail-bed sliding and shifting beneath her.

The thick iron rail frightened Bertha, and she stepped over it gingerly, holding her skirt high. She felt—foolishly, she knew—that something painful—a jolt of electrical current, perhaps, or surge of searing heat—would result if her sole or even the hem of her skirt touched its metal surface. When she reached the middle of the tracks, she paused with her skirt still raised.

The rails skimmed over the rough-hewn wooden ties like slick gray snakes, and they came together in two points, one to the north and one to the south. Bertha chose to face southward towards the depot, the place where, tomorrow, her journey to the college would truly begin. It would make everything seem more possible, she believed, if she saw the pitched roof of the small station, made sure it was still standing, that tomorrow morning she wouldn't find it burned to ashes or collapsed in a pile of splintered planks.

She released her skirt and with her arms partially extended as if she were crossing a narrow bridge, looked down and took a few tentative steps forward. She was alert for any unfamiliar sound, however faint, and held her bottom lip between her teeth.

At first, she planted a foot on every tie which made her move with an awkward, mincing gait, but then she tried them two at a time, stretching one leg ahead of the other. Soon she knew how far ahead to step without watching her feet. She focused on the point ahead of her where the two rails converged, and walked towards it with her arms swinging freely. She no longer listened for signs of approaching danger, following the path laid out for her without fear or calculation. But when she saw the Dayville depot in a clearing up ahead, she felt suddenly conspicuous and, like a startled animal, leapt over the rail to her right and into the tangled brush.

The river and the millrace were close by; Bertha could hear the hiss and rumble of their flow but she could not see them. Now, the invisible power of the rushing water called to her, and she felt compelled to the riverbank as forcefully as she had been drawn to the railroad tracks.

There was no clear path down to or along the banks of the river, and so she pulled aside a thorny branch and pushed her way forward through a tall patch of tuft-headed grass. Through the leaves of a sapling growing at river's edge, she could see the glint of sunlight on its dark water. She held the sapling's branches apart and realized that she had reached the place where the millrace poured back into the river, forming small whitecaps where the two streams collided.

Watching the river pucker and roil, Bertha was not tempted by its cool promise despite the heat. It moved in the same direction, following the path she had taken on the railroad tracks. She broke off a twig with two leaves attached, and dropped it in the water. The twig would soon be downstream, she thought, racing through the woods towards Danielson's giant factories.

Bertha looked up and across the river, past the millrace to the large main building of the Dayville Woolen Mill, quiet, she knew, on a Sunday. The bricks of the mill glowed orange in the sunlight and the windows revealed nothing but the empty blue of a reflected sky. Whenever she passed the mill on Main Street, she felt rather than heard the low throb of machinery hidden behind its walls. She had known mills like it—some smaller, one or two larger—all her life. Every village where her father preached had one, rectangular red brick structures with orderly rows of small-paned windows and a tower, more or less fancy, some with a clock, others with a bell.

When she was younger, the mills always made Bertha think of prisons or asylums, although she had never seen a prison or an asylum. But mills were mysterious places, filled with strange, unknowable people living lives so far from the comfortable familiarities of her own existence as to be born of another species. She had watched mill-hands, men, women and children, disappear through shadowy doorways, but she had never done so herself.

Whatever her future held, Bertha knew it held no mills. And, she vowed again as she had many times before, it held no cramped and dismal schoolrooms like the ones Florence endured. There would be no shabby little houses in muddy little villages in the years after college. She had no clear idea of those years, but sensed life in a city somewhere– Boston, New York, even Paris or Berlin—a literary life, perhaps, writing poetry, or a scientific one—she'd always liked biology and chemistry, the little she'd learned in high school. It didn't matter; she'd pay attention to it all, absorb it all, everything they taught her, let it lead her to a wider, richer world.

Bertha drew in a deep breath, filled with the odor of moist earth and of the restless water at her feet, and turned again towards the railroad tracks.

She headed northward now, moving steadily forward. She would have kept going, she almost believed, leaving her outgrown life behind, first to Worcester, and from there west to Springfield, and from there north to Holyoke, and from there uphill to South Hadley and the college, if her family were not waiting at home, expecting her for supper.

John Mellish sat across from his younger daughter at the round table in the center of the parlor, an open Bible between them. Just past seventy years old, he was a still-vigorous man of average height, with a broad face and eyes of translucent amber. His thick, neatly trimmed white beard was the same width as his high forehead and from the front his head looked rectangular.

Florence occupied one of the upholstered armchairs flanking the stove; Sarah reclined in the other. She had managed only a cup of coffee and a piece of toast at the evening meal and would have been in bed if not for the importance of the occasion. The light from a kerosene lamp on the table left Sarah and her older daughter in shadow and flickered on the faces of her husband and Bertha.

Her father seemed particularly solemn this night, Bertha thought, beyond the usual ministerial gravity he adopted at such times. She always felt a little uncomfortable with him in the pulpit or at family Bible readings. On those occasions he seemed distant and animated by a force outside himself. As a little girl, she'd thought the eyes of God shone from her father's face, and now he looked at her with the light of the lamp reflected in his spectacles. He cleared his throat and leaned forward, his hands resting on the table.

"The daughter we know will leave us tomorrow and never return," he said.

"What nonsense is that!" Sarah's voice was sharp as a claw. She rarely interrupted her husband during devotions, and was surprised at her own vehemence.

"I don't know what on earth you can mean by such a thing. What a thing to say!" Sarah huffed through her nose and shifted in her chair, further irritated by the shocked look on Bertha's face, which she knew was meant for her and not her husband. She did not glance over to gauge Florence's reaction, sure to be as dismayed as her sister's.

John Mellish stopped, his mouth half open. He was startled but not angered by his wife's rebuke. How strange his words must seem to her, sensitive as she was, about to say good-bye to their precious daughter. He wished he had bitten his tongue before the thoughtless sentence escaped him.

"I'm sorry, my dear," he said with a rueful smile; she answered with another huff.

John turned again to Bertha, sitting wide-eyed across the table. "What I mean to say is that you will leave your home and family to go out into a wider world and when next we see you—a blessed time that will come sooner than we think—you will be a changed, a wiser and more experienced young woman. That is all I intended."

John paused, waiting for the atmosphere in the room to settle into the hushed reverence he had hoped to create. He glanced at his wife, now leaning back in her chair, hands cradled in her lap, eyes half-closed. She had forgiven him, and he was grateful.

He'd selected a verse from Proverbs, appropriate, he thought, to the lesson he wished to instill in Bertha's heart. He had sensed a restlessness in her and a weakening of self-control that, he hoped, was only temporary, occasioned by the imminence of her departure.

He cleared his throat again, pushed his spectacles further up his nose and leaned closer to the lamp. He was a fine reader, his voice smooth, warm, and expressive. "Hearken to your father who begot you," he read, "Buy truth, and do not sell it. Let your father and mother be glad; let her who bore you rejoice."

Sarah was indeed mollified. She relaxed in her chair and opened her eyes to see her husband radiant in the lamplight. His white hair glowed like an aureole. Truly a man of God, she thought, and regretted her earlier disrespect.

John Mellish closed the Bible and laid his right hand on the table, palm upward. He looked at Bertha fondly, certain she would understand the gesture. But she stared as if she did not recognize the hand as a part of him, her father, but saw it as an alien thing, an unearthed root or a beached fish. He felt an empty place open in his chest.

"Please," he said, and there was something mournful in his voice. Slowly, Bertha drew her left hand from beneath the table and placed it in his, palm down.

"There will be temptations before you, even in the good and Christian place to which you go," John said, and squeezed her fingers. "Search for wisdom as for hid treasures; have right views of the evil of wrong-doing."

Bertha's eyes were fixed on her father. He had never focused his sermonizing so completely on her and she wished Florence were sitting by her side. She wanted to pull her hand away–her shoulder was awkwardly twisted and her father's grip was too tight–but there was nothing to do but endure.

"When you leave the daily guidance of your parents and dear sister," he continued, "you will need the fear of God in your heart. You will need to depend on the power and goodness of God that turns men and women from the thrall of sin and Satan. If you do, your heart will not be tempted by those follies that bring shame and ruin."

She saw the tiny flames before his eyes, one glowing in each glass oval of his spectacles.

Her father had often spoken to her about doing what was good and right. Of course she knew that sin permeated the world and that Satan was a real presence. She knew that some people didn't go to church on Sundays and that men gambled away their children's bread. She had seen drunken mill hands, both men and women, in the village streets, had overheard the whispers. But never had her father warned her so personally, so urgently or so nakedly. Never had he suggested that she might follow a path of ruin. She was ashamed that he thought her capable of such things.

At last, he released her hand. Bertha returned it to her lap and looked down to escape the brilliance of his gaze.

The silence grew heavy with her father's patient expectation and Bertha shifted in her seat. She should reassure him, tell him that she understood his message and would try with all her heart to live by its precepts. But she was not sure that she could. Her father himself had said that she might fail.

"Bertha, have you anything to say to your father?" her mother asked.

Bertha shook her head. "I don't know," she whispered. If she couldn't answer honestly, she wouldn't answer at all.

Florence, quiet until then, could no longer bear the look of pained confusion on her father's face and reached out to touch his arm, covered in the faded wool of his best frock coat.

"With such models as you and Mother have been," she said, "we can rest assured that Bertha will follow the path of righteousness even when she is away from us. I'm not worried for her."

In truth, Florence was not worried for the state of her sister's soul. She did hope, though, that Bertha would be happier at school than she had been, but then Bertha was smarter and stronger and it had been twenty years since Florence left Mount Holyoke.

Twenty years ago, the place was still a Puritan convent to many people, a cloister where farmers' and ministers' daughters trained to be teachers or missionaries, taught by generations of seminary-bred spinsters, governed by a Byzantine system of rules and bells, steeped in overwrought religiosity and boarding school primness.

Florence's chest tightened even now, just to think of it. She'd entered the school dreaming of missionary work in some far-off land. But she was awkward and shy and could not bring herself to confess in public her daily sins as all pupils were required to do and so spent each day choked with guilt at her failure of spirit and will. Bertha's Mount Holyoke, a full-fledged college now, would be a very different place, freer and more forgiving.

Florence remembered the portrait of Mary Lyon, hanging in the vestibule of Mount Holyoke's Seminary Hall. Square-faced, with a broad, sloping nose and thin mouth, the foundress sat in her picture like a block of New England granite. With her light blue eyes framed by crow's-feet, she scrutinized, gently but mercilessly, the generations of girls who passed before her. Florence had not survived that scrutiny but, she was certain, Bertha would.

Bertha lifted her head and glanced at her older sister with a look that Florence recognized as gratitude. "Florence is right," she said, turning to face their father. "I will always follow that righteous path."

So much trust in her father's eyes, and all of it placed in her. Bertha saw it shining through the flame-lit glass of his spectacles, an unquestioning, innocent trust, beyond betrayal. Under its weight, Bertha dropped her head once more. "At least," she said, "I will always try."

Chapter 3

The College

Bertha began her journey traveling north out of Connecticut on the tracks she had walked the previous day. With a Latin grammar open and unread on her lap, she kept her head down as if studying, afraid to catch the passing glances of strange men or recognize and have to talk with an acquaintance.

At Worcester's Union Station, she changed to the westbound Boston & Albany Railroad for the fifty-seven mile trip to Springfield through the woods and fields of central Massachusetts. After some confusion about her luggage and the correct platform, she boarded a car and found a seat next to a window. Her head hurt from coal gas fumes and she removed her hat and touched her forehead to the glass, but it was warm and offered no relief.

With her hat back on and her face resolutely turned to the window, Bertha watched the trees and farms rush by and tried to imagine the girls she would meet, her fellow students, her competitors, her potential friends. But the only models she could envision looked like Charlotte, or Hattie, or some other Dayville girl already left in the past, and so she gave up the effort.

Too self-conscious to find and unwrap the lunch that Florence had packed for her, Bertha ignored her hunger until it went away. At no point on the trip could she imagine relieving herself in a public place and so she held that, too.

At Springfield, the train reached the Connecticut River and she disembarked to catch the Boston & Maine to Holyoke, eight miles up the valley. Some of the other young women who boarded with her were clearly Mount Holyoke students; they scanned the car with obvious excitement. Several recognized old friends with squeals of pleasure and found seats together. Bertha took an aisle seat next to an old woman, hoping none of the girls would notice her, at least not yet. She was light-headed and her mouth tasted sour; she wished she'd eaten.

At the Holyoke station, a low-slung building of heavy gray stone, Bertha followed a cluster of girls across the platform to a man in dirty trousers and a shapeless hat. Hanging back until the others were done, she gave the expressman her baggage ticket and fifteen cents and was told to look for her trunk at the college in a day or two.

Anxious not to lose her guides, Bertha glimpsed them under a nearby railroad bridge and half ran to keep them in sight, along a wide, straight canal flanked by rows of large brick mills. She joined the small crowd gathered on a busy street corner just as the South Hadley stage arrived and was soon packed into the carriage for the hot and dusty ride to the college. They crossed the river over an iron trestle bridge. The water rushing over Holyoke's massive dam thundered to the left; behind it swelled the green Mount Tom Range. They soon left the chimneys of Holyoke behind and gently climbed through open farmland.

A spiked iron fence separated the college from the village of South Hadley. Bertha, a small obstacle in the crowd that flowed around her, stood outside the fence but faced Seminary Hall. The sleeves of her blouse were wilted and her wool skirt felt heavy in the September sun. Although she didn't know it, a speck of soot clung to her right cheek. Her hair, smoothed into a low bun when she left Dayville that morning, stuck out from beneath her black sailor hat. In one hand she clutched her father's old carpetbag, which held a few books, a change of clothes, a comb, a bar of soap, tooth powder and toothbrush, and a dark paisley shawl, a gift from her mother.

Seminary Hall was bigger than Bertha had imagined from stereographs brought home by Florence from her year at the school. In Florence's pictures, the building's wide wooden veranda had been white, but now it was painted the color of brownstone. With its red brick walls and its grid of identical black-shuttered windows, the building reminded Bertha of the mill she had stood outside just the day before. The resemblance unnerved her, as if she had traveled all this way and gone nowhere. No, she told herself, touching the hard reality of iron with the tip of one finger, the moment that she passed beyond this fence, nothing would be the same. One last time, she turned to look at the road she had just traveled.

Directly opposite Seminary Hall was an ancient burying-ground, the one Florence called God's Acre. To its left stood a substantial public school, built of brick. Further down, Bertha could see the simple shapes of wood-frame houses visible through the leafy branches of the elms that lined both sides of the unpaved road. She tried but felt no pang for the small wood-frame house she had left behind.

Two little boys and a slightly older girl stood outside the cemetery, watching the arrival of the college girls with their bags and bundles, tennis rackets and bicycles. As Bertha scanned the scene, the smallest boy caught her eye and waved. She waved back and the little boy stuck out his tongue. Without thinking, she returned the compliment and immediately realized how ridiculous she must look. Mortified, she ducked her head, clutching the handles of the carpetbag in both fists.

Bertha felt a presence, just behind her right shoulder. She didn't move, hoping whoever lurked there had not seen what she had done and would go away, leave her to slink off in peace.

"Excuse me," the presence said in a voice smooth as honey, "May I help you?"

Bertha had no choice; she turned to find a young woman, tall but delicate, with a small head and a cloud of light brown hair. The girl had large, melancholy eyes, a long nose and a wide, slightly crooked smile. She made no sign that she had witnessed Bertha's childish gesture.

"My name is Mabel Eaton," the young woman said, "I'm a sophomore at the college and I'm looking for a newcomer to help settle in.

Perhaps I can be of some use to you, Miss . . . ." She paused, her head tilted encouragingly, waiting for Bertha to offer her name.

For a moment Bertha wondered if Mabel Eaton mocked her, made fun of the helplessness she was struggling to conceal, but she saw that the girl's eyes were kind. She released one hand from the carpetbag but wasn't sure if she should offer it. She pressed her moist palm against the fabric of her skirt, just in case.

"Bertha Mellish," she said. Her voice sounded thick in her ear and she cleared her throat. "My name is Bertha Mellish."

Mabel Eaton made no move to take her hand. Instead, she reached out and gently brushed Bertha's face. "Just a little speck," she laughed, and flicked her fingertips with her thumb. "Come with me, Miss Mellish, and I'll show you where to go."

Mabel led her through the college gates, down a short path, and up the front steps of Seminary Hall into a small square room with bustling offices on either side and a winding staircase opposite the door. A long corridor passed through the space; the library was down the hall to the left, Miss Eaton explained, and down the hall to the right lay the chapel.

Bertha felt insignificant in that hive of self-important busyness, especially since Miss Eaton seemed so perfectly at ease. With calm sincerity Mabel acknowledged the many girls who greeted her and, if she could catch them as they passed, presented them to Miss Mellish. Bertha smiled tightly at each encounter and later realized that she could not remember any of their names.

Mabel left Bertha at the Registrar's Office with a promise to find her later and take her down to supper. A harried old woman in spectacles gave Bertha her preliminary course schedule and instructed her to prepare for entrance examinations in English Literature and American History. Another woman, equally preoccupied but younger, assigned Bertha's dormitory room and told her to check the bulletin board in the Chapel to find her designated table for meals. Bertha was informed where and when mail would be delivered and handed a printed page of rules.

—∾—

Punctual attendance at Sabbath morning services and at daily Chapel service was required of every student. Punctual attendance at daily meals was required. Students were to attend punctually to their domestic work. Students were not to enter the rooms of others in study hours. Students were expected to observe the silent half hour. Students were not to make calls, meet company, drive, or be absent from town without permission. Students were not allowed to walk alone outside the village limits.

Calls were not to be made or received on the Sabbath. Rooms were to be in order at half past eight every morning. Wardrobes were to be put in order and account books balanced every week. Lights were to be extinguished at 10 p.m. Studying was prohibited before the rising bell. Recreation time commenced at 4:30 Tuesday afternoon and ended at 6 o'clock Wednesday evening. Students were not to purchase or receive eatables, except fresh fruit. Regular exercise in the open air was required unless forbidden by the College Physician.

Bertha read the list as she sat on a bare mattress in a room on the third floor of the south wing of Seminary Hall. Her roommate had not yet arrived, and she was glad of the solitude after all the effort she'd spent acting confident, as if she knew what to do and where to go.

The room was narrow and opened onto the building's inner courtyard with no view of the mountains or river valley. It held two simple wooden beds, one against the wall on either side of the door. Each bed had a pillow at its head and a straight-backed chair at its foot; Bertha's carpetbag, still packed, rested on the seat of what was now her chair. The bare floorboards were painted a dull reddish brown, and the wallpaper was olive green, faded in patches, with a pattern of interlocking ferns and flowers picked out in gold. Bertha noticed a few bright sparkles on the black wool of her skirt, but it was some time before she realized that the wallpaper shed a fine dusting over the room.

The entrance to a small closet with built-in drawers and a washstand was located at the end of the left-hand wall, but Bertha chose the bed on the right because the door opened in that direction. The door was closed now, but if it was ever left ajar or if anybody ever came into the room without invitation, she would be safely hidden.

As she made her way down the south corridor, Bertha had glimpsed the interiors of other girls' rooms. Many had colorful rugs, velvet bedcovers, Japanese silk wall-hangings. Some had white lace curtains. Most had pillows–ruffled pillows, pillows with tassels, pillows with embroidered mottoes, pillows appliquéd with class years and secret society letters. A few were crowded with overstuffed armchairs and wicker rockers, small stands and stools, desks, writing tables, tea tables, chests of drawers, bookcases, potted plants. Almost all had photographs pinned to the walls, banners from Yale or Amherst, chromo'd advertisements, fashion plates, calendars, greeting cards.

But it wasn't the faded emptiness of her own room that disturbed Bertha. It was the unsettling intimacy of the place, the knowledge that other people had walked its floor, sat in its chairs, and laid in the bed that was supposed to be hers. She was anxious to meet the girl who would share this space with her, the stranger with whom she was meant to live, close as sisters. Bertha placed the list of rules on the mattress beside her and shut her eyes. She willed herself back to Dayville, and listened for Florence in the kitchen below, making supper.

The bell that had sounded at various intervals throughout the day now rang three times. Bertha knew it announced the evening meal but she made no move to leave the bed. Apart from her encounter with Mabel Eaton that afternoon and a few short exchanges with busy college officials, she had not had a real conversation with anyone else and did not want one now.

She would stay in her room and eat the sandwich and fruit left from the lunch Florence packed early that morning. She would study for her entrance examinations.

The bell rang three more times, followed by a soft knock on the door.

"Miss Mellish, may I come in?"

Bertha recognized Miss Eaton's voice and wished she would go away. A few seconds passed before she answered. "Yes," she said.

Mabel opened the door and peered into the darkening room. She wore a freshly starched white muslin dress; pinned to the bodice was a bunch of violets, a gift from her roommate. She had spent most of the afternoon organizing her things and remembered her promise to the awkward freshman just in time. Mabel rescued Bertha as naturally as she would have plucked a stray kitten from the streets, and now felt a disinterested responsibility for the stray's well-being. Besides, she wanted every new student to feel the welcoming friendliness of the place. She stepped further into the room and half-closed the door behind her before she noticed Bertha sitting still as a statue near the head of her bed.

"Oh, there you are," Mabel said, trying not to sound startled. She knew how to draw out the shy girls, how to coax them, how to move cautiously. "It's time for supper," she said. "You must be very hungry."

Mabel noted with surprise that Bertha had made no effort to clean her face or fix her hair. She still wore her rumpled traveling outfit.

"I'm afraid there isn't time to change." Mabel glanced around the sparsely furnished room and realized it had no mirror. Without one, Miss Mellish could not know how disheveled she looked. "We'll ask matron for a mirror tomorrow. Perhaps you'd like to stop in the lavatory on our way to supper?"

Mabel hoped Miss Mellish would take the hint, but the girl did not reply.

Bertha didn't speak because she was trying not to cry. Her eyes filled and her nose tingled and she didn't trust her voice. A tiny hiccup escaped her.

Mabel pulled a handkerchief from the sash of her dress. She gave the handkerchief to Bertha, who dried her eyes while Mabel smoothed her hair. Embarrassed to return the damp cloth, Bertha slipped it under the pillow at the head of the bed.

Mabel gently lifted Bertha by the arm; the girl did not resist. "Now," Mabel said with a hearty briskness she didn't feel, "Let's go down to supper before there's nothing left to eat."

By the time Mabel and Bertha arrived in the basement dining room, prayers and hymn singing were over. With a pinched half-smile, President Mead looked on as Mabel showed Bertha to her assigned table. Under the scrutiny of every eye in the room, Bertha pulled out her chair. It squealed against the wooden floor.

At the head of Bertha's table sat Miss Slater, instructor of Greek. She would rather have let the poor girl settle in unnoticed, but felt it her duty to call attention to Bertha's tardiness. Mrs. Mead would be watching.

"Welcome," she said, trying to sound kind, "I know it's very difficult these first few days, but we should all try to be punctual at meals."

Elizabeth Slater was thirty years old with a long, plain face. Still, the students considered her the most romantic woman on the faculty. It was common knowledge that she was engaged to a brilliant young man, a graduate student in German philosophy at Harvard, and that they carried on a prolific and passionate correspondence. Of course, no one had read the letters, but the girls encouraged Miss Slater to talk about her fiancé and, although she knew such confidences were inappropriate, she could not resist.

Miss Slater's mood depended from day to day on the quantity and the nature of the letters she received from her George. She sent him letters festering with self-reproach, seething with disgust at her vulgarity and coarseness, her irritable temper and her mental and spiritual unfitness to be his wife. He, convinced of his ultimate and inevitable failure, replied with letters drowning in despair and hopelessness. He was horrified that she had attached her fate to his and advised her to leave him.

They pleaded with each other to expose their innermost souls and they tormented each other with the demons these souls revealed. She longed to cover his hair and face with kisses and hold him in her arms to ease his pain. He apologized again and again for his inadequate expressions of love and she basked in these apologies. Theirs was a happy courtship.

Elizabeth Slater was calm that night and secure in George's love. She helped the girls to bread and butter, to dried beef and stewed apricots, to the plain cake that was their dessert. She tried to start a lively conversation, but her efforts fell flat. A few of the girls at the table were friends, but were gently reproached by Miss Slater and asked to include the entire table when they spoke privately to one another. All the girls were tired, most were awkward and shy.

Bertha ate a slice of bread with no butter, a bite of meat, and two apricots. Still smarting from the humiliation of her entrance, she kept her eyes fixed on her plate and spoke to no one. After the table was dismissed, she hurried back to her room.

The square of translucent linen, fragile as snow against the coarse mattress ticking, had neatly rolled sides. One corner, delicately scalloped, held a large "M" worked in a padded satin stitch that stood out in glossy relief. The letter was more exuberant than graceful, beginning and ending in two slightly mismatched spirals. The two sharp peaks of the "M" bent awkwardly to the right.

Bertha did not see these imperfections. Her own experience with handkerchief making was to hem the plain cotton ones her family used. The piece of cloth in front of her seemed to be born of an entirely different breed and, until the electric lights were turned off for the night, she examined its tiny stitches as she would the markings of a living creature. She wished she had a magnifying glass, even a microscope.

Each stitch seemed evidence of the depths of Mabel Eaton's patient goodness. Bertha imagined Mabel as she embroidered the first letter of her Christian name, saw her face held close to the cloth, the cloth barely stirred by quiet breaths, the bright hard needle held tenderly between pale fingers. She thought of the needle's movement as it pierced the fabric and wondered if Mabel had ever pricked herself.

When the lights went off, Bertha ran her finger over the letter, trying to read without seeing as a blind person might. Then, she gently folded the little cloth and, although no one was there to there to witness the act, returned it quickly and furtively to its place under her pillow. Using her mother's paisley shawl as a blanket, she fell asleep on the bare mattress.

Chapter 4

The Pepper Box

Bertha woke before any bell had rung. The room was dark except for a cool wash of moonlight and for several seconds she did not know where she was. The strangeness of the place sank into her bones and she lay immobilized. The thought of people sleeping in the rooms next to hers and above and below hers oppressed her, and she imagined she could hear a deep, slow, unified breathing. Her chest felt tight and the room seemed very warm. She left her bed, dressed quickly, pulled her shoes over bare feet.

With her hair unpinned, Bertha left the room. She tiptoed through a deserted hallway lit by red glass sconces, crept down three flights of stairs, found a door.

The sky to her left was lightening; below it a low hill rose in the distance. The rounded silhouette of the hill was topped by a small but distinct bump that Bertha could not identify.

She ran through the early morning fog as if invisible, unfettered as the leaves scudding at her feet. Cool air caressed her legs, naked beneath her heavy skirt. She paused, laid her hands on the wet grass, wiped her face with the dew on her fingers. She crossed a narrow bridge—she could hear but not see the brook that ran beneath–onto a well-worn path.

Twigs and dried leaves, acorns and small pebbles crunched beneath her feet. Beyond a smooth lake ringed with trees, she began to climb the hill's grassy slope, sometimes bending over to feel her way up with her hands. When Bertha neared the top, she saw that the bump was, in fact, a small, shingled building on a high foundation, with twelve sides and a pointed roof. In the strange half-light anything was possible—it might be the home of woodland elves, a hermit's retreat, a witch's lair—and she smiled at her own foolishness. She climbed the stairs of the little pavilion, tried its door, and went in.

In a moment of blind panic, Bertha realized that she was not alone. A figure, a shadow in the twilight, reclined on a bench along the wall opposite the door. The figure had no distinct features, no clear arms or legs, no obvious head set upon a neck. It seemed to writhe and twist, a snake or a caterpillar in a cocoon, and Bertha stared at it, paralyzed.

The figure struggled to sit upright, and Bertha could see that it was a girl, swathed in blankets from head to toe. When the girl was finally settled, she extricated one arm from her swaddling, leaned forward and lifted a small kerosene lantern that sat by her feet to the bench beside her.

Bertha watched, no longer frightened, although her heart still pounded.

The girl released her other arm, and Bertha saw that she held a small metal box in her exposed hand. She lifted its hinged lid, took out a match, struck it. The tiny flame flared, throwing monstrous shadows on the walls and ceiling of the mysterious room. The girl touched the burning match to the lantern's wick, waited a moment for the fabric to ignite, then shook the match until it died. Dropping its blackened remains to the floor, she slid the blanket from her head.

Her face was a perfect oval and her pale, perfect skin glowed in the light of the lamp. Bertha had never seen anyone so beautiful.

The girl looked at Bertha and shook her head. "Not to be rude, but you're an awful mess. You look like Jane Eyre wandering the moors, something like that. Maybe a mad woman from Shakespeare."

Bertha was shocked to hear the girl speak. Sitting silently in the lamplight, she might have been an exquisite ghost, an apparition, and Bertha would have left without disturbing her, slipping out the door and closing it as she might awaken from a dream.

"Are you deaf?" The question was more amused than sarcastic, and it clearly demanded a response.

"No," Bertha said, "I was just surprised."

"I'm Eva Newton," the girl said, as if the simple statement of her name were explanation enough of who she was and why she was there, in that strange place at that strange time.

"I'm Bertha Mellish," Bertha said, but her own name sounded tentative in her ears, as if she were asking a question.

"Well, Bertha Mellish, come over here and sit down. No sense standing there by the open door."

There was no "please" attached to this command, but Bertha didn't mind. It felt like a honor, to be summoned to Eva Newton's side.

Eva unwrapped one of her blankets and gave it to Bertha, who draped it over her shoulders and took her place on the bench. She felt suddenly at ease but didn't know if it was Eva herself or the effect of the light and the odd intimacy of the little room. "Have you been here all night?" she asked.

"Yes," Eva said, and wrinkled her perfect nose. "They put me in a room with a girl who looks like a cow. Ugliest creature I've ever seen. And she snores." Eva turned to Bertha, her mouth pursed prettily in disgust. "How do they expect me to sleep in the same room with someone like that?"

Bertha shrugged sympathetically, glad that she was not to be judged the ugliest creature that Eva had ever seen.

"I'm going to complain," Eva said, and Bertha nodded. "Her name is Myra Plumb." Eva paused and snickered. "Why, that's almost as bad as Bertha Mellish." She laid a hand on Bertha's arm and smiled.

It did not seem an insult, coming from Eva, but a statement of fact, pronounced without malice.

"I know," Bertha agreed, "I don't like it either." She felt a little guilty, renouncing her father's name. "Well, the Bertha more than the Mellish."

"Then you must have another," Eva said, and tightened her hold on Bertha's arm. She stared at the lamp. "I know," she cried, "Let's call you Beatrice." She pronounced it the Italian way: Bee-ah-tree-chay.

"That *is* better," Bertha said, and felt her face redden. Beatrices had dark eyes and ruby lips. They lived in Italy and inspired poets. Bertha suppressed a giddy smile, glad that the dim light disguised her childish pleasure.

"Where are you from, Beatrice?" Eva asked, releasing Bertha's arm. "I'm from Chicago."

Chicago, city of the great Exposition. Bertha had seen pictures of its wonders, the gleaming white buildings, the sparkling lagoons, the dizzying Ferris Wheel. All she had to offer was dull little Dayville.

"A town in Connecticut." Bertha, apologetic, shrugged. "I'm sure you've never heard of it."

Eva didn't ask for its name. "I'm only at Mount Holyoke because my father thinks there are no young men around." She snorted, dismissing the absurdity. "And I have an aunt in Northampton. She's supposed to watch over me, but she doesn't."

"My sister went to Mount Holyoke, years ago, before it was a college." Finally, some topic of possible interest to Eva; Bertha was relieved. "And so did my cousin, ten years ago. She's dead now. My cousin that is."

"Is that so?" Eva said. "Do you know anyone who goes to Mount Holyoke now?"

Bertha had to shake her head.

"A shame," Eva murmured. She seemed suddenly distracted, reaching a hand beneath her blanket. "Anyway, what are you doing up in the Pepper Box so early in the morning?" she asked, fumbling under the cloth.

Bertha hesitated, not sure what to make of the odd name. "Oh, I needed some fresh air," she said, trying for nonchalance. "I couldn't sleep, my room was so warm."

"Hmm," Eva said.

"I don't have a roommate," Bertha offered. It seemed so important, not to lose Eva's attention. Eva, still preoccupied, didn't seem to hear. "I mean, she hasn't arrived yet."

Ignoring Bertha's remark, Eva pulled a cigarette from somewhere under her blanket and lit it, her movements graceful as a dancer's. She inhaled deeply and blew the smoke in Bertha's direction. Bertha felt a tickle in her throat, but did not cough.

Holding the cigarette between thumb and forefinger, Eva offered it to Bertha. "It's good for the nerves," she said.

Bertha stared at the glowing tip. "No, thank you," she said, although she was tempted to take the dangerous cylinder and bring it to her own lips. And she would have, she told herself, if only she knew what to do with thing.

Eva withdrew the cigarette and laughed softly. "Of course not," she said.

"It's just that I don't like the taste," Bertha said. Her voice lacked conviction; she didn't expect Eva to believe her no matter how confidently she spoke.

"Of course not," Eva said again and took another puff.

"What's this place for, anyway, this pepper box?," Bertha asked, desperate to change the subject and regain some measure of control.

"Picnics, somewhere to tell ghost stories." Eva tapped her cigarette with exaggerated elegance and watched as the ash fell to the floor. "And if I tell you it's also called the spoon holder, then you'll know."

Snickering, her head cocked, she looked at Bertha.

"You don't know what that means, do you?" Eva sounded sympathetic, vaguely mournful.

Ashamed, Bertha shook her head.

"Well, little Beatrice, I can't tell you. Ask your mother about spooning." Eva laughed. "And it's also for this." She took another draw, crushed the cigarette on the bench beside her. She threw the butt across the room, where it lay visible in the morning light.

By now the cool, silver sky was shot with copper and the sun was rising on a cloudless day. The fog had disappeared. Eva extinguished the lamp and the two girls knelt on the bench by the window. The smooth humps of Mount Holyoke and Mount Nonotuck were visible to the north and west, one on each side of the river that carved a gap in the Holyoke range. Open fields and distant hills spread out from the break between the two mountains and to the southwest they could barely make out the tall red chimneys of Holyoke, five miles away.

In the full light of morning, Bertha was conscious of her half-dressed state and worried about getting back to her room unnoticed. She stood up, returned the blanket to Eva and straightened her clothes. "I . . . I have to leave," she said, embarrassed by the amused look on Eva Newton's face.

"Run back down before anyone sees you, Beatrice," Eva laughed, "because you *are* a sight."

Eva shook herself out of her blanket, arched her back and yawned without covering her mouth. She seemed in no hurry to leave. "Perhaps we'll meet again," she said.

For a moment, Eva's words sounded like a promise and Bertha forgot her embarrassment. Here, at last, was an invitation to a world she had only read about. Eva Newton—beautiful, worldly, a little dangerous—was making plans to see her again, plain Bertha Mellish the minister's daughter who, smart as she was, had never even held a cigarette.

Perhaps, Eva had said. *Perhaps* we'll meet again.

So it wasn't a promise or an invitation after all. It was a dismissal. She should never have let Eva Newton play with her, insult her name, blow smoke in her face, make her feel ridiculous and small. "Perhaps we will," Bertha said, trying for indifference.

She left the Pepper Box and retraced the route she had taken at dawn. Her escape through the fog seemed like a dream now, with the sun already heavy on her shoulders. Holding her arms tightly across her chest, Bertha passed a few students and one or two faculty on the stairs and in the hallway outside her room without lifting her head to greet them.

The room was still empty; no roommate yet. Using her faint reflection on the window glass, Bertha arranged her tangled hair. She was sure that the smell of smoke still clung to it and the idea disgusted her. Unwilling to face the crowded bathroom and with no washbowl and pitcher, she brushed her teeth with dry tooth powder and swallowed the salty foam. She dressed again, putting on her corset and the clean underwear that had been packed in her carpetbag, finishing just as the breakfast bell rang.

Chapter 5

Phebe Cutts

When Bertha returned from breakfast, she found a slight, pale girl sitting on the edge of the unclaimed bed, her knees together and her feet barely touching the floor. Her head was bent toward her lap although there was nothing there, no book or piece of paper that Bertha could see, and she jumped up with a small squeak when she realized someone stood in the open doorway, staring at her. That squeak seemed to prime the pump; the girl chattered on for nearly twenty minutes, barely taking a breath while Bertha arranged her things, gritting her teeth and nodding politely, trying not to think about Eva.

"My name's Phebe Alma Cutts," the girl informed her, "I'm truly eighteen, but everyone takes me for sixteen because I'm so small."

In her ill-fitting suit, Phebe did look like a child in grown-up clothes. She was thin and short with a head round as a pie. Her movements were quick and nervous and reminded Bertha of a small animal constantly on the lookout for a larger one.

"Just think, until yesterday I wore my hair in braids." Phebe giggled uncomfortably. "Can you imagine that, a grown girl like me in braids. But look at it now. My ma helped me."

Forced to turn her head, Bertha saw that Phebe's rusty yellow hair was pulled into a tight bun at the nape of her neck. "Very nice," she said.

"I come from a farm in New Hampshire, way up north." Phebe sat on her bed, watching Bertha and making no move to unpack her own small suitcase. "The closest town is Potter's Place. It's a funny name, I know. I've got three brothers and a sister. Let's see, there's Caleb and Sam, then Ben, then Emmalee. Emmalee's married, but everyone says I'll never get married. I'm kind of sickly. Besides, everyone says I'm not good-looking enough to get married." Phebe paused, perhaps hoping for a rebuttal.

"Oh, you're all right," Bertha managed.

"Do you really think so?" Phebe didn't wait for another half-hearted compliment. "My folks say they'll pay enough for me to go to college so I can come home and teach and earn my keep. I'm no good in the fields. I'm too puny. Besides, I took to studying better than any of my brothers." There was a hint of pride in Phebe's thin voice.

"Indeed?" said Bertha, disappearing into the closet.

Bertha had hoped her roommate would be a mature girl, maybe a sophomore or a junior, someone studious but stylish who would introduce her to real college life. She had not expected anyone as awkward and inexperienced as Phebe Cutts and she wondered if it were possible to change roommates. She imagined how much better it would have been with Eva Newton if Eva had not insulted her. For a moment, she dared to think of Mabel.

Still, she tried to be civil, even when Phebe tacked a garish advertising poster for Pears Soap and an insipid head of the weeping Christ on the wall above her bed. On her side of the room, Bertha hung a photograph of the Colosseum and a black and white engraving of Millet's *Angelus,* both pictures taken from the walls of the Mellish parlor.

Later that day, Bertha went to the basement storeroom where she found a plain cotton mat for their floor. And that evening, with Phebe scurrying behind, she followed a group of girls to the attic and located a cracked but serviceable mirror and a table with a scarred surface. They put the mirror in the closet and the table under the window. But neither girl had much in the way of decorative bric-a-brac or artistic textiles and, all in all, their room had a spartan shabbiness that only money or a reckless imagination could have transformed.

Phebe was still in the dining room, clearing up after supper. With any luck, Bertha figured, she'd have almost an hour before the girl returned to fill the room with her mindless chatter. After nearly three days together, Bertha had begun to treat the sound of Phebe's voice like the distant chirp of crickets, annoying only if she let it enter her mind and disturb her thoughts.

Her schoolwork done for the day, Bertha took four clean sheets of stationery, a pen with a fresh point, and a new bottle of ink from her small supply. She sat down at the table and arranged the paper and pen neatly on the blotting pad, next to a small glass inkstand.

Carefully, so no drop would be lost, she unscrewed the lid of the bottle, attached its spout, and watched as the blue-black liquid filled the glass. Usually, the sharp smell of ink triggered a vague excitement, as if putting pen to paper was the start of an adventure. Bertha liked to write and thought she was good at it; she could express herself more clearly in writing, was more interesting in what she said, could even be amusing. But she felt no excitement now, only dread.

This first letter home should have been a pleasure to write. There should have been so much to tell her family; she knew they would hang on every word, read the letter over and over, maybe share it with friends. Bertha was sure her father would show it to Dr. Hill, so filled with pleasure at Bertha's happiness that he would forget how painful such a letter might be to an old man who'd lost his own children many years ago.

But these few days at college were not what Bertha had imagined during those last long weeks at home; even now she could barely admit her disappointment. Sharing that disappointment with her family was unthinkable. Too much depended on her success. Even more, she could not bring herself to admit defeat so early in the game.

Bertha replaced the lid of the bottle and dipped her pen in the glass well. The legs of the table were uneven and she pressed down with her left arm to keep the surface steady as she wrote.

Mount Holyoke College
South Hadley, Massachusetts

Thursday
September 12, 1895

My Dear Family,

I have thought of you often since I left home, but I have not had a minute to write until just now. I had a pleasant and uneventful trip to the College. I didn't meet anyone I knew and so it was a quiet time when I could read and watch the passing scenery.

I was anxious to see what Holyoke was like since it is the largest town near the College, but was a little disappointed to find it somewhat dreary and not as bustling as I thought it would be. But I shouldn't judge yet because I only saw an area near the depot that had many factory buildings bigger than our mill but not nearly as picturesquely situated.

The drive out to South Hadley was lovely just as Florence described it and I am looking forward to investigating the woods and mountains around the College.

I am done arranging my classes and will tell you more about them after recitations begin in earnest. At meals, I sit at the table with Miss Slater. She is the Greek teacher and seems quite nice so I think I shall be comfortable with her.

My room is small but pleasant and my roommate and I have done a little decorating to make it more homelike. We have all the modern conveniences: electric lights and steam heat and there is a bathroom with sanitary fixtures down the hall. My pictures are hanging on the wall above my bed and they remind me always of the beauties of Art and Faith.

Bertha heard a faint noise behind her, a tiny creak and a whisper of air. She turned; Phebe had opened the door and now crept to her bed. With a deep and prolonged sigh, she sat down hard enough to make the springs squeak. Reluctantly, Bertha asked what was wrong. Phebe wrinkled her nose, shook her head and, without a word, lay down with her face to the wall. Bertha shrugged and went back to her writing.

My roommate is Miss Phebe Cutts and she is a freshman too. She is quite young and a little timid but I am sure that we will get on well as we get to know each other better. I have met some very lovely girls, especially a Miss Eaton who is particularly kind and whom I hope to call on soon.

The letter was stiff; Bertha could see that. It would please her father and mother, but for Florence's sake she should have made it livelier, embellished the descriptions, added a few humorous touches, invented a friend or two. But her heart wasn't in it. Next week she'd do better.

I hope this finds you all in good health.

Your loving Bertha

She put the letter aside, waiting for the ink to dry. After a moment's hesitation, she dipped her pen again. "*Dearest Florence,*" Bertha wrote on a fresh sheet of paper,

I never knew I would miss you as much as I do. I was so anxious to leave that I never gave a thought to what I was leaving. I am not happy here. How stupid I was to think it would be easy to find my place among so many strangers. I know I'm awkward with the other girls and don't know the right thing to say when they ask me questions or the right way to act in certain situations. I met a beautiful girl who made fun of me and made me feel like a fool. No one has invited me to her room.

The table wobbled noisily and Bertha paused to rest her hand. She glanced at Phebe, lying motionless on her bed.

I hate my roommate. She's stupid and ugly and she makes me feel sorry for her. She talks all the time, except right now when she's lying like a lump on her bed. I know you and Father would tell me to be charitable but I can't. I can't help feeling angry that I am stuck with her.

The words she had just written were thick and angular and tiny spots of ink freckled the paper. Bertha exhaled deeply and continued, writing more slowly.

More than anything, I want to become friends with Mabel Eaton. She was so kind to me on my first day here and has just the sort of gentle spirit that I wish I had. I know that you would like her. When she walks she seems to glide and she has the most beautiful eyes I've ever seen, a little sad. She is my ideal of a college girl and I want to do everything I can to foster a friendship with her. I wish I knew how.

Florence would understand; Bertha imagined her sister's sympathetic face. In just a few days, there would be a letter in response, counseling patience, promising Bertha that in time the people at the college would learn to love her just as her Dayville friends had learned, just as her family always had. Tears stung her eyes and she remembered Mabel's kindness that first evening before supper. She thought of Mabel's handkerchief hidden under her pillow. Some day soon she would return it, but not yet.

You must promise never to show this letter to Father.

There was no need to remind Florence to keep it from their mother.

Your loving sister,
Bertha

When the ink was dry, she folded the letters and put them in a single envelope that she addressed to Florence but didn't seal. The next morning, she removed the second letter and destroyed it. The first she sent home to her family.

Chapter 6

Measurements

When, on Saturday morning, Bertha's name appeared on a schedule posted on the bulletin board in the Chapel, she didn't dare ignore the summons. At her assigned time, she joined a small group of girls in the gymnasium. Told to disrobe to their undergarments, the girls took off their skirts and shirtwaists, their shoes, garters and stockings. They sat in their corsets and petticoats on a long wooden bench, clothes folded in their laps, waiting to be weighed and measured. Some of the thinner ones shivered although the air in the small gymnasium was not particularly chilly. A few looked nervously at the unshaded windows.

The girl next to Bertha was plump, her soft middle held in by a substantially boned corset. The girl's wide thigh rubbed against Bertha's leg and Bertha shifted away.

"I beg your pardon." The big girl looked hurt and apologized without sarcasm.

Bertha hadn't meant to be rude and, although she was a little annoyed at the other girl's sensitivity, quickly responded. "Oh, no need—it was my fault entirely. I'm afraid that I was crowding you."

The girl had a pleasant, open face and she seemed eager to talk. But as she opened her mouth to reply, a clipped, authoritative voice called Bertha's name.

"Miss Mellish, please!"

The plump girl closed her mouth with a smile and a shrug and the other girls paused to look at Bertha as she rose. They had done the same when each name was called, but Bertha felt the scrutiny particular to her. Her mother had never seen her in this state, and she had stopped undressing in front of Florence when she turned thirteen. At home she took off her stockings to wade in forest brooks, but never in front of witnesses.

Dr. Mary Lowell sat at a desk on a platform in the back of the room, waiting to write in large leather-bound account book. She watched with a frown as Bertha walked towards her, and she gestured for the girl to come forward more quickly. The doctor's face was long and square and her hair, parted in the middle and pulled tightly back, exposed her high forehead.

Miss Nellie Spore, teacher of elocution and physical culture and director of gymnastics, helped Bertha step up onto the platform. Bertha was told to stand behind a movable screen that hid her from the view of those in the gymnasium. A table with calipers, rulers and tapes and an odd sort of breathing apparatus stood behind the screen, along with a large scale and a chair.

Miss Spore instructed Bertha to place her clothing on the chair and then undress completely. Like Dr. Lowell, she was efficient but not unkind, and she waited several seconds before repeating her request.

"Please put those things down and take off your undergarments."

Bertha stared at her in disbelief, unable to imagine how she was expected to comply. Miss Spore gestured to a shapeless flannel garment hanging on the screen. "And then put on that drapery. You do understand how it is meant to be worn?"

Bertha didn't move.

"Don't be silly, Miss Mellish." Miss Spore spoke sharply. "We have no need of false modesty here. No one but Dr. Lowell and I will be able to see you and we are both trained in this science. Now undress yourself."

Bertha flushed in anger and shame and imagined slapping the woman's big, officious face. Instead, she dropped her clothes in a heap on the floor and undid the hooks on the front of her corset. She let the corset fall. She did the same with petticoat, chemise and drawers and quickly pulled the piece of flannel from the screen. It was crude unfinished tunic, made from two rectangles of cloth fastened at the top to create shoulders. Bertha slipped it over her head and was mortified that it hung open along each side. She held her arms stiffly down to hide her upper body but her legs were visible. Phosphorescently pale beneath a furze of brown hair, they had well-formed calf muscles and solid thighs. Bertha grasped the cloth in each hand in an effort to close the sides.

Miss Spore acknowledged the heaped clothes with a disgusted glance. Dr. Lowell looked up from her ledger. "Please step on this scale Miss Mellish," she ordered, "And let go of that garment." Bertha reluctantly obeyed.

"Please hold out your left arm, Miss Mellish."

Miss Spore reached beneath the flannel tunic and pulled the tape around Bertha's breasts, her hips, her waist, calling out the numbers for Dr. Lowell to record. She measured Bertha's standing height and sitting height. She measured the distance from Bertha's feet to her pubis, to her navel, to her sternum. She measured the girth of both of Bertha's biceps, elbows, forearms, wrists, thighs, knees, calves and insteps, and of her head, her neck, her chest both inflated and deflated. She measured the length of Bertha's arms from shoulder to elbow and from elbow to fingertip. As Miss Spore's cool fingers wound the tape around her body, Bertha thought of snakes. She felt like a cow at market.

And then she considered how, long after she was gone, these numbers, these measurements listed neatly as an accountant's, might serve as a formula for her re-creation, as a blueprint to reproduce the solid volumes of her body. At first, the idea seemed appealing. She imagined eternity in the quiet, sympathetic company of the casts of ancient statutes that stood in ghostly ranks in Williston Hall. Aphrodite of Melos would be her sister through time. But then she realized no measurements existed to calculate the structure of her face and she saw herself naked and chalk-white with her head blank and featureless as an egg. She shook off the conceit and realized that Miss Spore was speaking.

"Small scar on forehead." Miss Spore reported. "How did you get that?"

"I fell as a child," Bertha answered. Miss Spore pursed her lips impatiently, waiting for her to continue, but Bertha offered no further explanation.

Dr. Lowell stood up and walked behind the screen. She listened to Bertha's chest through a cold metal stethoscope, she thumped Bertha's back and asked her to breath into the apparatus on the table that measured how much air she could hold in her lungs. She examined Bertha's arms and her legs, feeling the bone and the muscle.

"What diseases or ailments do you have or have you had, Miss Mellish?" Bertha remembered measles and a few cases of the grippe. "Stomach problems? Constipation? Fainting spells? Backaches? Weak knees? Tonsilitis? Scarlet fever? Typhoid fever? Diptheria? Consumption? Any of these in the family?" Dr Lowell asked. "Apoplexy? Rheumatism? Kidney problems? Suicide?" Bertha shook her head.

Dr. Lowell stared at Bertha, a frown of concentration tightening her mouth. "Heart is well-functioning and I'm glad to see no extreme corseting but your back is slightly curved. You must improve your posture. Let's see if we haven't expanded your lungs by the time we measure you again. Your arm muscles are underdeveloped and suggest weakness, although your legs look strong enough. We want all our girls here to be as vigorous and healthy as we know they can be. Good diet and enough sleep are imperative; you look a little over-tired. Sleep more, my girl. A course of gymnastics training with Miss Spore will help you to address deficiencies in your upper body musculature and in your carriage."

Miss Spore, with robust arms folded over swelling chest, smiled triumphantly. Dr. Lowell patted Bertha briskly on the shoulder. "Now, on with your clothes, my dear, quickly. That wasn't so bad."

Bertha vowed never to set foot in the gymnasium again.

Chapter 7

Alone in Athens

On the first Sunday of the term, faculty and students passed through the college gates and joined the townspeople in a pious procession to the First Congregational Church of South Hadley. They passed the village green, soggy after several days of rain and ringed by a line of dripping oak trees and a low white fence.

Some of the older women, college teachers and local matrons, spinsters and widows, held black umbrellas over their heads against a fine mist. Men's bowlers and derbies and ladies' hats, trimmed with ribbons, feathers and flowers, shimmered with tiny droplets. Carefully dressed hair frizzed or went lank. Most of the ladies from college and town wore their best outfits and silently worried about damage to silk, velvet and fine wool. They picked gingerly through and around puddles and lifted their skirts to clear the mud.

Bertha walked beside Phebe. She was embarrassed to be so publicly associated with the girl and ashamed of her embarrassment. Bertha's black skirt and silk waist, the only silk waist she owned, were simple, but at least they were well-cut. Phebe wore the same ill-fitting suit she had traveled in, now dirtier and more rumpled than before, and she talked without pause, chattering on about a litter of kittens her brothers had drowned the month before. With her mouth set in a slight pout and her jaw tight, Bertha walked faster than usual. Phebe half ran in her struggle to keep up, and the two made a slightly ridiculous pair.

Eva Newton, arm-in-arm with a large and well-dressed companion, strolled a few yards behind Bertha and Phebe and watched their progress towards the church in shared amusement. Eva's friend was a freshman, the most famous girl at the college, niece and adopted daughter of Governor William McKinley. To Eva's delight, people whispered when Miss McKinley passed and they looked at her with something like awe.

With moist and breathless Phebe in tow, Bertha entered the church and found a half-empty pew in the back, underneath the sanctuary's overhanging gallery. She nodded to the trio of shy freshmen already seated there and motioned Phebe to enter first. Bertha followed, gathering her skirts and settling onto the wooden bench. She hoped that no one would come to fill the empty space beside her and that Phebe would turn her attention to her new neighbors. But Phebe fell silent and looked around with wide, pale eyes at the handsome room with its vaulted ceiling and rose windows. "Golly, it's big," she said.

The pews were almost full and the demure hum of Sunday morning conversation filled the white-walled space. The minister moved towards his place, the choir and the organist were poised to begin, and slowly, softly, like the arc of a sigh, the hum subsided into silence. At that moment, one of the sanctuary's two doors opened and Eva and her companion entered. They kept close to the back wall and with no sign of embarrassment, sat down in Bertha's pew, Eva next to Bertha and Grace on the aisle.

"Miss Mellish, how do you do?" Eva whispered with a sly smile. "I'm surprised to find you all the way back here. You were running to church so fast, I thought you'd be sitting right under the minister's nose."

Bertha turned in icy dignity, silently regarding the delicate turn of Eva's nose, the finely sculpted bow of her upper lip, the graceful arch of her eyebrows. Without jealousy, Bertha accepted her beauty but decided that it would not move her again. Eva's pert face wilted under her steady gaze.

Eva touched Bertha's hand. "Don't be angry, Beatrice," she murmured.

Bertha was surprised at the girl's easy surrender and softened by her plea. She hadn't thought her good opinion of any consequence to popular Eva, never considered she had the power to hurt her feelings. Bertha suddenly realized that her own will was at least as strong as Eva Newton's. There was no reason to avoid the girl who had once seemed so superior.

If, in the end, friendship proved impossible, Bertha decided that she could still make a study of pretty Eva, with her smuggled cigarettes and her impudence. She was a sort that Bertha had never encountered and her habits could be observed and analyzed in perfect safety, like those of a wildcat without claws.

Bertha smiled. "I'm not angry," she whispered as the congregation rose for the hymn.

The Reverend Jones finished the first prayer and stood at the lectern in the center of the platform at the front of the church, looking down at a page of the large Bible open before him. Reverend Jones was nearing the end of his career and had lost some of his physical vigor, but none of his Calvinist steel. He was the perfect caricature of a Yankee minister, tall and impossibly thin, with an Adam's apple jutting out from his scrawny neck like a swallowed stone.

Silent and grave, he surveyed the upturned and expectant faces in the pews for so long that some of the new girls, unfamiliar with his typical performance, grew anxious and shifted uncomfortably. With the bony finger of one hand, Mr. Jones adjusted his spectacles and with the other he slowly smoothed a yellowed page of the book. He cleared his throat with an unpleasant, rheumy sound and intoned: "One Thessalonians, Chapter Three: "Therefore, when we could bear it no longer, we were willing to be left behind in Athens alone."

"In Athens, *alone,*" the minister repeated, giving the final word a drawn-out, lugubrious tone that was almost a wail. He paused, again running his narrowed eyes over the congregation in a manner that was meant to be piercing. He fixed them on the students in the college pews.

"During the labors and struggles of his second missionary journey, Paul chose to carry on his difficult work as minister of the gospel among the unbelieving Greeks, among the sophists and the cosmopolites in Athens, *alone.*"

Reverend Jones was not pleased with the untroubled young faces before him. He raised his volume and lowered his pitch and recounted at length and in detail the tribulations endured by Paul and his converts. He described the tortures of their martyred flesh, the anguish of their souls when family and friends deserted them, the desolation they endured in filthy prison cells. And he reminded his audience that they, young and happy and protected as they seemed to be, would also suffer persecution—*should* also suffer persecution—if they were truly to live a life in Christ.

Reverend Jones saw a few shoulders sag, a few hands clasped to a few breasts, a few clouded faces, and felt newly vigorous.

"Even in halls hallowed by the spirit of Mary Lyon, you will be tempted to turn from the light of Truth into the dark void of Paganism and Materialism. Even here, in this little village where rum is forbidden by God's law and by man's, you will see the drunkard in the street and even here you will hear the siren call of luxury and of Mammon from the cities around you."

Another pause. Reverend Jones straightened to his full, skeletal height and his hollow cheeks burned.

"And here, like Paul, you are in Athens, *alone.* Here you tread strange paths and eat and sleep in strange rooms, away from all those who love you best. Indeed, all the paths of this world and all the rooms of this world are strange and only true faith in Christ can guide us through them to the gates of Heaven."

Reverend Jones stopped again. This time he was gratified to hear a chorus of small, suppressed sobs. Now he turned his attention to the villagers, who had grown comfortable in their seats, and while he chastised them soundly for the places of iniquity flourishing under their noses, the college girls recovered. Freshmen were the hardest hit not, he would have been disappointed to learn, out of spiritual anxiety but from simple homesickness. Phebe snuffled noisily into her dirty handkerchief and considered both the sinfulness of her soul and how far she was from her family, together without her in the chilly New Hampshire farmhouse she had known all her life.

Eva found the sermon boring and the teary girls laughable. She poked Grace and rolled her eyes but got no response. The big girl's elbow rested on the arm of the pew and her cheek was pressed like a pink pillow against her fist. Eva saw that her lids were half shut and that moisture glistened at one corner of her mouth. Disappointed, she turned to Bertha, but Bertha was looking intently forward and paid no attention.

Although it seemed as if she were transfixed by Reverend Jones and his oratory, she was not. Bertha had been born into sermons, steeped in them. She had heard many ministers play the prophet far more convincingly than the old scarecrow now in the pulpit and she was more than familiar with 2 Thessalonians 3 and whatever lessons it might hold for a wavering or a steadfast Christian.

She knew the pitfalls that threatened her body and her spirit; she remembered her father's farewell admonitions. At first, with upright head and lowered eyes, Bertha had watched as Eva's gloved hands played restlessly with the lavender silk of her dress. Then, without changing her pose or expression of pious concentration, Bertha examined the rows of heads in front of her and tried unsuccessfully to find Mabel's.

In Athens, alone. With a melodramatic throb, the minister's words drifted through the heavy air into Bertha's consciousness. The phrase was familiar and had never meant anything in particular to her, but now it struck with the force of a revelation. On the hard oak pew, with Phebe Cutts on one side and Eva Newton on the other, she understood in one crystalline moment the unalterable truth of her condition.

In the small cell of her Dayville bedroom, she'd been seduced by the sentimental college stories she read in magazines. She'd listened too closely to accounts of happy times at Wellesley from Hattie Darling's older sister. She'd succumbed to false hope and for a time–even during her first days at college–believed that the gates of friendship would open for her and she would enter that sunny place where soul-companions strolled arm-in-arm, laughing brightly and sharing lofty thoughts.

Now, in bitterness and pride, she realized the enormity of her self-deception. The hearts of the girls who sat in ordered rows before her, their spines stiffened by corsets, some scratching their hair with dirty fingernails, some coughing, some sneezing, some squirming, some leaning gracefully, some listening with sweet faces of earnest piety, all seemed unspeakably distant and unattainable. In a state of exalted isolation, Bertha felt herself the most abject and the most superior of beings. She was now certain, as she had sometimes felt before, that she was marked by a fate different from that of other girls, and took grim pleasure in its inevitability.

Other girls might jump recklessly into the warm ocean of experience and play like mermaids in the waves. They might find loving husbands and bear legions of rosy babies, they might die after long and useful lives, mourned by multitudes touched by their warmth and goodness. Bertha was sure that she would not. The ocean was too treacherous, the husband and babies and loving friends ghosts of an impossible future. Whatever became of her, whatever honors she achieved, whoever she met and no matter how many years she lived, Bertha knew she would follow her path alone.

The exquisite pathos of the thought brought tears to her eyes, but she resolved to hide her struggle in silent forbearance. *In Athens, alone.* Her private watchword. From that moment on she would present herself in a friendly manner, without conspicuous brooding or obvious attempts at solitude. She believed herself now immune to disappointment, inoculated against the intimacy she had mistakenly supposed she craved.

Thoughts of her parents and Florence came unbidden to her mind and, not wanting to spoil the perfect bleakness of her mood, Bertha quickly dismissed them. Now she felt Eva's impatient tap on her arm. She turned and Eva, eager to share her mocking opinion of the preacher and the sniffling girls, rolled her eyes. Bertha answered with a knowing little smirk and a tiny, resigned shrug.

Pleased that she had won Bertha back, Eva's eyes flashed in momentary triumph.

Chapter 8

The Button Field

After the scrambled disruption of the first week, most students and faculty were glad when the routine of college life took over. The small community, in its green and peaceful world, settled into a measured order of existence marked by bells and guided by the familial decorum of mealtimes, by the dignifying calm of daily chapel services, by the discipline of regular recitations.

The freshmen began to walk more confidently along the paths from Seminary Hall to the classrooms in Williston Hall and the still-unnamed Science Building. They began to believe that academic success, even honors, might be theirs. Fewer of them struggled against tears during meals and chapel. The bolder ones joined clubs and attended receptions and began to make names for themselves as all-around girls, jolly and friendly, ready to help with decorations or invitations or whatever business needed to be done. They hosted spreads in their rooms and were invited to share homemade fudge and welsh rabbit in the rooms of sophomores, even juniors or seniors. They rowed on Lake Nonotuck at the foot of Prospect Hill, played tennis on the courts behind Williston, tried the new game of basketball with energy and enthusiasm in the cramped and outdated gymnasium in the rear of the main building.

In a few weeks, some among the teachers would notice a thrum of anxiety disturbing this happy, busy hive as essays and problems became due and upcoming examinations threatened. Newly formed groups of friends and acquaintances would harden into cliques; colorless, hard-working grinds would fade into the periphery of social existence. And the freaks—girls so awkward, so lacking in any physical or mental grace, so repellent in personality that they could only be likened to sideshow oddities –would be viewed with pity and disgust and then pushed beyond the pale.

Even as a sophomore, Mabel Eaton—serenely patient, good-natured to all, genuinely modest, unflinchingly generous–transcended the merely all-around. Many teachers as well as students predicted that Mabel would end her college career as senior class president. Most of Eva Newton's classmates called her, with her style and her means, a swell. She wasn't enough of a selfless worker to be all-around, and laughingly declined every office or responsibility asked of her. In the opinion of their fellow freshmen and those in the upper classes who deigned to notice, Phebe Cutts was well on her way to becoming a freak and Bertha Mellish had the makings of a grind.

But not, the others sensed, a typical grind. She didn't walk the campus paths with the hunched scuttle of most grinds. Her face wasn't pinched with worry, her eyes weren't puffy from long hours reading by kerosene lamp. Bertha moved calmly through her days with the corners of her mouth turned slightly up, as if sharing a pleasant secret with herself. She seemed to enjoy her Cicero, her Livy, her Horace, her Latin composition, her Herodotus, her Odyssey. She had no apparent difficulty with Higher Algebra or Trigonometry. She wrote essays for Rhetoric with little obvious effort. Bertha worked conscientiously, but never desperately, and was invariably correct when called upon in recitations. She usually had a book in her hand, even when she strolled outside, and sometimes read while walking. To the other girls she seemed unnaturally self-possessed, intimidating to some and irritating to others. "Who does she think she is?" they asked, and saw no reason to invite her to their rooms.

Strangely enough, though, some girls noticed, Miss Mellish and Eva Newton occasionally were seen walking together, up Prospect Hill or out into the village. Miss Mellish sometimes visited Eva in Eva's room although, the more observant of the watchers reported, Eva never went to Miss Mellish's. Eva's society sisters were curious about her association with the odd and distant freshman, and Eva laughed mysteriously at their questions. "Miss Mellish is a very deep thinker, very original," she explained. "We talk about moral philosophy and the wisdom of the ancients when we're together. We discuss the unanswered questions of existence. Most people can't understand the intricacies of her thought, but I can." Eva encouraged Bertha's growing reputation for eccentricity. She had no desire to introduce her into her own circle of friends and have them judge Bertha just an ordinary girl.

On a crisp Wednesday afternoon in October, Bertha and Eva sat together under a tall oak tree at the far end of God's Acre. Bertha leaned against a lopsided headstone, her back covering the inscription scratched in gaunt letters on its worn red surface: *John Preston dyed March ye 4 1727. The first here buried.*

"It must have been lonely," she said, more to herself than to Eva.

Eva was on her side facing Bertha, her head propped on one hand. An open and half-eaten box of chocolates lay on the grass between them, near Bertha's feet and within Eva's easy reach.

"What must have been lonely?" Eva asked, lifting a piece of chocolate from its bed of ruffled pink paper and holding it with exaggerated daintiness between her thumb and forefinger.

Bertha hesitated. It was a strange thought, she knew, and she hadn't meant to say it aloud. "Nothing," she said. "Never mind."

"Oh, Beatrice, don't be tiresome. Tell me what you meant."

Bertha played with a tuft of grass. "Just that it must have been lonely for John Preston, all those years he spent by himself, the first one buried here. Before anyone else joined him, I mean." She leaned slightly forward, tensed, waiting for Eva's response. Now that it was out, she was moved by the poetic melancholy of the idea. Certainly Eva would be too.

Eva popped the chocolate into her mouth. "But he couldn't have felt lonely," she said, the candy thickening her words. "He was dead."

Bertha leaned back against the stone and crossed her arms; Eva must have sensed her disappointment. She pushed the box closer. "Don't be morbid, Beatrice. Why think about dead people when you can eat chocolate!"

The sky was clear, the scent of pine drifted on the breeze, the sun warmed the grass. Eva was right. Bertha smiled and took a piece. It was her fourth of the afternoon and tasted of mint.

Eva also chose another. She bit it in half with her even white teeth, chewed and swallowed. "That's enough of that one," she announced, dropping what was left back in the box.

She did the same with the rest of the chocolates until the box held nothing but half-eaten pieces with their creamy insides exposed. Bertha watched in fascination as Eva methodically mashed every piece with one finger, each cracked brown shell collapsing into pastel goo. Bertha had never witnessed such sublimely wanton destruction and was both repulsed and impressed.

"There," Eva said as if finishing some long and difficult task. She put the lid on the box. "I've had a taste of everything I wanted and I only ate half as much. Not a bad strategy, don't you agree?" Eva licked a last trace of chocolate and orange cream from her forefinger.

"I guess so," Bertha answered with an indulgent shake of her head. After all, the chocolate was Eva's; she could waste it if she chose. Still, she might have saved some for later.

Eva lay flat on her back, stretching and flexing the fingers of both hands, "I like you, Beatrice" she said, looking up at the sky, "because you don't judge me or ask me why I do what I do. That's such a stupid question. Why does anybody do what they do? They do it because they feel like doing it."

"No they don't," Bertha said, so forcefully that Eva turned her head in surprise. "Most people do what they do because they think they should."

Eva was on her side again, resting on her elbow. "You're right about that. Take someone like Mabel Eaton, for example. I don't think she's ever done anything just because she felt like it. She's just too good for that."

Bertha felt her face grow warm; she wasn't sure if it was from anger at the insult to Mabel or shame that Eva had somehow guessed her secret, might even know about the handkerchief. But she had never breathed a word about Mabel to Eva, and Eva had never been to her room. Eva couldn't know that she went to meetings of the YWCA just to watch Mabel play the piano and, if she was lucky, share a word or two.

Bertha rested the back of her head against the gravestone. Maybe Eva wouldn't notice her flushed cheeks. Maybe the cool air would calm them.

"I wouldn't know," she said. "I've barely met Mabel Eaton."

"And what about you?" Eva leaned towards Bertha with a quizzical smile. "Do you do what you think you should or what you feel like doing?"

Before Bertha could answer, they heard a faint rustle, like a squirrel moving through dead leaves.

Eva sat up. "What's that?" she asked.

A slight figure stepped gingerly through the crooked headstones.

"It's Phebe," Bertha said, "What on earth is she doing here?"

Phebe kept her head down and made no sign that she had seen them, although she was headed in their direction. They watched in silent annoyance as she picked her way over the uneven ground, pulling her skirt tight to keep it from brushing the stones. About four feet distant, she suddenly raised her head, as if on cue.

"Oh, my goodness!" Phebe exclaimed, "I didn't see you. I was taking a walk and I just didn't see you until this very moment. Isn't that funny, to be so near someone and not even see them."

Phebe's voice trailed away and she looked plaintively at Bertha. Her ears stuck out through her lank hair, pulled tightly back and glistening in the sun.

Bertha gave her a nod and a stiff smile. "Hello, Phebe."

Eva stared in open rudeness. Still, Phebe stood her ground, arms stiff by her sides, eyes darting from one face to the other.

"It's such a pretty day, don't you think?" Phebe spoke quickly and without plan, as if a torrent of words could crack their reserve. "On days like this at home, I used to go on long walks all up and down the hills. I used to have a dog that would follow me everywhere I went, but that dog died last winter. Oh, no, wait, he died two winters ago. Do either of you have a dog?"

Eva stood up without acknowledging Phebe's question. Her expression had softened, and she addressed Phebe politely, as if she had just joined them. "Well, Miss Cutts, Miss Mellish and I were about to take a walk to the Button Field. Would you like to accompany us? Bertha, do urge your roommate to come."

Bertha, puzzled, looked at Eva and seconded the invitation without enthusiasm.

Too surprised to answer, Phebe only nodded. Her pale eyes moistened. "Oh, yes, please," she managed.

While the other girls brushed and straightened their skirts, Phebe noticed the box of chocolates still lying on the grass. She looked from it to Bertha and then to Eva, but neither seemed aware of the precious item. Side by side, they took a few steps forward.

"Wait!" Phebe cried, "You've forgotten this." With an awkward lurch, she picked up the golden box, its cover embossed with a bouquet of roses. She gasped. She had expected it to be empty but now felt the weight and movement of the sweet morsels still nestled within.

Eva turned back. "Oh you keep it," she said. "I'm done with it."

With the chocolate box pressed tightly to her chest, Phebe followed Eva and Bertha westward out of the cemetery and away from the college through patches of stickers and beggar's-lice and the feathery spray of waist-high goldenrod. Holding the box in two bent arms made walking difficult through the brush and down a gentle slope, but Phebe refused to loosen her grip. Soon the girls came to a scrub-covered field, their boots sinking into the dry sand.

"This," Eva said with a sweep of her arm, "is where the buttons grow in the summer. Look around and you'll find lots of ripe ones ready to be picked."

Phebe scanned the stubbly earth but could find no plants. It resembled no growing field she had ever seen.

"Look down, look down at the ground," Bertha instructed impatiently.

Phebe's confusion made Bertha uncomfortable and a little guilty. She kicked at the sand with her toe and uncovered a large white button. Phebe stared at it, open-mouthed, and then began to scuffle clumsily, rooting and digging with her boot. Most of the buttons she exposed were white and flat, some with four holes, some with two, polished clean by years in the sand.

"Why, they look like potatoes!" she cried in amazement.

Crouching, Phebe released one arm from her box just long enough to dig up a small brass button that she examined as if it were a jewel. Balancing it carefully on her outstretched palm, she carried the button to Bertha and Eva.

"How do you suppose they got here?" Phebe asked, her voice soft with wonder.

"Didn't I tell you they grew here?" Eva spoke to Phebe in a singsong cadence, as she would to a child. "If they didn't grow here, how else could they have gotten here?"

Phebe stood, thinking. Again she clutched the box with both arms, the brass button now sheltered in her fist. "Maybe girls lost them here," she said.

Eva shook her head. "But they're not all girls' buttons."

After a moment, Phebe's face brightened and she straightened her shoulders. "I know! There must have been a button factory. It burned down and the buttons scattered everywhere."

Eva sighed. "No. There never was any button factory here."

With a look, Phebe appealed to Bertha. Bertha shrugged. "She's right. There was no button factory."

"Maybe they washed down from the graveyard!" Eva laughed, shuddering in mock horror.

She turned and began to walk up the brambly hill towards the cemetery and the college. Bertha followed quickly and Phebe, burdened now by the button as well as the chocolate, trailed them both. The sun was low behind them. Phebe shivered and sniffled loudly but the other girls were too far ahead to hear.

Once inside the college gates, Eva joined a group of strolling friends and Bertha reported to the dining room to set her supper tables. Phebe went directly to their room and shut the door. For a moment, she considered locking it but didn't dare. She placed the brass button in the center of her pillow and then sat on the edge of her bed, her feet barely reaching the floor. She settled the golden box on her knees and aligned it so that the roses lay with their blooms at the top.

As a lesson in self-discipline, Phebe tried to move slowly. She considered how many chocolates might still be inside and cautioned herself against expecting too many. She would eat only one before supper and then only one a day until they were gone.

Breathless, Phebe opened the box.

Phebe had little experience with store-bought chocolate, or chocolate of any kind, but once before, in the prim upholstered parlor of a lady's house, she had been offered a piece from a box similar to this. It had been a small, shiny oval, with its smooth surface topped by a tiny hardened peak and she had eaten it in four small, deliberate bites. For a moment Phebe stared at the crushed chocolates, stuck to each other and to the crumpled pink paper, and could not figure out why they looked so different from what she remembered.

She picked out a piece and put it in her open palm, just as she had done with the brass button, and brought the palm close to her face in the darkening room. She saw the chocolate's lacerated edges and the traces of concave scars left by teeth and felt a momentary twinge, more disappointment than disgust, just before she lowered her head and, with a grunt, shoved the piece into her mouth.

When Bertha opened the door, Phebe was still sitting on the edge of the bed, her head down, her thin neck straining forward and her back bent almost double. In the few seconds before she turned on the light, Bertha saw Phebe grab a handful of dark matter from the box on her knees and bring it to her face. Phebe froze in the flash of electric light, her hand pressed against her ravening mouth. Chocolate smeared her cheeks, her chin, the tip of her nose, the front of her white blouse and she stared at Bertha with her pale eyes bulging in frenzy and shame.

"Stop that! Stop it!" Bertha strode the few feet from the door to Phebe's bed and snatched the box off her knees. The few remaining crushed and tooth-scarred pieces went flying, scattering over Phebe's worn bed quilt and the mat-covered floor. Bertha lifted her other arm in a quick and violent gesture and had to force herself not to hit Phebe. She stood, awful as an Old Testament prophet, over the limp and cowering girl.

"Look at you!" Bertha sputtered in rage. "You, you're disgusting! You look like a. . .a . . . a filthy animal, covered in dirt—covered in worse than dirt. Where is your dignity? How could you eat another person's refuse?"

Bertha stopped abruptly and lowered her arm. She tossed the empty box onto Phebe's quilt and sat down on her own bed across the narrow space. Suddenly, she was very tired and no longer angry. Phebe was crying now with full-blown sobs. She hadn't changed position; her knees were together, her feet skimmed the floor, her body curled inward. She didn't cover her face with her hands, which lay motionless on her lap, and tears ran down and mixed with the chocolate on her face. Her nose began to drip but she made no move to wipe it. Above her head hung the picture of the weeping Christ.

The picture was a black and white lithograph, taken from a painting famous fifty years before. Christ wept over Jerusalem's sins with his long, softly bearded face tilted and turned gracefully to one side. Two tears, fat, round and glistening, balanced on his gaunt cheek. Christ raised his right hand, delicate as a woman's, in a gesture as much of despair as of blessing. Bertha watched Phebe, wretched as any of God's creatures that she had ever seen, sob beneath the tender, mournful hand of Christ. Bertha watched her with detachment, her rage dissipated, even her repulsion fading. She tried to feel pity but realized that mercy was the best she could do.

"It's all right, Phebe," she said quietly. "Stop crying and get a handkerchief. Clean yourself up and we won't talk about this again."

Phebe silently obeyed and walked with her head down in an exaggerated show of penitence to the washstand in the dark closet. When she came out, her face had been wiped almost clean but she wore the same stained shirtwaist.

"Clean off your bed and the floor and throw the rest of that mess away." Bertha continued to watch with her arms folded and her face calm but stern. Phebe picked up the remains of the chocolate and the pink paper and put them in the bottom of the box. The rose-covered lid still lay on the bed and Phebe looked at it and then, imploringly, at Bertha. "May I keep the box?" she whispered and Bertha, after a moment, nodded.

Phebe made a hurried and furtive trip to the trash-room down the hall, where she left the evidence of her shame, returning with the empty bottom of the treasured box. Under Bertha's impassive eye, she took the brass button still lying undisturbed on her pillow, placed it in the box and carefully replaced the lid. She sat again on her bed with the box on her knees. She waited, nervous and fidgety. She felt that there was something she was supposed to say or do but had no idea what was expected of her. She could not bring herself to meet Bertha's gaze and her stomach hurt. Her eyes began to fill.

"Phebe," Bertha finally said, "I'm going to tell you about the Button Field. Of course you know that buttons don't grow there."

Phebe sighed and her wan face reddened. "I'm not stupid, you know." Her voice was plaintive and resigned, as if she knew it would be futile to press the point.

"Of course you're not stupid. I never meant to imply that you were. I just meant that you already understand nothing supernatural is involved."

Phebe sat up straighter and pushed some loose clumps of hair away from her face and anchored them behind her ears. She listened attentively as Bertha spoke.

"About two miles from the field there used to be a paper mill. They had to cut the buttons off the rags they used to make the paper and these buttons were thrown into the rubbish heap along with bits of rag and other trash and then this heap was dumped on the field and spread all over as fertilizer. The rags disappeared, but the buttons remained. That's it– no magic and no mystery."

Phebe shifted her knees and felt the little brass button skid inside the box. That tiny golden nugget, delicately filigreed, could have nothing in common with cow dung and straw or the smelly pulp of a paper mill.

"I see," Phebe said softly. Although she accepted Bertha's explanation, she didn't believe it, at least not for her button. Her button was different and, Phebe was sure, had lodged itself deep in the sandy soil in some other, miraculous way.

Part Two

Sophomore Year, September 1896 - June 1897

Chapter 9
Recreation Day

On the first Wednesday of the semester, Bertha relaxed in a cushioned rocking chair in the room—the largest in Seminary Hall–that Eva Newton now shared with Grace McKinley. A shaft of afternoon sunlight fell on her from an open window; she set the chair in gentle motion and closed her eyes. This year, she reflected, was starting out much better than the last.

Unlike Eva, Bertha hadn't asked for a different room or a new roommate and had fully expected to be back with Phebe. Whatever fate God chose for her she'd planned to accept. She was surprised, then, to find that she'd been assigned a nicer room—one with a view of the hills and fields towards Holyoke—and a new roommate, a pretty freshman from New Haven who put up a Yale banner and had her own chafing dish, and who spent most of her waking hours in the company of two friends she knew from home.

Through the window, Bertha heard the thump of distant drumbeats. A monument to the town's Civil War dead, now thirty years gone, had been unveiled on the village green that morning. The solemn speeches and prayers were long over but the band played on and many of the college girls still joined the villagers in celebration; Grace McKinley was down there yet. But Bertha had been summoned to witness another unveiling: a new cycling outfit fresh from Eva's Chicago dressmaker.

"Bertha! Don't fall asleep!"

Eva's command roused her; she opened her eyes, leaned forward.

Ferocious in her excitement, Eva tore at a large parcel, scattering shards of brown paper. She dumped its contents on her bed and dug her fingers in the jumble of fabric as if it were a pile of gold.

"I want to try on everything this minute," she said, "You have to help me."

Amused by the naive urgency of Eva's desire—she seemed more a child of five than a woman of nineteen—Bertha didn't mind playing nursemaid. She rocked forward, propelled herself from the chair.

Eva's hands shook; Bertha helped with buttons, laces, hooks. After fifteen minutes of concentrated effort, Eva was ready. She stood before the full-length mirror that straddled one corner of the room, turning from side to side, admiring, transfixed by her own reflection.

The jacket hugged her body, the skirt fell a few inches below her knees.

"I want to wear this outside." Eva said. "I want to wear this in the village."

Bertha hesitated. She looked at Eva's exquisite little boots, the slim turn of her ankles, her calves swathed in black and thought of the crowd outside the fence. "Mrs. Mead wouldn't approve," she said, although she knew her objection carried no weight.

Eva ran both hands down the front of her skirt. "All the more reason to do it," she said. "Let's get my bicycle."

Eva rode her gleaming black bicycle the short distance from the storage room underneath the gymnasium to the college gates; Bertha followed behind. Just inside the fence, Eva stopped and swung her leg back over the saddle, dismounting like a boy. Together, the two girls surveyed the street.

The band played ragged and out of time in the ornate bandstand on the green. Peanut vendors, lunch wagons and tables selling doughnuts hunkered in the shade of the elms that lined the road. Children darted between strolling couples, clusters of young men and young women came together and drew apart, guided by some mysterious magnetism. Here and there, a bearded veteran of the Grand Army of the Republic in a uniform either too big or too small shuffled by on a cane or the supporting arm of someone younger.

Bertha glanced at Eva's face and saw a feral intensity there that confused her. Eva's eyes moved restlessly over the scene as if she were looking for something particular; Bertha had no idea what that might be.

"Here," Eva said, tilting the bicycle towards Bertha, "You hold this. I don't want to catch my skirt in the spokes."

Bertha took the handlebars. For a moment, she considered mounting. Once she'd watched Charlotte Cogswell speed down the road on such a machine; there was no reason she couldn't ride just as well, with a little practice. But the bicycle was Eva's and not hers; Bertha merely kept it upright and wheeled it forward while Eva, unhampered, led the way.

Eva turned out of the gate as if heading to church. Then, without a word, she crossed the street towards the village green, not pausing to see if Bertha followed.

A fence ringed the green with its new granite obelisk. Men, a few old, most young, leaned against its wooden rails. Some had taken off their jackets and lounged in vests and white shirts, their hats raked over their eyes. Some ate, shucking peanuts and throwing the shells on the ground, and some, because the town was dry, drank bottles of soda pop.

Eva reached the fence first and waited for Bertha with her hands resting on her hips. Together, they began to walk the length of the fence, Eva taking small, mincing steps. With a laugh, she turned her attention to Bertha and spoke with self-conscious animation, loudly enough to be heard over the brassy music.

"You really ought to try a wheel," Eva said, "Riding one is such fun. You've never felt anything so fast."

Suddenly, she stopped and bent at the waist to adjust a button on her gaiter. Then, with a slow, sweeping motion of her hand, she smoothed the back of her skirt.

With conspicuous stares or hooded glances, the men at the fence watched. One or two of the older ones averted their eyes and even the rougher boys in shirt-sleeves made no audible comments or rude remarks. Still, the air around them prickled with an energy that frightened Bertha. When Eva stood up, her face was red. She grabbed the crook of Bertha's elbow and kept her eyes fixed on the ground.

"I've had enough of this," she said. "The music, if you can call it that, is giving me a headache. Let's go home."

They walked away quickly, Eva pulling at Bertha's arm, Bertha struggling with the bicycle. Close to the college gate, Eva slowed. "I'll take that now, Beatrice," she said, "You must be tired."

Bertha liked the feel of the bicycle in her hands, liked the thought that everyone they passed—even the men at the fence—imagined her a strong and independent woman, a cyclist. Reluctantly, she returned it. As they started down the path towards Seminary Hall, she crossed her arms and refused to look while Eva explained just how easily she had learned to ride that past summer.

But there was Mabel Eaton, coming up the path towards them. Bertha uncrossed her arms and quickened her pace.

"Miss Mellish! Miss Newton!" Mabel called, "How lovely to see you both!"

Since the beginning of the term, Bertha had tried to without success to arrange a chance encounter with Mabel. Now, unprepared for such a meeting, she found herself with her heart pounding, staring dumbly at Mabel while both Mabel and Eva looked at her. Bertha felt herself blush.

"Well, Miss Mellish, I hope to see you at more YWCA meetings this term." Mabel was used to filling silences and never let them grow to be uncomfortable. "I've heard that you have a lovely manner in recitations," she continued, "Maybe you can lead us in prayer someday soon."

Eva gave a soft, almost inaudible snicker and began rolling the bicycle a few inches forward and then a few inches back.

"I'm sorry if I'm keeping you, Miss Newton," Mabel said, without a trace of sarcasm.

"Now that you mention it, Miss Eaton, I do have to put my wheel away. Perhaps it's best if I leave you two alone."

Eva glanced at Bertha with a knowing smile, as if some secret passed between them. But Bertha did not acknowledge the look and

Eva quickly mounted her bicycle and sped down the path and out of sight.

Bertha was calmer now and her breathing slower. For the first time since their encounter a year ago, she raised her eyes to meet Mabel's. They were brown, warmed with gold, the color of oak but soft as velvet.

"May I call you Mabel?" she asked.

"Of course," Mabel said, "if you'll let me call you Bertha."

They both smiled and Bertha reached for Mabel's hand. When she thought about it afterwards, she could not explain what had driven her to be so bold.

"Last year, when I was new and didn't know a soul, you were very kind to me." The words came out of Bertha's mouth before she formed them in her mind.

Mabel pressed Bertha's hand and gently drew hers from its grasp.

"It was my pleasure," she said. They stood together in the afternoon light with Mabel's face in shadow and her hair lit from behind. "And my duty."

Bertha flinched.

"No, not a duty, please forgive me," Mabel said, "Sometimes I get a little preachy." She paused and touched Bertha's arm. "I'm having some friends to my room next Tuesday evening, for a spread. I hope you can come. I'll put an invitation in your mailbox."

For a moment, Bertha wondered if Mabel's offer was merely penance for her remark about duty. And what if it were? Bertha smiled her acceptance.

"Tuesday, then." Mabel turned to leave, abruptly stopped. "Oh, yes," she said, "I just remembered there was something I wanted to ask you. I know this sounds silly, it's been so long, but do you remember a handkerchief of mine that you borrowed last year?"

Bertha's smile froze and turned brittle.

"I only realized it was missing this summer," Mabel explained, "when my dearest friend from home asked about it. She made it for me, otherwise I wouldn't bother you."

That treasured piece of linen, the one link to Mabel that was hers and hers alone—a fraud. Bertha's chest hollowed, as if she had no heart, no lungs, nothing but a barren cage of bones. She forced herself to breath.

"I remember the handkerchief," Bertha murmured as if reaching back to a vague and distant past. "It was the first night, when you came to get me for supper."

Some hands other than Mabel's worked the needle. Some strange girl held the cloth in her thick, rough fingers and tugged and pulled the thread into that misshapen token of a friendship between Mabel and someone else, someone far closer and with a much greater right to Mabel's love.

Stay calm, Bertha told herself. Don't give yourself away.

"I think I gave it back to you," she said, trying for a convincing blend of certainty and doubt, "I think I handed it back to you."

Mabel looked puzzled but not suspicious. She offered no challenge. In the face of such trust, Bertha felt guilty. Still, it was impossible to confess the truth.

"I might have kept it, I'm afraid I don't remember," she said. "I'll check my room and I'll write to my sister at home. Maybe it's mixed up with my things. I am sorry, but I haven't seen it since that night. If I did have it and I lost it, I am truly sorry."

Her apology, though false in particulars, was sincere. Bertha looked at Mabel with genuine remorse.

"Please, don't let it trouble you," Mabel said. "It's only a handkerchief—I have others. I'm sure I took it back that night and then lost it. Please don't be upset on my account."

Bertha noticed a slight tremor in her voice, a hint of tears, and understood just how much Mabel hated to cause distress, however mild.

"Thank you," Bertha said and held Mabel's gaze.

The village band was silent, the peanut and doughnut sellers packed up and left, the families carried off in their buggies and their wagons. For the first time that day, the air was still. The girls who came in from the village and those who walked in pairs or in groups or alone on the campus lawns and paths seemed unusually quiet, as if glad to hear nothing but the faint rustle of leaves in a mild breeze.

Bertha had never known a moment so perfect and so poised and she had never seen anyone so beautiful as Mabel with her sad, understanding eyes and the corners of her crooked lips drawn up in a small, beseeching smile. Bertha wanted to hold her, rest her cheek against the halo of her hair. Mabel said good-bye; Bertha stood alone on the path just long enough to attract the curious stares of passing girls.

After supper that evening, walking the red-tinted hallway to her room, Bertha considered the strange and unsettling direction the day had taken. She wondered what she and Mabel might talk about on Tuesday evening, and remembered the weight of Mabel's hand in hers. Over the next few weeks, Bertha decided, she would make for Mabel a fine linen handkerchief embroidered with an "M" to substitute for the imposter that, as soon as it had served as a model, she would destroy.

Deep in these imaginings, Bertha did not hear the light, rapid patter of footsteps until they were directly behind her. She turned to face Phebe, wan and thin in the same over-sized suit she had worn last September. Phebe opened and closed her mouth several times like a fish and then, without a word, turned and ran back the way she had come.

Chapter 10

Miss Slater

Platters of reheated steak, eggs and potatoes sat on the long, white-clothed tables that filled the dining hall; the air was thick with their smell. Elizabeth Slater wasn't hungry, but for appearance's sake she took a potato and a small piece of meat. Waiting for the girls to fill their plates, she stared into the building's enclosed courtyard, visible through a window to her left. How awful the life of a prisoner, she thought, shut away from the world.

By the morning of the second Sunday of the term, Miss Slater was already worn out and impatient with herself and everyone around her. She thought her teaching days would soon be over, but George's work was not going well and he would not marry without his degree.

The unseasonable heat of the day oppressed her. The thought of the long Sabbath before her almost made her cry. First was this interminable morning meal, then the tedious Sunday service, then dinner, then the lonely afternoon hours of letter-writing or reading, then supper, then the solemn and serious prayer meeting before bed.

The day before, Mrs. Mead had asked her to lead that Sunday evening service and she'd struggled furiously to decline. She tried to explain that her conscience told her not to, that she didn't have the power or the talent or the will to lead or inspire the college. She didn't say so to Mrs. Mead, but it sickened her to think about uttering the grim pieties expected on such occasions. But Mrs. Mead would not accept her refusal. A very unpleasant conversation ensued and at the end of it Miss Slater still found herself responsible for the evening meeting.

Elizabeth Slater was a Christian woman. Only by loving and giving herself to others could she do Christ's work, she believed, and, by so doing, find him. And she longed to find him. She'd had enough of sin and retribution, the awful silences of a cold New England upbringing, the sting of belt leather, the horrors of hell.

The fourteen girls, seven on a side, each helped themselves as the platters made their rounds and then, with straight backs and folded hands, looked to Miss Slater.

"Miss Slater?" the girl seated to her right whispered. "Miss Slater?" she asked again, more loudly.

Miss Slater started. "I beg your pardon," she said and picked up her knife and fork. "Do begin."

For several minutes, they ate in silence, sawing at their tough meat, taking polite and restrained forkfuls of potato. The six freshmen at the table were particularly self-conscious and ate smaller bites and dabbed their mouths more frequently than they would have done at home.

She should be drawing these new students out of themselves; Miss Slater was acutely aware of her failure. She was sure that all the other tables were lively—she heard laughter coming from Cornelia Clapp's–and that Mrs. Mead was taking note of her indifference and would later remind her of her duty.

In desperation, she turned to the girl on her left, a nervous new student who kept her eyes fixed on her plate, intending to ask how she liked the college. Before she could muster the energy to speak, Helen Calder, seated halfway down the table, came to the rescue of both the teacher and the timid freshman.

"You must all try basketball!" Helen exclaimed to no one in particular, looking around the table with a good-natured smile. She had been biding her time and was pleased with herself for breaking the awkward silence. "You all simply must try it!"

Helen, tall and broad-boned, was captain of the Sports Association. Like many other girls at Mount Holyoke, she'd recently taken up the new sport of basketball, invented just a few miles down river at Springfield College.

Miss Slater listened gratefully while Helen amused the table with a description of the game and its attractions. All of the girls turned towards her, their faces bright as if warmed by a genial sun. All, she noticed, except Miss Mellish. Miss Mellish continued to eat, cutting her meat with the precision and focus of a surgeon. She was not, it seemed, oblivious to Helen's conversation; occasionally a hint of a smile or a glimmer of amusement passed across her face. But she had clearly removed herself to eavesdrop, like a foreigner in a strange land feigning ignorance of the native tongue.

Bertha Mellish had made Elizabeth Slater uncomfortable from their first meeting, early last year when the girl was late to supper. Without excuse or apology, she had accepted the teacher's gentle reprimand so calmly that the older woman found herself flustered. Miss Slater was disconcerted to find Miss Mellish a student in three of her Greek recitations, sitting in the center of the first row. She was grateful for the massive lecturer's desk that separated them. Standing plain and frowzy behind its polished surface, she hoped something of its authority was reflected in her face.

When, during the second week of classes, Bertha Mellish began to answer questions and present translations, her voice had a rich dignity older than her years. Elizabeth Slater was sure then that Miss Mellish could see her for the fraud she knew herself to be, a coarse and common woman despite her two Wellesley degrees.

Yet, towards the middle of that first term, she came to realize that Bertha Mellish had no interest in exposing her secrets and was neither a performer nor a competitor. There were even times when it seemed that the other girls, the dull-witted and the sharp, had all disappeared and that only she and Bertha remained, as if all of her mental energy, all of whatever wisdom she had managed to wrestle into her possession, all of the poetry that grew like moss in the darkness of her soul was directed at this strange girl with impenetrable eyes.

By the time classes resumed for the second term, Miss Slater was disappointed that Miss Mellish had not approached her outside of class and barely spoke to her at meals. She knew that, as the adult and the teacher, it was her responsibility to reach out to the young woman, invite her for a walk or for tea in a parlor or even her room. She had done so for other students who interested her less. In truth, she was waiting for the girl to come to her. She wanted to know that she had, in fact, reached Miss Mellish's heart.

Swept along by the force of Helen Calder's enthusiasm, nearly all of the girls at the table had agreed to join her in the gymnasium for a basketball lesson. Not that Sabbath afternoon, of course, but the next day.

Helen turned to her right, where Bertha Mellish sat. "I don't see you much in the gym, Miss Mellish," she said, "You must come down tomorrow, too." Helen did not expect her reserved neighbor to accept, but felt it only polite to include her in the general invitation.

Bertha wiped her mouth with her napkin and smiled softly. Last year she would have declined, but now she understood that this invitation and, more importantly, Mabel's, were signs of a challenge that she must meet and master. If she tried hard enough, she might yet claim something of a place for herself inside the college circle. And, she realized, it would be a relief to describe, in all honesty, both Helen Calder's basketball lesson and Mabel Eaton's reception in her letter home.

"Thank you, Miss Calder, I would be pleased to join you," Bertha said, "but I'm afraid I won't be much good."

"Nor shall any of us!" In the seat across from Bertha, a hitherto silent freshman with a scrubbed face and rimless spectacles had summoned all of her courage to offer this observation, which was met with general laughter.

For once, Miss Slater did not chide the girls when they broke naturally into smaller groups and the rest of the meal passed pleasantly. The irregular rhythm of their chatter, punctuated by an occasional guffaw from Helen Calder, relieved her of any responsibility and she drank the last of her coffee with one elbow perched on the edge of the table. She found herself watching Bertha Mellish, who had been drawn into conversation by the brave freshman flush with her public triumph.

Miss Slater could not hear their words, but Miss Mellish seemed more engaged than usual. She looked directly at the other girl and there was a little more animation in her face when she spoke.

At the end of the meal, under Mrs. Mead's direction, the students and teachers tucked their napkins into rings, laid them neatly at their places and left their seats. Bertha stayed behind, one of the crew of students assigned to clear up after breakfast. By the time she'd scraped and stacked her dishes, all the rolling carts were taken and she was forced carry the dirty tableware to the kitchen.

Leaning over to collect the last of the plates, Bertha thought she heard her name in the echoing clatter of the room. A trick of the ear, she figured, and wiped her forehead with a damp and wrinkled sleeve. But she heard it again, more clearly, and when she straightened to scan the room, she noticed Miss Slater standing by the door, looking in her direction and motioning her forward with two bent fingers. Some reprimand, Bertha sighed, some reminder of a broken rule. Mrs. Mead's emissary, sent to warn her about reading too early in the morning or walking too far from the college.

Miss Slater, now that she had the girl's attention, wagged her fingers vigorously, softening the command with a smile. She should have done this a long time ago, she realized, broken the ice between them. How selfish she had been, expecting Bertha to make the first move.

The girl approached slowly, shoulders drooping. She stopped a few feet away, that familiar expression on her face, opaque, unreadable. "Yes, Miss Slater," she said.

"Come outside." Miss Slater stepped forward, touched the sweat-soaked fabric of Bertha's sleeve. "I'd like to talk to you, and it's much too warm in here."

The girl didn't move or change expression. "But I have my tables to finish," she said, with no hint of defiance or complaint.

"Of course you do." Miss Slater pulled back, crossed her arms. "They certainly must come first."

She hadn't meant to be sarcastic but couldn't keep the bitterness from her voice. She didn't blame the girl, choosing to clear dirty dishes on a beautiful Sunday morning. A minister's daughter, most likely—there were so many of them here, drilled in duty from the moment they were born. And duty, Miss Slater knew, was a burden not easily set down.

"I'm sorry," she said, "I spoke too sharply. Please come to my room this afternoon, after you've finished your chores and had a chance to rest. For some time I've been meaning to talk to you. You're a fine student in Greek; perhaps you'd like to tutor a freshman."

Miss Slater paused, waiting for Bertha to express delight in both the personal invitation and the professional compliment. For a moment the girl said nothing, although Miss Slater heard her draw a quick breath and saw her eyes widen under her dark brows.

"Thank you," she said, "What time shall I come to your room?"

Bertha hoped her tone was sufficiently grateful. She was mortified to have insulted Miss Slater by choosing to finish her domestic work. She was furious with herself for failing to convey just how much she appreciated the older woman's attention. She was sure she had clumsily trampled the first tender shoots of what she scarcely dared dream would grow into a respectful friendship.

"We can talk before supper," Miss Slater said, "Shall we say half past four?"

Chapter 11

Fire

From Prospect Hill, the lazy curls of smoke hanging in the still air above the courtyard were barely visible. To drowsy eyes, lulled by a full day of Sabbath decorum, they hardly registered. To dreamy minds, they might have been tufts of disintegrating cloud drifting slowly to earth. Except that the wisps rose upward and grew into darker, fatter billows.

Bertha reached Miss Slater's door promptly at four-thirty and stood in front of it for several minutes, practicing her greeting. "Good afternoon, Miss Slater," she whispered, "Thank you for your kind invitation." She drew a breath, knocked twice softly. No answering sound from within. She knocked again, harder than she'd intended. When Miss Slater opened the door, Bertha was relieved to see that she smiled, no trace of annoyance on her face, so often sharp and strained.

"Good afternoon, Miss Slater," Bertha said. "Thank you for your kind invitation."

"I'm glad to see you, Miss Mellish. Please come in." With an open hand, she invited her guest across the threshold, closing the door behind her.

Miss Slater's room was the first faculty sanctum she had ever breached, and Bertha tried not to scan its contents too openly. She'd expected something more scholarly, a retreat with bookcases rising from floor to ceiling, oil paintings on the walls, maybe a fragment of Greek statuary and a piece of Roman glass displayed on a table.

Miss Slater's room was sparer and neater than most student rooms, but it too had its potted plant and its rocking chair, its framed prints and embroidered pillows. A large bookcase and an oak desk scattered with paper and pens dominated the wall opposite the bed. Bertha saw no unusual artifacts, nothing to suggest a broadly lived life. She tried not to show her surprise or disappointment. And then it struck her, the lesson of this room. Miss Slater was not so different, after all, just a woman, educated, yes, but human. Perhaps they could be friends.

Miss Slater followed Bertha's gaze, saw it light on a framed photograph resting on the desktop.

"That's Mr. George Rogers," she said, unable, as always, to temper her pride. "We're engaged to be married." She moved towards the desk, intending to retrieve his picture.

The sounds were indistinct but audible: muffled shouts and the quick, soft thump of running feet. Miss Slater stopped, looked quizzically at Bertha.

"What on earth is that commotion?"

When Miss Slater opened the door, tendrils of light gray smoke drifted into the room. For a moment the two women watched as the room slowly clouded.

Stinging eyes brought Miss Slater to her senses. She ran into the hall, fanning both hands in the air around her head; she heard Bertha follow. They hugged the wall, saw three girls hurry by, their forms softened by the thickening haze. The first dragged a bulging blanket, the second struggled with an armload of clothes, the third carried a mandolin.

Miss Slater caught the arm of a passing teacher, Netta Haffner, an older woman trained in Chemistry.

"Where's the fire?" she asked, her voice hoarse. "How close?"

Miss Haffner, handkerchief to mouth, squinted at Miss Slater. "In the gymnasium. For now," she answered, her words muffled by the wadded cloth. She lowered her hand, coughed. "We must get everyone out," she said, pulling free from Miss Slater's grasp.

Miss Slater pushed Bertha in the direction of the Seminary wing, westward, far from the gymnasium. "That way," she said, "go that way, into the old building!"

Bertha left; Miss Slater hurried in the opposite direction, a shepherd in search of her flock.

Bertha did not follow Miss Slater's orders. There was still time, she was sure, for a trip to her own room, one floor down on the same northern wing. She'd seen no flames, felt no real heat. If she worked quickly she could save her things, *her* things—not much to most of the girls, she knew, but things that had cost her father and her mother and her sister dearly, things given in love, things meant to be protected.

The door was open; Bertha's roommate had already made her escape. The girl's bed was stripped bare, her shelves empty and walls cleared of pictures. Nothing but a broken teacup and a single stocking remained on her side of the room.

Bertha tore the bedclothes from her mattress, spread out a sheet. On it she threw most of her clothes, all of her books, her letters from home. She knotted its corners, spread the second sheet. In that she wrapped her feather pillow, her blanket, her mother's paisley shawl. She dragged both bundles to the window, thankfully open, and wrestled them up and out. A glance downward told her they'd landed near a scattering of similar packages. Later, she reassured herself; I'll find them later.

The pictures—the Colosseum, Millet's *Angelus,* behind glass in wooden frames–would have to stay. Bertha accepted their possible loss. But she was not ready to give up the contents of her trunk, stored in the attic: her new woolen skirt and her winter jacket, a pair of thick-soled boots, warm flannels, Florence's re-cut black silk dress. There might still be time, if she hurried.

On her way to the door, Bertha noticed Mabel's handkerchief, exposed on the mattress. She snatched it up, slipped it into the cuff of her blouse, ready to head eastward towards the attic stairs.

—ꟺ—

The fire, begun stealthily and secretly in the dark beneath the gymnasium, feeding on desiccated timber and dust, was exuberant. Now it played merrily through the gym, climbing the ropes that hung from the exposed beams of the ceiling, jumping and somersaulting along the polished floorboards, springing from the wooden rowing machines on the ground to the balcony high along the wall. It waved its black smoke and its bright flames like banners through the shattered windows and it forced its way through the brick walls into the south and then the north wings and up the cramped stairwells and the elevator shaft. Then, in a final explosion of ferocious glee, it burst through the old gym's roof and brought it, cracking and groaning, down.

A distant crash and a small tremor sent Bertha, barely over the threshold on her way to the attic, scurrying westward. She ran, hands over her nose and mouth, coughing, propelled by sudden terror, past open doors and figures moving through the thick gray air like frenetic wraiths, women with lamps, pillows, pictures, men with desks, rocking chairs, tea tables.

Near the end of the long hall the smoke was lighter and Bertha no longer imagined flames licking at her heels. She slowed to catch her breath. All she had to do was reach the door to the old Seminary wing and from there make her way out of the building.

On her left, she saw the door to Phebe's room, closed.

So what, she told herself. So the door is closed.

In that moment, she truly hated Phebe for her insatiable need, for her wan pale eyes, for her innocent trust and her utter helplessness. Bertha opened the door and peered into the room. "Phebe!" she called, her voice hoarse and impatient.

One side of the room had been cleared. On the other, Bertha recognized the faded quilt on the still-made bed and the framed picture of the weeping Christ.

"Phebe! Are you here?!"

No answer. Bertha turned to leave.

A faint sound, a series of tiny squeaks. Bertha followed them into the room's windowless closet and found Phebe there, huddled in its furthest corner, whimpering.

Bertha grabbed her by both thin wrists. Phebe's hands, she saw, were tightly curled.

"Get up!" she ordered, jerking the girl upright.

Clutching Phebe's arm, Bertha dragged her out of the closet and across the room. Limp as a doll until they reached the door, Phebe strained against her ferocious grip.

"I can't leave him!" she cried, "I can't leave him to burn!"

With a few vicious yanks, Bertha forced her out of the room. She pulled the girl down the hall, pushed her into the safety of the west wing. Through it all, Phebe's right hand remained curled, although Bertha did not notice.

The fire was no longer playful. It was hungry and impatient and in no mood to be distracted by water from firemen's puny hoses. With single-minded gluttony, it raced forward through the building's parallel wings, sucking on old roof beams until they shriveled, licking plaster and lath walls until they disappeared. It smashed oil lamps and barely noticed the explosions. It crashed out windows, tore down brick cornices, fouled the air with its thick, sour breath. And when it had devoured everything it could in the north and the south wings, leaving brick walls like brittle husks, it followed its gargantuan appetite westward and feasted on Mary Lyon's dream.

By sunset, even the stalwart Seminary building, that sturdy box built sixty years earlier for Mount Holyoke's first daughters, surrendered to the fire. Its walls and windows were invisible behind the flames, tall and twisted as monstrous trees. Billows of black smoke twinkling with golden sparks poured into the darkening, red-streaked sky. The burning building lit up the surrounding countryside and its glow could be seen as far away as Springfield, thirteen miles down river to the south.

At seven-fifteen, the roof beams and the great center cupola came crashing down. Then, one by one, the big chimneys tottered and wavered. Each struggled to stay upright, like a drunkard fighting for dignity, but each ultimately fell. Two lurched forward and shattered on the lawn. The others shuddered and collapsed where they stood, telescoping downward into the flames.

The crowd had grown steadily since news of the fire first spread outward from South Hadley until it numbered in the thousands. There were more people elbowing each other on the main street and village green than had come to celebrate the Civil War monument unveiled just five days earlier. The electric cars left Holyoke dangerously overfilled until that city's Street Railway Company put additional trolleys into service to handle the demand. Any man or boy with a bicycle pedaled up as fast as he could, families hitched their horses to wagons, carts and carriages, those with no other transportation walked or ran along dusty lanes and paths until they reached the excitement.

While the sun was shining and the fire burned merrily in the building's rear, the crowd had been happily entertained. Children laughed as they watched an old lady teacher carry Mary Lyon's portrait to safety, holding the framed canvas in front of her like a shield. Everyone who saw her chuckled at the strapping student who emerged from the building burdened with two tennis rackets and a shotgun. They encouraged the men who rescued rocking chairs, bookcases, tea tables, desks and set them down in haphazard groupings across the campus lawn. And they cheered in approval when the police dragged a ragged hobo, caught pilfering from one of the white bundles that also littered the place, off to jail.

But now they stood in silence with darkness behind them and searing flames reflected on their skin and in their eyes. The heat had driven them back, past the line of elm trees with scorched bark and shriveled leaves, and across the wide unpaved street. The air that day had been calm and still, but now the fire itself created violent gusts and drafts that sent the flames roaring and whistling in sheets hundreds of feet high. The walls of the building, still standing, formed a massive chimney that shot cinders like a meteor shower into the air and onto the roofs of the wooden houses across the street and the heads and shoulders of the watching people.

Many of the college women and girls sat among the graves in God's Acre as the building burned. Mabel Eaton watched in solemn melancholy, thinking of Mary Lyon's faithful spirit and how sad it must be on this awful, terrifying night. Eva Newton watched with something like joy at the glorious destruction, troubled only by visions of her bicycle, stored in the basement under the gymnasium, reduced to a puddle of warped metal and melted rubber. Elizabeth Slater sat with her head in her hands, distraught beyond tears at the thought of George's letters turned to ash and vapor by the flames. And on the steps of the village school, a few yards south of the graveyard, President Mead sat with College Treasurer Lyman Williston. After a brief storm of hysterical tears, Mrs. Mead rallied and now, as the old place went up in smoke, the two busily calculated the value of Mount Holyoke's insurance policies.

Bertha had held tight to Phebe's wrist down the smoky halls of the old building, across the crazily furnished lawn and through the gawking crowds into the cemetery. Once out of her room, Phebe no longer struggled and, weakly whimpering, did her best to keep up with Bertha's single-minded progress.

"Here," Bertha said as she released Phebe and pointed towards the soft grass in front of a headstone, "Sit down and don't move until someone tells you to. You're all right now." She turned to leave, hoping to find Miss Slater, or Eva, or Mabel somewhere in the dusky confusion.

Phebe did as she was told, although she kept her distance from the gravestone. She remained in a quiet huddle as the sky grew dark and the roar of the fire erased all other sound. But when the roof and the cupola fell she jumped up and went to stand among the watching crowd.

Phebe's pale face and hair glowed like the embers floating in the air around her. She stood completely still with unblinking eyes and she held her left hand outward, palm upward as if hoping to catch the sparks like snowflakes as they fell. In her right fist, she clutched the little brass button, its pattern pressed into the flesh of her palm. Her lips moved as if in prayer, but the words were audible to no ears but her own.

By nine o'clock, most of the Holyoke firemen had been relieved of duty, along with the South Hadley Falls hook and ladder company and the Northampton men who had arrived in time to save the college library, demolishing the corridor that connected it to the main building. By eleven-thirty, most of the onlookers and the helpful volunteers had left and the homeless Mount Holyoke faculty and students had found shelter, some with generous villagers, some in the town's schoolhouse, some in the college's remaining buildings. Portions of Seminary Hall kept falling until midnight and those sections that did not succumb remained as lonely sentinels over the ruins. By one o'clock the streets of the village were empty except for a few firemen who kept watch all night, dousing the tenacious flames that occasionally burst from the lingering pall of black smoke, and the policemen who guarded the deserted grounds, decorated with their ghostly furnishings.

Chapter 12

Miller's Cottage

Bertha, along with eleven other girls—Phebe among them—and two teachers, one of them Miss Slater, was assigned to a good-sized, musty old house half a mile down the Holyoke road. It took Addie Miller, the shrewd spinster who owned the place, a day to calculate her profits before agreeing to rent to the college and move in with her brother and his family. The house had a big kitchen and seven other rooms but no bathroom and no steam heat, two inconveniences that sent one student home after a single night.

On the day after the fire, after several hours of searching, Bertha found both of her bundles, damp and sooty but otherwise undamaged, and joined other girls bound for Miller's cottage on a creaky old wagon. When the group arrived, they swarmed the house and laid claim to various rooms, juniors and seniors taking most of the sunny, stove-warmed downstairs spaces, sophomores and freshmen making do with what remained.

Upstairs, four students settled on a room to the left of the second floor landing. To the right of the landing, each teacher was given a small front bedroom.

Hidden behind the back wall of the students' upstairs room was a rectangular chamber, hardly wider than a closet, accessible by a small door. It now held a bed, but its original use was unclear; perhaps it was meant for storage. It had one small window and delicate traces of ancient water stains on its plaster walls. Every girl who saw it curled her nose in disgust and a few declared that they would go home if forced to sleep there.

But Bertha liked the little room, safe as a cocoon. No one else, she was sure, would want to share the space with her and so she volunteered to take it.

After one happy night alone, another girl was assigned to the house and, because all the other rooms were full, her cot set up in the space that Bertha had already come to think of as her own. But the girl, a freshman, made no attempt to disguise her unhappiness and by the next afternoon she'd left the college, although her cot stayed.

The following morning, Bertha received a new trunk. It held replacements for the most essential items she had lost: a winter jacket and boots, a flannel skirt, some waists and some linens, a few books. Bertha was grateful but guilty. With so little to spare, she had already cost her family more than they could comfortably afford. She hoped somehow to repay them. At the very least, she resolved, from that point on anything she wanted or needed would be purchased with money she earned herself. How she might earn that money was still unclear, but she had until the summer to decide.

For that night and the next, content in her small bed with a kerosene lamp and a pile of books resting on the scarred surface of a rickety bureau, her new clothes neatly folded in its drawers and her trunk safely stored, Bertha thought her plan a success.

Phebe had, by default, ended up as one of four girls in the upstairs bedroom. The girls were strangers to one another, thrown together only because each realized in her own way that her presence in the nicer rooms below was inconvenient or unwelcome. One of the girls, Lina Stubbs, was a freshman, only eleven days at the college. Emma Preston and Sally Green were sophomores, separated from the companionship that each had painstakingly cultivated during her first year at school.

For several nights, Phebe's new roommates barely hid the disgust they felt in her presence. Lina tried not to stare at her filthy clothes or react to the sour odor that followed her like a cloud. Emma and Sally were less circumspect in their looks and gestures; they curled their lips and shook their heads behind her back, not caring if she caught them should she turn.

Bertha slipped stealthily through the room, constantly vigilant, determined to avoid meeting Phebe's eyes. She remembered them on the night of the fire, round with fear, but now she saw that they glittered feverishly.

It had begun to dawn on Phebe that she among others must bear some personal, particular responsibility for the flames. She knew there was talk of a new Mount Holyoke rising from the ashes, but was shocked when she overheard a girl call the disaster a blessing in disguise. God's message might be obscure, Phebe understood, but the fire that rained on their heads was *not* a reward.

Phebe had always thought of her soul as a gray mass, thick and featureless as fog, but the fire had annealed that shapeless lump into a brilliant, sharp pebble lodged in the center of her chest. She strung her button onto a double thickness of cotton thread and tied it around her neck so that it hung inside her clothes at exactly that place where she now knew her soul to be.

A mark on the wall beside her bed looked like a snake, so she found a small nail and scratched a cross over its coils. The wind that moved the trees at night spoke in tongues. She felt as if every nerve was exposed and the pain was exhausting and exquisite. Nothing she saw, nothing she heard either awake or asleep was without meaning. God called to her through every atom of His creation and she strained to catch each word. She tossed restlessly at night and said strange things in her sleep.

On the morning after their fourth night together, the girls who shared her room quickly conferred. Then, as Phebe stood dressed in her suit that still smelled of smoke, they told her she would have to leave.

"Talk to Miss Hooker," Emma advised. "She'll find you another place."

After an awkward moment in which nobody spoke, Emma, Sally and Lina, exchanged rueful glances and went downstairs to breakfast. Phebe, her forehead wrinkled and her mouth open, watched them go.

Phebe did not talk to Miss Hooker. She skipped breakfast and morning chapel and her scheduled recitations and spent the day searching for the miracle she was certain would occur. At the bottom of a pile of worthless things, behind some mess of tangled furniture, in some overlooked corner, Christ waited for her. His cheeks might be scorched and his robes charred, but the fat, moist tears of suffering and love would still drip from his eyes. And when she found him, Phebe would know she was forgiven.

She visited every building on campus as well as the school across the street. In each place, she inspected the collection of unclaimed items with an intensity of purpose that made her oblivious to the stares of the people around her.

An hour or so before sunset, she stood at the edge of the ruins and reluctantly accepted that the weeping Christ left hanging on her wall had not been transported by any agency human or divine out of the burning building. With nothing to eat or drink all day, she felt light-headed. She would have given up except for the certainty that in this one final place her mission must be fulfilled, and so she scrabbled through the ashy wasteland on her hands and knees in the waning light of the cool October evening.

It was fully dark by the time she returned to Miller's Cottage, empty-handed. The front door was unlocked, and Phebe shut it softly behind her. She stood for a moment in the gloom of the entrance hall before creeping forward to mount the stairs that led to the second floor. Her footfalls were barely audible; the floorboards' intermittent creaks attracted no attention.

Phebe hesitated at the top of the stairs. To her left was the room from which she had been banished, to her right the dark hallway where the older women lived. Phebe was prepared to spend the night curled on the floor of the landing until she remembered Bertha's space, hidden behind the wall. She sucked in her breath, raised her shoulders, and opened the bedroom door. With one hand cupped as a shield against her face, she ran across the room, slipped into the sanctuary.

In profound darkness, Phebe felt she could not breathe.

"Bertha?" she whispered, believing the other girl lay asleep, invisible somewhere in that darkness. "Bertha?"

Phebe held out both hands and shuffled forward, searching for something solid and familiar. When her shins hit the hard edge of a wooden cot, she wasn't sure what she'd found until, bending over, she felt the sway of its canvas. Without another call to Bertha, Phebe lay down and was asleep before she thought to say a prayer.

Chapter 13

Phebe's Dream

The air was clear, finally free of the smell of damp ash that had clung to it for days. Bertha was glad to be walking through the chilly night under a waning moon and a sky speckled with stars. It was almost nine o'clock and she was returning to Miller's Cottage after an unexpected meal eaten with Eva in the cozy house that Eva and seven other girls now called home.

Eva and Bertha had met that morning between recitations in Williston Hall when each recounted her adventures during the fire, although Bertha left out her rescue of Phebe. Then Eva invited her to supper at Mrs. Johnson's.

Mrs. Johnson was a motherly widow who fed her new charges well. Bertha smiled and laughed with the others more naturally than she had since leaving her own home. When it was time for her to walk the quarter mile to Miss Miller's, Mrs. Johnson fretted over her warmth and safety and insisted that Bertha take the largest and brightest kerosene lamp the house had to offer.

When she entered the house, Bertha dimmed the lamp. In the upstairs room, the girls were all in bed, writing letters or reading. They looked up when she entered, and Bertha nodded briefly, wishing them good night.

"There's someone in there," Sally said, gesturing towards Bertha's door with her head. "I was up here earlier, reading, and I heard someone run across the floor and open your door."

Miss Hooker must have assigned another girl to the cot. Bertha's jaw tightened. "Who?" she asked.

Sally shrugged. "I don't know. I had my back to the door. When I turned, I saw someone go in, just part of her skirt and her foot."

Sally glanced at Emma; Bertha saw a smile pass between them.

"Maybe it's that Phebe," Emma said, and laughed.

Why Phebe should be there and not in her own bed was a mystery and an outrage; Bertha held the lantern to her sleeping face and poked her roughly in the shoulder.

Two pokes and Phebe did not stir; Bertha pulled her hand away.

Her torpor was so absolute that Bertha might have thought her dead. Her feet, hands and head stuck out like a marionette's from the brown wool of her suit, the outlines of her body hidden by the heavy fabric. The skin on her face, pulled taut over every bone, was bloodless beneath a pall of dirt. One arm hung over the side of the cot and the other lay bent across her body, its hand curled in the middle of her chest whose rise and fall were the only signs of life. Both hands and wrists had a chalky cast that Bertha realized was a covering of ash.

Bertha leaned over to examine the curled hand and saw that the knuckles were scraped and streaked with blood. She smelled smoke and the warm, sweet odor of unwashed hair.

Phebe groaned. Startled, Bertha retreated to her own bed, placed flush against the end wall of the narrow room. Even so, only the width of the bureau separated her from Phebe's feet. Bertha made room for the lantern on the bureau and sat on the edge of her bed.

Phebe was restless now. Her mouth twitched and grimaced, her closed lids fluttered. Suddenly, she sat upright, eyes open but unfocused. "I should have burned," she said in a hollow voice. "I wish I had burned."

Bertha stared at Phebe in open-mouthed horror. Then, without thinking to take the lantern, she escaped through the large bedroom and stood shivering on the dark landing outside its door. She remembered Miss Slater, her room a few feet away.

In the days since the fire, she had seen Miss Slater both at meals and in the hallways of the cottage. The two greeted each other politely and expressed concern for the other's well-being, but Miss Slater seemed distant and did not offer a new invitation.

"Miss Slater!"

Elizabeth Slater finished her letter to George—one pen stroke and she was done–before lifting her head. She thought she recognized the voice, but it was late, nearly ten o'clock, and she was not dressed for visitors.

"Miss Slater! It's Bertha Mellish. Please, Miss Slater, may I speak with you?"

All of her clothes lost to the fire, Miss Slater wore a nightgown borrowed from a shorter, broader colleague, woolen socks but no slippers, an old shawl draped over her shoulders. Her hair was down, falling in thick waves she'd always thought out of keeping with her spare features.

Still, the girl's tone was urgent. "One moment, please," she said.

Bertha stood outside her door, still in skirt and blouse. Even in the dim light of the hall, cast from a lamp inside her room, Miss Slater recognized fear in the girl's eyes.

"What is it, Miss Mellish? Is something wrong?"

"I'm sorry to disturb you, but it's Phebe Cutts. She's supposed to sleep in that big bedroom"—Bertha gestured toward the right—"but she's in my room. She doesn't look well and she's saying strange things." Bertha spoke uncharacteristically fast and seemed out of breath.

"Strange things?" Miss Slater echoed. She recognized the girl's name—a small, timid creature, always in a soiled brown suit–but had never shared a table or exchanged a word with her.

"She's talking in her sleep." Bertha's voice shook; she sounded close to tears. "She said, she said she should have *burned.*"

"I don't know Phebe Cutts well," Miss Slater said, "I'm not sure I can help."

Still, she told Bertha to wait and returned with the lamp. With Bertha in the lead, they crept into the hidden room without disturbing the girls asleep in the large bedroom.

Miss Slater set the lamp on the bureau and leaned over Phebe as she lay, asleep again. The brighter light and the movement seemed to disturb her and she opened her eyes.

"Phebe?" Miss Slater's voice was low, and she touched the girl's cheek. "Can you hear me?"

Phebe stared at an invisible point somewhere above Miss Slater's head.

"Bertha, do you have any water? And a towel."

Reluctantly, Bertha pulled her washbowl and pitcher from under her bed. Both were full, ready for the bath she planned to give herself in the morning. With a twinge of regret, she brought the bowl and her only clean towel to Miss Slater.

Miss Slater dipped a corner of the towel into the washbowl, wrung it out and began to wipe the residue of ash and dirt from Phebe's forehead.

"Phebe, wake up." Miss Slater kept up the soft chant. "Phebe, wake up."

She had been so hot before, but now she felt better and could see more clearly. The smoke had gone away somehow. She could see that someone, a woman, was looking down at her and saying her name and wiping her face with something cold, wonderfully cold. She sat up so she could be closer to the woman.

"Phebe, Bertha tells me that when you were asleep you said something. Do you remember what you said?"

There were so many words to understand and she was not sure where she was or how she had come to be there. She knew it was Bertha standing there, listening, but she did not recognize the woman. But the woman's voice was kind and Phebe wanted to please her.

"I don't know," she said. Her voice was thick and slow and she swayed a little as she sat. "I had dreams."

"What did you dream?" the woman asked.

There was a cow with red eyes that gave blood instead of milk. There was a dark well so deep it had no end. There was a woman with flaming hair and a serpent's tongue. Phebe saw the pictures but could not describe them.

"I don't remember," she said.

The woman knelt on the floor beside the cot and leaned forward until her head and Phebe's almost touched. "Bertha heard you say that you should have burned," the woman said, "Why would you say such a thing?"

She had never meant to tell anyone, that secret too terrible and too true to speak aloud. That she had, was proof of her degradation. "I should have burned," she said in a strangled whisper.

The woman was so close that her hair brushed Phebe's cheek.

"But why?" she asked.

How was it possible the woman couldn't see? The corruption of Phebe's spirit was, she knew, stamped on her face and it emanated from her body like a foul and unmistakable smell.

"Because I am a sinner," she finally said.

The woman drew back and her kind face hardened. "What does a young girl like you know about sin?"

There, in the space between herself and this wretched child, Miss Slater saw her own father, his gray eyes cold as ice, his whiskers covering his jaw and chin and climbing halfway up his cheeks. She remembered the horror of days spent under his inquisition and nights passed alone in a dark shed, punishment for the laziness, the willfulness, the selfishness that disfigured her character and imperiled her immortal soul. Miss Slater recognized Phebe as a specter from her own past, an unwelcome reminder, a threat to the precarious balance of her current life.

Miss Slater could not meet Phebe's eyes and no longer wanted an answer to her question. Using the edge of the cot for support, she stood up and turned towards Bertha.

"Phebe needs to go home," she said. "She's clearly been affected by the excitement of the fire and must rest. I'll ask Dr. Lowell to telegraph her family tomorrow."

From her place beside the bureau, Bertha watched Phebe's face crumble like paper in a fist. Her mouth was pursed and tears trickled into the creased flesh around her eyes, but she made no sound. With a movement of her head, Bertha signaled Phebe's distress.

At the sight of the poor girl's tears, Elizabeth Slater knew she could not send her home and began to see her relation to the girl in another, clearer light. Perhaps she had been led to this pitiful creature for some greater purpose. Who better than she to understand the perverted nature of the child's upbringing and thus, with patience and love, show her the true Christian way. She would explain her revelation to George in her next letter and was sure he would agree.

"You shouldn't think so much about your failings, Phebe," Miss Slater said, "You've done things that are wrong, I'm sure, and I'm sure that you've had unchristian thoughts but I also know that you are *not* a sinner."

She knelt again and turned Phebe's face to hers. "Your heart is not sinful. God would never punish you so horribly. There's nothing you could have done that would make him want to punish you like that."

She paused, searching Phebe's round, blank eyes for a glimmer of understanding, a hint of acceptance.

"Christ's true work is love, not revenge. If you think you've done wrong, if you've been selfish, or. . . or envious, or if you've lied, or if your life seems bitter, or if it seems empty. . . ." Miss Slater realized that she was speaking too loudly and too fast. "Phebe," she whispered, "think of the light that shines away all darkness."

The girl stared back, her face a pale and distant moon.

Miss Slater stopped again, frustrated. Even as Phebe's future hung in the balance, she could not convey the urgency behind her words. "Do Christ's work, Phebe. Love and give yourself to others."

Miss Slater turned to Bertha. "Bertha, do you understand? Will you help me show Phebe what I mean?"

Bertha started and glanced quickly to the side, as if Miss Slater intended the question for someone standing at her shoulder. She'd watched the scene, a play in which she had no part. It terrified her now, to be drawn into something so beyond her capacity. Her stomach dropped, as if she'd been handed a scalpel and asked to open the body of a patient. She shook her head.

"Will you help me, Bertha?" Miss Slater asked again.

Such a look of trust on her teacher's face; she'd seen that look before, in her father's eyes, a year ago, the day before she left for college.

If Miss Slater believed she could do it . . . . . Bertha clenched her fists and pressed them against her skirt. "Yes," she said, "I'll help."

Miss Slater smiled, and turned back to Phebe.

"Are you hungry?" she asked, sweet as a mother.

"Yes," Phebe said, and in one awkward movement she leaned forward and laid her head on the woman's shoulder.

When Bertha returned from her errand to the pantry with hard crackers and a plate of cold potatoes, Phebe was standing half-dressed in the center of the cramped space. Miss Slater washed her using Bertha's bowl and towel. A filthy petticoat hung from Phebe's waist and a small button on a string hung down to the hard spot between her tiny breasts.

Bertha and Miss Slater turned away when Phebe stepped out of her drawers and petticoat and furtively washed herself. When she was done, Bertha handed Phebe her spare nightgown, whose hem piled in white folds around the small girl's feet. Then Phebe lay down on her cot and nibbled a hard biscuit until, with Bertha and Miss Slater watching, she fell into a calm and dreamless sleep.

Chapter 14

Titan's Pier

Her congratulatory duty done, Eva left Grace's room in the Hotel Woodbridge. You'd have thought Miss Grace McKinley was elected president yesterday instead of her uncle, Eva huffed to herself, acting so high and mighty. Thank goodness she was finally free of the girl.

Eva had no plans for the rest of the recreation day. She wandered onto the village green, irritated by the activity around her, by the shouts and scuffles of small boys and the excited chatter of men who punctuated their political bluster with wagging fingers. She walked once around the green, stopping as if interested at the memorial to the Civil War dead, and wondered where Bertha might be.

In the past month, the two girls had seen each other several times a week. Bertha ate supper with her more than once and when Eva's new bicycle arrived two weeks ago, she let Bertha ride. This particular afternoon was as good a time as any to give her another try.

Eva hoped that if she strolled in the direction of Miller's Cottage, she might meet Bertha, as if by accident, walking towards the campus. Eva—although not by conscious design–never put herself out for the sake of Bertha's company. If the two happened upon each other or Bertha chose places where Eva was likely to be, Eva welcomed Bertha into her orbit with the careless charity of a queen.

Sometimes, though, Eva, caught up in the theatrics of her own storytelling, glanced at Bertha and saw in her face a patient detachment, as if she watched Eva through the lens of a telescope. At those moments, Eva felt diminished and a little desperate. And, recently, she sensed something more dangerous upsetting the delicate imbalance of their friendship. Bertha now went on frequent walks with a teacher and a few days ago had even refused Eva's invitation to supper in order to visit the woman in her room.

So Eva was disappointed to see Bertha come up the gently rising sidewalk some distance ahead with Miss Slater at her side and pathetic Phebe Cutts trailing behind. Both Bertha and Miss Slater wore plain woolen jackets against the November air and Bertha's black tam o'shanter perched like a pancake on her head. Miss Slater held the curved handle of a basket in her left hand and she walked with a broad open stride, both arms swinging. Bertha matched her speed and Phebe broke into a shuffle whenever she fell too far behind.

Eva would have slipped behind a house until the trio passed, but she was annoyed by Bertha's easy companionship with the teacher, the way their shoulders sometimes brushed and their heads bobbed in counterpoint. It was a challenge she couldn't resist.

'Bertha!" she called and waved her hand high above her head. "Beatrice!"

Bertha waved in return but, since neither one picked up her pace, it was a good minute before they were finally close enough to speak. After a formal introduction to Miss Slater and a nod in Phebe's direction, Eva learned that the group was on its way to a mid-afternoon picnic in the Pepper Box on Prospect Hill.

"How pleasant," Eva said and waited a few awkward moments before Miss Slater invited her to join them. Without a glance at Bertha, Eva accepted. "May I suggest, though"—and here she turned to Bertha with the hint of a conspiratorial smile—"that we find a more adventurous destination?"

Elizabeth Slater thought it only right that she voice concern about possible rain and Phebe's ability to walk any distance. Eva observed that, although there were clouds, the air was dry and didn't feel like impending rain. And Phebe, dressed in donated clothes slightly less ill-fitting than her old suit, insisted that she was as strong as any of them. "I always walk," she said, her voice quavering, "I can walk for miles."

"Well then!" Eva exclaimed and clapped her gloved hands, "Let's go to Titan's Pier!" Smooth as satin, she slipped between Bertha and Miss Slater and took the younger woman's arm. She pulled Bertha tight against her side and, whispering gossip into her ear, took over the lead of the newly formed procession.

It was possible, with too much time spent on the grounds of the college or in its buildings or even in the center of the village, to forget the river flowing about a mile to the west. Hidden behind elms and oaks and by the slope of its banks, the Connecticut moved languorously through a landscape of farms and fields. It curved down through the Hadley plain until, after running straight for a time, it looped twice in a shallow "s" and then cut a deep gorge through the mountainous ridge that rose in irregular humps from the fertile alluvial soil.

On its west bank, the Mount Tom Range paralleled the river until it took a turn to the east and, terminating at Mount Nonotuck, disappeared under water. Reappearing on the other side as the Holyoke Range, the ridge, with Mount Holyoke as its dominant peak, now ran perpendicular to the river.

The river narrowed and deepened through this gorge and its current accelerated. Here the water looked darker and was agitated by eddies and erratic clusters of small, irregular ripples. On the west side, the slope of Mount Nonotuck gradually decreased and the mountain met the river peacefully, with a muddy beach and stands of scrubby brush and flat patches of exposed stone bearing the footprints of prehistoric creatures. But the Holyoke Range on the other side rose steeply from the river as naked rock, in a triangular wedge fifty feet at its apex with forty more hidden under water.

The wedge, divided vertically into two unequal parts by a deep cleft, was formed by an outcropping of basalt, a place where the mountain's volcanic bones poked through its skin of soil and vegetation. Its surface, a patchwork of gray and red ochre flecked with pale green lichen, was irregular but crystalline, with interlocking planes whose crisp edges were outlined in deep brown. A few pine and hemlock saplings grew on its flatter surfaces.

The massive structure, formed eons before when molten lava rose from the earth, then cooled and contracted, looked strangely unstable. Its overlapping, parallel columns of stone jutted over the water, apparently without support. Yet the formation seemed deliberately constructed, as if some mythic mason had carefully cut and finished individual slabs and blocks of stone and then painstakingly fitted them together into an enormous puzzle.

When Professor Edward Hitchcock, the great geologist of Amherst College, explored the site in the 1830s, he recalled the freakish rock formations on the northern coast of Ireland and knew they were formed of the same stuff. With the Giant's Causeway and Fingal's Cave in mind, Professor Hitchcock–hoping the name would attract visitors to the lonely spot–christened it Titan's Pier.

Sixty years later, Titan's Pier was better known and more frequently visited, although most people agreed that it was seen to best advantage from the opposite bank of the river. Pleasure parties or fishermen in small boats would row from the Mount Nonotuck side and pull up onto a small beach that curved around a protected cove on the upriver edge of the pier where the water was still. When the water was low, some intrepid hikers, usually local boys and young men from Amherst College made their way towards it from down river, climbing carefully over smaller rock outcroppings and muddy banks to enjoy a smoke under its precarious canopy.

The top of the cliff was easier to reach, accessible off the unpaved carriage road that ran through South Hadley northwest to Mount Holyoke and then Hadley. About three miles out of the village, the road took a turn towards the river and cut through the mountain's rocky spur before continuing due north. This stretch of road had long ago been christened the Pass at Thermopylae by Amherst geologists in homage to the narrow place between the mountains and the sea so bravely (and unsuccessfully) guarded by ancient Greeks in their fight against the Persians. A modest version of its namesake, the Pass was bordered on the right by a face of dark stone and on the left by a treacherous drop to the river. A crude plank fence ran along this edge until the land between the road and the river widened and travelers seemed out of danger. Visitors to Titan's Pier knew to leave the road there, where the fence ended.

After almost an hour of steady walking, the women reached the Pass and turned left at the last fence post. Bertha, Eva and Miss Slater had all unbuttoned their coats to the cool air and everyone's boots and skirt hems were coated with dust from the road which was pocked and rutted by hoof prints and wheel tracks.

They now walked on a narrow path between oaks and pine trees through ankle-deep drifts of rustling needles and dry leaves. Dark gray humps of exposed rock swelled and bulged under their feet like the backs of petrified whales. Eva led the way, not stopping until she reached the ledges at river's edge. Bertha came next, moving easily over the uneven surface. Miss Slater was burdened by the basket and her sense of responsibility towards Phebe and she dropped back, waiting for the girl to catch up.

Eva stood on a flat slab, roughly diamond-shaped, with a corner that jutted into open air like the prow of a ship. She inched forward until the toes of her boots lined up with the edge of the rock and then, with her feet spread and her knees bent, leaned forward. The breeze twisted loose strands of hair around her face, and her skin, usually pale, was flushed.

Bertha was close behind Eva, intending to follow her onto the diamond-shaped rock. But now she stopped some ten feet back, reached out and called her name. It was more a question than a command, and Eva did not respond.

"Eva! Move away from there!" Miss Slater ran towards them, leaving Phebe standing with both hands over her mouth and her eyes wide with horror.

Eva straightened and stepped back from the edge. She turned around to face the others and laughed. "Did you think I was going to fall? Or jump, perhaps?" Eva spoke without malice or sarcasm; she seemed genuinely amused by their concern. "I have a very good sense of balance. And I've always felt like I could fly. Although I've never actually tried it."

Miss Slater shook her head. "I do wish you'd come off that rock," she sighed.

Nothing she could say or do, Elizabeth Slater realized, would compel Eva to obey; she found herself admiring rather than disapproving of such willfulness. She set the basket down on a patch of level ground and sat on top of a low, rounded rock. From there, the craggy edge of Titan's Pier was not visible. Still, she could see the two girls and beyond them a view across the river to Mount Nonotuck, its autumn reds and oranges subdued against the overcast sky. Miss Slater was determined to keep the girls in her sight until they were safely back from the edge. She was sure that if she didn't, when she looked again they would be gone.

Bertha had stepped onto the rock where Eva still stood, a foot from the edge, but could not bring herself to join her friend. She had never considered herself afraid of high places, but now she was certain that, with one move forward, she would lurch and fall.

"Come here, Bertha!" Eva held out her hand. She wiggled her fingers impatiently. "Come here so you can look over the edge. You can't see the rock formations unless you do."

Bertha reached out, put her hand in Eva's black-gloved palm. She was sure that Eva, in playfulness, would pull her forward too quickly. But Eva held her steady; Bertha shuffled to her side. She allowed herself to be guided to the edge, but kept her eyes resolutely focused on Mount Nonotuck.

"Look down," Eva whispered. She released Bertha's hand, but put an arm around her shoulder.

The ledge on which they stood extended beyond most of the fractured, crystalline surface of the cliff, and so Eva and Bertha looked directly into the water below. The water was a livid gray, metallic and steely, like something molten rather than liquid.

Bertha, dizzy, said nothing. She imagined that a pebble or a twig, falling into it, would descend through suffocating muck. The sharp peaks of submerged rock, barely visible beneath the leaden surface, terrified her. They were evidence of a subterranean world, deep beyond measure, that descended into the earth beneath her feet.

"I've heard that boys jump off of this place, into the river," Eva said.

Without thinking, Bertha pressed herself more tightly against Eva's side. "But isn't that very dangerous? There are rocks under the water."

Eva withdrew her arm from Bertha's shoulder. "Well, to do it safely you'd have to push yourself forward so you'd land past the rocks—you'd have to take a running leap. But you could do it, and then swim across to the other bank."

Bertha tried to see herself deliberately stepping off the edge of the cliff towards the repellent water below but could not.

Once again, Eva leaned deeply forward. "Just think of it, sailing into the air like that. It would be like flying. It would *be* flying." She turned towards Bertha, her eyes flashing. "If I were a boy, I'd do it!"

"I would too," Bertha said.

"You don't really mean that, Beatrice." Eva gave Bertha a wry smile.

"You're right," said Bertha, smiling in return.

Eva turned back to the water and her face grew serious. "But *I* do."

Phebe sat on the ground near Miss Slater's legs, the warm folds of the woman's skirt pressed against her side. Yet, even from her nest of leaves, Phebe did not like this place, and she was disappointed that Miss Slater had allowed Eva to join and then divert their little party from the familiar slopes of Prospect Hill. Phebe had never seen the jagged rock formation, either in person or in pictures. Although she couldn't see it now from where she sat, the name alone suggested sinister forces.

She tried to remember what she had read about Titans and thought that they were something ancient and powerful in Greek myth. She considered asking Miss Slater but didn't want to expose her ignorance. She watched Eva and Bertha as they stood on the edge of the cliff, their dark figures silhouetted against the cloudy sky, and envied their careless courage. She wondered what they would do if a great creature, a towering man-beast with gleaming horns, suddenly rose from the abyss she imagined gaping below them.

"Phebe?" At the sound of Miss Slater's voice, the creature disappeared. "Phebe, help me lay out the picnic things. It's time we thought about eating."

Phebe scrambled to her feet. Together, they emptied the contents of the basket– a jar of strawberry jam from Addie Miller's pantry, soda crackers wrapped up in brown paper, three apples, two knives, a spoon, and a mason jar filled with water–onto a square of white cotton. When everything was arranged on the pristine surface of the cloth, they stopped to admire the modest luxury of their meal.

"How pretty this is." Phebe touched the jar of preserves and glanced at Miss Slater, as if expecting a rebuff.

"It *is* lovely, like melted rubies," Miss Slater said, smiling at the girl until a sudden panic gripped her, a feeling that she'd lost something precious. She spun towards the cliff.

The girls were still there, thank God. Now they sat at the edge of Titan's Pier, their legs dangling in thin air. She called their names, her voice sharp. "Bertha! Miss Newton! Come and have something to eat!" They did not seem to hear.

Phebe jumped up as if she'd been stung by a bee. "I'll go get them," she said.

Without a glance backward, she walked towards the cliff like a man resigned to the gallows. At the edge of the diamond-shaped rock, she stopped. Bertha and Eva turned, visibly surprised.

"Phebe, I never thought you'd come this close!" Bertha said.

Phebe felt a tiny flutter of pride and raised her chin. "Miss Slater says it's time to eat."

"Now that's a good idea!" Eva slid away from the edge. Holding her skirts clear, she stood up and helped Bertha do the same. They ran past Phebe, towards Miss Slater and the picnic.

Phebe meant to follow, took a step in that direction. But then she stopped and turned back to face the cliff. Slowly, cautiously, her arms outstretched and her knees bent, she crept onto the diamond-shaped ledge. Her breath was shallow and she whimpered, but she made it to the edge and, for one vertiginous moment, looked down.

All she saw was a blur of gray and brown before escaping to safer ground. Even so, she felt exhilarated and physically bigger than she ever had before. She wondered if the others had seen her. As she ran back to join them, Phebe felt for the little lump cushioned beneath her layers of flannel and wool and pressed it triumphantly with her thumb.

"I'm sorry we don't have another apple," Miss Slater said when Phebe sat down again by her feet, still panting slightly. Phebe glanced from face to face but no one said anything about her accomplishment.

"I'm afraid we didn't know Miss Newton would be joining us when we packed our provisions." Miss Slater opened the jar of preserves and released the bright, sweet smell of strawberries.

"I don't want an apple, Miss Slater." Phebe took a cracker from the pile in the middle of the cloth, but didn't raise it to her mouth. She could no longer keep it to herself. "I went to the edge!" she cried. "I went to the edge of the cliff and looked over!"

"How very brave," Miss Slater said. Phebe blushed.

Eva raised the jar of water. "To the brave Miss Cutts!" she shouted and took a gulp. She passed the jar to Bertha.

"To the brave Miss Cutts!" Bertha echoed and drank as well.

On the cloth in front of her, Bertha had four crackers with jam and a small pile of apple slices. Now, slowly and voluptuously, she ate one of the tart white crescents.

Phebe concentrated on her own share of food. Eva had split one of the apples and, without warning, tossed half to her. The apple had fallen cut side down, but Miss Slater cleaned it with water from the jar and now Phebe chewed a bite thoroughly, as much to show Bertha that she could exercise self-control as to make the apple last.

Eva, already finished, stood up. She threw her apple core and watched it vanish in a pile of leaves, then left the picnic cloth for an almost level patch of ground beneath a nearby pine tree. There, as the others looked on, she waltzed on a carpet of needles in the arms of an invisible partner, her skirt swaying to imaginary music. After a few turns, she dropped dramatically to the ground and fanned her face with her hand.

"That looks like very good exercise," Miss Slater said.

Miss Slater wanted to maintain a dignity appropriate to her age and to her role, but she could not stop herself. She felt her cheeks redden even before she spoke again.

"Have you, Miss Newton," she began. "Have you, that is, have you ever danced like that with a, with a . . . partner?" She was sure that Bertha and, somehow, Eva—even Phebe—knew that she was thinking of George. She brushed a scattering of crumbs from her skirt to cover her embarrassment.

The older woman's confusion made Eva feel not only immeasurably worldly in comparison but also a little protective. Such an angular, plain, hard-shelled woman, stuttering like a schoolgirl. Eva remembered talk of Miss Slater and her fiancé. "Do you mean, Miss Slater, have I ever danced like that with a gentleman?"

"Well, yes."

"Oh, my goodness, many times!"

Miss Slater leaned forward, staring at her with an almost voracious curiosity. Bertha wore a look of patient amusement—as if she'd heard it all before—and so Eva focused her attention on the teacher. She didn't bother to gauge Phebe's reaction.

"Oh, I've been to any number of dances," she said lightly. "When I'm home in Chicago, of course."

Eva paused, letting her casual admission sink in. Strictly speaking, dancing—girls paired with girls—was forbidden at Mount Holyoke, but as long as it wasn't flaunted under the noses of President Mead and the older faculty, it was tolerated. Friends could partner off if they liked and not get into serious trouble. But dancing with a man on campus—they all knew that was grounds for expulsion.

"But Miss Slater, haven't you ever danced with your fiancé?"

Eva knew the question was rude and when she saw Miss Slater's mouth tighten, prepared to apologize and retreat. But the icy look lasted only a moment before the older woman's face fell.

She shook her head. "No, I've never danced with him." Elizabeth Slater looked down at her hands, resting in the valley of cloth between her knees. They were rough and worn and she noticed a small smear of jam on one of her thumbs. "I've never danced at all. In my family, we. . . . In my family, we didn't do such things."

Without a word Eva got up and stood, her hands on her hips. "Then why not do it now!" Her voice was playful but commanding.

Miss Slater looked up, startled. The idea was preposterous, the suggestion rude. But Eva had her arms outstretched and, even as she stood, she seemed infused with the same energy that moved the branches above their heads. Her invitation was irresistible. Miss Slater awkwardly raised herself from her low rock and, with a glance at Bertha who gave her a smile and a barely perceptible nod, followed Eva to the space under the pine tree.

After some initial fumbling, Eva grasped Miss Slater firmly by the waist and, approximating the brassy exuberance of Sousa's *Washington Post March* with her voice, led the woman in a vigorous two-step over the uneven ground. Miss Slater—half a head taller than her graceful partner, heavy on her feet and stiff, stumbling on bits of rock, twigs, and ropy tree roots—followed as best she could.

Soon, though, Elizabeth Slater stopped thinking of herself as ridiculous, stopped berating herself for her clumsiness, stopped telling herself that plain, coarse women had no right or reason to dance. She threw back her head and looked up into the sky, soft and downy as a feather bed. She began to laugh. Eva joined her and the two bobbed and spun until they fell down together, still laughing.

Phebe and Bertha had moved closer to watch the spectacle, and they stood side by side. Phebe's mouth was open in an amazed half-smile and she held her hands to her face. She had never seen grown women act this way and found it both disturbing and compelling. She felt privy to some secret ritual that, she was sure, from this moment on would bind her to the others in private fellowship. She had never before been allowed such a privilege. She began to laugh along with the two dancers, first in hesitant giggles and then in shrill, raucous peals, utterly abandoned, that left her doubled over and out of breath.

At first, Bertha enjoyed the scene as she had savored the adventure of the cliff's edge and the taste of the simple food. She smiled and even clapped in time to Eva's music. But by the time the dance ended and

Eva and Miss Slater sat near each on the ground, happy and flushed, her smile had faded and she didn't feel like laughing. She told herself that she was worried about Miss Slater, that Eva had tempted her into this foolish situation in order to humiliate her, to spread the story around the college and amuse her friends with a description of the Greek professor's performance.

But she knew it wasn't concern for Miss Slater's reputation that troubled her. Bertha understood that, no matter how long or how hard she might try, she was incapable of doing for Miss Slater what Eva had done with one impulsive act. She might discuss Greek literature and Greek grammar with Miss Slater and she might help her in the saving of lost souls, but she could never pull her away from the duty that oppressed her or lift the burden of her conscience. Not for the briefest of free, unfettered moments could she ever teach Miss Slater to dance.

And Eva, Bertha thought bitterly, had found in Miss Slater a more interesting and rewarding challenge on whom to test her attractions than Bertha, a mere student, serious and plodding, could ever be. Bertha had hoped that for both Eva and Miss Slater, individually and for different reasons, she had a special role to play, that, at least in the circumscribed universe of the college, she held a place, however small, in each woman's life that no one else could fill.

Bertha turned to Phebe who was now laughing in little hiccups. "Oh, stop it!" she snapped. The sound died in Phebe's throat and she looked at Bertha with hurt, moist eyes. Bertha, furious and ashamed, turned without another word and went to pack up what was left of their picnic.

Chapter 15

A New Year

On the second evening after the picnic, with Phebe away from their tiny room, Bertha took out the small square of white linen she had cut and hemmed but not yet embroidered. Working feverishly by lamplight, she stitched the letter M with its spiraled ends and tilted peaks. Each stab of the needle reminded her of the fate she'd allowed herself to forget: alone in Athens. Mabel was no more her friend than she was the day they met; Eva and Miss Slater needed each other more than they did her.

The next morning, she took Mabel's original handkerchief to the outhouse and dropped it there. She put the imposter between two thin sheets of cardboard that she wrapped in white paper. She drew a sprig of violets on the front of the package and wrote "Mabel Eaton" in the most florid hand she could. The package went deep into her bureau drawer; she wasn't sure if she would ever give it to Mabel.

Bertha nursed her wounds for a week. But when first Miss Slater and then Eva sought her out to ask if something was wrong, she could not resist. So much for resolve, she told herself. She apologized for her coolness, blamed schoolwork.

And, although she never said she was sorry, she began to treat Phebe with more patience than before. For some reason, Phebe did not seem as freakish as she had once appeared. She didn't seem to scurry as much; she seemed to chatter less. She kept herself cleaner.

For two or three evenings each week until the students and faculty left for the Christmas holiday, Bertha and Phebe joined Miss Slater in her room in Miller's Cottage. They arranged their chairs near a register that sent up meager wafts of warm air from the stove in the room below. They drank tea while one of the two house cats, a brown tabby with a loud purr, lay at their feet or in one or another's lap. Sometimes Eva joined them, bringing cake or fruit or candy or a pair of gloves or scarf or hat she didn't need. Sometimes Miss Slater read out loud but, more often, she talked about her George. She described how she met him, introduced by a mutual friend in a lecture hall in Boston, how she could tell from the moment she saw him that he was a man of superior feeling, how she knew from the instant their eyes met that they shared a special sympathy. Even Eva listened attentively.

Three days before Christmas, Mr. George Rogers came to South Hadley to escort Miss Slater to Boston for the two-week recess. He walked from the streetcar stop outside the college to Miller's Cottage in the late morning sunlight, a thin layer of packed snow crunching under his feet. He found his fiancée, already dressed in hat and coat, waiting for him in the cramped hallway just inside the door. In the brief privacy of the moment, they shared a hurried embrace. "George, my love," she whispered into the dark fabric of his coat before he picked up her traveling bag and led her out the door.

The two walked together with her arm hooked over his elbow. Each wore the supremely happy and slightly dazed expression of someone surprised by great fortune. Miss Slater didn't notice her student until they'd almost passed and Bertha called her name.

At the sound, first she and then George stopped. She didn't drop his arm, and was pleased that Bertha could see her as a lover, however chaste.

"Bertha, how nice!" She noticed that Bertha's face seemed unusually animated and her eyes were bright. She had never realized what a warm, deep brown they were. "Miss Mellish, may I present Mr. George Rogers. George, dear, this is Miss Bertha Mellish."

The two acknowledged each other with stiff smiles and nods. Mr. Rogers was a thin man, two or three inches taller than Miss Slater, with rounded shoulders, a sparse, blond mustache, thick spectacles, and a black felt bowler that sat high on his head. There was nothing romantic or heroic in him that Bertha could see. He looked to her like a bookkeeper or a bank clerk.

I'm so glad we met today," Miss Slater said. "I saw Phebe at the cottage earlier this morning just before she left, but you were nowhere to be found. I did want to say good-bye and wish you a pleasant holiday with your family."

"Thank you, Miss Slater. I hope you have a pleasant holiday, too." Bertha felt foolish parroting the words, but the man's presence made her teacher seem suddenly unfamiliar.

Mr. Rogers picked up the traveling bag he had dropped to the ground. "I'm sorry, my dear, but if we don't say good-bye to Miss Mellish, I'm afraid we'll miss our car." He looked at Bertha gravely. "I do apologize, Miss Mellish. I hope someday to have the pleasure of a longer conversation."

Bertha watched the pair trudge up the street and felt almost sorry for Miss Slater, so clearly deluded about her ponderous, prosaic Mr. George Rogers. But the feeling passed, and she returned to her own happiness.

It had all been so much easier than she'd imagined; she was sorry she hadn't done it sooner. With no more time to waste, that very morning Bertha retrieved the package from its hiding place, marched herself to the house where Mabel lived, forced herself to knock on the door and, painfully aware that she was uninvited, asked for Mabel.

But, of course, Mabel had been so kind; what else would she be? Mabel drew her in the door, led her to her room, settled her on the bed, made her tea. Mabel sat down next to her, admired the drawing of the violets and the lettering of her name. She carefully unfolded the paper and tenderly set it aside, separating the two pieces of cardboard to reveal the handkerchief inside, precious as a pearl.

"Oh, Bertha," she cried, after Bertha explained that, since she had lost the original, she felt it only right to make a replica, as close to the first as she could remember. "You went to so much trouble, you dear girl!"

Bertha had listened in proud confusion as Mabel marveled at the accuracy of the pattern, the neatness of the stitching, Bertha's generous sacrifice of time. "I shall treasure this," Mabel said and held the cloth to her cheek. "I shall treasure it always."

Bertha, still glowing, reached the cottage and, grateful that Phebe was gone, packed her few clothes in an old suitcase borrowed from Miss Miller.

After Bertha's unexpected visit, Mabel returned to organizing her things. Luckily, her train did not leave for several hours; she'd had time to be a good hostess. As she put the last shirtwaist in her bag, she noticed Bertha's handkerchief lying on the bed.

She picked it up with a rueful smile. Its scalloped edges were angular. The large "M" was clumsily drawn. The stitching was uneven. There were tiny pulls in the linen's surface and thick knots on its underside. It looked to Mabel like the work of a child, and she shook her head indulgently. What a sweet, awkward girl that Bertha Mellish was. Mabel added the handkerchief to her bag and, when she unpacked its contents in her room at home, put the little folded square in the bottom drawer of her bureau and forgot it there.

A letter was waiting for Bertha when she returned to the college on the first Wednesday of the new year. She had checked her mail slot looking only for official notices. Since she'd just come from home and had no correspondents other than her family, she was surprised to pull out a small white envelope with a return address in Boston. The name of the sender, written in a neat hand above the address, was not immediately familiar.

Mrs. George Rogers. When she recognized the man's name, her first thought was of Miss Slater's fiancé. Why on earth would that man's mother write to her? But she realized the idea was ridiculous and, even before she opened it, Bertha knew what the letter would say.

A white rose petal, brown along the edges but still moist, fell to the ground when Bertha unfolded the single page. She stooped to pick it up before she read.

Boston, Massachusetts
Saturday, January 2, 1897

My Dear Bertha,

I have the happiest news to tell you! Mr. George Rogers and I were married the last day of the year, in a quiet ceremony. We had thought to wait until he finished his degree, but after we saw each other again, we just could not postpone it. I don't know if you can understand, at least not yet—someday I'm sure you will—just how much we had to be together.

Please break the news gently to poor little Phebe. I will miss you, quiet, serious Bertha, but I worry for Phebe. I think I have come to mean too much to her and I am afraid she will slip back to that terrible state in which we found her. I know it is asking a great deal of you, Bertha, but look after her. Please don't think me selfish for leaving you with her. My husband needs me more and caring for him is now my sacred duty.

Please tell Miss Newton, too, although I am sure my story will be the topic of gossip for some time to come. President Mead was furious when I told her. I broke the news first with a telegram and then screwed up my courage and spoke to her on the telephone. I hope I can forget the terrible things she said about my character and I am trying not to take them to heart.

Please write to me at the address on the envelope, although it is temporary. I would be so happy to know that you send me your good wishes.

Your friend,
Elizabeth S. Rogers

That night, Bertha told Phebe. They sat beside each other on Bertha's bed, and Bertha put her arm around Phebe's shoulder as the girl sobbed. The next morning, Bertha wrote a curt note of congratulations to her former teacher before throwing Miss Slater's envelope and its contents into the belly of a stove. She did the same with each of the letters that appeared in her mail slot until, after a month, they stopped.

Three days after Bertha told her Miss Slater was gone, Phebe received a letter of her own. The event was so unusual she read the address on the envelope four times before she was convinced it was meant for her. Her parents never wrote, sending whatever message they needed to convey through one of Phebe's brothers in his terse and infrequent letters, usually written when someone was sick or newly dead.

At first, Phebe didn't recognize the name of the sender written high in the envelope's left corner, but when she did, she pressed it to her face and smelled the delicate scent of roses. Her hands shook as she carefully unsealed the flap.

Once a week from that point on, Phebe found an envelope in her mailbox. Each week, Mrs. Rogers reassured Phebe that, wherever she might be, she would always remain Phebe's friend and guide. And each Sunday afternoon, with a dictionary, grammar and Bible close by, Phebe struggled happily with her reply.

When the first letter came from Mrs. Rogers, Phebe ran with it to Bertha. But Bertha refused to read it and wouldn't let Phebe describe what it said or repeat Miss Slater's excuses.

When, early in their correspondence, Mrs. Roger asked Phebe to tell Bertha just how much she missed her young friend and how sorry she was that Bertha seemed angry, Phebe didn't have the courage. And two weeks later, when Bertha asked her if Miss Slater had written again, Phebe lied. "No," she said, with a slight quiver in her voice. "no, just that one. I never wrote back." Whether Bertha believed her, Phebe couldn't tell, but she never asked again.

Chapter 16

Eva

"Croupous pneumonia, Mrs. Chandler. Your niece has croupous pneumonia."

Dr. Mary Lowell spoke impatiently into the telephone's short trumpet. She had spent a long night caring for her newest patient and wanted to dispense with this duty as quickly as possible so she could get a few hours' rest. "It is a disease quite easily diagnosed and one that I have no small experience with. It is particularly prevalent this time of the year when winter is well underway. February is a particularly dangerous month. I will leave it to you to contact Eva's parents as you see fit."

Dr. Lowell drummed her fingers on the surface of her desk.

"Now, Mrs. Chandler, there is no cause to become so agitated. In my experience, healthy young women like your niece recover nicely with no ill effects. The illness itself is not pleasant, certainly, but we do not need to discuss transferal to a hospital."

The telephone line amplified Mrs. Chandler's shrill voice; the doctor could no longer contain her irritation. "Well, of course you may come and see your niece, but there is no reason to bring another physician for consultation. The case is quite uncomplicated, I assure you. Yes, yes, I will be ready to receive you at"—Dr. Lowell paused to look at the gold watch that hung from her waist by a chain—" one o'clock this afternoon." Another pause. "Fine, Mrs. Chandler. Now I must say good-bye."

Dr. Lowell returned the earpiece to its cradle and pushed the telephone away. She normally took pride in the instrument, one of the few private telephones on campus, and saw it as a symbol of her importance to the college and a badge of her authority but now she was too tired and indignant to care.

Pride was the mortar of Mary Lowell's character. It had gotten her through the slights of a girlhood when her strong face with its square jaw attracted no admirers and through the rigors of a medical training that she was expected to fail. It guided and supported her in the years she spent as assistant superintendent in the gray granite hulk of the Maine Insane Hospital before coming to Mount Holyoke College as resident physician and lecturer in physiology.

Dr. Lowell was only in her thirties, although the students thought her older. When she caught them out unprotected in the rain, she ordered them back home to put on their overshoes. When she saw them opening packages from friends or relatives, she made them throw away the edible gifts she deemed unhealthy. She hectored fat girls into exercise and forced skinny ones to eat. Dr. Lowell was especially pleased with her performance during the fire and made it known to students and faculty alike that she had been the last one to leave the burning building.

Eva Newton had been brought to the infirmary just before four o'clock the previous afternoon, half dragged and half carried by two frightened young ladies whom Dr. Lowell immediately sent away. There had been more than the usual number of respiratory illnesses that winter and Dr. Lowell did not want to encourage their spread.

"Wash your face and hands with soap and hot water," she had advised the two students, "and go early to bed." No, she told them, they would not be able to visit their friend for several days, maybe not for as long as a week. It was now a few minutes after eight in the morning and, except for some brief naps in a chair beside Eva's bed, Dr. Lowell had not slept. She got up from her desk, intending to leave her office and go upstairs to her private residence, but went instead to the room where her patient lay.

Eva was in one of two beds that flanked a table covered by a fringed woolen cloth, thick and mossy green. A picture of horses drinking from a stream hung in a gold frame on the wall next to Eva's bed. She was alone; Dr. Lowell had moved the room's previous occupant, a freshman suffering from grippe, into a recently vacated bed in the infirmary's other, larger ward.

Dr. Lowell walked to the bedside and freed Eva's wrist from a tangle of sheets. She felt for the girl's pulse and was gratified to find it soft and regular, although her breathing was still a little quick. "Just as it should be," she said aloud, as if to defend her course of treatment to the absent Mrs. Chandler.

Eva was on her back, her head propped up by two pillows, apparently in a deep and untroubled sleep. Dr. Lowell knew that the effects of the morphine injection, given when Eva proved unable to bear the pain in her side and the hard, dry cough that made it worse, would wear off in several hours. "We'll see then how it goes," she said and touched Eva's pale, hot forehead. Before leaving, Dr. Lowell went to each of the room's two windows, raised their shades and opened the sashes several inches. "Excellent," she murmured as a gust of February air chilled the room and a shaft of morning sunlight fell across the body of the unconscious girl. "Fresh air is the best medicine."

By the time her aunt arrived that afternoon, Eva was no longer in a morphine stupor. She lay on her right side, flat in the bed facing the wall, with her knees drawn up and her arms folded against her chest. She had managed to push the two pillows away from her head and onto the floor, where Mrs. Chandler and Dr. Lowell found them when they entered the room together. Dr. Lowell had been away from the sickroom only a few minutes arranging to hire a village woman as a nurse, and was humiliated by the discovery. After snatching the pillows and placing them firmly on the other bed, she addressed her visitor. Her embarrassment made her especially brusque.

"What you must understand, Mrs. Chandler, is the nature of Miss Newton's illness. Pneumonia is what we physicians call a self-limited disease. It can be neither aborted nor cut short by any known means at our command. We can only try to make the patient comfortable and allow the disease to run its course." Dr. Lowell crossed her arms and she and Mrs. Chandler moved closer to the patient.

Eva's exposed cheek shone with a brilliant, startling patch of red like a heavy-handed smear of rouge. Her mouth was open and a sore had formed on the edge of her bottom lip. Her breathing was fast and labored and each time she exhaled she emitted a soft, involuntary grunt.

She gave a short barking cough, and a rusty, viscous thread ran from her mouth to the white sheet beneath her. Dr. Lowell moved to wipe it with a towel. She noticed visible throbbing in Eva's temple and knew that her pulse was bounding, too strong and abnormally fast. Eva coughed again and groaned.

"Eva," Mrs. Chandler said. She laid her gloved hand tentatively on the girl's shoulder. "Eva, it's your Aunt Priscilla. How are you feeling?"

Eva looked up. "I want to ride the horses," she said. She shifted restlessly. "Why can't I ride the horses?" She coughed three times, deep, crackling spasms.

"Eva has a very high fever and is somewhat confused," Dr. Lowell explained. "Her temperature will remain elevated until the crisis occurs some days from now. That is the typical progress of the disease." She motioned Mrs. Chandler towards the chair at the foot of the bed. "Please sit down."

The doctor turned to the bedside table and poured water from a pitcher into a glass, then shook a medicinal capsule from a small brown bottle into the cupped palm of her hand. She sat next to Eva on the bed, cradled her head and shoulders with one arm and placed the capsule onto the girl's tongue. She reached for the glass and before Eva had a chance to react, poured the water slowly into her mouth, taking care that she did not choke.

Dr. Lowell glanced at Mrs. Chandler, who sat on the edge of the chair and seemed anxious to leave. "That was a dosage of Dover's powder," the doctor explained in the precise, slightly peevish tone she used with slow students. "It is a compound of opium and ipecac. It will ease the pain and allow Miss Newton to sleep. When she is calmer, I will administer hydrotherapy." Mrs. Chandler looked at her blankly. "Cool water baths and ice packs," the doctor clarified.

Mrs. Chandler did not know her niece well. After her sister married and moved with her new husband to the Midwest some twenty years ago, their visits had been rare. She had seen Eva twice as an infant, two or three times as a child and, since the girl's attendance at Mount Holyoke, no more than once a semester. There was not much of her sister or herself in her niece—Eva's looks and disposition came from the Newton side—but she liked the girl, thought she was charming and, above all, felt personally responsible for her well-being. Mrs. Chandler rose abruptly from the chair. "I really must telegraph my sister and brother-in-law. I cannot have their dear child's health entirely on my shoulders."

"Certainly," Dr. Lowell replied coolly from her place on Eva's bed. She stood and acknowledged Mrs. Chandler's good-bye with a sharp nod. "I am sure that if they choose to come, before they arrive the crisis will have passed and Eva will be convalescing nicely."

Dr. Lowell, to her great satisfaction, was right. The crisis that she anticipated came even sooner than expected and on Saturday, Eva's third day in the infirmary, her fever broke, her pulse slowed and her respiration seemed easier. Although the cough and pain persisted, they were less severe, and Dr. Lowell had to caution Eva to maintain complete rest until the state of her lungs returned to normal. Eva's parents were due to arrive on Sunday afternoon after two arduous and anxious days of travel, and Dr. Lowell declared Eva able to receive a few student visitors that morning.

These visitors were allotted an hour after morning chapel. They were allowed to wish Eva well one at a time and permitted to stay no longer than five minutes. They were instructed by Dr. Lowell to speak softly and to do or say nothing that would excite the patient. All of Eva's society sisters came. Together, they had ordered roses from a florist in Holyoke. Grace McKinley came with a bag of plump hothouse grapes and ate a stem before leaving them in a bowl on the bedside table. One friend brought a small book of inspirational poems and another left a hand-embroidered bookmark. Bertha was not able to get to the infirmary until a few minutes before eleven, and she was the last of Eva's visitors.

She entered the room slowly, afraid of what she might find, and took her seat next to Eva's bed. To her left was the table, now covered in gifts, with the roses, six red ones in full bloom, placed in the center in a simple glass vase. Bertha could just make out their scent. Eva was again on her back, propped up by pillows, her eyes half-closed. She wore a clean white nightgown with ruffles at the neck and wrists, with a thick woolen shawl draped over her shoulders. She seemed exhausted and unaware of Bertha's presence.

Bertha felt a chill as soon as she entered and now noticed that both windows were open to the winter air. She wondered if that was dangerous to the patient but did not think she should disturb anything in the sickroom.

"Are you cold, Eva?" she asked, half rising from her chair. She leaned forward and pulled the shawl tight, tucking it so that the nightgown was fully covered. Her face brushed the top of Eva's head and she smelled a pungent mixture of dried sweat and something bitter and medicinal. She hesitated, suspended in that awkward position, and then touched her lips to Eva's hair.

Eva seemed asleep. In the stillness, Bertha heard the whistles and crackles of her breath. One of Eva's hands lay uncovered on the blanket and Bertha took it in both of hers, pressing Eva's palm against her own. She studied Eva's face. The porcelain sheen of her skin was marred by the sore on her lip and another at the base of a nostril. There was a coarse ruddiness in her cheeks, but the delicate carving of her features was unchanged. Perhaps, though, the skin clung a little closer to the bone.

"Eva, you frightened me," Bertha said, thinking she could not hear.

Eva stirred and her mouth twitched. She opened her eyes and turned towards Bertha with a smile. "I've always frightened you, Beatrice," she whispered. "This is just the first time you've admitted it."

Bertha laughed in surprise and relief and squeezed Eva's hand. "I won't deny it now," she said, "You're right."

Dr. Lowell entered the room holding her watch. With a sharp movement of her head, she signaled Bertha to leave. "I heard laughter. Miss Newton must have perfect rest. Unless you can maintain the proper decorum in deference to your friend's health, miss, you are not to visit her again."

Bertha and Eva exchanged quick glances and furtive smiles.

Bertha leaned forward. "I'll come again tomorrow," she whispered.

Eva's parents arrived after dinner. Although they were tired from their journey, both went immediately to the infirmary and spent the rest of the day by their daughter's bedside. They watched her while she slept, wiped her forehead with a cool cloth when she grew restless, fed her broth or lemonade when she was thirsty, read to her or sang when she turned fretful.

Mrs. Newton insisted on taking over all of the nursing duties and, even after it grew dark, would not go to the hotel with her husband. She would spend the night with Eva, sleeping in the empty bed. Mrs. Newton had never wanted to send Eva so far away to college and during the long hours on the train from Chicago could not keep herself from saying so. She insisted that she hadn't meant it as a reproach to her husband, but he took it as one. Now, after he had gone and she was alone in the moonlit room watching Eva sleep, she was sorry that she had blamed him.

Even in her youth, Harriet Newton was never a beauty like her daughter. She had always been a little in awe of the girl even when Eva was a small child. Once, when Eva was four years old and tiny and exquisite as a doll, the two had gone walking in a park near their home. A large dog came charging in their direction, and it had been Eva who waved her arms and commanded him to stop. Harriet had a son, four years younger than her daughter, who was more like herself. She understood and depended on him and she loved him as much as she loved Eva, but he did not fascinate her the way that his sister did.

Mrs. Newton slept lightly, alert to every noise. She got up once to close the windows and another time to relieve herself in the chamber pot rather than fumble her way to the bathroom. A volley of hard, wrenching coughs sent her racing to Eva's bed.

"Oh, my poor, dear child," she said, as she had years ago when Eva suffered from the measles. She tried to make her drink, but the water ran down the sides of Eva's mouth, onto her neck and into the ruffles of her nightgown. Mrs. Newton wiped it away with her fingers. She went to a basin on the table, folded a damp cloth into a cool compress. She laid the compress across Eva's forehead and, repeating the process every ten minutes, sat with her until daybreak.

Mrs. Newton was dozing in the chair when Dr. Lowell arrived at seven. She jerked awake and turned to Eva. "She seems to be sleeping comfortably," she reported, but her tone was unsure, as if she needed the doctor's confirmation.

Dr. Lowell went first to the windows and re-opened them. "We must keep the room well-ventilated." She turned to Mrs. Newton and approached the bed. "You are an admirably vigilant nurse," she said and gave the woman an approving nod. "Now, if you please, let me examine the patient. There, please stand over there." She motioned to the foot of the bed.

Dr. Lowell found Eva's wrist and, as she felt for the pulse, looked closely at the girl's face. She turned Eva's hand so that the girl's fingertips rested in her palm and she bent her head to inspect them. Eva's breathing had not markedly changed, but Dr. Lowell discovered that her pulse was weaker and more rapid than it had been the night before. Eva's lips and the base of her fingernails were tinged with the faintest hint of purple.

Mrs. Newton closely followed each of Dr. Lowell's movements and noticed every shift in her expression. She saw the doctor's mouth tighten.

"Is everything all right?" she asked and stepped forward.

Dr. Lowell hesitated; when she answered her voice was shrill. "Yes, yes, of course." She paused and continued more calmly. "Although we must take care of the heart. If you'll excuse me, I'll return with some medication."

Dr. Lowell retreated to her office and shut the door. She stood in front of the wooden cabinet that spanned the length of the narrow room and scanned its rows of brown glass bottles, each carefully labeled and arranged, tallest on the bottom shelf, shortest on the top. She sighed and crossed her arms. Digitalin now or strychnine? Perhaps just a dose of whiskey or a whiff of aromatic of ammonia.

When Dr. Lowell returned with a hypodermic containing one-twentieth of a grain of digitalin, Mr. Newton was standing by his daughter's bed.

"She doesn't know me," he said. His voice was both plaintive and accusatory. "Her color is not good."

Eva's condition did not improve as the day wore on. Dr. Lowell tried another dose of digitalin, recommended by most experts as the best way to strengthen a weakening heart, but Eva continued motionless and the purple cast of her lips and fingernails turned blue. Mr. Newton insisted that Dr. Brownlee, Mrs. Chandler's personal physician, be summoned from Northampton and Dr. Lowell did not protest.

Dr. Brownlee arrived at four o'clock that afternoon and ordered a subcutaneous saline infusion. Dr. Lowell arranged the apparatus, a rubber bag and tube attached to a length of hose and a hypodermic needle, which Dr. Brownlee inserted into the skin of Eva's thigh. Still, her pulse did not grow stronger and her breathing turned quick and shallow, almost a pant. The two doctors agreed that strychnine, in the massive dose of one-twelfth of a gram given by needle, was absolutely necessary.

By ten o'clock, Eva's face was gray. Her skin was cold and clammy to the touch. Her pulse had grown so faint that neither doctor could find it in her wrists. Her heartbeat was slow, weak and irregular and her chest barely rose or fell. With her parents kneeling by her bedside, willing every agonizingly slow and labored breath until there were no more, Eva died that night.

A memorial service was held in the village church on the Sunday after Eva's death. The spectral Mr. Jones had retired and the new minister, young and energetic with an earnest throb in his voice and a probing, sympathetic gaze, enumerated Eva's virtues and offered comfort and hope to the weeping congregation. By then, Eva's body was no longer in South Hadley; it had been prepared for the journey and taken back to Chicago for the funeral as soon as Mr. Newton, wild-eyed, his face gray beneath the shadow of an unshaven beard, could arrange it. Two of Eva's society friends were selected by Mrs. Mead to represent the college at the funeral and, terrified, they accompanied the parents. Grace would have gone, too, except that she was called to Washington to attend the inauguration of her uncle.

Before they left the college, Eva's parents had asked to meet their daughter's friends. Students who wished to pay their respects could visit Mr. and Mrs. Newton in a room at the hotel. Bertha did not go. She had caught a glimpse of them on Monday when, as promised, she went to visit Eva. It was in the afternoon, later than she had planned, and Bertha was sure that she would find Eva sitting up in bed, complaining playfully about her tardiness.

But she had stopped in the open doorway of Eva's room when she saw the man and woman huddled beside the bed. They turned to look at her with expressions of such desperate hope—they must have thought that she was the doctor, bringing salvation in the form of some untried remedy—that she backed away and ran out of the infirmary without a word. Bertha did not know how she could face them now that Eva was irrevocably gone, and she did not know what she could possibly say in the face of such despair.

Bertha and Phebe left the church in silence. Bertha had not cried during the service and her face was uniformly pale. Her jaw was tense and her mouth had the tight, determined set that warned Phebe not to speak. Phebe held a handkerchief to her eyes and she staggered slightly as she walked through the mud, thick as pudding on the road back to Miller's Cottage. Bertha slowed her own pace and took Phebe's elbow but still said nothing. It had rained the night before and would rain again that afternoon. The sky was a solid, ashen blanket of cloud.

"Bertha! Bertha, please wait!"

She would have ignored Mabel's plea if Phebe hadn't stopped and turned around. Bertha released Phebe's arm and slowly pivoted, reluctant to face the sweet sympathy that Mabel was sure to offer.

Mabel covered the short distance between them with her hands outstretched, palms upward, as if blessing or beseeching. She had offered solace to grieving friends and relatives before and when she was at home that Christmas had rallied the faith of a recently bereaved widow. She first greeted Phebe with a quick and pitying smile before placing a hand on each of Bertha's shoulders. She leaned inward and touched Bertha's cheek with her own.

A few days earlier, Bertha might have moved forward to meet Mabel's soft embrace but now she stiffened and, after a moment, pulled back.

"I know that Eva was your friend." Mabel still held Bertha's shoulders and she looked searchingly into her eyes. She expected to see them fill with tears or gaze back in sadness. Their steady self-containment unnerved her. "I am truly, truly sorry," she said and dropped her arms.

Bertha stared at the mild, tender-hearted girl before her and felt a surge of unexpected anger. "Can you tell me," she asked," can you explain to me why it was necessary for her to die?"

Bertha's question was clearly a challenge, not a rhetorical lament, and Mabel looked at her in confusion.

"I know this is difficult," she said, "but you must know that God's purpose and plan is beyond our understanding. Much as you miss Eva, you must take heart that she is beyond all suffering, that she. . . . that she is happier now."

"How do I know that she's happier? She seemed happy enough when she was alive." Bertha spoke without consideration, shocked at her own words; all the promise of redemption, all the hope of resurrection, all the visions of an eternity spent in the presence of God that she had absorbed since childhood seemed, in that instant, to vanish.

She'd seen death before—Grandmother Lane with her eyes and her mouth half open, the infant son of a neighbor laid out in a tiny coffin, the funeral of Cousin Alice May in Boston three years ago—but none of these nor any of the Dayville deaths she'd heard about (mill workers crushed by their machines, riders thrown, swimmers drowned) seemed so pointless, so unfair. Bertha remembered Eva on Titan's Pier, leaning into the wind like a sail or a kite, free and brave as anyone she'd ever known.

Mabel sighed and shook her head. She looked at Bertha sorrowfully and without rancor. "You cannot let your faith be shaken by this. We all die. We must accept that fact and we must accept that only God knows when and why."

Phebe had been standing slightly behind Bertha, listening intently with the handkerchief bunched against her mouth and her eyes wide. "Will Eva go to hell?" she said, directing her question to Mabel.

"What makes you ask such a thing?" Bertha demanded, before Mabel had recovered from the strange suddenness of Phebe's words.

Phebe, cowed by Bertha's vehemence, shrugged timidly before answering in a small, uncertain voice. "Well, it's just because she didn't seem . . . well, she just didn't seem so, so very careful of things."

Bertha and Mabel stared at her as if expecting more. Phebe tried again. "What I mean is, she didn't seem very sorry. She never seemed truly sorry for anything she did." Phebe was pleased with this explanation and grew more confident. "I don't think Eva truly was a. . ." she hesitated, then lifted her chin defiantly. "I don't think Eva truly was a Christian." As soon as the words were out, Phebe flinched, as if expecting a blow.

Mabel, her mouth open and her hands pressed to her throat, stared at Phebe in dismay. "Miss Cutts," she began, "you mustn't . . . ."

Bertha took Phebe's arm. "I'm sorry, Mabel," she said abruptly, forcing her into wounded silence. "I appreciate your kind words, but Phebe and I have to go."

With Phebe keeping pace by her side, Bertha continued the walk that Mabel had interrupted.

"Phebe," she said, "You may be right."

Phebe beamed in confused pride although she wasn't sure what Bertha meant.

"I never heard Eva acknowledge Christ." Bertha spoke quietly, as if to herself. "She *was* careless and thoughtless. I cannot imagine her in paradise." Bertha smiled. "I don't think she'd like it there." She turned to Phebe. "But even if she isn't saved, I can't believe she's lost."

Phebe, anxious to please, was about to nod in agreement. But she hesitated and reached for the small, hard lump that still hung beneath her clothes. "I think God will give her what she deserves," she said clearly and steadily. It was the only revenge against Eva that Phebe ever took.

Chapter 17

Rain

"And what are your living plans for next year, Miss Mellish?" The question came from Sally Green, seated across the table. There was a note of amused condescension in the girl's voice, and she flashed a sly glance at Phebe, who sat on Bertha's left, toying with her food.

Every girl at breakfast except Bertha and Phebe had shared her dreams for the long-anticipated move into the college's four new dormitories. Since the last day of May, more than a week ago, girls had pored over the plans on display in Williston Hall with the thoroughness of explorers preparing for an expedition. Was it better to be near the ground or higher up? How close should one be to the matron, to the bathroom, to the stairway? Was a bigger closet more important than a bay window? A single room or a double? Many delicate negotiations were still underway, to find or keep a compatible roommate or to break those ties and set out alone.

Bertha did not immediately respond. She was glad that her mouth was full when Sally posed the question and she shot a quick look at Phebe, who now stared at her plate with her fork lolling in her motionless hand.

She had not talked to Phebe about next year. Bertha wanted a room by herself, but couldn't bring herself to break the news, and so deliberately kept silent or changed the subject whenever Phebe broached it.

Bertha wiped her mouth and looked evenly at Sally. "I haven't decided yet."

With a dainty but incredulous snort, Sally shrugged. "Well, you'd better do it soon! We'll be choosing rooms in a few days."

Phebe laid down her fork and with her head still bowed, leaned towards Bertha. "I have to talk to you," she whispered.

Phebe would ask to share a room, of course. She would plead with her round, pale eyes, and, in her puny helplessness, remind Bertha of the responsibility passed on to her by Miss Slater. Bertha clapped her own fork down on the table, a small outlet for her resentment.

"Why?" It gave her some satisfaction to make Phebe explain what was so perfectly clear.

Phebe shook her head. "Not here," she said. "In our room."

Even if their attention seemed elsewhere, Bertha knew that most of the others at the table strained to hear their murmured conversation. "All right," she said and swallowed the last few bites of her meal, dreading that moment when she would agree to Phebe's beseeching demand.

Bertha stood in the open doorway of their hidden room with her arms folded, leaning against the jamb. She refused to break the ice, and waited impatiently for Phebe to begin. But Phebe knelt wordlessly beside her cot and reached into the darkness beneath its sagging canvas. She pulled out a large black book. A Bible, Bertha saw. Phebe slipped a small white envelope from its pages.

"I got a letter," Phebe said. She stood, facing Bertha.

Bertha felt a sickening drop in her stomach. So Phebe had lied. So she and Miss Slater had shared a correspondence through all these difficult months.

"So I see."

Phebe did not move to give her the envelope. "It's from my brother," she said.

Relief made her weak; Bertha raised one hand to the door-frame. "Shall I read it?" she asked.

"No." Phebe was embarrassed by the letter's scrawled penmanship, by its mistakes in spelling and grammar, by its blunt and crude vocabulary. "No. I can tell you what it says."

But Phebe could not find the courage to speak; for a moment the only sound was the girls' breathing and the faint rhythm of raindrops hitting the shingled roof above. The rain had begun the night before and continued throughout the morning, sometimes light, sometimes in a heavier barrage. Now it fell in a regular, steady shower.

When Phebe finally spoke, she kept her eyes fixed on the worn, scuffed boards beneath her feet. "It says I have to go home," she said. Her voice was flat. "Mother is poorly and I have to go home. Emmalee just had her baby and she can't help."

Phebe sat down on the cot behind her. She put her face in her hands but did not cry. The crumbled envelope fell to the floor.

"Well, you can leave right after examinations and help your mother over the summer." Bertha did not see why Phebe was making so much of the situation; she tried to be encouraging but her tone was dismissive.

Phebe lifted her face from her hands and shook her head. "You don't understand. They say I have to come home right now. And . . ," Phebe inhaled sharply, making a sound like the first gasp in a sob, "and they say I can't come back."

"What do you mean?"

"It's simple, really." Now Phebe's voice was strangely calm. "My mother and father can't pay any more. They always told me I couldn't stay for the whole four years and now it's time to go home." Phebe shook her head and shrugged. "If ma hadn't gotten sick I could have taken my exams but now I can't." She looked directly at Bertha. "Anyway, it doesn't make any difference."

"Of course it makes a difference!" Bertha was indignant at the selfishness of Phebe's parents. Even more, she was angry at the girl's meek acceptance of their tyranny.

Phebe smiled without bitterness or humor. "No," she said, "it really doesn't matter. They don't care back home. As long as there's a school that will pay me to teach, they don't care."

"When do you intend to leave?" Bertha asked.

Phebe looked down at her hands. "Today," she said.

Without real hope that she'd agree, Phebe asked Bertha to go with her to the train station. But Bertha said yes, and they rode the electric car to Holyoke through the insistent rain in silence.

They stood together for several awkward minutes until the train arrived that was to take Phebe northward to the depot at Potter's Place where, a few hours later, she would find a brother waiting in the family's loose-jointed farm wagon to take her home. At this last moment, Bertha leaned forward and kissed Phebe on her cheek. And, just before she turned to mount the steps into the train carriage, Phebe pressed a small, hard wad of paper into Bertha's hand. "I want you to have this," she said.

Even with the train and Phebe gone, Bertha did not immediately examine the gift. To her surprise, she did not feel lighter or happier free of the responsibility that had dogged her for almost two years. She walked slowly from the Holyoke depot, trudging up the hill at Dwight Street with the folded paper in her closed fist.

The rain pummeled the cloth dome of her open umbrella and it soaked the bottom of her skirt. With the small burden apparently forgotten in her hand, she boarded an almost-empty electric car at the stop in front of City Hall. When the car crossed the river out of Holyoke, Bertha watched its dark, churning water crash over the dam onto the granite blocks below.

At last, Bertha turned to the object in her hand. She unfolded a piece of lined paper, torn from a composition notebook, and found in it a small brass button tied with a long, doubled strand of cotton thread, no longer white. Bertha stared at the threaded button in confusion before she realized where she had seen it before. She remembered that it hung around Phebe's neck the night Miss Slater washed her, and she remembered the day two Octobers ago, when Phebe picked it up from the sandy soil of the Button Field and showed it to Bertha and Eva as if it were something precious.

Bertha tightened her fist around the button and, small as it was, felt it press into the flesh of her palm. What kind of ridiculous talisman was this for Phebe, she wondered. And why did she give it to me? Does she expect me to tie it around my neck? Bertha opened her fingers and looked again at the button. It seemed to her the embodiment of Phebe's naïve ignorance, a worthless object transformed by the girl's confused mind into something . . . . Bertha stopped. Into something beautiful? Was that possible?

The sheet of paper that had covered the button still lay in Bertha's lap and now she noticed writing on its inner surface. She smoothed it open with her empty hand. *This helped me and gave me strength,* Phebe had written in careful cursive, *and now I hope it will help you, too.* In smaller letters below, Phebe gave her address in neat block printing. *Please write to me,* the note ended, *Your friend Phebe.*

Bertha folded the paper and slipped it in a pocket. She held the button in one hand. When she left the electric car at the stop outside the college, she gripped the handle of her umbrella in the other but did not unfurl it against the rain, which now fell in drenching sheets.

Bertha turned away from the college and crossed the street, stumbling through the rivulets that gouged their way through its sodden dirt. Her hair lay dark and slick against her head, and her clothes, drenched through, stuck to her body and wrapped around her legs like seaweed. She crossed the muddy ground of God's Acre, passed the stone of John Preston's grave, and staggered down the overgrown slope that led into the marsh that was the Button Field.

Bertha dangled the brass button by one end of its grimy thread and held it up before her eyes. She could barely discern it through the suffocating rain. She spoke loudly, mixing her words with its incessant roar. "What help was this to you, Phebe?" she shouted and the water ran into her open mouth. "What strength did it give you? What luck did you ever have?"

Bertha dropped the button into the water-logged sand at her feet. It rode on the surface and so she pushed it down with the toe of her boot until no trace of the button or its trailing thread remained. "And what luck would it have brought me?" she whispered.

The rain fell in torrents the rest of that Wednesday and through the night and continued as drizzle the following morning. The unseasonable and prolonged downpour forced the Connecticut River beyond its banks, inundating meadows and crop-laden fields. The rain washed out beds and trestles along the routes of the Boston and Maine railroad, stalling trains and causing two wrecks, one of them fatal. A boom in Bellows Falls, Vermont, could not contain its load against the pull of the flood and burst early on Thursday morning, sending several million feet of unmilled logs rushing down river. The restless, bobbing flotilla crashed into the boom at Turner's Falls, Massachusetts, itself trying to hold four million additional feet of timber. It gave way too and the force of the combined drive breached the boom at Holyoke at six o'clock on Saturday morning.

The avalanche of wood reached the Holyoke Dam and hurtled over its edge. The logs hit the whirlpool at the dam's foot and shot back into the air before pounding its now-submerged granite blocks. Once back in the current of the river, some of the logs lodged against bridge piers, trees or other projections along the way, some were caught, fished out and tied to trees for future salvage, and some were born down the swollen river and released into the waters of the Long Island Sound. A few made it all the way to open ocean.

Part Three

Summer and Junior Year, June – November 1897

Chapter 18

Home

Florence carried a platter of ham and fried eggs from the kitchen into the small dining room whose blowsy floral wallpaper had faded to a dusty pink. There were six chairs around the oblong table, and she could barely squeeze between them and the sideboard, a heavy old-fashioned piece purchased by her parents soon after their wedding. The linen cloth laid on the table was clean, but its surface was flecked with yellowish stains. Florence hid the largest under the serving plate.

Florence shared with Bertha and her father the wide Mellish forehead. Her hair, pulled off her face and fastened in a bun high on the back of her head, formed a soft pouf around the exposed skin of her forehead. A tiny mole like a spot of velvet nestled between her ear and the end of her right cheekbone. She thought that shirtwaists and skirts were too youthful for a woman of her age and always wore high-necked dresses, dark wool in the cool months and, at home in the summer, subdued calico prints in rusts and browns like the one she had on that day.

Seated in the chair closest to the kitchen door, Sarah Mellish noted Florence's clumsy ploy with ironic amusement. No need to hide the state of the family linen from these two guests. She cared nothing for the good opinion of old Dr. Hill whose rapid decline over the past few months struck her as self-indulgent. And, as her doctor, Henry Hammond knew every bodily secret that she chose to share. Sarah felt a tickle of loose hair against her neck but did not adjust it. She had always taught her girls that a lady never groomed herself in public.

Bertha sat in a chair between her mother and Dr. Hill, pressed between the table's edge and the wall at her back. She could not easily get in or out of her place to help Florence who, in any case, had refused her offer. Still, Bertha did not like to sit while her sister worked; she was sure the two guests were silently calling her lazy. Sarah caught Bertha slouching in her chair and, with her hand hidden by the tablecloth, poked the girl in her knee.

Reverend Mellish, at the other end of the table, watched Florence closely, eager for his supper. His digestion was excellent, although he took care not to overeat. John Mellish complimented his elder daughter on the aroma of the meat and looked to Dr. Hill, seated on his right, for confirmation. The old doctor was fumbling with his silverware and did not seem to hear. But Dr. Hammond, on the minister's left, enthusiastically agreed, and Florence, who had accidentally bumped his chair twice while laying out the meal, felt warmth in her neck and then her face. She hurried back to the kitchen.

She returned with a bowl of boiled potatoes and another of green beans, laid them on the table and sat down in the empty place next to Dr. Hammond. As Reverend Mellish offered a blessing, they all bowed their heads except for Dr. Hill, who reached for a nearby biscuit.

For a few minutes, all that could be heard in the room was the faint sound of chewing, the occasional clink of metal against china and the buzz of a fly. The screen in the open dining room window had a large hole that Reverend Mellish had not yet repaired and a plump, slow-moving insect had come to share their meal. Sarah flicked her hand impatiently as it neared her plate and the fly escaped into the kitchen. A cool breeze rattled the shade that was pulled halfway down against the light of the summer evening and Florence gratefully felt its breath against her warm cheek. Dr. Hammond broke the silence to request the salt shaker and she lifted it from where it rested on the table to her left and placed it in his hand.

He thanked her with a smile. An admirable woman, he thought, with natural refinement and a sensitive heart, but too constrained by duty, perhaps by timidity. Henry could never look at Florence without a twinge of sympathetic regret.

Henry Hammond had no beard or mustache; the round knob of his chin was clean-shaven. His hair was thin on top, with a few long strands that he carefully swept from one side to the other and held in place with a dab of hair oil. But his hair grew thicker along the sides of his face and it jutted outward in long wiry tufts from the bottom of each ear to just above the collar of his black frock coat. During the war, he had seen an officer in full military dress sport such whiskers and they seemed to him dashing, gallant and even a little exotic. He grew his own and had worn them ever since, although they were sparser now and contained more coarse gray hairs than dark ones.

The doctor had a weak heart, the result of rheumatic fever and overwork in his younger days. As an army surgeon, he had seen and done things in the terrible war of his youth that still visited him in his sleep. He saw piles of severed limbs, organized by type and neatly stacked, and naked men, thin as skeletons, marching by in endless rows. Dr. Hammond had entered Richmond on the day of its fall and sometimes the city's flames consumed the ghastly army of his dreams. Sometimes his heart fluttered in his chest like a trapped bird or thudded heavily against his ribs.

When Florence first met Dr. Hammond, she smiled to herself at his overgrown sideburns. But over the past few weeks, with his wife away caring for her ailing father, he had called more often at the Mellish house and she had come to know him better. Now his whiskers were simply a part of his facial geography, as natural and necessary as any of his features, and as he took the small glass shaker from her with a gentle nod, Florence could not remember why they had once looked so odd.

Henry Hammond seasoned his potatoes and then turned to look diagonally across the table at Bertha. He knew her to be a quiet girl but since his arrival at the house about an hour earlier she had barely spoken a word. Now she seemed particularly listless and without appetite. Dr. Hammond believed in education for women but he thought that Bertha might have driven herself too hard at school. He took a doctorly interest in her condition.

"Bertha, my dear, how was your time at college this last year?" he asked.

John Mellish didn't wait for his daughter's reply. From his place at the head of the table, he reported to Dr. Hammond that Bertha had done very well indeed in all her subjects. She had excelled in French, in Rhetoric, in Greek, in Bible study and in General Chemistry, a scientific course that she had just taken up. In fact, Bertha had been invited to join the Debating Society when she returned to school in the fall. It was an honor, he assured his listeners, open only to the school's top scholars.

Out of appropriate humility, Reverend Mellish tried to contain his enthusiasm, but his open face beamed. He was also concerned that Florence might find some painful memory triggered by Bertha's triumph, but if she had regrets about her own short academic career, Florence gave no hint. She smiled at her sister across the table. Dr. Hill, whose absorption in his food seemed absolute, stopped eating with his fork halfway to his mouth. "Chemistry!" he snorted. "For a girl!"

Strangely, Dr. Hammond noticed, Sarah Mellish did not seem moved by her husband's praise of their daughter, and had a strained, sour look through it all.

Dr. Hammond turned again to Bertha and half raised his water glass in a gallant gesture. "Congratulations, Miss Bertha! You are certainly entitled to rest and enjoy yourself this summer!"

At the end of his good-natured remark, Dr. Hammond felt a growing tension. Sarah gave Bertha a sharp look, Florence glanced worriedly at her mother and John Mellish frowned in his wife's direction.

Bertha seemed unaware of the brief, silent communication among her family. She looked directly at Dr. Hammond and answered in a firm voice. "I'm afraid not. I'm going to work this summer." She stopped and drew a breath. "I've secured a position at the mill."

Dr. Hammond looked momentarily surprised before he caught himself and composed his expression. Mill work was not what he expected of a Mellish daughter. And, clearly, some family disagreement was at work. Although hesitant to insert himself, he felt a sudden sympathy for the girl. He thought perhaps she was asking for his help and he saw a core of desperation in her unwavering gaze. He tried to keep his tone matter-of-fact, hoping that a neutral interest in her plan would help Bertha respond to her family's objections.

"I admire your diligence, Bertha, although I still think that rest is important, too. What will you be doing? Bookkeeping, typewriting, clerical work in the mill office? These are all excellent ways to learn about business and acquire useful skills for later employment."

Sarah Mellish broke in. "Well you'd think so, wouldn't you. No, our Bertha has it in her mind to be a mill hand. She wants to spend all day in one of those nasty rooms with those filthy, dangerous machines." Sarah glared at Bertha and shook her head. "Why a girl with two years of college education, a girl from a fine, educated family would want to rub shoulders with those. . . . ." Sarah's color was unnaturally high and she broke off, breathing rapidly.

"Florence," Reverend Mellish instructed, "please fill your mother's glass."

Florence did as she was told although Sarah did not take the proffered water. Florence touched her arm. "Mother, there's no need to be so upset," she soothed, "Mill work is respectable."

Sarah had her wind back and she pushed away her daughter's arm. "Yes, if you're an Irish girl or a French one! Do you have any idea how many children those French women have?"

She looked wildly from Dr. Hammond to her husband but neither man responded. The doctor wore the expression of sympathetic attention he used with querulous patients.

"Haven't you seen them strutting around the town as if it were theirs? Some of the women look like harlots. And the men!" Sarah stopped and beat the linen tablecloth with her fingers, a puny outlet for her rage.

Reverend Mellish, embarrassed by his wife's show of temper in front of his two friends, looked sorrowful. "Sarah, dear," he said, his voice soft with gentle reproach, "Sarah, dear, we cannot hold ourselves above others. Pride. . . ." He shook his head. "Pride," he repeated.

In truth, he was chastising himself as much as his wife. He did not want Bertha to work among the mill hands any more than her mother did, but he couldn't find any Christian reason to forbid it. The blessedness of honest work and of humility. How in good conscience could he deny these virtues to his own daughter?

Bertha spoke again, directing her words to Dr. Hammond as if her mother's outburst had never taken place. "I won't be in the office. They have no need of anyone there. I'm going to work in the finishing room."

Dr. Hammond nodded thoughtfully. "Ah," he said, "that's a quiet, clean place."

Dr. Hammond turned from Bertha to her mother. All the fervid animation of her anger had dissipated and she sat, deflated, with her shoulders stooped and her limp hands in her lap. She usually did not carry herself like a woman nearing seventy, but now the doctor was reminded of her age.

"Mrs. Mellish, you can rest easy! Bertha will have nothing to do with dangerous machinery."

"Small comfort," Sarah Mellish answered in a hoarse and brittle voice. "So now you see how poor we really are."

Chapter 19
The Mill

It was almost noon. Bertha had been at work since seven that morning, seated at a table whose surface was propped up at an angle by two sticks, one on each side. She held her face inches from the coarse woolen broadcloth that draped over the sloping board. The muscles in her neck and shoulders tingled and her eyes burned.

The idea had come to her on the train back to Dayville, when she first caught sight of the red brick tower in the distance. She would spend her summer doing mindless tasks in a place where there would be no need to remember or think or speak. She would be a mill girl, one of a crowd, nameless and untroubled.

Absorbed in her task, Bertha was oblivious to the movement around her. She did not notice when the women and girls who worked beside her at the row of twelve tables stood up to remove and fold their finished cuts of cloth and to adjust new ones over their boards. She paid no attention to arrival of men and boys who brought piles of fabric from the weaving rooms to the burlers and who delivered the burled cloth to the menders on the other side of the long, whitewashed room. It was what she had wished for, this obliteration of everything and everyone beyond the focus of her eyes.

A dull ache settled in her lower back. She gripped the tweezer-like burling iron between the thumb and first two fingers of her right hand with unnecessary force and moved the tool awkwardly over the freshly woven fabric, which was tacky with its last residue of animal oil and smelled musky in the room's moist air. Filaments of wool floated lazily in the sunbeams that shone through a row of tall windows behind the burling tables. Some of the fibers stuck in her throat and tickled her nose, but she fought to suppress a sneeze.

The black cloth absorbed whatever light fell on or around it and made it difficult for Bertha to find the imperfections that it was her responsibility to fix or to mark for the mender. Each burler had an identifying number that she wrote in chalk on each completed cut of fabric, and each burler had a page in the overseer's book. Although she was to be paid by the piece, Bertha was more concerned that no mistakes be traced back to her than she was with piling up finished cuts.

She looked for bits of foreign matter nestling against the wool's unnapped surface: a strand of weaver's hair, a tiny strip of weed gathered long ago in a pasture somewhere out West, a miniscule fiber of jute rubbed from the inside of a bag that once held the raw shearings of sheep. She searched for knots in the cloth to be drawn out between the burling iron's two points and then carefully excised with scissors. A small slip would leave a hole for the overseer to discover and the menders to resent.

There were runners, pulled-in sections that distorted the edges of the fabric, to be released, gently and slowly, without breaking the fibers of warp or weft. There were mistakes in weaving to be marked with chalk and left for the menders, flaws in the cloth's own structure visible only through the slightest change of value, the merest hint of a darker darkness, a horizontal sliver of a line, perhaps three inches, maybe six, in the blackness of the cloth.

Bertha inspected every inch of the surface in front of her, tortuously, obsessively, as methodically as an archeologist, although on her third day as a burler, she was not imagining herself or her task in such romantic terms. The finishing room was, as Dr. Hammond observed, one of the quietest in the mill, but the incessant clacking and pounding of the machines on the four floors above— the looms, the carding machines, the spinning machines, the fulling machines, the shearing machines, the napping machines—and the grinding of the gears and the belts and the shafts that powered them filled the buildings and the mill yard with a palpable, throbbing presence. In the room where the burlers and the menders sat, this presence was felt more than heard. It permeated Bertha's mind and drove away thought.

She had to stop. She closed her eyes, drew her shoulders together and tilted her head back until the sinews of her neck and the slight rise of her Adam's apple bulged against her skin. Her hands, one with the burling iron and the other holding a pair of scissors, hung in the air, just level with her chest. Bertha held that position for only a few seconds before the finishing room overseer, making his way down the aisle between the bank of windows and the backs of the seated burlers, stopped to the right of her bench. She straightened and went back to work.

"Look sharp there, girlie. Mind you don't tip over." His tone was falsely jovial and slightly menacing.

Bertha did not acknowledge his presence or his comments and hoped the man would leave. She could hear his breathing at her side, moist inhalations through open lips. He now stood directly beside her and she sensed that he was leaning over to examine her profile.

"Oh, I do apologize," he said in a tone more mocking than contrite, "I beg your pardon. You're the new young lady." He emphasized the last two words suggestively.

Bertha realized he was toying with her in some way she did not understand, yet felt she was expected to respond. She turned her head in his direction and looked up into his face, pink and glistening with sweat. The flesh on his neck swelled and met the roll on his chin and the collar of his white shirt and the wings of his black bowtie cut into its soft surface.

The overseer stood with his short arms folded over a belly encased in a black vest, and looked at her appraisingly. After a moment, he snorted and his mouth hardened and lost its insinuating sneer. He regarded her sternly.

"Can you do this work or not?" he asked.

Bertha tried to keep her voice steady. "I can do it well enough, I guess, Mr. Aldrich." she said, "I'm a little slow, I'm afraid." She had hoped to sound dignified and unruffled, but her words came out ingratiatingly humble. She had never answered to a boss before and had never been required to perform a task for which she felt so utterly incompetent.

"Well, speed it up, then," he ordered and moved on to the next table.

Bertha kept her head down and pretended to pick at the cloth while she watched the man's movements out of the corner of her eye. She saw that his attention was now absorbed by the girl at the next table, seated barely five feet away. Bertha raised her head, turned it to have a better but still discreet view.

The girl sat upright with her head and arms raised, working on the upper half of her fabric. Aldrich stood behind the girl's bench with the swelling arc of his belly pressed against the curve of her back. He leaned in as if to inspect the cloth, and he raised his left arm and passed it over her shoulder so that the damp hollow under his arm crushed the white folds of her shirtwaist. He stood like this for nearly a minute and the girl did not resist or recoil, barely hesitating as she plucked, rapidly and surely, with the burling iron in her right hand.

Bertha was shocked by the intimacy of the scene, and repulsed by the thought of the overseer's touch. She continued to observe the girl even after he had left. French-Canadian, like most of the hands, she stood out from the other French girls, who were generally modest in attitude and dress. Bertha had noticed this difference two days earlier when she watched the girl walk carelessly to her bench, late, on Bertha's first day at the mill.

She was slight but well-formed, with a waist cinched so tightly that a big man's hands could circle it. Her shirtwaists hugged the contours of her upper body and her breasts strained even the apron that she wore to protect her clothes. When she arrived in the morning and left at night, she wore her straw sailor hat tilted saucily forward and not, like the other girls, flat on her head like a plate. Her hair was yellow, dull as straw, and when her hat was off, darker hair was visible at its roots. Her cheeks were unnaturally pink. Her eyes were a pale, clouded blue and seemed too big for their sockets. She often dipped her head slightly and looked up through her lashes, especially when talking to men.

Although the two looked nothing alike, something in the French girl's bearing made Bertha think of Eva. She tried to imagine that it was, in fact, Eva who sat near her in the damp, wool-hazed room, fresh and cool with a teasing smile on her perfect face, but the ghost of her dead friend would not be conjured.

The girl turned suddenly towards Bertha. Her eyes were narrowed and suspicious. "*What are you looking at?*" she asked sharply in French.

Bertha started guiltily, then shook her head and shrugged as if she had not understood the girl's obvious question. Bertha spoke perfect, fluent French—the Parisian kind taught to her first by her mother and then at college—and she had heard the Canadian version often enough to be familiar with that. But she honestly did not know how to answer. I am looking at a shameless young woman, she thought. I am looking at a strange creature bred in some world beyond my experience. I am looking at something ugly and fascinating. I am looking at the memory of my beautiful friend. She could say none of these things and so kept silent.

The French girl dropped her tools in her lap and, with a fist pressed against each hip, twisted her body towards Bertha. "*I said, what are you looking at? Are you deaf or just stupid?*" Her voice was loud and high-pitched and cut easily through the finishing room's dense air.

The wan fourteen-year-old sitting at the table to the girl's right and the plump middle-aged woman at the table to Bertha's left paused in their burling and, with smirks of suppressed amusement on their faces, waited for Bertha's response.

Bertha focused on the few inches of black wool in front of her as if nothing else existed in the world, but she knew that her cheeks burned, more from anger than shame.

"*Oh, Yvette, she doesn't understand French, can't you see.*" Bertha's neighbor to the left called this observation to her friend, sending it past Bertha as if she were invisible.

"Ah, an ignorant Irish!" Yvette spoke in heavily accented English. She tossed her head and snorted before reverting to French. "*No wonder she's slow and stupid.*"

"I am not Irish," Bertha said abruptly and without thinking, a slight tremor of indignation in her voice. The experienced burler who had trained her and who now sat at the far end of the row of tables, was Irish. She had been patient enough that first day, given that time spent with the newcomer reduced her own pile of finished cuts. But her voice had often risen in exasperation at her pupil's clumsiness and Bertha still smarted from her condescension. The woman was tough and raw, with a coarse accent and big red hands, and Bertha did not want to be associated with her.

"Eh, *Anglaise*–even worse!" Yvette waved her left hand dismissively.

The plump woman stopped working and pivoted on her bench until she faced Bertha. She leaned forward with a conspiratorial look. "College?" She inflected the one word as a question and, although she seemed to be trying to say it in English, she used the softer "g" of the French. "You go in college, yes?"

Bertha glanced towards the woman and, again, gave an uncomprehending shrug before looking away. The woman waited a moment and then threw up her hands in defeat. She looked past Bertha to Yvette.

"*I heard that this girl she was in college. That's what Hortense told me she heard the boss say to Monsieur Bennett. He said that she is a very educated young lady, a very smart girl.*" The plump woman raised her eyebrows and chuckled. "*She doesn't say much for a smart girl.*"

Trapped between the two women, Bertha was unwilling to come to her own defense. Under no circumstance would she now admit to understanding their words and she began to take grim pleasure in considering all that she might learn just by listening.

Yvette, still sitting with arms akimbo, looked at Bertha in mocking pity and laughed. "*Well, she must be a very bad student in that college of hers, or she wouldn't be taking her lessons here.*"

A tall, thick-set man in rolled-up shirtsleeves dropped a load of cuts on the floor in front of Yvette's table, and she looked up at him with a sly smile. He winked in reply and, just as the noon whistled shrilled, jerked his head as an invitation for her to follow.

Bertha stayed at her bench while the room quickly emptied. The eleven other burlers and the twelve menders dropped their tools at the first note of the steam whistle, shed their aprons, grabbed their hats and the various lunch pails and paper bags stowed under their tables and rushed out the door to the mill yard beyond. The youngest girls ran, while Bertha's plump neighbor and the two or three other women her age exited with more dignity. Yvette sauntered out on the arm of the tall Frenchman and soon Bertha was alone. With the distant machinery temporarily stilled, the room seemed strangely listless, inert rather than peaceful.

She turned on her bench and sat facing the window. She watched as a gaggle of children scampered into the yard, each clutching the handle of a metal pail and looking for the mother or father or older sibling whose lunch, hot from the kitchen, the little boy or girl was charged to deliver. She watched the tired hands, male and female, emerge from the brick building with their clothes and hair and skin flocked with wool, and she watched them come to life again in the fresh air of the yard.

The formless crowd broke into smaller groups or into pairs. She knew that some who left the yard headed to the rows of tenements built just along the edge of the mill complex while others walked in the opposite direction towards the boarding houses located near the depot and the livery stable. She saw that some remained in the yard, eating their noon-day meal on the few patches of grass that grew within its confines along the shallow banks of the mill race.

Bertha considered her options. On her first two days, she had left with the others and, unnoticed in the crowd, slipped away to a quiet spot along the stream some distance from the mill. Now she wanted fresh air and a walk to stretch her legs but did not like the thought of crossing the mill yard so conspicuously alone. She could eat her lunch--a peach and a chicken sandwich grown warm over the long morning hours–there at her table. Florence had tried to convince her to make the mile-long walk home for dinner each day, but Bertha had refused, arguing that the noonday break was too short. She preferred to remain in the uncomfortable room rather than face the friendly curiosity of her father and sister or her mother's disapproving frown.

A German grammar was packed in the paper bag along with her food, and Bertha moved her bench closer to the window to study from the book while she ate. She was settled with her back to the window when she heard footsteps and then a deep, male voice. She looked to her left and saw Mr. Aldrich standing some fifteen feet away, at the door of the small glassed-in cubicle where he kept the finishing room records and account books. He stood with his broad back towards her and his legs spread apart. His arms were not visible to Bertha, and she imagined them fat as sausages, crossed and resting on his belly's broad shelf. He rocked slowly back and forth on his heels and his head moved as if he were speaking.

The overseer was not alone. His companion, a much younger man–perhaps twenty-two to Aldrich's fifty and at least four inches taller–faced Bertha. He wore the clean white shirt and necktie of a manager, and a gold watch chain looped across the front of his neatly buttoned vest. Although most of the other men at the mill, workers and supervisors alike, had mustaches, some so long that they covered the entire upper lip, others neatly waxed and curved up at the ends, this man's face was clean-shaven. He had dark eyebrows and dark curls that covered most of his forehead. His lips were full but pale and he had a long, oval face with a jaw just square enough to keep him from beauty.

Bertha sat frozen, at first merely afraid of discovery. But something other than fear kept her motionless on the bench and as she studied the young man she did not think of escape or plan her next move.

The young man listened patiently as Aldrich, now punctuating his words with stabbing gestures, continued to talk. But after a few minutes he looked away from the gesticulating man and noticed Bertha sitting in the light of an open window, a book on her lap and a sandwich gripped in one upraised and immobile hand. He caught her looking at him, clearly staring.

Before Bertha could drop her eyes, he smiled. Even at this distance, she could see that his smile was open, complete and unforced and in its warmth her embarrassment disappeared. Without conscious effort, she smiled in return. Aldrich had not noticed the young man's brief inattention and now he grabbed him by the elbow and propelled him out of the room. The young man, as he passed through the doorway, turned and touched his hand lightly to his forehead in a parting salute.

Chapter 20

Sunday

Reverend Mellish, wearing the frock coat that had done him Sabbath service for nearly fifteen years, walked between his daughters on the road that ran from their house towards Main Street. He moved briskly despite the July heat, helped over the unpaved surface by the point of his walking-stick. When he paused to rummage in his coat pockets for a handkerchief, his daughters stopped too, and watched anxiously as he wiped the sweat collecting under his broad-brimmed hat.

Their father seemed unusually distracted that morning. He had taken nothing but a cup of coffee and a slice of bread for breakfast and had fidgeted in his chair, absently twisting small clumps of his beard. With uncharacteristic impatience, he'd urged his daughters to hurry through their own meal and didn't answer when their mother asked what on earth was wrong with him.

The minister folded the handkerchief and returned it to his pocket. The three resumed their journey until they reached the railroad tracks that cut diagonally across the road and through the center of the village. Florence took her father's arm to steady him over the obstacle, but Reverend Mellish pulled away.

"I'm afraid that I have to leave you here, my dears. You go up to the church without me. I must. . . . I have an errand to attend to in Danielson this morning." Reverend Mellish looked down at his walking stick as he spoke and dug a little hole in the dirt with its tip. When he was done, he glanced at Florence, who gave him the lovingly disappointed look of an indulgent parent.

"Papa, you know Mother doesn't think it's right." She paused before continuing more sternly. "And I'm not sure that I think it's right either."

Confused and hurt, Bertha looked from her father to Florence. Clearly, neither one had given a moment's thought that she was excluded from their cryptic conversation.

"What on earth are you talking about?" she asked her sister, but it was her father who answered.

"I occasionally attend service in a church in Danielson and I have been asked to preach there today." Reverend Mellish had regained his parental dignity. He stood up straight with his stick hooked over one arm and his hat sitting plumb on his head.

Florence turned to Bertha. "Father means the Advent Chapel."

"May I go with you?" Bertha asked.

"No," Florence said, but their father took Bertha's arm.

"I would certainly enjoy the company. And you might find the experience illuminating." He looked at Florence and smiled with the easy benevolence of victory. "You're welcome to join us, my dear, but I understand if you choose not to."

Reverend Mellish and Bertha turned into the nearby yard of Kennedy's livery stable, where the old minister had made arrangements for a delivery cart and driver, idle on the Sabbath, to carry him the three miles to Danielson and to bring him home some hours later. When he pulled out his thin purse, Mr. Kennedy waved it away and sent them off with a tip of his hat and slap on the thick flank of the dray horse.

The driver left them in front of a brown clapboard structure the size and shape of a middling one-story house. A few shallow steps led to its front door. Through its open windows, they heard a rich and resonant voice, a woman's. Reverend Mellish slowly twisted the doorknob, wincing slightly as it squeaked. He entered the chapel with

Bertha close behind and removed his hat. The room was hot, without a breath of air coming through the open windows.

Ten crude wooden benches were arranged in parallel rows with an aisle down the middle. Three or four people, alone or in pairs, sat on each bench. Reverend Mellish indicated a space near the door for Bertha, while he slipped into the second row.

In front, behind a table, stood a tall woman in a rusty black dress and an old-fashioned bonnet whose projecting brim framed her jowled and florid face. She gripped the table's edge, barely moving, while her voice filled the room and her eyes performed a dramatic dance. They swept upward in exaltation, dropped in despair, fixed the assembled worshippers with a stern and penetrating gaze.

Most of the worshippers were women, old or middle-aged, as shabbily dressed as the speaker. They looked to be farmer's wives, or struggling spinsters getting by on a few bits of dressmaking, or the widows of bricklayers or butchers. A few men of the same type were scattered among them.

The woman's voice grew louder.

"How prepared are you?" she thundered, pivoting her head from one side of the room to the other. Her eyes bulged and her cheeks quivered.

The question, accusatory and urgent, died into silence while the woman raised one arm and thrust her outstretched hand towards the ceiling. "Do not be deceived," she bellowed, drops of spittle flying from her mouth, "do not be fooled by Satan's lies. Hearken to the truth: the signs of the times tell us that He is coming soon!"

She lowered her arm until it was level with the heads of the congregation and, with index finger extended, passed it over her listeners. A few shrank back at the gesture but some leaned towards it; all had tears glistening in their eyes.

The preacher aimed her finger at a tiny woman, face shriveled as a walnut beneath her bonnet. ""And what have *you* done in preparation for His arrival?" Her voice was softer now, not unkind, almost sorrowful. The old woman clasped her hands beneath her chin and faced her interrogator with a beatific smile. "I have prayed," she said, "I am ready."

The preacher woman moved on, directing her question from one rapt listener to the other, until she came to Bertha, seated on the end of the bench near the door. "And you, young woman, what have *you* done?"

Now the woman lingered and she and the congregation paused in expectant silence. Until this point, Bertha had observed the performance with some amusement and a little disdain, wondering what possible interest her father could have in such a primitive display. She had felt so distant, so utterly without connection to the ignorant people seated around her that, for a moment, she did not believe they could see her.

Bertha nearly turned around to look for some other, visible woman who must be standing in the space behind her bench, the real object of the preacher's attention, and she remembered that strange night in the cell she shared with Phebe, when Miss Slater stared at her too, waiting for an answer. If not for her father, Bertha would bolted through the nearby door.

Everyone in the stifling room looked at her, their bodies twisted on the hard, unsparing benches and their heads straining in her direction. On their worn, guileless faces Bertha saw how anxious they were for her immortal soul and how boundless and generous was the hope they offered her. But the weight of these gifts was suffocating, and Bertha did not want them. Finally, she managed a small shrug. As she lowered her head to stare into her lap, she avoided glancing towards the bench in the second row where her father sat.

The preacher woman moved on to other, more responsive targets and now she rested her hands on the table. Suddenly, she seemed too tired to stand and a raw-boned, bearded man jumped up and brought a chair to her side. She collapsed into the seat and for a long, hushed moment seemed insensible until, as if waking from the dead, she roused herself. On her feet again, she leaned against the tabletop and raised her head heavenward.

"I know you are coming, Lord, be it on a cloud of perfect whiteness or in the violence of a whirlwind or in the heat of fiery flames. I know that you are coming, Lord, and I pray that we may be ready to receive you." She paused and closed her eyes, and when she spoke again, there was nothing theatrical in her voice. She sounded like a child yearning for its mother or a wife whose husband has been too long at sea. "May you come soon," she whispered and sat down.

"Amen," the congregation sighed.

They sang a ragged and tuneless hymn and then the bearded man invited Reverend Mellish—Elder Mellish, he was called– to the rudimentary pulpit. John Mellish spoke of God's compassion and held his listeners by the calm authority of his voice. Under his influence the gaunt old spinsters and rock-plagued farmers opened their tightly clasped hands, breathed more easily, let their coiled shoulders drop.

But he did not allow his listeners to grow complacent. Guilt born of sin grew and festered within the dark recesses of each and every heart, he reminded them, within every man and woman in that room. Confess your sins, beg forgiveness, expose the cancer of your soul to God's searing light. This, Elder Mellish promised, was the path to salvation.

Like the preacher woman, he searched out individual members of his audience as he spoke, and, for a moment, directed his words to each upturned, earnest face.

He found himself glancing at Bertha. He was sorry that she had been singled out earlier and felt for her in her embarrassment. Still, when it happened, he found himself praying for his daughter to be moved. He prayed that she would throw aside her reason and her reserve and give in to the power of the moment. He prayed that Bertha would let him know that she was ready. But when he saw her there, sitting so out of place among those sad-eyed souls, he remembered just how young she was. Life had not yet taught her its harsh lessons. She would learn in time. He only hoped those lessons would not come too hard or too late.

Chapter 21
Hell

Sarah Mellish lay on her back with her eyes shut and her hands resting palms-down against her ribs. An hour before, her husband and daughters left for church. When she heard the front door close behind them, she took off the cotton wrapper that she wore downstairs to breakfast and draped it over the chair beside her bed. Now she was dressed only in a under-vest and a pair of knit drawers that hugged her legs down to the knee. She could feel the beating of her heart against her left thumb and for a time was conscious of nothing but its rhythm.

Sarah fell asleep and slept heavily until a sound outside her window—the rattle of wheels against the nearby road or a blue jay's chatter—roused her. Gripped with the half-formed panic of the abruptly awakened, she stared up at the bed's sagging canopy. She studied the fabric's pattern of fruit-filled cornucopia, twisted into fat spirals that alternated with extravagant bursts of foliage. Although these bursts looked more animal than plant in the strange faces they suggested to her drowsy eye, she grew calmer.

The canopy was a heavy wool damask, once the rich color of claret but now muted by age and dust to an ashen mauve. Every summer, Florence attempted to take it down for cleaning and storage and every summer Sarah refused to let it go. She needed the comforting veil of its presence to hide the blank white ceiling above and, beyond that, the infinite breadth of sky that rose to a heaven she could not imagine. Sarah had known her husband, borne her children, and passed countless solitary hours under the canopy's protection and she had a vague sense that God would arrange for her to die in its absence.

The heat finally drove her from her bed. Sarah slowly raised herself to her elbows and then, in a burst of irritable energy, sat upright and swung her legs over the edge of the high bedstead. Light-headed after so long on her back, she rested a moment, looking down at her bare feet. They were pale and fine-boned and she realized with a bitter smile that they were the best-preserved and most youthful part of her body.

Sarah slid forward and stood up. She shuffled the short distance to a washstand pushed into a corner near the foot of the bed and, once there, steadied herself with a hand placed lightly on its oak surface. A small cotton towel, freshly laundered, lay folded to Sarah's left. On her right a china pitcher, filled with water by Florence early that morning, resting in the hollow of a matching bowl. A mirror attached to two vertical uprights rose from the back of the stand and Sarah adjusted its angle until she found her face reflected on its surface, which was smooth except for a few pits where the metallic backing had chipped away.

Sarah dragged her fingers down the skin of both cheeks, pulling her mouth into a grotesque pout. She pressed the sides of her face until she felt bone beneath the pulpy flesh and then impulsively raised her hands to unpin her hair. Once brown, Sarah's hair was now gray, a mixture of shades from silver to steel. It was coarser than in her youth but still shiny, and it fell below her shoulders. She shook her head and let the loosened strands obscure her face.

She tilted the mirror downward and could now see only that portion of her body from the base of her neck to her navel. Encased in the ribbed cotton of her vest, she did not find her form as displeasing as her face. She turned to look at herself in profile and, although satisfied with the effect, was soon distracted by the sweat-dampened hair that stuck uncomfortably to her forehead and neck. Sarah picked up the towel and, rather than pour water from that vessel into the bowl, dipped it directly into the pitcher. She raised the dripping towel and squeezed it weakly with both hands before bringing it her face.

Water ran steadily from the fringed ends of the towel down Sarah's neck and she shivered gratefully at its chill. It soaked her shoulders and a u-shaped section on the front of her under-vest and when she took the towel from her eyes, she saw that the saturated fabric clung to her, translucent, revealing the pale pinkish-yellow of her skin. The sight and, particularly, the sensation of the wet cloth were strangely unsettling and made her think of a day, years ago and also in the heat of summer, when she had felt another such taut, cool membrane against her body.

One Saturday afternoon, with their infant daughter asleep at a neighbor's house, Sarah and her husband, barely two years married, went for a walk in the woods beyond their village and found a small pond hidden behind a curtain of bramble bushes, the water tinted brown by leaves that lay like a carpet along its bottom. Hot, tired and alone in the world except for the creatures–insect, animal, and bird—that skittered in the underbrush and in the trees, they forgot for a time that they were minister and minister's wife.

John swam naked and Sarah wore only the thin cotton chemise that remained after she had discarded bodice, skirt, petticoats and corset. They played together in the cool, shallow water, laughing and splashing like children. Then, like the first couple after the Fall but without consciousness of shame, they embraced with no thought beyond the smooth, slippery corporeality of their legs and their arms, their mouths conjoined, Sarah's hair spread on the water, brown and slick as the leaves below, her cotton shift floating filmy and delicate as the spider webs draped from twig to twig on the banks of the pond.

Again on land, they had felt suddenly awkward and turned from each other to button their damp bodies back into their clothes. But for a few days afterward, Sarah had caught her husband glancing in her direction– once as she sat in a pew while he spoke from the pulpit– with a look so intimate that she blushed even as she returned it. She remembered that look now, standing before the mirror in her cramped, low-ceilinged bedroom, where the air felt depleted even with the windows open and where a deep breath drew in the faint, sour smell of mildew.

With her right hand gripping its handle and her left hand supporting it from below, Sarah raised the heavy, water-filled pitcher until its lip hung poised above her head. She tilted it forward, her arms shaking with the effort to hold the pitcher aloft and direct its flow, and a thin stream dribbled onto her hair and down her face. She wanted a torrent, a cataract to drench her as completely as that dark New Hampshire pond had drenched her forty years before, but her arms gave out and the pitcher crashed to the floor.

It broke into several large pieces, scattering shards across the room. With tears of frustration blurring her vision, Sarah stood in the puddle and watched as water spread outward from her feet and soaked into the cracks between the floorboards. She did not think to find a dry towel or a rag to mop it up nor did she bend to pick up the pitcher's larger remnants.

After a moment, her disappointment turned to anger and, without considering their jagged edges, she kicked at the fragments. One of them spun lazily away and Sarah, a tiny drop of blood on the tip of her left toe, crossed the wet floor with its crumbs of shattered china and, grabbing her wrapper from its chair and her slippers from underneath the bed, went to the parlor to wait for Florence. "I dropped the pitcher when I tried to fill the wash bowl," she would say to her daughter when she returned, alone, from church, "You should have done that before you left."

Reverend Mellish had asked that the cart and driver meet them at the town green instead of the Advent Chapel and, with more than half an hour until it was due, father and daughter walked the short distance down Main Street towards Davis Park. They both felt constrained and did not talk; Bertha was unsure if she should apologize and her father did not want to ask a question or make a comment that might suggest disapproval of her behavior in the chapel. When they arrived at the park's triangular wedge of grass, Bertha followed her father along one of its well-packed dirt paths towards a bench whose back touched the trunk of a tall oak tree.

The old man sat down with a sigh and rested his hand on the handle of his upright walking stick. Bertha settled next to him, smoothing and compressing the fabric of her skirt. Reverend Mellish turned towards his daughter and in a silent gesture of conciliation patted the gathered folds of black sateen that fell over her knee.

"What a lovely place to rest," she offered in return.

They sat together in the shade, surveying the pleasant scene around them. They admired the steep six-sided roof and carved railings of the town's bandstand visible straight ahead and they studied the Soldier's Monument to their left, with its pensive bronze youth raised high on a granite pedestal, one fist forever clutching the barrel of his upturned rifle.

Bertha now felt comfortable with her father, no longer humiliated in his eyes, and she was encouraged to ask a question that might seem rude. "Papa," she began, "Papa, why do you mix with such people? They don't seem. . ." she hesitated, remembering her father's frequent warnings against the sin of pride, "they don't seem quite our. . . quite your sort of people."

Reverend Mellish regarded his daughter indulgently. "No, they're not well-educated. They're not refined in their dress or their habits. But they are more sincere and more direct in their faith than many polite ladies and gentlemen in prettier churches."

"But the woman who preached. She was so. . . loud. And she made such gestures and such faces. She even. . . .," Bertha broke off, embarrassed for a moment but determined to continue, "she even spit!"

Reverend Mellish chuckled. "Yes, she did," he agreed with a nod. "But her odd faces and her. . .her indelicacies are of no importance. That she truly believes, that she feels her faith, that she sees it and hears it with every atom of her soul—*that* is important."

Bertha stared into the hazy blue of the summer sky and tried to imagine how she herself might experience such faith. As a tiny ember glowing in her heart, perhaps, shooting its heat towards the tips of her fingers and her toes, finally engulfing her body in invisible flames. But she found herself wondering if this spiritual heat would travel through her veins or her arteries—she could not remember which moved outward from the heart–and all she could feel was the warmth of the air against her face, the hard slats of the bench against her back, and a rumble of hunger in her stomach. She turned again to her father.

"Do you believe with that kind of faith?'

John Mellish hesitated. "I try," he said.

"But do you believe that the world will come to an end soon, as that woman warns?"

Again, the minister considered. "Well," he said and absently twirled the metal point of his walking stick in the grass between his feet, "well, I'm not sure. There are many things happening in the world today that do look terribly, terribly bad."

He shook his head and thought of the greed and the hatred, the poverty and despair, the violence and the prurient horrors that he knew blighted every hour of every day in the dark places of the world and in the big cities and even the tiny hamlets of his own nation. He stopped and looked up at the bronze soldier silhouetted against the sky. The soldier's gaze, implacable and serene, met his.

Reverend Mellish blinked firmly and continued. "But then things have been very bad in the world for many centuries and yet God allows it to continue. Are we worse today than ever before? I cannot say."

Now he looked directly into Bertha's face and his voice had a strange urgency that made her draw back. "But the Lord *will* come. Whether sooner or later doesn't matter."

He released his walking stick and let it fall to the ground. One of Bertha's hands rested on the bench between them and now he grasped it in both of his. Startled, Bertha thought his hands with their mottled, parchment skin looked too fragile to grip with such strength.

"Bertha, look at me." His command was gentle but absolute and she obeyed. "We must always prepare for the day of judgment that will come when He returns. You do understand that, Bertha, don't you? That we must live our lives and prepare for death knowing that we will all be judged?"

Bertha nodded. Her father seemed suddenly conscious of his zeal and, smiling apologetically, released her hand. He looked around as if searching and then leaned over to retrieve his stick.

She'd never planned to mention it. It belonged to another world, another life. "I knew someone at college who died," Bertha whispered.

"What was that, my dear?" Her father was upright again, his stick held vertically between his knees.

"I knew someone at college who died," she repeated, fixing her eyes on a neat pyramid of cannon balls resting at the foot of the soldier's tall pedestal.

"How sad," her father said. "Was she a friend of yours?"

Bertha counted the cannon balls before answering. There were twelve, as far as she could tell, maybe thirteen. "I suppose she was a friend." She hesitated, considering how much to reveal. "But I didn't know her very well. We weren't close."

Bertha turned to her father and for a moment was afraid that his sympathetic look would make her cry. She pressed her lips together and swallowed.

"I don't think she thought much about these sorts of things. About her future, I mean. I don't think she prepared herself before she. . . before she died."

Bertha remembered Phebe's judgment of Eva, but was not sure she should repeat it to her father. She decided to take the chance and spoke quickly but firmly. "I don't think she truly was a Christian," she said and saw her father's forehead contract and the lines between his eyebrows deepen. "But she wasn't a bad girl," Bertha reassured him, "she did some good things, too. She was generous and. . . and she could be kind."

Reverend Mellish shook his head, his face still drawn in a troubled frown. "That will do the poor girl no good at the judgment seat."

Bertha thought again of Phebe and her prophecy. "Will she go to hell, then?," she asked lightly, as it didn't matter. But she held her breath while she waited for an answer and was surprised to see her father's expression soften.

"Bertha, you ask a more interesting question than you know. You wonder why I come here to this place and worship with these people." He stopped and his next words shook with anger.

"I have never accepted the hell of my fathers," he said, "I have never accepted the hell that you fear awaits your friend. I have never believed that a loving God would be so cruel as to torment his children throughout eternity. I have never preached such a God or such a hell, not at least for a very long time."

Reverend Mellish felt for his handkerchief and wiped his face from his forehead to the irregular edges of his beard. He blew his nose into the cloth and returned it to his pocket. It seemed to Bertha that her father had forgotten not only her question but her presence and she sat quietly waiting for him to continue.

His composure restored, he turned again to Bertha. "You see, my dear, in the Adventist faith there is no hell."

"And no heaven?" she asked without thinking.

"Oh, no. There is a heaven. God is just and he rewards. And he punishes, but he punishes justly." Reverend Mellish had resumed his usual patient, pastoral tone.

"In the old Puritan faith of our fathers, Bertha, the soul lives eternally and, if it is not saved, it will suffer eternally. But in the Adventist faith, if the soul is not saved, it will cease to exist." He paused and looked to see if Bertha understood.

"Cease to exist?" she repeated. The idea was chilling and seemed too enormous to comprehend.

"It dies." Reverend Mellish pressed the fingertips of one hand together and then quickly opened them, a magician's gesture. "It's gone. Our Father will draw the darkness of oblivion over those poor souls. It is a terrible fate, certainly, but far better than suffering the heat of eternal fire. Or suffering an eternity banished from the divine presence."

"Is Eva, then . . . is her soul gone? Has everything about her"–Bertha had to steady herself to repeat the phrase–"ceased to exist?"

He shook his head gravely. "Not yet. The poor girl's soul will sleep the sleep of the dead until Judgment Day. And then, if she is found to be beyond salvation, well, only then will her soul. . ." he, too, found himself faltering and he cleared his throat, "only then will she cease to exist."

They sat without speaking until Reverend Mellish noticed the delivery cart roll down Main Street and stop at the edge of the park. He stood up briskly and held out a hand to his daughter. She seemed distracted and did not respond. "Come along, my dear." He tried to be sprightly; no need for Bertha to dwell on such gloomy thoughts this beautiful day. "Let's not keep Florence and her dinner waiting."

Chapter 22
Mr. Spaulding

Roy Spaulding, charged by his boss to recalculate the day's tally of finished cloth, left the mill nearly half an hour after the six o'clock closing whistle. By the time he turned left from the mill-yard onto Main Street and headed up its gradual incline towards the village, only a few stragglers were still trudging their way home to supper. One of them was a solitary woman, and Roy found himself walking directly behind her, although at a good distance back.

He was struck by the woman's measured, deliberate gait. Her skirt stopped just above the ankles, and he saw her lift first one foot and then the other clear of the dirt path, extending it slowly forward and setting it firmly down. Her head tilted sharply on her upright neck. From shoulder to elbow, the woman's arms pressed against her sides and did not swing. Her forearms and her hands were not visible. She moved so soberly and seemed so transfixed that he wondered if she might be praying.

Roy was over six feet tall, with long legs and an easy stride. He realized that he would soon overtake the woman and, not wanting to disturb her, shifted to the right in order to widen the distance between them. She had just crossed the iron-railed bridge that spanned the mill-race when he found himself about to pass her, and he glanced to his left to confirm what he had suspected.

But he had been wrong, and he chuckled when he saw that the woman—a girl, really–was holding an open book in both hands and attempting to read as she walked, navigating as cautiously as a blind person through the soft light of the summer evening. The girl raised the book closer to her face and dipped her head, but did not acknowledge Roy's presence. The effect was comical, and Roy slowed his pace to hers.

"Excuse me, Miss," he said, smiling as he moved to her side, "excuse me, but aren't you afraid you'll trip? That's a dangerous thing you're doing."

She stopped, lowered the book and turned her head. She looked directly at Roy's face, with no girlish modesty in the fierce composure of her gaze. "I don't know you," she replied, "and I don't think I should be spoken to or laughed at by a stranger." There was a childlike indignation in her reprimand that Roy found appealing.

She opened her mouth again, inhaling sharply as if she had more to say. But she broke off and dropped her eyes, and a flush rose from the band of skin visible above her high white collar and spread quickly into her cheeks.

Roy, distracted by a sudden feeling that he'd forgotten something important, barely noticed her confusion. Then he had it: the girl he'd seen a week or so earlier, sitting by herself in the dusty heat of the finishing room with a book in her hand. "Wait a minute!" he exclaimed. "I know you! You work at the mill. I've seen you there."

The girl looked up, gave a short nod and smiled, a self-conscious flexing of her lips that quickly faded. She seemed tentative and shy, a surprising change from her initial self-possession. Roy liked her the better for this vulnerability. He held out his hand.

"I'm Roy Spaulding," he said and when she offered her hand in return, he shook it once and then released it to tip his hat, a brand-new derby.

"I come from Ashland—Ashland, New Hampshire, near Squam Lake. I'm down here to work for a while," he explained. "I'm assistant to Mr. Bennett. He's superintendent at the mill." He paused. "But then I guess you know that . . . that Mr. Bennett is superintendent."

"Yes," she said, looking down. "Yes, I know." Her voice was prim and a little loud. She raised her head, bolder now. "I've been at the mill since June," she said, "My name is Bertha Mellish. I work as a burler in the finishing room."

She smiled again and Roy thought she was nicer looking than he had first judged, although he wouldn't call her pretty. Soft cheeks and lips, but a strange severity around the eyes. And no real grace in the way she stood, with her feet close together and her hips locked.

"Of course, Miss Mellish, that's where I saw you!" Roy gestured towards the book that she now held against her chest, one thumb tucked inside to mark her place. "You had a book then, too." He leaned slightly forward, as if to read the title on its spine. "Is it the same one or have you gone on to another?"

When Bertha realized that the rude young man who'd interrupted her walk was the same young man who had caught her staring at him from her seat by the finishing room window, she was dumbstruck. It had been just over two weeks since that encounter and, although she kept a secret vigil, she had not hoped for more than another glimpse and never expected—never really wanted– an actual meeting. Once, she had tried to plan what she might say to him if their paths happened to cross at the mill, if he were to come in and stand near her table, or if they passed in the yard or brushed by one another on the stairs. But Bertha could not bring him to life in her mind's eye—her image of him was too vague, a tall man with dark hair and a broad smile—and, even in her imagination, she could not script a conversation.

Now she knew his name, and he knew hers. And, although she'd humiliated herself by blushing, by standing mute, by speaking loudly, by answering his questions stupidly, he seemed content to stay. He hadn't seemed to notice her confusion and he seemed genuinely excited when he recognized her from the mill. He asked questions as if he really cared about her answers. There was a puppyish quality to him, but without awkwardness, a buoyancy of spirits that lifted him beyond guile and above suspicion. To Bertha's fascination, he moved, and spoke, and laughed like a man who saw no danger in moving, or speaking, or laughing.

She glanced down at the volume in her hands, as if a little startled by its presence. "Oh," she said, "I guess it is the same one." She knew that she should tell him its title, but a German grammar was an odd book for a young woman to be reading while walking on a summer evening and, Bertha realized, she did not want Mr. Spaulding to think of her as odd.

"And what is it, Miss Mellish?

Bertha smiled ruefully and handed him the small, brown book. "You can see for yourself," she said as he read the title page. "It's a little dull."

"Not at all!" He leafed through its pages, finally stopping at one in the middle. He tried to read a few words, but the Gothic type and foreign words flummoxed him and he let out an appreciative whistle. "Too much for me, Miss Mellish," he said as he returned the book with a quizzical tilt of his head.

"I'm only working in the mill for the summer. When I go back to college in the fall, I plan to take a course in German." Bertha stopped, sure that she sounded like a boastful child.

"College!" Mr. Spaulding stood with his feet apart and his hands tucked into the pockets of his trousers. He rocked on his heels and shook his head with a few broad, emphatic sweeps. "I envy you, Miss Mellish. I graduated from high school, but I never did make it to college." He paused, and looked at her with exaggerated but good-humored suspicion. "But where are your spectacles? My mother told me that all college girls wear spectacles."

Bertha hesitated, but only for a moment. "Oh, I've left them at home," she said," I only wear them when I'm studying by candlelight." The easy wit of her reply, so perfectly in keeping with the spirit of his question, astonished Bertha. She was nervous but excited, anticipating the challenge of a game whose rules she did not fully understand. She waited anxiously for Mr. Spaulding's next remark.

Miss Mellish now had color in her cheeks and Roy took some pride in the thought that he had put it there. He considered paying her a compliment—what a shame it would be to hide her eyes behind glass--but, clearly, she wasn't a girl experienced with compliments, and he was afraid she might take it too much to heart.

"Tell me more about your college work," he said. "I'd study science, if I were in college. Do you?"

Before she could answer, a noise, a cacophonous mixture of trills and cackles like a flock of mismatched birds, distracted them. They turned to see a rag-tag parade of children approaching, clearly from the tenements that clustered in rows beyond the mill. The children followed in the wake of a boy, perhaps ten, who struggled to propel the rusting carcass of a bicycle.

The apparatus had no pedals, no chain, and no seat. The rear wheel was a bare wooden rim. The front tire was flat. The rider, shoeless, scrambled forward on the tips of his toes with the main bar of the frame pressed against his crotch. He wore a pained but determined expression and would not be distracted by the boy who repeatedly poked a stick into the spokes of the rear wheel, or the girl who sauntered behind, grabbing at the metal stump where the saddle should have been. Other children, some barely old enough to toddle on their own, skipped and squealed, laughed and pointed, clapping their hands in joy at the ridiculous tenacity of their pied piper.

Roy shared an amused look with Miss Mellish, then chuckled and shook his head. The boy's hard work for so little reward struck him as both admirable and sad. "Excuse me for a minute, will you, Miss Mellish?" he asked and, after receiving a nodded assurance that she would stay, walked briskly towards the spectacle. A few of the children ran away, but most watched in silence as he approached. The boy on the bicycle seemed oblivious to anything outside his own efforts at locomotion.

"That's a hard way to ride a wheel!" Roy called as he neared the struggling rider. "Let's see if we can make it easier." He grabbed the bicycle by a handlebar, forcing it to a stop. The startled boy flinched and, in a frantic, high-pitched voice, blurted something in French, a language Roy did not understand.

"Easy, there, kid." Roy spoke soothingly, as he would to a skittish colt. "Easy there. I'm going to make things a whole lot more fun, if you'll let me. Lift your feet up off the ground." Roy, grinning, held on to the bicycle with one hand and, with the other, pointed at the boy's dirty feet and motioned upward.

The boy, no longer frightened, looked puzzled. Then, in a flash of understanding, he lifted both feet and tucked them against the sloping bar at the front of the bicycle's frame. Roy swung his right leg over the bare rear wheel and straddled the bicycle behind the boy. With his boots planted easily on the ground, he reached forward around the child and grabbed both handlebars.

"We're off," he shouted and ran the boy and the bicycle up Main Street, with the jubilant crowd of children scrambling to keep pace. Bertha watched for a minute before hurrying to join the motley procession, her book clutched in one hand and the other pressed against her hat. She forgave Mr. Spaulding the question he had asked and then forgotten. She laughed at his long legs, furiously pumping, and at his grunts as he manhandled the boy and the bicycle over the unpaved road, its surface crisscrossed by wagon and carriage tracks and pocked with innumerable hoof-prints.

Bertha reached the railroad tracks, hot, exhilarated and out of breath, just as Mr. Spaulding dismounted and returned the bicycle to the beaming, speechless boy. "You take it from here," he panted, leaning forward with his hands on his thighs, "It's a heck of a lot easier going down!"

He exhaled noisily and took off his jacket and his hat, exposing his flattened hair and damp shirtsleeves, one of which he used to wipe his forehead. With his jacket hooked on a finger and draped over his shoulder, he loped to Bertha's side to fan the air near her face with the brim of his hat.

"Thank you," she said, flustered by his attention and the intimacy of the gesture. "But please don't trouble yourself. I'm quite fine." She was sorry, though, when he stopped. She moved a hairsbreadth closer, leaning towards him without shifting her feet.

"No trouble," he said as he dropped his arm, "I was cooling myself, too." He turned and pointed to the boy on the bicycle, now halfway down the hill. "Take a look at that kid. He's a persistent little Frenchie. Make a good hand some day."

Together, they watched the boy skitter and wobble, his bare feet scuffling to keep the wheel in check, with his winded but still enthusiastic entourage close behind.

"I've got a pair of brothers at home," Mr. Spaulding said, a little sheepishly, "Sometimes I forget and act like a kid myself."

Bertha had never stood this close to any man younger than Dr. Hammond. She had never stood this close to any man so much taller than herself and, as she raised her face to Mr. Spaulding's, she felt delicate and doll-like and a little giddy. She had never stood this close to any man who had worked so hard in the warmth of a summer evening and who, at rest and in his shirt-sleeves, radiated heat and a strong, unfamiliar smell. All Bertha could manage was a silent, understanding nod. "That was a very kind thing for you to do," she finally said, "you made that poor child happy."

He shrugged–out of modesty, Bertha hoped, and not indifference-
-and put on his hat. Under the dome of his black derby, his face became serious and he glanced up at the darkening sky. Bertha followed his gaze. Sunset was not far off. "I'm afraid I've kept you, Miss Mellish," he said, and his voice sounded stiff. The air around her went hollow.

"May I see you safely home?" he asked, and the evening was again thick with moisture and with the invisible presence of crickets and frogs, chirping and croaking in the nearby woods and millstream. She smiled, wanly though, and shook her head.

"Thank you, Mr. Spaulding, that won't be necessary. I live just a little way down the Attawaugan road. I don't want to inconvenience you." Bertha could not have reasonably explained the presence of a strange young man to her parents who, by this time, would certainly be waiting by a window or to Florence, who might at this moment be coming out to find her, an unlit lantern in one hand and a match safe in the other, while supper grew cold on the kitchen table.

"Well, then, good evening, Miss Mellish. It's been a pleasure." He gave a small bow and a smile as warm and enveloping as the one she still remembered from the finishing room, and resumed his journey up Main Street.

Bertha turned onto the Attawaugan road. After a few steps, she could not resist one farewell glance in Mr. Spaulding's direction. She was disappointed, even a little surprised, that she did not catch him doing the same. Still, it did not occur to her until later that night, as she lay awake in bed, to wonder why he had not pointed out the certainty, or even expressed the hope, of another meeting.

Chapter 23

A Picnic

After one quickly eaten sandwich, Bertha left Dr. and Mrs. Hammond and Florence sitting in their portable chairs under the canopy of a wide-branched oak. With no particular destination in mind, she moved slowly, her head down, considering which of the young women scattered here and there over the picnic grounds might greet her intrusion with a measure of grace.

The August air was moist, with a gusting breeze that stirred the trees and jumbled together all the smells around her, the pine sap and trampled grass, the inescapable odor of horses, the hint of something edible, chowder, perhaps, or fried donuts, the mingled scents of perfumes and toilet waters, soaps and hair oils.

By the time Bertha thought of her old schoolmates Charlotte Cogswell and Hattie Darling, kind-hearted girls that she saw most Sundays at church, she found herself under a large tree near the lake. She sat down, planning to search for Charlotte and Hattie from that vantage point, secluded but with a broad view of the area.

And there they were, directly in front of her but many yards away, two in a cluster of spectators following the progress of a baseball game. Even from behind and at this distance, tall, solid Charlotte was impossible to mistake and the slight girl standing next to her had to be Hattie.

Bertha scrambled to her feet and took a step forward, relieved and unexpectedly happy to have found them. But her excitement faded as quickly as it flared and she caught herself in mid-stride. The two were so easy in each other's company. The last time she spoke with them, the previous Sunday, a week ago that day, Charlotte and Hattie described a trip to Providence and she had nothing to offer in return.

Truly, what did she have to talk about? Her happy adventures at college? Her fascinating work at the mill? Her chance encounter with Roy Spaulding? Bertha retreated to her place under the tree.

At first, she wished she'd brought a book, then considered escaping into the wooded area at the edge of the picnic grounds. But the day was warm and Bertha lay on her side, growing comfortable and lazy, certain she was the object of no one's attention. Occasionally, someone wandered by the grassy area to her left, engrossed in a dish of ice cream or a sandwich, unconscious of her scrutiny, quiet as she was and camouflaged by dappled light.

For a time, she turned to watch the fat-bellied rowboats bobbing on the lake to her right, the young men in them resting on their oars, the young ladies skimming the surface of the water with their fingertips.

What if she were one of those girls? What if Roy Spaulding sat across from her in a gently rocking boat?

Bertha sat upright, ducking her head as if the image in her mind could be seen on her face. Agitated, she picked up a twig and in a patch of exposed earth scratched all the inflectional forms of an irregular German verb, embellishing the ends of each letter with so many loops and flourishes that the individual words grew illegible in a network of arabesques.

A sudden cheer from the ball game distracted her. She looked up from her calligraphy in time to see a tall man lope across what she could only guess was home plate. When he raised both arms in the air, Bertha dropped her stick. She could not distinguish the details of his clothing or make out his features, but she recognized the outline of his form and the buoyant elasticity of his movements.

It had never occurred to her that Roy Spaulding might be there. She had seen him in the mill several times since their meeting on the road, always in passing but always with a smile and a shared greeting. Yet she had no idea what he did outside the mill, knew nothing of his daily habits, his social activities, or his friends. She did not know which village families welcomed him as an intimate. She believed he boarded in a house on High Street but, the few times she had found a reason to pass its door, had never seen him enter or leave. He did not attend her church. She had not encountered him at the dry goods store, the livery stable, or the depot. He existed in her mind without history or context and, until this moment, she had shared him with no one. Now she sat, unable to move but desperate to push her way through the crowd and claim a place by his side.

Emma Hammond beat an irritated tattoo on the wooden arm of her hammock chair, its striped canvas unsuitably bright against the mourning dress she wore in honor of her father, barely a month gone. She was hot despite the shade of the oak tree and annoyed with her husband, too engrossed in the action of a nearby baseball game to help entertain Florence Mellish who sat to Emma's left, stiffly upright on a straight-backed wooden camp chair.

Emma did not know the woman well; the Mellishes were her husband's protégés and it was his invitation that now burdened her with Miss Mellish on this oppressive August day. Still, she knew her duty and with as polite a frozen smile as she could muster, considered what topic of conversation they might have in common. Emma was a married woman, widely traveled and, in her own way, a patroness of arts and letters. Henry had once mentioned that Miss Mellish wrote poetry but Emma discounted such a story. She was, as far as Emma could discern, a middle-aged schoolteacher, a spinster keeping house for her parents, a woman rendered by temperament and circumstance deficient in imagination and incapable of romance.

Although Miss Mellish had a pleasant face, it was marked by a permanently anxious air. Miss Mellish, Emma thought with amusement, always looked as if she had a pie in the oven she was afraid might burn. Emma sighed—inaudibly, she hoped—and cleared her throat.

"Miss Mellish," she asked, "Do you think rain will come this afternoon to spoil our picnic?"

Florence, balancing a plate on her knees, had just taken a forkful of angel food cake. She chewed rapidly and in the moment before she was able to speak, brushed the corner of her mouth where she felt a nestling crumb.

"Oh, I don't know if I can make such a prediction, Mrs. Hammond." Florence's voice caught on the hastily swallowed cake. With a muffled cough, she looked up at the clouds that had gradually accumulated since mid-morning.

"Those puffy white clouds—cumulus I believe—might very well be harbingers of rain. They could grow into cumulonimbus—thunderheads—but then they could also stay as they are now." Florence taught the classification of clouds to her older students and was pleased that she could offer Mrs. Hammond a seriously considered answer to her question. "But it is quite humid," she added, "And there is a rising breeze. It might rain, Mrs. Hammond, although I hope it does not."

Emma stifled a yawn. Leave it to a schoolmarm to make even simple conversation tiresome. "Hmm," she murmured, and turned towards her husband. "Henry, I think Miss Mellish would like a glass of lemonade. Could you fetch one, please?"

With no sign of impatience, Dr. Hammond looked away from the game. "Of course," he said, adjusting the tie he had loosened in the heat of the day.

Florence held up both hands, palms outward. The plate on her knees shifted. "No, please. I don't . . . I really don't . . . ."

Dr. Hammond smiled at Miss Mellish and wagged his finger. "No protests, please. I'm happy to do this small service." He turned to his wife. "And a glass for you my dear?"

Emma considered. "No," she said, "I'll have an ice. You know how much I like ices."

When Henry was gone, Emma glanced at Miss Mellish, who sat silently studying her half-eaten cake. Poor woman, she thought, no husband of her own.

Satisfied, Emma relaxed into the curve of her canvas chair and lazily scanned the picnic grounds. Something caught her eye, a figure siting under a large tree near the edge of Alexander Lake, and she roused herself to lean forward.

"But isn't that your sister?" she said, pointing. "I can barely make out the features, but I do believe it's Bertha."

Florence followed the line of Mrs. Hammond's arm, hoping she was wrong.

"Hmm," she said, although she knew at once it was Bertha. "It might be, although it's very hard to tell."

"Of course it's she," Emma sniffed, "Surely you can see that."

Florence squinted and craned her neck, pretending to reconsider. "Yes," she reluctantly admitted, "it does look like Bertha."

Mrs. Hammond made three sharp clicks with her tongue. "But I thought Bertha was with her friends all this time. That's where she said she was going when she left us hours ago." She shook her head, as if such behavior was beyond comprehension. "How strange, to sit alone like that."

She turned to Florence with a look of patronizing sympathy; Florence, humiliated, answered with a pinched half-smile.

When my husband returns," Mrs. Hammond said, "I'll have him find a party of young people for Bertha to join."

"That won't be necessary." Florence spoke sharply; she'd had enough of Mrs. Hammond's honeyed condescension. Let the woman think her rude. "I'll talk to my sister myself."

She stood up and the plate on her knees slipped to the ground. It broke neatly into three pieces. For a moment, the two women stared at the wreckage.

"I'm sorry," Florence whispered, and knelt on the ground by Mrs. Hammond's feet.

"It's nothing, Miss Mellish," Mrs. Hammond said, her voice cool and steady. "Think nothing of it. It's just old crockery, of no value."

Mrs. Hammond pulled a handkerchief, hemmed in black, from her sleeve. As Florence handed her the shards, she meticulously wiped off every crumb of white angel cake and every dark speckle of dirt. And then, one by one, she laid each piece in a basket by the side of her chair while Florence watched the painstaking process.

"Bertha!"

She looked up, startled. Florence stood over her with her arms crossed and clamped against her chest. Her face was flushed.

"You are making yourself conspicuous." Florence's voice was low, her words clenched as if she struggled to contain them. "People notice such things, you sitting off by yourself like this."

Bertha resented her sister's tone. Florence had no right to attack her. Florence cared too much what other people thought. Florence should go away and leave her alone.

"It's my business where I sit," Bertha said.

Florence's eyes narrowed. "Look over there," she said, jerking her head towards the ball-field. "I can see Charlotte and Hattie from here. How would they feel, if they saw you sitting alone like this? They'd think you didn't like them."

Bertha couldn't remember the last time she'd seen her sister so angry. She stood up to face the onslaught, folding her arms in deliberate mimicry. Best to look unfazed, she decided, even a little amused.

"I cannot understand your willful disregard for simple good manners."

Without lowering her chin, Bertha averted her eyes. She refused to respond. Florence had not spoken to her like this since she was a child, and she would not submit now to such treatment. Bertha steeled herself for the next accusation, but all she heard was Florence's ragged breathing. She glanced back.

Florence was looking past her, towards the lake. She was pale now, tired and sad, her mouth and shoulders slack.

"Never mind," she said.

Instantly, Bertha was sorry. She'd never meant to upset Florence, make her kind and patient sister angry, cause her worry. And after all those letters she'd sent from college, every one of them designed to keep Florence happy.

Bertha uncrossed her arms and dropped her head. "I didn't mean to be rude." She couldn't keep a beseeching tremor from her voice. "I didn't mean to embarrass you."

Florence smiled in gentle absolution. "I know," she said and brushed some tiny remnants of bark from Bertha's shoulder. "You never do. I understand. Now go and find your friends."

Hattie noticed her first.

"There you are!" she called, as if Bertha were expected. "Where have you been all this time?" She reached for Bertha's hand, drawing her in.

Charlotte looked over, grinning. Loose coils of hair sprouted from beneath the brim of her straw hat and were jostled by a stiffening breeze. "Hello, Bertha," she said, "how wonderful to see you!"

Bertha tried to think of something interesting to say. But Roy Spaulding was in a field just a few yards away and she could concentrate on nothing else. Desperate, she looked up. "I hope it doesn't rain," she said.

Charlotte and Hattie followed her gaze. For a few moments, the three young women studied the gathering clouds, irregular billows in shades of yellowish gray. Like old bruises, Bertha thought.

Charlotte shook her head. "No," she said, "We just won't let it rain."

"That's right," Hattie agreed brightly. "It just can't rain, not if we don't want it to."

Bertha bit her lip, trying to let Hattie's simple-minded faith go unchallenged. "I *hope* it doesn't rain," she finally had to say, "but if it's going to rain, there's nothing we can do to stop it."

Charlotte laughed, a forced chuckle. "I like Hattie's way of thinking better."

"No," Hattie murmured, "Bertha's right."

The three girls stood in awkward silence until Charlotte's brother Will, fourteen years old and big-boned like his sister, hurried towards them, shouting and waving his cap.

"We won! We won!"

Roy Spaulding followed close behind.

Bertha's first impulse was to run. She wasn't prepared to confront him in person, not now and not in front of all these people. But she stood, unable to move, during Will's enthusiastic account of the baseball game.

"Will, enough!" Charlotte laughed and pulled on the bill of his cap. "Let someone else get a word in!"

Mr. Spaulding turned to Charlotte. "I am sorry, Miss Cogswell," he said with a smile, "I've been as rude as Will here." He bowed slightly, with deliberate and humorous formality. "A pleasure to see you this afternoon, Miss Cogswell."

He looked at Hattie. "And I apologize to you, too, Miss Darling," he said, with the same flourish.

Before he could turn to Bertha, Charlotte interrupted. "Miss Mellish, I don't believe you know Mr. Spaulding."

"Thank you, Miss Cogswell," Roy said, giving Bertha her salute, "but I have had the pleasure of Miss Mellish's acquaintance. When I first met Miss Mellish, she was deep in the pages of a book."

Bertha hesitated, not sure if he was making fun of her. "I do like to read," she said.

"Bertha was the very best student in high school, boy or girl," Hattie announced and hooked her arm through Bertha's. "We've always been so proud of her."

Charlotte nodded vigorously. "Bertha is Dayville's prize scholar!"

Bertha, embarrassed but pleased, shook her head.

Will came to his sister's defense. "But, Charlotte, all three of you girls went to college."

"Yes, but Bertha is the only one to stay." Charlotte turned to Mr. Spaulding. "I've done with Wellesley, you see. I learned what I wanted there and now I've come home to my music."

"Charlotte has a lovely voice." Hattie too, addressed Mr. Spaulding. "She'd never tell you this herself, but the church choir missed her so much, they just begged her to come back and lead them."

Hattie released Bertha's arm and clasped her hands behind her back. "I never really went to college," she said softly, looking down at her feet. "I was at Lassell Seminary until this summer, but now I prefer to be at home. I studied a great deal while I was there, and I don't want to study any more." She raised her eyes to Mr. Spaulding, prettily flustered. "I'm not as clever as Miss Mellish and I don't sing anywhere near as well as Miss Cogswell."

Bertha did not like the way Roy Spaulding leaned towards Hattie, a tiny, almost imperceptible advance, and she did not like the way he tilted his head and looked at her as if she were a precious little thing.

"Yes, well, there's so much more that I want to learn." Bertha was desperate to turn Mr. Spaulding's attention from Hattie Darling. "I'll stay the four years at Mount Holyoke and then, maybe, go for a higher degree."

Bertha was not sure how to continue, now that everyone in the group except Will, who had wandered off in search of food and younger friends, was looking at her in polite expectation.

What was the question he'd asked her that evening on the road, before they were distracted by the boy and his bicycle? Science. He'd wanted to know about science. "I'm particularly interested in the physical sciences." Bertha glanced in his direction. "I had a course in chemistry last semester and I especially liked the laboratory work."

Mr. Spaulding seemed attentive, with his eyebrows raised and his lips slightly parted, but Bertha knew that a word from Hattie would distract him. She pushed on, barely considering what she said.

"I found it so, so interesting, so exciting, measuring chemicals and mixing them, seeing how they reacted, how they changed in color, how they smoked or bubbled, the smells they made. I . . ." She broke off, self-conscious.

"The way you describe it, it does sound amusing," Charlotte said.

"I never did care for science." Hattie wrinkled her nose. "Last semester, they wanted me to cut up a little frog, but I just couldn't harm the pitiful creature, even if it was already dead."

Charlotte and Mr. Spaulding laughed at Hattie's tender-hearted logic, and she looked at them in delighted confusion. Like a puppy that has pleased its master, Bertha thought, disgusted. Time to escape, she realized, to make some excuse and go back to her place by the lake. But then Roy Spaulding turned away from Hattie and Charlotte, leaving them to discuss the horrors of dissection.

"I bet I'd like chemistry too if I had a taste of it," he said, "but what I really want to do is study geology. There's so much to learn from rocks." He paused, not sure how to explain himself. "They're so old." He shook his head in frustration and looked at Bertha, expecting to see a hint of boredom or, even worse, patient tolerance in her expression. But she was watching him closely, with a serious intensity he had never seen in a girl. She seemed to understand the awesome import of the word. "I mean so *old*," he repeated.

Bertha nodded. "I've seen fossils," she said. "There's a collection of them at my school." She thought of the dark blocks of basalt displayed in Williston Hall and the strange, three-lobed footprints impressed in their rough surfaces. "I think it's very. . . it's extraordinary to see the marks of creatures who died thousands, I mean hundreds of thousands, of years ago." She worried that she might be talking too much, but Mr. Spaulding seemed interested in her words. "It's hard to believe that they ever walked the same earth as we do now. And we only know they existed because the rocks tell us so." She paused, feeling warm and a little reckless. "We only know them because of the marks they left behind."

Roy could not quite figure out how he felt, listening to this girl. Although there was a spark in her eyes that he had not noticed before, he felt no desire to flirt with her, flatter her, or continue the harmless game of pursuit that he had begun the first time they met. It wasn't that he considered her unappealing, it was just that she seemed so. . . so compact, like an egg, or a smooth-shelled nut. He saw no invitation in her movements. He could not imagine kissing her, although he noticed her lips, full with a little pout. He had no plans to kiss her, but when he talked to a nice-looking young woman, the possibility of a kiss usually played somewhere in the back of his mind. Still, he liked her and thought the two of them shared a certain view of things. Roy was sure that, if she were a man, they would end up friends. He admired her way of speaking and her bookishness and figured that he could learn from her. And, he suddenly realized, he wanted her to think the same of him.

"Miss Mellish," he said, so enthusiastically that Hattie and Charlotte stopped in mid-sentence and looked over, "I've got a book for you, something better than your German grammar! I've read it a few times and I could lend it to you. It isn't about science, but there's a natural philosophy of life in it that I think you'd like."

Bertha nodded, speechless at the offer, so personal yet so casually and publicly made. She was afraid that she would accept too eagerly and struggled to control her voice. But just as she opened her mouth to say yes, thank you, a loud clap of thunder startled her and a sudden gust of wind blew her skirt against her legs, snapping it out like a flag.

"Bertha!" Dr. Hammond, disheveled and out of breath, ran towards her carrying an open umbrella. "Bertha, I'm afraid we have to leave immediately." He reached Bertha's side and took her elbow, glancing apologetically at the others. "Of course, it's not just the rain. It's also the lightning that's sure to come," he explained as he hustled Bertha away.

Chapter 24

Mr. Spaulding's Book

More than a week passed; Bertha thought he had forgotten. But, late in the afternoon of the tenth day, Mr. Spaulding passed her table and, with a conspiratorial smile, pulled the book from his vest and dropped it in her lap. Taken by surprise, she had no time to thank him before he was gone.

She glanced to the left. If nobody was looking, she would pick it up, maybe even read a sentence or two; the temptation almost overwhelmed her. She glanced to the right. Yvette, her burling iron frozen in her hand, was openly staring with an unpleasant smirk on her rouged lips. Bertha set her jaw, pretending not to notice. She slipped the book under her apron and went back to work; it lay heavy as a brick in her lap.

When, at last, the closing whistle sounded, Bertha lingered at her table until the finishing room emptied. Hands shaking, she drew the book from its hiding place. The same size as her brown German grammar, its cover was bright blue stamped with a border of silver foliage. The title, also silver, was written in spiky, swelling letters: *Collected Essays of Colonel Robert Ingersoll.*

She opened it, hoping to find Roy Spaulding's name written inside the front cover, perhaps, or on the facing page. But the name wasn't there, or on the two blank sheets before the title page. Still, the book was his, and carried the invisible mark of his touch. She raised it, smelled the sharp scent of ink and new paper.

The table of contents was five pages long; so much to read. Did Mr. Spaulding. . . . did Roy expect her to start at the first page and go straight through to the last? Bertha closed the book and held it tightly in both hands.

Was there some particular passage, a sentence, even a word, a message he meant for her to find? What if she did not recognize this message? What if she misunderstood it?

And when it was time to return the book and give her opinion, what if she disappointed him? What if he realized that no true sympathy had ever, could ever exist between them?

Bertha wished he had never lent the book. Desperate, she fanned through its leaves until, as they sped by, she caught sight of one dog-eared corner. Here, then, was her sign.

"What Shall We Do to Be Saved?" read the title at the top of the marked page. She began to read, as apprehensive as she was excited.

By the time she reached the middle of the page, Bertha had to stop, amazed. Colonel Ingersoll did not believe in hell. He did not believe in a god that damned most of his creation to eternal fire in order to save them. Her father, she realized, had said almost the same thing just a few weeks before. Still, there was something exhilarating in this man's way of putting it, something fresh, as if the stifling air of the Advent chapel, of all the chapels and churches she had ever endured, was stirred by a cool, clear breeze.

Bertha turned to the next page and noticed a darkly penciled "x"" in its left-hand margin.

"I like a man who has got good feeling for everybody," she read.

At the bottom of the page, two x's and an exclamation point: "I believe in the gospel of cheerfulness, the gospel of good nature, the gospel of good health." She scanned the few remaining pages of the essay but found no other marks. Bertha shut the book, laid a hand on its cover.

Did the fate of every human being rest on things as simple as friendly conversations, hearty handshakes, well-regulated diets? The idea disturbed her more than any attack on orthodoxy. It had no grandeur and no mystery, this revolutionary creed, this blow struck against the power of an angry god and in defense of helpless humanity.

But then she imagined Roy, sitting with the book open before him, maybe at a desk with his long legs stretched out and the lamplight warming his face, maybe in the shade of a tree with his back against its trunk, the pencil in his hand, smiling and nodding in agreement as he read those simple truths, thinking perhaps of her as he marked them with his vigorous x.

He must be right. With the exception of her father, Roy Spaulding lived his personal creed, as uncomplicated and clear as water, more completely than anyone she knew, even Florence. Even Mabel, pious and perfect as she was. She thought of the poor boy with the bicycle, and how Charlotte and Hattie brightened in Roy's presence.

What else could matter, but the kindness of one person to another? What greater gift could there be than the generous opening of one heart to another? Wasn't such kindness, such generosity, mystery and grandeur enough?

Bertha was sorry for her skepticism and made a vow. Although it wouldn't come as naturally to her as it did to Roy, she would take his gospel to heart. She would live her life as he did, in the few weeks remaining to her at home and, more importantly, in the months ahead of her at school. Alone in Athens. She would banish that selfish phrase forever.

Good nature, good humor, good health, good feelings for everyone. Mercy and forgiveness. Kindness and generosity of spirit. How much happier she would have been these last two years, if these had been her watchwords. Bertha put the book in her paper bag, where it rested against the German grammar, and she left the finishing room filled with the resolve of a new convert.

Bertha turned the iron knob and pushed on the heavy door that led out of the building, thinking ahead to the cheerful greeting she'd give her mother. The door didn't move. She tried again, then a third and fourth time, twisting the knob and rattling the door as if sheer determination could unlock its bolt.

A scuttling of rats in the empty space behind her.

Fighting panic, Bertha spun around, searching for an open window.

The sound, she discovered, came not from rats, but from two people pressed together in a corner of the stair tower, lit by a shaft of late summer sun. Bertha recognized the figures, although she could not tell what it was they did. They faced each other, the thick-set Frenchman in front of Yvette, Yvette pushed into the corner, so close that his body could not be distinguished from hers. They did not seem aware of Bertha's presence.

The man held Yvette by her waist. Her skirts were raised and Bertha could see her leg, covered in a black stocking halfway up the thigh and then left naked, a band of pale flesh bisected by the strap of a garter. Her leg hooked behind the man's knee and her arm gripped his head, forcing his mouth against hers. The man rocked his hips back and forth in short, hard thrusts and with each one, the couple grunted, his a deep groan of animal exertion, hers soft and impatient. Bertha did not realize that she, too, moved, however slightly, to their rhythm. Her breath grew rapid and shallow and she felt a strange restlessness, mental as well as physical, an almost desperate urgency for the thing to end.

Suddenly, they stopped. The man slumped forward, resting his weight on Yvette, whose head tilted back against the wall behind her. His arm dangled by his side and Yvette's leg was limp, her foot barely touching the floor. She did not push him away or lower her skirt. The man breathed heavily through his open mouth.

Bertha had never seen two people do the thing that she watched in silent fascination, had never heard it spoken of, had never read about it. But she had a vague notion of what it was that they did and she sensed that it was wrong. She knew that she should cover her eyes, stop her ears, flee. But she could not will herself to move, to run back into the finishing room, to hide until they were gone, to wipe her memory clean of the image.

Bertha stood, flushed and guilty as the girl half-naked before her. Guiltier, because she, unlike that ignorant girl, had been armed since childhood with the sword of decency and the shield of self-control.

She had been taught, at home and at church and at school, how to keep those weapons sharp and polished, always at the ready. Yet, presented with a clear and unequivocal test, she had failed, disgracefully, utterly, absolutely.

Still, no one knew of her failure or had witnessed her disgrace. If she could steal away undetected, sneak into the finishing room and climb out a window, the secret would remain hers. She looked towards her refuge and calculated how long it would take to tiptoe across the unprotected space to its door. In her left hand, she still gripped the paper bag that held her books. She pressed it to her chest and, with a glance towards the couple, took a cautious step forward. At that moment, the man raised his head and turned towards her. Bertha froze.

"Eh!" His cry was more an inarticulate yelp than a word. He jerked to attention and pushed himself away from Yvette who, unexpectedly released from his weight, stumbled a few steps forward.

"Who the hell are you?" The man, his pants crumpled below his waist and his shirt-tails hanging, stood with his legs apart and the fingers of both hands curled. For a few moments they stared in silence, Bertha with her mouth open, clutching the bag, the man wary yet combative, sizing up his opponent.

The man's shoulders dropped and he relaxed his fingers. He tilted his head and looked at Bertha through narrowed eyes.

"What are you doing here? What's in that bag, eh? What are you stealing?" The man's voice had deepened and he barked the questions confidently, like someone—a policemen, a teacher–used to wielding authority.

Still, she could not interpret the sounds emanating from his mouth. He seemed to her like a snarling animal, a barrel-chested dog.

The man walked towards her, adjusting his shirt and buttoning the front of his pants with exaggerated care. He now looked more self-satisfied than belligerent, and he had a twisted, unpleasant smile on his lips.

Bertha could barely breathe. She could not will her legs to move and she could not continue to meet the man's insinuating gaze.

She stared down at the floor beneath the scuffed toes of her boots before shutting her eyes. She did not want to see him again, to acknowledge his presence or even allow his existence. If she only waited patiently enough, quietly enough, if she did not show a sign of humiliation, or of fear, or of shame, if she did not indicate by any movement or sound or even thought that she had, in fact, seen what they all knew that she had seen, then both the man and the girl must somehow vanish, taking with them all evidence of this encounter.

The sharp tap of heels against the wooden floor told her that Yvette had left the corner and was also approaching. Bertha smelled something sweet and musky, a scent that made her think of Roy Spaulding standing near her in the summer sun. She raised her right hand and pressed it against her closed lids, as if to obscure the picture in her mind. Yvette spoke in French, her voice shrill and impatient. "*Oh, leave her alone. She doesn't know what you're talking about anyway. Just open the door and let her go.*"

Moments after Yvette's petulant order, Bertha heard the rattling of metal against metal. The man must be a watchman, searching through his keys for the one to fit this lock. She could not keep herself from looking and raised her head. The man held a thick iron key, attached to a metal ring, that he slowly slipped into the keyhole and then, just as slowly, turned until the bolt tripped.

At the sound, Yvette grabbed Bertha's arm, catching a handful of shirtsleeve near the shoulder. The color of the girl's face in the darkening room reminded Bertha of unwashed wool.

"You don't say nothing."

Bertha could not tell if the girl was offering a plea or issuing a warning. Yvette released the fabric of her shirt and the man twisted the iron knob, swinging the door just wide enough so that Bertha, as she escaped into the cool evening air, was forced to feel the pressure of his body.

Once home, she could not begin the practice of Roy's creed as she had hoped. She complained of headache and went immediately to her room, refusing Florence's offer of supper on a tray. She shut the door and, with no key for its lock, pushed a small, straight-backed chair against it. Without rolling up her sleeves or opening the neck of her shirtwaist, she walked to the bureau and, awkward as a goose, plunged her face into the washbowl. When her breath gave out, she counted slowly to ten before raising her head with a gasp. She dried her face on a coarse cotton towel, rubbing until her skin burned.

Bertha opened the bureau's top drawer and took out a small cake of complexion soap wrapped in pleated tissue paper, the last of a box that Eva had not liked and passed to her. She tore the delicate paper and, with both hands submerged, wrestled it into a lather so violently that the water in the bowl churned and spilled over its lip. Her hands still covered in soap, she methodically dried both palms and each finger. Even so, she was sure that anything she touched would be marked by a stain, not like a dirty fingerprint or a smudge of ink, but with an insidious, ghostly trace of something moist, like oil or acid. She left the book wrapped inside the paper bag, and, with the towel over her fingertips, knelt down and gently pushed it into a far corner under her bed. Clutching the damp cloth in her hand, she sat down heavily on the edge of the mattress.

Chapter 25

Florence's Book

When Bertha was fourteen, she experienced a sharp pain in her right side that lasted for two days. On the morning of the third day, she woke to find her nightgown, bed-sheets and the inside of her thighs stained with blood. The discovery was frightening but not entirely unexpected–Bertha had heard whispers of such a thing from other girls—and, realizing that her secret would inevitably be exposed on the next washday, turned to Florence for help.

Florence was calm and did not mention the ruined linens, but when she explained to her younger sister that this unpleasant manifestation was, in fact, perfectly natural, a necessary milestone on the path to maturity, her voice was strained and she looked at Bertha's hands instead of her face. She had left the room and returned with a small, red-bound book, her name penciled in neat script on the inside of its front cover.

From its pages, written more than twenty years earlier, Bertha learned that the seeds of a flower resided in a slender green stem called a calyx. She read that pollen was like the father of a baby-plant, and that bees carried this life-dust from one flower to another on their legs, leaving it in each mother-flower's seed-bearing blossom. She read that eggs were like seeds that grew inside a mother hen's body and that if a father chicken infused an egg with his life force, a chick would form inside that egg. And she was told that human beings, the highest and most perfect of God's creatures, shared and were bound by the same process of generation as the plants and the animals.

Bertha read with disbelief that she, like all females, carried eggs within her. She was told that the germ of life lay dormant in those eggs, each one waiting to be fertilized, to be touched by the power that only a father could give. And Bertha learned that when a girl crossed the threshold of womanhood, as she had just done–when that girl was physically able even if mentally and morally unready to become a mother—from that delicate and dangerous point forward, once a month, the eggs that had not been infused with a father's life force would leave her body in a cleansing wash of blood.

Bertha did not know if the eggs hidden somewhere inside her body were perfectly round and joined together in a slippery mass like frog roe in a pond or if they were tiny, oval and thin-shelled like a chicken's. Both images disgusted her. And, horrified, she realized that in some still-mysterious way, perhaps without her knowledge, those eggs might now be fertilized and she would become a mother. From that day forward, Bertha understood, she would have to be vigilant.

But what should she be on guard against? How, she wondered, did a father's life force, animal or human, infuse a mother's egg? By what magical or mechanical means did the two come together? The book had told her that male fish expelled a whitish fluid but beyond that it was silent. Bertha did not know if the life force of a human father was also liquid, pale and milky, or if it was dusty like the pollen carried on the legs of a bee.

Bertha went back to the book and although she searched every page found no answers. Frustrated, she returned it to her sister. "Thank you," she said while avoiding Florence's eyes, "This has been very helpful.'

But she remained troubled and could not stop pondering these questions, although she was sure they were dangerously carnal. She reasoned that an opening of some sort was necessary for the life force—liquid or dust—to find its way from the father to the mother's egg. Through the mouth? An ear? A nostril? The first seemed likely, but she dismissed the last two possibilities as ridiculous.

Could this opening be the same as the place through which discarded eggs left a woman's body? Bertha, alone in her room at the time, blushed at the idea but recognized its logic.

When she was eight years old, Bertha had seen two horses in a field acting strangely and she asked the friend out walking with her, a farmer's daughter, what it was they did. They were playing, her friend said. Bertha had not been satisfied. What kind of play? Getting married, the little girl explained, they were playing at getting married. Bertha, still perplexed, felt stupid and let the matter drop. Now, at fourteen, it struck her that what she had witnessed in the field that day was, perhaps, some form of animal infusion.

Still, Bertha could not imagine how any substance might travel from another human being and actually reach that place hidden between her legs. Except for those private moments when she undressed or took a bath or, most embarrassing to consider, visited the outhouse, it should be and always was covered. Was a woman expected to lift her skirts and—here Bertha buried her face in her hands– take off her underclothes in front of another person—a man? She refused to believe that anything so humiliating could be part of nature's plan.

Maybe—and she hoped this was the case–the infusion could pass through cloth. Or maybe it *was* conveyed through the mouth, as she had initially thought. In either case, she realized with some relief, if she kept her distance, she probably had nothing to fear. And, finally, she took comfort in the hope that human beings, imbued as they were with spirit as well as trapped in flesh, might undertake the process of infusion more delicately than horses. A brief touching of bodies, an exchange of breath, a whispered prayer, and, she was sure, God joined male and female.

But the man and woman Bertha watched in the mill that evening had been as heavy-limbed and mindless as beasts. Fertilization. There could be no other explanation for what she had seen. The word made her think of dirt. Yvette, brazen as the man, was certain to become a mother. Bertha knew from gossip overheard at the burling tables, exchanged around her in the French she pretended not to understand, that Yvette and the man were not married. There had been nothing sacred in their union, no hint of divine love in their coupling, no gentle congress of souls as well as bodies. In a moment of brutal clarity, Bertha now grasped the enormity of the sin committed before her eyes and her complicity as its witness.

Chapter 26

Prayers

She resolved not to sleep. She would sit up at the small table that served as her desk and use the dark hours of the night to reflect on her recent behavior. Maybe, then, she could regain the serenity of mind and buoyancy of spirit she'd briefly enjoyed before the encounter in the stair tower. At the first light of dawn, she'd exchange her soiled clothes for clean white linen. In the morning, she'd meet her family's innocent and trusting eyes with a clear conscience. She would retrieve Roy Spaulding's book from the shadows. And, when she saw Roy again, she would answer his friendly smile without a blush.

Bertha rose, dislodged the small chair from its defensive position beneath the doorknob, set it in front of the table. She paused before sitting, listening for the soft footfalls of her father and sister downstairs. Her mother, she knew, was in the room next door, enjoying the oblivion of guiltless sleep in her oversized bed. Bertha rested her wrists on the edge of the table. She wove her fingers in a pious ball, closed her eyes and bowed her head.

Her first thought was a familiar prayer. "Our Father. . . ." she began but abruptly stopped and shook her head.

"I like a man with good feeling towards all people," she whispered. "I believe in the gospel of cheerfulness, the gospel of good nature, the gospel of good health."

Bertha repeated the sentences, over and over until they lost all meaning. As she murmured, her shoulders sagged and, with an involuntary sigh, she fell asleep with her cheek resting on her clasped hands.

She sat at her burling table, picking mechanically at the cloth. She did not find it strange that the finishing room had no walls and no ceiling and that a tall pine tree grew next to her chair. She heard a whimper and, turning to her left, nodded briefly at Phebe, who held her iron tightly against her chest while tears dripped down her pale cheeks.

Yvette, as usual, was Bertha's neighbor to the right. When Bertha glanced in that direction, she saw that the girl's skirt and petticoat were lifted and the skin of her thighs shone pale as the moon. Yvette felt Bertha's eyes on her and she turned, speaking softly in a taunting, lascivious purr. Many of her words were strange, words Bertha had never learned in her French lessons, but she understood enough to glare at Yvette in humiliation and impotent anger.

Yvette stood up and shook out her skirts with a seductive smile on her small, sharp face. She leaned over and put her mouth against Bertha's ear. "*You know what I mean,*" she whispered. "*You know just what I mean.*"

Yvette straightened and arched her back. Her yellow hair, once bunched and piled on top of her head, was now undone, a tangle of frizzled strands that fell below her shoulders. Her skin glowed unnaturally red, as if blood had pooled in the center of each cheek. She placed one hand on the white shirtwaist that was pulled taut against her rounded stomach and rubbed it once, slowly.

"*I saw you,*" Yvette hissed and drew on a cigarette held loosely between two fingers of her other hand. She exhaled as she turned to leave, and the smoke stung Bertha's eyes.

Bertha lay on her back in the long grass that grew at the base of the burling tables. But the tables and the people seated at them had disappeared, along with the tall pine tree, and, although she did not rise to investigate, she believed herself alone and at rest in a vast meadow. The blades of grass surrounding her were stiff and unbending and ringed her body like a cage of straw. She stared up into a flat and featureless sky whose gray-green translucency reminded her of the frozen surface of a pond she had skated on one childhood winter. When she tried to lift a hand towards it, she found both arms tingling and immobile. Her legs, she discovered, were useless too.

She felt the pressure first on her chest and, with her arms heavy at her sides, raised her head and tilted it as far forward as her neck and shoulders would allow. She could see nothing resting on her sternum, no pile of stones, no curled up cat, no grinning little demon with popping eyes nestled between her breasts. The sensation of weight spread to her stomach and she was about to lie back when she saw an indistinct shape hovering above the sharp grass.

The shape grew larger and she recognized it as a head. Soon, she saw a figure's shoulders and torso, its arms swinging by its sides, and its long legs breaking a path through the stalks. Although the figure remained indistinct as it approached, as if caught in a shadow, she knew it was Roy Spaulding. By now, the strain on her neck and shoulders was unbearable and she was forced to lie flat.

"Beatrice!" Roy called, pronouncing the name in the Italian way.

"How did you know?" she whispered.

"Beatrice," he said again, and she could tell, although she couldn't see, that he was kneeling in the grass by her feet. She closed her eyes.

Her feet were bare and so were her legs. She could not feel his hands, only the movement of air around her legs and the prickling of nerves under her skin. The pressure on her chest and stomach disappeared and moved instead to the place between her legs.

She wanted to touch him and when she tried, she found that her arms were free. She raised one hand towards where she thought his cheek must be. She could feel the warmth of his breath against her face and the barest brush of his lips against hers.

"Bertha? May I come in?"

Although Florence had retired at her usual time, worry over her sister kept her awake. Bertha did not normally rush to her room without taking supper. She had looked unusually pale that evening and, Florence thought, seemed almost furtive in her movements. Barefoot and in her nightgown, Florence tapped once on the girl's door before opening it. She held a single candle in an old-fashioned holder and, by its flickering light, saw Bertha asleep at the table. She tiptoed to her side.

"Bertha, wake up." Florence leaned over and gently shook her arm. Bertha stirred. "You can't stay like this all night," Florence said and raised the girl's shoulders from the table. "Here, now, stand up," she instructed and, with Bertha groggy and submissive, Florence patiently prepared her sister for bed.

For several days and nights after her dream, Bertha could not bring herself to retrieve Roy Spaulding's book. The few times she glimpsed him at the mill, she looked away until all chance of meeting had passed. She was disturbed by how often and how clearly his voice and his touch came back to her, surprising her at the supper table, at the burling table, in the early morning darkness when she lay sleepless in her bed. She hoped their memory would fade before she had to talk to him again or even open the pages he'd entrusted to her.

But the night before she was to finish at the mill, Bertha realized she had waited too long. Of course she couldn't read the entire book in time to return it to Mr. Spaulding and tell him what she thought. She felt an unfamiliar panic. She had never been given an assignment she couldn't complete, had never gone unprepared to an exam, had never been asked a question in class that she couldn't answer. That her first failure should be with Roy Spaulding was unthinkable.

The only solution was to take the book to school, read it there and, as soon as she was done, send it back with her apologies and a thoughtful but light-hearted letter. Certainly he would send a letter in reply. She fell asleep imagining their correspondence and their next encounter, when she came home at Thanksgiving.

Bertha spent her last day at the mill praying they wouldn't meet. When she stopped at the superintendent's office to pick up her wages, she was certain she'd find him there. But then she overheard one clerk tell another that Mr. Spaulding had gone home to Ashland for a visit, and she could breath again. Luck was on her side; she could write in evident sincerity that she had brought his book to the mill. And she could tell him how sorry she was to have missed him.

Chapter 27

Engaged

Although she hadn't asked for one, Bertha found herself assigned to a private bedroom in brand-new Porter Hall, an airy top floor room with a window facing the mountains. At the end of a hallway, it was far from the bustle of the first-floor parlors and the dining room. A paradise, Bertha thought, after the closet she had shared with Phebe in Miller's Cottage or their drab and dusty room in Seminary Hall.

On her first night back at the college, Bertha turned to the only essay that truly mattered, the one Roy Spaulding had marked. Elbow on the table that served as her desk, head propped on a fist, she began at the beginning and read each word with growing excitement. She and Roy now shared a dangerous, free-thinking secret.

But she didn't understand just how powerfully, how uncannily, even providentially, Roy's voice was speaking to her through its pages until she reached the essay's final passage.

"Next to eternal life is eternal death," she read, "Hearts of dust do not break; the dead do not weep."

Cease to exist. She thought of the terrible phrase uttered by her father on that summer day, when, sorrowfully but firmly, he had pronounced the likely fate of poor, dead Eva. The image of utter annihilation, the silence of the infinite void that he had prophesied for her lost friend horrified Bertha more than any fiery vision.

But that was not the eternity offered in Roy's book. In that eternity, the dead belonged to living nature; they were motes of dust, beyond sorrow and pain, murmuring in the streams, floating in the clouds, bursting in a foam of light upon the shores of the world.

Bertha's breath caught in her throat and she laid a hand flat on the page. Nodding in solemn agreement, she reached for a nearby pencil and, with its newly sharpened point, left a small but distinct "x" in the margin beside the passage. After a moment she closed the book and, handling it as reverently as a Bible, placed it on its side on the top shelf of the bookcase that stood beside her desk.

The college was not the same as when Bertha left in June. The new dormitories were complete, the grounds around them smoothed and seeded, the signs of demolition and construction hauled away or erased.

The place where she had spent most of the last two years of her life was scrubbed of its patina, its texture of age and association and memory, and Bertha was glad of the transformation. She wanted to re-enter the life of the college without the recriminating shades of Phebe, Miss Slater, and Eva waiting for her in some once-familiar corner. And, she believed, in this bright and busy new world she would forget what she had seen in the mill and no longer be visited by those frequent dreams from which she awoke with feelings of shame and regret that lingered for hours.

Yet she could not shake the suspicion that some of the girls—Mabel Eaton in particular—could sense the unhealthy turn of her mind, that they could see in her face, through a clarity of vision reserved for the pure and good, evidence of the physical debasement that consumed her. Bertha wanted to live the simple creed of cheerfulness that Roy had offered her in more innocent days, and she wanted to be friendly, to take an interest in the topics that animated the girls at her table in the dining room of Porter Hall, to surprise everyone who had known her before and thought her aloof, or awkward, or strange.

But the effort was exhausting and, Bertha finally realized, futile. Although she could read difficult texts in Greek and Latin and measure and mix chemicals with a patience learned in the tedious summer hours spent at her burling table, she could not concentrate on the life around her. When she shared a conversation with Mabel (whose physical proximity now embarrassed her and whose sweetness, once so enthralling, struck her as naïve), or listened to the basketball stories of Helen Calder, (who sat next to her at meals), she could not focus on their faces or their words. They seemed to drift by her, like creatures in an aquarium. Or maybe *she* was the floating creature, separated from them by a transparent surface that would not yield to her touch or even retain her fingerprints.

Two weeks into the new term, Bertha made a sign for her door, a small piece of stiff cardboard with a loop of black ribbon. She wrote the word "Engaged" in bold black script. Most girls reserved such signs for desperate moments—the night before an exam or the hours before an essay was due–, but from that point on Bertha displayed hers whenever she was in her room. The scrap of cardboard became her guardian, her talisman. Since she began its use, not a single person, as far as she knew, had knocked on or called her name through the door.

If anyone did come to see her (and it gave Bertha particular satisfaction to imagine Mabel on such a mission), the sign politely but firmly offered her excuses. Miss Mellish is within, it said, but regrets that she is too busy to accept your kind invitation. Miss Mellish is sorry that her studies prevent her from walking with you. Miss Mellish is afraid that she simply has no time to join you in conversation. The intruder, her fist poised to knock, would lower her arm and tiptoe away.

Chapter 28

The Shell

The inside of the turtle shell was smooth and cool against her cheek. Bertha, lying on her left side with her knees drawn up and pressed against her chest, barely fit into the tight, domed space, but she liked its feeling of enclosure. Her head rested near the opening at the back of the shell and her feet pointed towards the empty space where, when the ancient creature was alive, its head and two front legs would have protruded.

Strictly speaking, the shell had never housed a prehistoric terrapin, although Bertha did not know this. It was a cast, made of plaster, hard and gray as stone. The gigantic skeleton of another prehistoric beast, a portion of which she could see from where she lay, was also a cast. So was the nearby carapace of an ancient armadillo whose skull was attached to its body by a flexible steel rod. Bertha had lightly tapped this skull when she walked past it on her way to the turtle, and it had bobbed in a slight but friendly greeting.

The school was at supper and Bertha, on this eighth day of November, was alone in the dim, dusty museum on the second floor of Williston Hall. She had visited the museum often in past years, studying with curiosity and a touch of wonder its bones and shells and fossil footprints, its glass cabinets filled with fragments of rock, desiccated insects, and small stuffed birds. She had learned from Eva that adventurous freshmen, egged on by sophomores, climbed into the rear of the turtle shell and wriggled out the front, but she had never tried it herself. In those days, the inside of the shell looked small and dark; she might not be able to escape.

But when she wandered into the museum soon after her return to school in September, it was more than curiosity that drew her to the bones and the footprints. The empty turtle shell no longer frightened her. These artifacts seemed now to embody the unconscious dust of eternity described in Roy Spaulding's book, as if some of its particles, whirling and spinning through time, had been pulled together and made concrete.

Fleshless and immutable, they offered proof of an existence beyond desire, the promise of an absolute and perfect peace. She had run her hands over the hard outer surface of the turtle shell and, arms outstretched, leaned against it in a grateful embrace. Finally, making sure there were no witnesses, Bertha had, for the first time, climbed inside. Curled up in the shell's warm silence and cushioned by her skirt, she had fallen asleep.

Bertha shut her eyes and breathed with a slow, deliberate rhythm, but now her goal was not to sleep. She wanted to calm a restlessness she felt more and more powerless to dispel, a persistent sense that something about her had permanently altered in ways that she had neither anticipated nor desired. She imagined herself an unborn chick or an infant turtle still in its shell, alive but unburdened by consciousness or will.

The idea was comforting and made her smile in the darkness until, out of nowhere, she thought of Yvette and the half-formed being that by now must be growing inside her. Bertha tried to bring back her pleasant fantasy, but the picture of the girl, belly distended under her tight clothes, persisted until it was replaced by the vision of a small shape, something like a tadpole, hidden beneath Yvette's white shirtwaist. The shape had tiny hands and feet attached like flippers to its body and black, unblinking eyes in a bulbous head.

The monster disappeared and in its place Bertha saw a miniature infant, nestled just as she was in some quiet interior space. The infant had pink skin smooth as porcelain and delicately modeled fingers and toes like those on a doll that, years ago, she had flung to the floor and shattered in a fit of childish rage.

Then, guiltily, Bertha returned to a notion that had taken root in her mind soon after her first dreams of Roy, a preposterous conceit, improper and impossible, that she now found increasingly difficult to keep at bay and, once in her thoughts, to banish. What if, in those dreams or in the waking moments when they would not leave her memory, his life force had somehow passed to her? What if Roy Spaulding had given her a child, not in the disgusting way that the Frenchman had given his to Yvette, but as gently and chastely as a shared thought?

Perhaps, at this moment, she carried within her body a tiny spirit, pure and perfect as that porcelain doll. Bertha maneuvered her right hand through the tight space and placed it on her stomach. She held her breath and, for almost a minute, allowed herself to feel the flutter of a faint but steady heartbeat. When her need for air broke the spell, she inhaled sharply.

Don't be stupid. She said the words out loud. Don't be a fool.

Bertha shook her head in disgust and bumped it against the shell's hard plaster. With that small pain, she realized that her left side had fallen asleep and her back was sore. She was suddenly worried that supper might be over and the corridors and stairways of Porter Hall filled with girls before she could return, unnoticed, to her room. Bertha straightened her legs and, unable to raise her arms, squirmed forward until she emerged head-first from the back of the shell. She dropped to the floor with a thud and, after a quick look at the watch pinned to her blouse, hurried through the glass doors of the museum too quickly to notice Professor Cornelia Clapp, sprightly and compact as the grasshoppers that she loved to study, passing by with a freshly mounted display of butterflies in her hands.

"Hello there! Come and see what I've got!" Professor Clapp called, but the girl was running and did not hear.

Chapter 29

Letters

A rising murmur of voices signaled the end of supper and the emptying of the dining room below. Still breathless from her run across campus in the fading twilight, Bertha opened the door to her room and transferred her sign from the inside to the outside doorknob.

With her sign in place and the door shut, she played no part in the world outside that room. Over the past few weeks she had begun to perceive—and the perception gave her great relief–that unless she showed herself among her classmates and teachers, she did not, so far as they were concerned, exist.

Bertha realized she was hungry. Two weeks ago she'd stopped going regularly to meals; the smell of the dining room sickened her. No one questioned her absence or told her to return. She kept a stock of food in her bureau, bought down in Holyoke with money left over from her summer at the mill.

On her way to the bureau she pulled the cord of the electric lamp, which threw a cone of harsh light over the room and left the corners in shadow. Inside the topmost drawer she found three apples, spotted and slightly flaccid, and a paper bag half full of soda crackers next to a modest pile of underclothes. She retrieved a handful of crackers and ate them quickly, unconscious of their taste or texture.

Instead of hunger, Bertha now felt a nervous flutter in her stomach. Without thinking to close the bureau drawer, she hurried to the bookcase across the room where a stack of note-paper, almost a quarter of an inch thick, lay on the top shelf beneath Roy Spaulding's book. She slid the papers free, carried them to her desk, and placed them on a newly-laid sheet of green blotting paper.

The letter to Roy Spaulding would begin with an apology and an appreciation of what she'd read. She would tell him how much the essay meant to her. She would ask him a question that required a reply and she would say how truly grateful she was. This had been Bertha's plan, from the moment she returned to school.

Yet the first time she sat down to write the letter, she realized its terrible power and the pen froze in her hand. The wrong tone or a badly chosen word could destroy whatever good opinion Roy Spaulding had of her. The letter might reveal too much. It might not say enough.

Dear Mr. Spaulding, she managed to write early in September. *I have no excuse for my failure to return the volume that you so generously entrusted to me.*

She crossed that out and tried again.

Dear Mr. Spaulding, Please forgive my irresponsible retention of the volume you lent me.

Dear Mr. Spaulding, Please accept my apologies for the tardy return of your book.

Dear Mr. Spaulding, I am very sorry to have kept your book so long.

For two weeks, Bertha covered every aborted effort with angry lines so thick with ink they soaked through and made tiny gashes in the paper. But by then the familiar loops and curves of his name and the repeated confessions of her guilt seemed a kind of incantation and she left them exposed. The words began to flow more easily from her pen.

By the end of September, she wrote:

My Dear Mr. Spaulding, I find solace in the lessons of your Mr. Ingersoll. I am not preoccupied with death, but I have been close to it and the thought that we, all of us when we die, will be like drops in a stream of water comforts me. I feel that you must think so too.

In the middle of October, she wrote:

Dear Roy, I hope you won't think badly of me for using your given name, but I know that we are friends. I find so much of you in your book that when I read it I can hear the words spoken in your voice. I hope you won't mind if I keep it just a little longer.

The sense of urgency that had at first compelled her gradually faded away. It was better to find the perfect words than to send the wrong ones off in haste. And, when this awkwardness between them was over, she would share the ink-stained pages with him as a record of her struggle and as proof of her constancy.

Bertha picked up the topmost letter in the pile, written the seventh of November, just the night before.

My Beloved Roy,

I cannot wait any longer to tell you how I feel. I haven't said a word to anyone, I haven't told a single person how much I think of you, how full my mind and heart are of you. We hardly know each other, I mean we haven't spent much time together, but I feel that you are always with me, that you are closer to me than anyone I have ever known.

Now, my dearest Roy, I have something incredible to tell you. It will sound impossible, I know, and I hardly believe it myself. There was a time– there have been many times since our last meeting when I have felt that we were together in body as well as spirit. I feel that you are holding me in your arms. I guess these must be dreams but they seem real to me. I only hope that you, far away as you are, have some sense of what I mean.

Your own Beatrice

She brought the paper to her lips, gently laid it down. Maybe she would address it tomorrow, maybe even send it. No, she reconsidered, not yet. But soon; she could tell that the time was approaching.

Chapter 30

Freytag's Pyramid

"As Herr Freytag has shown us, as we've seen in his analysis of the tragedies of the Greeks and of Shakespeare, narrative, compelling dramatic narrative, has a structure that must be followed."

As she spoke, Professor Clara Stevens raised her right hand along a diagonal axis and then dropped it, inscribing two sides of an invisible triangle. She stood in front of the classroom window, where the autumn sunlight made a halo of the frizz above her temples, and gazed benevolently at the girls seated shoulder to shoulder in the three rows of chairs before her. Professor Stevens was proud of the easy control she wielded in the classroom, judging herself a firm but gentle commander, friendly but not familiar, who inspired respect rather than fear.

"Now, I have a new assignment for you . . . ." She paused with a knowing smile and raised her eyebrows. Her eyeglasses shifted on the bridge of her nose. "No objections, young ladies, or I'll add something more."

Most of the students responded with brief sighs or faint groans, and Professor Stevens was pleased with their performance in her little comedy. The room rustled with the sound of turning pages and girls shifting in their seats as they readied their pens.

"We have, of course, spent the better part of this term studying Freytag's analysis of this structure, and we have employed his symbolic pyramid to examine the plot construction and character development in the novel as well as in the drama."

Martha Sprague, seated in the first row on the far right next to the door, had allowed her attention to wander; she seemed to stare fixedly at the floor and not, Professor Stevens silently noted, at her. Without interrupting the smooth flow of her words or betraying irritation, she strolled to the girl's chair and stopped, so close that the bottom of her skirt grazed Martha's boot.

"Miss Sprague," she said, "could you please remind us of the five parts of Freytag's pyramid."

Martha's head jerked up. She looked confused, as if she had been sleeping. Professor Stevens waited, a patient but triumphant curl to her lips. She did not like Martha and could not help enjoying her embarrassment.

"No, my dear?" Professor Stevens did not believe in humiliating students in front of their peers and her question was more mournful than sarcastic. In the ensuing silence, she turned and walked to her desk, centered in the front of the room. She stood behind it and rested both hands lightly on its surface. "Someone else, then?"

Helen Calder's arm shot into the air. She was a big, exuberant girl, not quick or clever. Professor Stevens would have preferred to call on someone else, but Helen's raised hand, waving from the middle of the second row, could not be ignored.

"Yes, Miss Calder."

Helen lowered her arm and looked briefly at the ceiling before she spoke. "The five parts are. . .let me see. . . .the first part is the introduction. Then there is the. . .the rising movement comes next, I think. Then the third part, the. . .the part in the middle when it all comes together. . . ."

Professor Stevens could stand it no longer. "Thank you, Miss Calder. Let us give someone else an opportunity to speak." She scanned the assortment of students who, by arm movements or eager expressions, invited her attention.

She was about to call on Harriet Wells, conspicuous in the first row, when another student, almost hidden from view at the far end of the third row, caught her eye. Professor Stevens recognized her as Bertha Mellish, an impressive scholar whose written work was disconcertingly excellent in form and content but who never chose to exert herself in class. Bertha, as ever, showed not the slightest interest in attracting her attention, yet did not lower her eyes to deflect it, and her composure suddenly struck Professor Stevens as unbearably rude.

"Miss Mellish, perhaps you would care to help us."

Professor Stevens hoped, as a gentle lesson in humility, that the girl might fumble through her notes while looking for the correct answer. But, to her disappointment, Bertha answered in a clear and steady voice.

"The five parts of Freytag's pyramid are: first, the introduction; second, the rising movement, third, the climax, fourth, the falling movement, and fifth, the catastrophe."

A few of the girls exchanged looks of surprised admiration; a few rolled their eyes. Professor Stevens crossed her arms and nodded her approval.

"Nicely done, Miss Mellish, nicely done," she said, but received no grateful smile in return.

Professor Stevens straightened her eyeglasses and cleared her throat. "Now, as to your assignment. You will demonstrate your understanding of Freytag's pyramid by writing an original story structured according to the five parts that Miss Mellish has just listed. You have the next week to complete your narratives. They will be due, then, on Thursday one week from today, the eighteenth of November." She stopped, troubled, and realized her mistake. "I correct myself. Since the eighteenth, as we know, is Founder's Day, you may leave them for me in my mailbox in the office of Mary Lyon Hall before Tuesday the. . . that would be the twenty-third, the day we leave for our Thanksgiving holiday." She fixed the class with a mock glare. "I expect to find them in my mailbox early that morning."

She waited until the furious scratching of pens subsided.

"Your first concern, of course, is to find a suitable subject for your story. Don't search too far afield. You are not Shakespeare, certainly, nor Aeschylus, and I do not want to read your versions of their tragedies."

Professor Stevens felt particularly adamant about her next point and she marked each phrase with an emphatic shake of a half-closed fist. "Look to your own world, your own time, your own experience," she urged, "Examine the lives around you and find the poetry and tragedy in them."

The bell signaling the end of the period rang and spoiled the effect of her closing exhortation. Professor Stevens dismissed the class with a nod and a frown. She noticed, however, that Bertha Mellish did not immediately join the other students as they pushed their chairs aside and jostled to the door. She sat with her elbow resting on the widened arm of her chair and her head propped on a closed fist, and she did not get up to leave until the last of the girls was gone.

Chapter 31

La Petite

Hilda Klemm. It had the right sound, a clumsy strength, suitable to a burler in a woolen mill, raised on a Massachusetts farm. Bertha thought the name had the same heavy gracelessness as her own. Marie Racine, on the other hand, was light, appropriate to a dainty, delicate figure. *La Petite.* That would be Marie's sobriquet and the title of the story.

When Bertha first identified her characters and an inkling of the plot that would draw them together, the story was just another assignment to be dutifully fulfilled. Soon, though, it came to accompany her on walks across campus. She felt an unfamiliar excitement, a sense that maybe this, this story-telling, was the thing she was meant to do. Over the next two days it kept her awake at night and infiltrated her dreams. She filled page after page with notes and failed beginnings, destroying them all. Greek, Trigonometry, even Chemistry–nothing now but irritating chores. The letter to Roy was put aside; she could not concentrate on both.

Late Sunday night, Bertha wrote what she knew would be the story's opening lines: *Hilda Klemm, the only hand of German extraction to work among the Irish and the French at the Mattawaugan woolen mill, had been there for almost two years. It was June.*

There was no Mattawaugan mill. The made-up name came easily to Bertha; she thought of the mill along the Attawaugan road that ran past her Dayville home. But the view that Hilda admired through the open windows of their burling room had nothing to do with the familiar hills of northeastern Connecticut. Hilda saw craggy mountain peaks outlined against a northern sky, mountains that looked something like the ones near the college but wilder, more like mountains that might be found in New Hampshire.

A new hand appeared in the burling room that month, a dainty tiny thing, trim and perfectly French from her brown leather shoes to the aigrette in her straw hat. She had bright hazel eyes and pink cheeks and a cheerful disposition that drew people to her.

There was something of Eva's look in Marie Racine, Bertha knew, but Eva had been perfect and Marie was not. Marie had never known her mother and the abuse of a brutal father left her with one shoulder slightly higher than the other. Hilda only noticed the flaw because, on Marie's first day at the mill, some of the hands whispered about the little deformed girl.

Hilda was slow and awkward at her work but Boss Darley ordered her to train the new hand at burling. Marie was dexterous and quick, and she lightened Hilda's load both with her skill and her light-hearted chatter. Marie sang as she burled and also at noon, when the Irish and the French forgot their feuds and gathered together to listen.

Besides Hilda, Marie made another special friend among the mill hands.

French Joe was six feet three and well-proportioned and he caught Marie's eye one day as he lumbered by with a load of cuts. "What a jolly big dance floor," she exclaimed, and there's my partner!"

Imagining French Joe made Bertha uncomfortable and she tried to dwell as little as possible on his features. She did not want to decide whether he had a dark moustache or curly black hair. She knew that he had to be as tall as Marie was tiny and as well-muscled as she was frail, but it was a struggle to keep both Roy Spaulding and the thick-set Frenchman from serving as his models. Still, nothing bad would come of this. Although her high spirits had overtaken her modesty, Marie was a good girl, good as Hilda. Bertha even had a wedding planned. Maybe two, one for each.

The rest of June and all of July passed happily, with Hilda and Marie burling side by side in a room filled with sunshine.

Bertha remembered, with uncomfortable clarity, the thick summer air in the Dayville burling room and the clatter of distant machines. She remembered the cool and curious stares of the women around her, the leering face of the fat overseer. She remembered Yvette and the man in the stair hall. But when she remembered Roy glancing over his shoulder at her from the open doorway, she smiled despite the tears that unexpectedly stung her eyes. She went to bed, his presence still with her.

Late the following afternoon, after a day of interminable recitations, Bertha hurried back to her room, anxious to continue the story. With the sign on her door and the door firmly shut, she sat at her desk, dropping a letter from Florence she'd found in her mailbox.

These days, letters from Florence seemed to come from somewhere very far away, a foreign place, and what was in them had nothing to do with Bertha's current life. Once she'd read the letter, she'd be forced to reply and it was harder now, inventing things to keep Florence happy.

But Florence's envelope stared up at her, pale and accusatory. How would your sister feel, it scolded her, if she saw me lying here? Don't you know how eagerly she opens *your* letters? With a sigh, Bertha sat down and slid the envelope towards her. She could read it now and answer it later. It won't take long, she admitted, just a quick look and then she could turn to the story. She owed Florence at least that much.

Father was well. Mother, the same as ever. The weather had been quite wet. Dr. Hammond came to supper. Dr. Hill was poorly. Charlotte Cogswell sang beautifully at church. It was all as Bertha expected and she skimmed Florence's careful handwriting until a name in the last paragraph caught her eye.

I've saved the most interesting news for last. Your friend Hattie Darling is engaged to be married, to a young supervisor at the mill. His name is Mr. Spaulding, and I believe he comes from New Hampshire. The wedding is set for Christmas, so you will be able to attend.

Please do write soon and tell me how you are. Mother and Father send their love along with mine.

Your sister,
Florence

Chapter 32

Hilda's Letter

"Mary Dear, at last you have asked me to tell you the whole story of your mother."

So now it was a letter—Bertha smiled bitterly; she knew more than enough about letters—a letter from Hilda addressed to Mary, the innocent offspring of Marie's reckless, selfish sin.

Bertha sat this Tuesday afternoon on a carpet of fallen oak leaves halfway up Mount Holyoke with a pencil in her hand and paper pressed against a book balanced on her knees.

"I linger over those bright days," Hilda wrote, *"Darkness and sorrow came too soon."*

The story was different now. Bertha was different. What foolishness, to plot a happy ending for Marie, even for Hilda. Had she really thought they'd end up dear friends and beloved wives, each with a baby on her knee? In the terrible hours since Florence's letter, Bertha saw it all, the fate they had in store, the fate they'd always had in store.

One morning in August, Marie was late coming to the mill. She had received permission from Boss Darley for one hour's leave, but she had been absent two.

A transgression that might have lost Marie her job, if work were not so pressing. Marie was a good hand, the best burler in the room, and Boss Darley might have kept her on if he hadn't witnessed something he could not forgive.

Boss Darley kept watch for Marie through open windows and caught sight of her hurrying up the dusty street towards the mill. He saw her stop in front of the mill to speak with French Joe, bent under a heavy load of cuts he was bringing around.

Bertha did not explain why Marie stopped to talk to French Joe or what it was they said. But Marie should have known better than to invite gossip. She should have known better than to smile at French Joe and entice him with her eyes. She should never have stood close to him, with the promise of her body visible through the fabric of her clothes. She should have known what French Joe wanted.

Marie's dismissal notice was ready by the time she reached the finishing room.

Marie, resolutely and without tears, walked out between the row of machines and burling tables, speaking or signing a kind good-bye to the sympathetic, excited hands who watched her pass.

The green blotter, once pristine, was covered with random blots and streaks of ink. Bertha's Tuesday supper, a pile of soda crackers and an apple, lay within reach of her hand and she grabbed the fruit and dug the tips of her fingernails into its flesh. The sweetness it released sickened her and, without thinking, she threw it across the room. She wiped her fingers on the blotting paper before picking up the pen, but the smell of overripe apples lingered.

Marie's friends were poor. Her father's house was a place of misery. Even Hilda could not offer Marie a place of refuge.

French Joe took Marie to his cottage over the hill, but she could not be his wife. In Canada years before he had parted from his wife.

The sentences were clipped and flat and hid more than they revealed; Bertha knew she could have told much more. But, she thought, better to leave some things unsaid.

The news reached the mill. Marie's former friends shook their heads in unforgiving pity. Everyone, that is, except Hilda.

One day before the summer was over, Hilda wrote, *I visited French Joe's lonely cottage. Looking down the lane towards the cottage, I caught sight of my poor little friend bending over a patch of bright asters in the yard.*

(Bertha thought of Phebe, scuffling in the sand on the day she found her button.)

But Marie disappeared before I could reach her, and the house was locked and still..

I spent my winter days in the noisy loneliness of the mill, shut in by its glazed windows from all the world outside.

But Hilda had not forgotten Marie.

"Once more I tried to see my poor girl. In May, five weeks after her baby was born."

The words were out; Bertha laid down her pen and imagined Professor Stevens peering through her spectacles at the shocking phrase. Let her wonder, Bertha thought with a hint of resentful pride, let her wonder how Miss Mellish ever came to learn about such things.

Nine months had passed since Marie's temptation and fall; Bertha knew enough to calculate the timing of the birth. Marie went to live with French Joe in August; she had a baby the following May. Bertha had tried to keep the specter of Yvette from her mind but now she saw the man and the girl again, joined together in the corner of the mill. She shook her head, but the image remained. For a moment she smelled the odor of damp wool mixed with something sweet. For a moment she remembered how she'd felt standing next to Roy Spaulding the summer night they'd met outside the mill.

Enough. She picked up the pen, determined to finish the scene.

The little house looked desolate and uncared for, unlike anything that could belong to Marie. There was no one in the yard, no visible life in the house. I sat down on a step to wait. I had to see Marie, to help and comfort her. I had heard rumors at the mill, that Marie was not herself, that French Joe had twice brought her back from the river road.

Bertha turned the sheet face down on the blotting paper. She tossed that night in bed, picturing Hilda sitting motionless on the step, waiting for Marie.

Chapter 33

Catastrophe

The room was dark when Bertha woke up, a little before seven o'clock on Wednesday morning. She lay on her back, breathless from the sudden awakening and from the lingering effects of a dream she could not fully remember. There were monsters in it, that much she knew, full-grown versions of the amphibious creatures she'd imagined growing inside Yvette, swimming in murky pools, slithering through mud.

She fought the urge to pull the bedclothes over her head, shifting slightly to watch as the light of a cloudy morning infused the muslin curtains. After a time, she heard the soft and irregular tapping of raindrops on the roof above her head and, as she listened, the rhythm grew stronger and steadier.

The sound was hypnotic and she felt no compulsion to sit up, get out of bed, wash herself and dress, do any of the small chores required to begin the day. She wasn't tired, not in any physical sense, but felt mired in a kind of paralysis. She wanted to hold the pen again but could not will herself to move.

A flurry of voices in the hall, a volley of closing doors, and the sound of receding footsteps told Bertha as clearly as any clock that it was seven-thirty; the girls were going down to breakfast and then on to whatever recreation day pleasures they had planned. Lulled by the rain, she fell back to sleep.

When Bertha woke again, the room was brighter. Only an occasional drip from the eaves or the window frame broke the silence. Whatever paralysis had gripped her earlier was gone and she regretted the hours wasted in sleep. She threw back the covers, hurried to the bureau to check her watch. Ten-thirty; the morning half gone.

She splashed her face at the washstand, dried it on her nightgown. She left the nightgown in a heap on the floor, put on the same shirtwaist and skirt she'd left in a pile the night before, rolling the sleeves past her elbows.

Without opening the curtains or turning on the electric light, Bertha sat down at her desk, dipped her pen.

I sat on the step in the warm sunshine, Hilda wrote, patient and still, hoping for some sign of Marie. As I waited, I thought sadly of the happy days that had been and of the sad days that were and were to be.

Bertha repeated the last sentence out loud. She liked its solemn rhythm and, for a moment, wished she could show it to someone.

Hilda looked up, although she heard no sound, and saw her friend disappear around a far corner of the house. She called, but Marie did not look back.

"Was I mad to pursue her, Mary?" Hilda asked all those years later, "Had the sight of me, stirring bitter memories, recalled the dreadful purpose that twice before drove Marie to the river road?"

Dreadful purpose. Bertha stopped and reread the two words. They had the tone she wanted, mysterious and grand. She remembered the phrase from newspaper articles describing the fates of remorseful embezzlers, ruined merchants, spurned lovers, fallen women, outcasts, pariahs, madmen.

The word dreadful terrified her. Not the puny "how dreadful" of today, but the dreadful she'd heard in the sermons of her childhood.

Dread had made her heart pound in her chest, dread had shaken the pew beneath her and sent the room spinning. She dreaded that inevitable moment when she would stand as a sinner before the heavenly throne, she dreaded the possibility that she might someday suffer the torments of hell (torments that her father now said did not exist), and she dreaded just as deeply the infinite darkness of winter nights that left her calling for Florence from her bed.

Yet, somehow, in the wordless terror of such dread, Marie had found purpose. She was hurrying to meet the very thing that most human beings struggle with every last pulse of bone and blood and sinew to escape. It must take just as much strength, Bertha thought, to look for death as to hide from it. No, she reconsidered, it must take more.

Marie had left the road and was running now, straight towards the mountains. Hilda pursued, never gaining but never falling behind. They ran together down a hill, across a stream at its foot, and up a slight incline through a narrow belt of hemlock trees that skirted the foothills of Mount Holly.

Let Professor Stevens think I mean Mount Holyoke, Bertha thought. Maybe I do.

They continued forward along paths that wound through broken ledges and boulders. Suddenly, the paths stopped at the base of a steep and craggy slope and, for one brief moment, Marie seemed to hesitate.

Just before the catastrophe, Freytag teaches, there is an instant, a slip in time, a moment when hope flickers and the inevitable might not happen.

"Surely, she would not, could not go further," Hilda remembered, "In despair, I called to her."

And then, inexorably, the catastrophe.

Marie ignored Hilda's cry. She began to climb.

The way she went, Hilda knew, led straight as death to the river on the other side.

Hilda followed, clinging to the rocks, until she reached the western summit.

There she saw Marie, starting down the northern face of the mountain, a treacherous slope covered with a precipitous mass of trap rock. She watched in helpless horror as Marie reached the belt of trees that clothed the steep base of the mountain just above the river and vanished into them.

Eva stood at the edge of Titan's Pier, facing the river. She was very far away, barely more than a dark, delicate shape silhouetted against the empty sky. Bertha, stumbling over the rocks and tree limbs that littered her path, was afraid Eva would disappear before she could be reached. But she waited, and when Bertha was close enough to hear her speak, she turned, held out a gloved hand, and whispered an invitation. Bertha raised her arm, hesitated and drew back. Eva, with a small, sad shrug, turned again towards the river.

Bertha jumped up from her chair, heart pounding. The voice, it seemed, came not from inside her head, but from somewhere just outside her ear and for one irrational moment she expected to see Eva standing nearby, smiling triumphantly. It was not exactly a dream; Bertha did not remember feeling drowsy, her pen was still gripped in her hand, she had not slumped onto the desk. But it was not precisely a memory, although it recalled details of the picnic at Titan's Pier just over a year ago. What she had just seen and heard, Bertha finally decided, was some kind of visitation. She was not ready to concede that the ghost had been real, but Eva's words echoed in her mind and for some minutes kept her from sitting back down at the desk, able to write.

Time stopped as Hilda waited in paralyzed agony at the summit of Mount Holly. Suddenly, she heard a sound that told her that the river had its own. She flung herself down the rocky slope, lost her hold and fell. They found them both that night; Marie floating at rest in the river, no death agony in her still face; Hilda bruised, half-covered with small stones, crumpled at the foot of a low cliff.

If the struggle of a character has taken hold of her entire life, Freytag teaches, then the author must make the complete ruin of that life necessary, inevitable and impressive.

Hilda did not die, but lay ill for many months. During her long, slow convalescence, she thought happily of Marie. There was no reason to grieve for her now. "Heaven's mercy," Hilda explained to Mary, "had led her out from her shamed, stifled life to a guiltless death."

The rain started again, heavy and insistent, and the room grew darker. Bertha raised the page to her eyes and, although she could smell the ink, she was barely able to decipher the words. She knew them, though, and repeated them, at first hesitantly and in a whisper and then, once again, out loud. When she finished, she felt the sting of unexpected tears and then a small, rebellious thrill. *Guiltless death.* Let Professor Stevens think about that. Let Mabel.

Yet this was not the end Bertha had envisioned for Marie when she first set her on the road to catastrophe and filled her with dreadful purpose. Marie had sinned in life and she had sinned even more grievously in her death. She was an adulteress and then a murderer, taking for herself what was God's alone to take. No hell, no eternal suffering, but no reward— that was the end prophesied by her father. Marie would cease to exist in body and spirit. She would become nothing.

But, as she wrote, Bertha regretted the sorrow Marie's suicide would cause Hilda. She thought too about the young girl Mary who, in the end, would have to live with the knowledge that her birth led, however innocently, to her mother's death.

And, as time went on, Bertha began to wonder if Marie's utter hopelessness might not be, in fact, her absolution.

Now Bertha understood the truth, a truth she felt more than believed. Marie did not defy God when she leapt into the river; she sought escape by the only means possible and therefore her action was natural, inevitable, inarguably right. Marie betrayed the love of her friends and made herself the object of pity and disgust. Her failures and regrets drove her to the brink of madness. If God is merciful–and Bertha hoped that he was –then the promise of release from such unhappiness was his gift.

"Hearts of dust do not break," Bertha whispered, remembering the words from Roy Spaulding's book, "The dead do not weep." She imagined Roy saying them to her, just to her, and for a moment she forgot that he was lost to her forever. She was comforted, and knew Hilda would be comforted too.

Bertha saw Marie gently floating, her eyes closed, her face without mark or blemish, her mouth curved in a peaceful smile. Then she saw Eva dissolve into a falling cascade of sparks that fell, one by one, onto the surface of the water, flickered and were absorbed.

The story was complete but for one final revelation. Certainly Mary had guessed it by now, but Hilda had to make it official, permanent and irrefutable.

"Marie's baby was left to me by the dead mother and the living father," she wrote, "and I loved her as Marie's self. Yes, darling, that was you."

A tiny baby, just over one month old, wrapped in a square of clean white flannel, its face pink and perfect, its infant-blue eyes bright as marbles, impossibly small in the hands of the tall man that held it out to her like a gift or a sacrifice. Bertha crossed her arms on the desktop and laid her forehead in the cradle that they formed. She began to cry, softly at first, an almost silent flow of tears that trickled down the sides of her nose and onto the green blotting paper.

The twang of banjo music and off-key singing filtered in from the room across the hall, and now she cried audibly in sharp irregular grunts. She sat up with her elbows on the desk, folding her hands as if to pray, and rested her forehead on her clenched fists. The tears ran down her cheeks and fell onto her skirt.

Her grunts turned into sobs and then, as the rain pounded without form or rhythm against the roof and the window, into high, wordless keens.

She raised her head and pressed her hands, wet with saliva and tears, to her open mouth, trapping the inchoate sounds in her chest. Her body rocked with the effort but, gradually, her gasps grew shallower and less frequent until she sat quietly, hunched in the chair with her hands still covering her mouth. She slowly drew them away, wiped them twice across her eyes and cheeks and dropped them, palms down, on her lap.

The rain had let up but still fell steadily, and Bertha could again hear the sounds of banjo playing and singing, joined by occasional bursts of laughter. She stared down blankly at her hands, noting without reflection the stain of black ink on her right middle finger and the too-long, irregular edges of her nails.

Then the words came back to her in a revelation as swift and hard as a blow to the stomach and she doubled over, raising her hands to her ashen face. *A shamed, stifled life.* The shame was hers and the stifled, suffocated life was hers. The world she had made for herself, she understood now as never before, was no larger than a single bedroom in Porter Hall.

Bertha shut her eyes, felt their soft bulge against her fingertips. In perfect darkness she remembered that self-important watchword, taken years ago as a freshman. Alone in Athens. She grimaced, pressed harder. The ideal of exalted isolation she had nurtured during her first two years was a childish conceit born of selfishness and spite. Her friendships, barely worthy of the name, had been failures and the fault had been entirely hers. She had allowed that foolish prophecy to guide her and now, more terribly than she had ever intended, it was fulfilled.

Suddenly exhausted, she crept through the late afternoon dimness, an even gray tone that drained everything in the room of color, to lie face down on the unmade bed. A sick emptiness in her stomach reminded her that she had eaten nothing that day, but she had no desire for food. She put the feather pillow over her head to muffle the sound of rain and of girls returning to their rooms before supper.

Miss Slater. Bertha had tried not to think of the teacher since the day she threw her letter in the fire, but now she remembered Elizabeth Slater the way she had looked when she talked about her George, when the lines of her plain face relaxed and her eyes softened. Bertha now understood the meaning of that transformation, as Miss Slater promised someday she would. But when it had mattered, when she had been given the chance to demonstrate the depth and generosity of her friendship, Bertha had coldly refused to allow her teacher happiness.

Phebe–Phebe who had been her special responsibility. That silly button on a string, Phebe's miraculous button, heartlessly thrown back into the sandy field. Bertha groaned beneath the pillow and pressed it more tightly to her ears. She had been thoughtless and impatient and, in the end, had spurned Phebe's confidences and scorned her sorry little token of affection. She should have kept the button and the grimy scrap of paper that Phebe had pressed into her hand at the Holyoke train station and she should have sent the girl just one short line, just one single hint that she still remembered they had once shared a life.

And Mabel. She had held the sympathetic warmth of Mabel's nature in contempt, a contempt that exposed the hollowness of her own heart. She had succumbed to that long-ago attachment, that mortifying schoolgirl crush, out of weakness, and ever since her release from its bonds, she had been ruthless in showing Mabel just how little she cared, just how completely indifferent she was to whatever scraps of kindness the girl tried to give her and now, when she might have taken nourishment from those scraps, she could not ask for them.

Eva. She didn't want to think about Eva.

Bertha, breathless beneath the pillow, lifted it from her head. She lay still for a moment with her cheek flat against the sheet and then, slowly, sat up and swung her legs over the edge of the bed.

On her way to the bookcase, she pulled the dangling cord of the overhead lamp and squinted in its sudden light. She retrieved the pile of letters, placed the desk chair directly beneath the lamp and sat down. In the glare of the electric bulb, she read each page.

By the time she reached the end of the last letter, Bertha's face and neck burned, as hot with shame as if she had read her confessions in public. She should never have exposed, even to herself, the restless figments of her imagination. Feelings that had seemed so natural and right when they flowed from her heart, now, in the clear light of self-examination, showed her just how ridiculous she had become.

She had written impassioned letters that she could never send to a man she hardly knew and who never thought of her. She dreamed of his touch although he had never touched her, she caught his scent although he was hundreds of miles away. She almost believed that, through some mysterious process defying all laws of nature, she could have a child with him, without degradation and without disgrace. Somewhere in her mind had lived the unspoken promise of marriage. She had lost herself in thoughts that she had no reason or right to dwell upon, tempting herself with lover, husband, child—rewards that she, with conviction and resolve born of arrogance, had renounced years ago. And she had been right to renounce them.

One by one with a meticulous care, Bertha tore the letters into small, irregular pieces, each with no more than one incomplete pen-stroke visible on its surface, and sent them drifting to the floor.

She would have cried again if she had been able, but her desolation was beyond tears. She would have shared her grief, if she could have found words to describe it and if she had left herself even one friend to turn to. She might have burdened her father or Florence with her unhappiness if they had been there to comfort her, but she knew in her heart that, even then, she could never bring herself to destroy their illusion of a bright, good girl.

A guiltless death. Wasn't that, in fact, the catastrophe she had been planning for herself all along? She had spent her entire life first laying the foundation and then building the walls of her prison, brick by brick. Today she had recognized and acknowledged that prison; perhaps soon she would find the courage, with heaven's mercy, to escape it. She closed her eyes and, sitting motionless with the fragments of paper like snow at her feet, followed Marie over the mountain's rocky slopes to the cliffs above the river. But the precipice on which Bertha stood was a diamond-shaped rock and the steel gray water she looked into was the same she had seen once before and feared. "Push yourself forward so you'll land past the rocks," Eva advised, just as she had a year ago, "Take a running leap."

Part Four

Afterwards

Friday, November 19, 1897

Elizabeth Mead took a sip of tea and rested the cup and saucer on her lap. She leaned back into the velvet upholstery of her favorite chair, deep maroon with substantial arms and legs of carved mahogany and feet like lions' paws. The shades were down, the curtains drawn tight, and the fire gave off a comfortable warmth. She sighed and shut her eyes, savoring the memory of yesterday's triumph.

She had been right, after all, to postpone Founder's Day. November eighth would have been too early; the eighteenth had been perfect. The day was fair and mild from morning until night (while the eighth dawned overcast and ended in light rain). The red walls of the cottages (made from new bricks intermingled with those salvaged from Seminary Hall) showed nicely against the cloudless sky, and the bare-branched trees, the oaks and elms and the big black walnut that survived the fire, looked stately rather than sepulchral in the bright sunshine. Their fallen leaves crinkled cheerfully under the feet of the guests as they strolled the college paths, shaking their heads in wonder at Mount Holyoke's transformation.

And Mary Lyon Chapel. The weighty grandeur of its stone exterior, the soaring height of its sloped ceiling, the graceful strength of its exposed wooden beams and pointed arches, all of these reminded Mrs. Mead of the ancient churches she visited while in England, years ago with her husband by her side and more recently in the company of her daughter.

Just this morning when she led the college family in its first service in the new chapel, the hymns, sung in the students' eager young voices, had never sounded so sweet. Mrs. Mead opened her eyes and smiled. She looked up at the mantel over the fireplace, at a framed photograph too small to be seen clearly. You would be proud, Hiram, she thought. This isn't the South Hadley meetinghouse you preached in, thirty years ago. She was forty-nine when he died and well beyond the romantic illusions of youth, but she loved her husband and now at sixty-five, at this moment of accomplishment, she felt his absence more keenly than she had in years.

One last sip and the tea, pleasantly tepid, was gone. She put the cup and saucer on a low table by her side, next to the remains of a light supper brought in on a tray, and settled again into her chair. She let her head fall back and roll slightly to the left.

After more than a year of incessant worry, of pleading for money, always more money, after endless meetings with trustees and alumnae, after haggling with architects and contractors, after carefully radiating a hopeful optimism that she was often too exhausted to feel, the vision that she had of a new Mount Holyoke, even as she watched the fire consume the place that she loved, had been realized, and now, at last, she was able to rest. Not that everything was complete, of course; there was so much more still needed, more buildings, more equipment, more faculty, and Mr. Williston was always reminding her how close their finances were to the bone, how much more she would have to charm from prospective benefactors. Mrs. Mead exhaled sharply and frowned. Plenty of time to pick up with all that tomorrow, she scolded herself. Don't spoil these few precious moments. She laid a hand against her chest and, for each rise and fall, counted slowly from one to ten until her hand slipped to her lap and she fell asleep.

She woke with a start to a series of short, timid knocks and glanced at the clock on the mantelpiece. It wasn't particularly late, barely eight o'clock, but she was not accustomed to visitors approaching her in her private rooms after dark. Mrs. Mead smoothed her hair with both hands and straightened the ruff on her collar before speaking.

"Who is it?" she said. She did not try to hide her annoyance.

"Mrs. Mead, excuse me. It's Mary Bradford." The voice from the other side of the door was tentative and its tone surprised her. Mary Bradford was a brilliant Latin teacher with a university degree and, although not strict enough for the president's taste, typically was not unsure of herself with her superior.

"Come in, Miss Bradford." She softened her voice, and by the time the door opened she was sitting straight-backed in her chair with a polite smile on her lips. Miss Bradford stood with her hand on the knob. Her chin, always a little weak, trembled. "Yes?" Mrs. Mead asked, no longer smiling.

Mary Bradford had a kerosene lantern in one hand and she held tightly to the doorknob with the other. She had run from Porter Hall to the president's rooms in Brigham Hall, not a long distance but enough to wind her, plump as she was. After a moment, she felt steady enough to close the door and place the lantern on a flat-bottomed wooden chair, but she did not move further into the room.

"Um," she said, holding her clasped hands against her stomach. "Um," she began again, trying to sound composed, even a little nonchalant, as if she were reporting a minor difficulty, something that might have waited until morning. "I, uh, I'm afraid there's a student missing, Mrs. Mead," she said and averted her eyes to study the dwindling fire. The president, she knew, had little patience with those who failed to meet her own high standard of duty, and Miss Bradford was sure that the guilt she felt was written on her face.

Mrs. Mead rose abruptly in a rustle of black silk. "What do you mean?" she demanded. "Which student?"

Mary Bradford forced herself to look at Mrs. Mead. "Bertha Mellish," she answered.

Mrs. Mead was of course familiar with the name—she knew the name of every student at the college– but could not associate it with a particular young lady. She nodded, not wishing to expose her ignorance to the teacher.

"She has a room by herself in Porter Hall but she isn't in it," Miss Bradford continued, "she. . . . '

Miss Bradford was irritatingly slow in her explanation and Mrs. Mead interrupted. "She must be visiting, then. What makes you think she's missing? Have you inspected the building?"

"She has her engaged sign on display." Miss Bradford leaned against the door. She thought she might cry.

Porter Hall and the students who lived there were her responsibility, hers and Cornelia Clapp's and the matron's but, Mary Bradford felt, particularly hers. She was the one Porter residents went to with their quarrels; she was the one who comforted homesick freshmen; it was with her (although she felt herself inexpert in such matters) that some girls shared their innocent romances. If Professor Clapp played father to the house—bringing insects trapped in bottles and jars to show at supper, leaving in the morning with her high-water boots and butterfly nets–then she was mother, and every child in the house was hers to watch over.

"Please, Miss Bradford, explain the situation." Mrs. Mead was standing with her hands on her hips, her eyes narrowed and her lips pursed.

Miss Bradford gathered herself and tried to speak firmly. "Helen Calder and Harriet Wells, who live on the same floor as Miss Mellish, came to me this evening, not more than twenty minutes ago. They were wondering, they said, because neither of them could remember seeing Miss Mellish at any time today and they thought she might be ill in her room." She paused for breath and considered asking for permission to sit down, but Mrs. Mead did not look open to distraction. "I knocked quite loudly for several minutes and then I tried the door. It was unlocked, but Miss Mellish was not in her room." She remembered a disturbing detail. "And her bed was neatly arranged."

Mrs. Mead stared at Mary Bradford, puzzled. "But why did the young ladies wait so long?" she asked. "Surely they could have knocked on the door themselves and inquired after her earlier?"

"They said they didn't feel comfortable disturbing her, with her engaged sign in place."

Mrs. Mead drew her skirts close to avoid upsetting the small table and approached the other woman. "When is the last time they remember seeing her?"

"Helen said Miss Mellish was at dinner yesterday afternoon."

"And when is the last time *you* saw her, Miss Bradford?"

Mary Bradford looked down at the floor. "In my class, perhaps on Monday."

The president gave one precise, deliberate nod. "I see," she said and, with a slight turn and a few steps forward, retrieved a woolen shawl that hung from a hook on the wall near the door. She draped it over her shoulders.

"Show me to her room," she said with studied calm.

Elizabeth Mead strode along the path from Brigham to Porter Hall through the November darkness, with a sliver of moon visible among the stars and Miss Bradford, her lantern swinging wildly, struggling to keep up.

Daniel Hill, the college steward, sent Mr. Lyman and Mr. Thayer down to the lake to check the boathouse for a missing craft and to investigate the weeds and grasses along its banks, while he and Mr. Smith searched Prospect Hill. He told Mr. Kinney, Mr. Battersby and Mr. Allen to do the best they could in the broad fields and stands of trees that led from the dormitories to the college's furthest boundaries. Miss Bradford went from building to building, making vague inquiries of each matron about unfamiliar visitors or overnight guests, and Mrs. Mead, with her closest and most discreet assistant, Miss Louise Cowles, inspected, one by one, all the hallways and classrooms of Williston Hall, the Science Building, the Library, even Mary Lyon Hall and the chapel. At eleven o'clock, as arranged, the men gathered in Mr. Hill's office in the basement of the new administration building.

"No sign," said Mr. Lyman, speaking for them all, "Too dark."

Daniel Hill, his arms folded and his long face grim, nodded. "We'll try again tomorrow morning," he said and, with a glance towards the door, dismissed them. "Not a word," he ordered. "Not one word."

He waited until their footsteps had died in the empty hallway and then left to report to President Mead in her office upstairs.

When Daniel Hill opened the door, President Mead was at her desk, Miss Cowles standing guard at her shoulder. Miss Bradford sat hunched and miserable in a chair pushed almost to the wall.

"No sign of the young lady, Mrs. Mead," Daniel said. He stood in front of the president's desk with his hands clasped behind his back. "We'll try again when it's light."

He waited in silence, he and the two teachers, staring at Mrs. Mead. Although she was a good ten years his senior, Daniel had always found her a good-looking woman. She had a kind of liveliness around her mouth, and pretty skin, soft like a peach and barely wrinkled. Now, he thought, if someone were to touch her cheek, it would feel like ice.

"There is no more to be done until morning, then." Mrs. Mead looked directly at Daniel and spoke with deliberate emphasis. He was sure he understood her point. No calls to the police, no general alarm. He had been right to order the men of the college to keep silent.

Mrs. Mead placed both palms on the desk and stared at the backs of her hands. Daniel thought she might have fallen into some kind of trance, and he wished Miss Cowles or Miss Bradford would speak up. To his relief, the president raised her head.

"The young lady is certain to show herself soon," she said, with such conviction that he thought he might believe her. "We all remember unfortunate episodes in the recent past." Mrs. Mead gripped the arms of her chair, fixed her attention on poor Miss Bradford. "Last term, you'll remember, the freshman who left the college without a word and went home to her mother. And a year ago, the girl who. . . ." She paused, lips tight. "The girl who eloped with a young man."

As if she were cold, Miss Bradford hugged both arms against her chest. "Yes," she said, "I remember."

"Well, then," the president continued, "Miss Mellish has probably gotten herself involved in some more innocent escapade—perhaps she's gone to visit a friend, or she has stayed overnight in one of the other dormitories."

Mrs. Mead stood up with an energy that surprised Daniel. She smiled, but the effect seemed to him more desperate than encouraging. "There is no need to excite the whole school," Mrs. Mead said as she led the way out of her office, "or bother anyone else."

Or let this get into the papers, Daniel thought.

Saturday, November 20, 1897

Miss Bradford's eyes were red when she took her seat at the head of the breakfast table; Helen was sure she was wearing the same clothes as the night before. When the teacher said good morning, her voice was flat and a little hoarse. Helen gave her a quizzical stare, but Miss Bradford refused to look her way. She must be avoiding the sight of the empty chair, Helen figured, and shifted noisily in her seat, hoping to catch Miss Bradford's attention.

Helen elbowed Harriet, sitting to her left. "Still gone," she said in an audible whisper that stopped all conversation at the table.

Mary Bradford offered the girl a look of sad reproach. President Mead had made it very clear last night, when interrogating Helen Calder and Harriet Wells, that discretion and restraint were absolutely essential for the good of the college, but Helen evidently had not taken the lesson to heart.

The teacher spread her napkin on her lap before responding. "You're right, Miss Calder, Miss Mellish has decided not to join us for breakfast." Miss Bradford looked around the table with what she hoped was uncompromising sternness. "Even so, that observation should not be the subject of gossip."

"But did she ever come home last night?" Helen meant no disrespect, but she knew soft-hearted Miss Bradford was only making a show of displeasure. Besides, by now the whole school must have some idea that a student was missing, and Helen felt a certain duty to acknowledge that fact in the light of day. A few of the girls at the table stifled gasps at her question; some waited for an answer with open mouths.

"Helen, please!" Miss Bradford cried.

"I'm sorry," Helen said, "but I'm worried. We're all worried." She turned to Harriet, who nodded in solemn agreement.

Mary Bradford glanced away from the rapt faces at the table and bit her lower lip. "I'm worried too," she whispered, "I don't know where she might have gone."

I ought to know, she thought, as she had all through the sleepless night. I should have taken more care. I should have paid more attention. She shook her head and raised the napkin to her mouth. Suddenly conscious of the gesture, she dropped it back into her lap. "Mrs. Mead will brook no gossip," she said stiffly, "We must all comport ourselves with discretion until Miss Mellish's whereabouts are confirmed."

Chastened, the young ladies returned to their breakfasts, picking at their eggs and sharing looks of wide-eyed curiosity.

"Of course," said Helen after a few moments of general silence. "But do her parents know?"

Captain Murphy broke off his conversation with the lieutenant—"what do you know about boxing anyhow" was his parting shot–and picked up the receiver on the telephone's third ring. "Yes, it is," he said and waited. "No, the Chief's not here."

The lieutenant, with nothing better to do, propped himself against the long wooden counter with his arms folded and watched the captain. The captain was short and broad, just this side of fat, with red cheeks and a bristling moustache that, as he listened, began to twitch. With his free hand, he groped for a pad and pencil. The lieutenant sensed something good and leaned forward.

"And when was she was discovered missing?" Captain Murphy, his eyebrows raised, shot a look at the lieutenant and motioned him with a flick of his head. He hurried around the counter and stood next to the captain, straining to read his notes.

"And a description of the young lady?" Murphy gripped the pencil awkwardly in his fist as he wrote, pressing hard against the paper. He raised his head from the telephone's mouthpiece. "Go get Mack," he ordered, and the lieutenant, excited by the turn in what had threatened to be a dull morning, loped away from the counter and down the hall to see if the detective was in his office.

"Detective Mack will be there soon," Murphy promised with a trace of wounded pride in his voice. He didn't know this Mr. Hill, steward of the seminary up in South Hadley, but the man seemed a little too high on his horse, advising him, a Holyoke police captain, how to do his job. "Sure, I'll tell the Chief and the patrolmen." He listened, beating the pencil impatiently against the pad. "Right. Yes. Yes." Murphy slapped the receiver back into its cradle and reached along the counter for the official register. He wasn't any neater with a pen than he was with a pencil and, absorbed in recording the particulars of the complaint, didn't hear the approaching footsteps.

A man, young and slight, reached the counter. He watched for a moment in silent amusement as the captain worked laboriously on his chore. "So, Captain Murphy," he said, "What have you got for me this bright and early morning?"

The captain's hand jerked and he looked up with a scowl. "Damn it, Webster, you made me blot!" He laid down the pen and wiped his fingers against a leg of his trousers.

"My apologies. So sorry." Earl Webster rested his forearms on top of the railing that separated the officer's side of the counter from the civilian's. "Can I see what you're writing?"

"You're a pain in my ass, you know that, Webster."

Murphy smiled in spite of himself. He enjoyed stringing the kid along, the overdressed little fop, but in the end he always gave him the story. He liked to search the evening paper for his own anonymous contributions to its columns and point them out to his wife. "Anyway, what have *you* got for *me*?" Murphy asked, puffing out his cheeks and folding his arms over the blue wool of his jacket.

Webster reached into the pocket of his overcoat and pulled out a cigar, slightly bent. He held it up, daintily, between his thumb and index finger. "Will this do?"

Murphy snorted. "Keep it." Tired of the preliminaries, he leaned forward. "There's a young lady missing from the college in South Hadley." He emphasized the word missing, knew Webster would get his insinuation.

"You don't say!" Webster whistled through his front teeth and stood up. He took a small pad and a pencil from his other pocket, the one without the cigar. "Since when?" he asked.

"Since last night, the man from the college says."

"The young lady's name?"

Murphy searched his scrawled notes, squinting. He ran his finger below two barely legible words. "Looks like Bertha, Bertha M-e-l-l-i-s-h."

Webster, the name in his note pad, turned away from the counter without a word. No more time to waste on the thick-headed captain; the minute the news spread, his scoop would be gone. If he filed before two o'clock, the story would run in that evening's paper.

But he remembered his manners and paused. "Thanks, Murphy," he said, glancing back and touching the brim of his derby. "I owe you a cigar. A new one."

First the police and now the parents. By eight-thirty, Elizabeth Mead faced the inevitable. The missing girl had not returned; the discreet search and cautious inquiries had yielded no clues. She sat at her office desk with her head supported by a fist and reviewed the telegram she would soon ask Mr. Hill to send, its text distilled from a paragraph of delicately worded prose. *Mr. John Mellish, Dayville, Conn.*, she read, *Regret cannot locate your daughter. Please inform if returned home. Holyoke police notified. Trust God she is safe. Elizabeth Storrs Mead, President, Mount Holyoke College.*

She shifted her eyes and stared at the closed door, its upper half glazed in frosted glass that made everything seen through it vague and insubstantial; she could read "Office of the President" spelled out in gold and black, but the letters ran backwards. When two blurred forms appeared at the window, she asked them in before they could knock.

"Mr. Hill," she said, indicating the chair that faced her desk, "please sit down."

She waited while the steward ducked his head in awkward acquiescence and settled in the chair, tucking his legs under the seat and resting his hands on the knees of his trousers. She turned to Miss Cowles, who stood just inside the door, caught in a shaft of raking sunlight. Mrs. Mead worried that the strain was too much for her; she looked unusually pale.

"Miss Cowles, please ask Dr. Lowell to find a photograph of Miss Mellish, and to bring it and the ledger with her measurements to me." She glanced at Mr. Hill. "The police will certainly need them," she said and looked again at poor Miss Cowles. "Then, my dear, please try to get a little rest." Miss Cowles, her eyes wide behind her spectacles, nodded several times but did not move.

Until this moment, the missing girl's surname had meant nothing to Louise Cowles; she had seen so many young women come and go over the decades, had learned and then forgotten so many names. But a revelation suddenly came to her, from whatever dark recess of her memory she could not say. "There is another Miss Mellish," she blurted, her voice unnaturally high.

"Yes, of course," Mrs. Mead said, "Florence Mellish, the elder sister."

Miss Cowles shook her head. No, she was now quite certain, there had been another one. Alice May Mellish–that was it. A whisper of tragedy had arrived in her wake, she recalled. It was before President Mead's time, during Miss Blanchard's rule as principal. Rumors of a mad father had followed Alice Mellish, of a man once important, a senator or something like, someone high up in government gone suddenly insane, taken to the national asylum in Washington to die a wretched, raving death. It seemed to her now that she had first heard the story from Cornelia Clapp, recounted in low tones in an empty parlor in the old seminary hall some ten years earlier.

"Alice May Mellish," Miss Cowles said, "She was a student shortly before you arrived."

"I am not familiar with that name," Mrs. Mead replied. "Is she a relative of some sort? Are you suggesting a connection? Does this observation have any bearing on the case at hand?"

Miss Cowles hesitated. She wanted to answer yes to each question with all the pride and certainty she could muster, but was loath to give Mrs. Mead information that might in fact prove false.

"I don't know," she was forced to admit. She had not felt like much of a help during this trying time. She was too nervous, more of a worry than a support to Mrs. Mead. Finally, here was something she could offer the investigation, a real contribution, a genuine clue and, she resolved, she would do everything she could to find out.

By a stroke of luck, Webster found a streetcar waiting in front of City Hall and was outside the college fence in a little over twenty minutes. But he was intercepted on his way to the president's office by the school's dour, tight-lipped steward and made to sit on a bench just inside the entrance to the administration building. He was warned; any attempt to wheedle information out of a student or teacher or anyone connected with the college in any way would result in forcible and permanent ejection from the grounds, and a guard had been recruited to enforce the order. An old crone in spectacles kept watch from a little room whose door opened opposite his bench. Webster had asked her name but she pursed her lips and shook her head in reply. No blood from that stone, he knew.

When Detective Patrick Mack reached the college some fifteen minutes later, he was amused to find the reporter cooling his heels, slouched and petulant as a child. "I just might have something for you shortly, Mr. Webster" he said with deliberate condescension, "Try to be patient." He removed his gray homburg, held it to his chest and turned sharply on his heel. "Excuse me, ma'am," he said to the lady watching from the small office, "I'm Detective Mack of the Holyoke Police Department. Could you please point the way to the President's Office? Mrs. Mead and Mr. Hill are expecting me."

Webster waited until the detective was well down the hallway before slipping out the door of the building with a parting wave to his helpless guard. Just a stroll around campus, he thought, just a few harmless questions.

Detective Mack allowed his hat and overcoat to be taken from him by Mr. Hill and hung on a rack in the corner but he politely refused Mrs. Mead's offer of a seat. He liked to stand when he questioned witnesses; he thought it gave him a certain advantage. Patrick Mack was a big man, almost six feet tall and barrel-chested but, as he noted with pride each morning when he dressed, without an ounce of fat. At fifty-one, his hair had gone gray and he kept it cut close to his head. His cheeks and chin were clean-shaven, smooth as a young man's. He positioned himself by the side of the lady's desk so she was forced to swivel in her chair and look up.

Mrs. Mead nodded curtly. "Excuse me, Detective Mack," she said, turning to Mr. Hill. "Please tell Miss Bradford to bring those students we have identified to my office." With a suspicious glare at the detective, Hill left the room.

"Perhaps you'd care to see a picture of the young lady? I also have a detailed record of her physical characteristics." Mrs. Mead gestured towards a carte-de-visite photograph and a large bound ledger lying on her desk.

Mack was curious to see the photograph, but he did not like his subjects to take the lead. There was something unwomanly about this person, and it annoyed him. She wore her mantle of authority too easily. She did not exhibit any of the feminine nervousness he was used to and, in fact, liked to assuage in such situations. "In a minute, Mrs. Mead, but some questions first, if you don't mind."

"Certainly." She rolled her chair back a few inches and waited with her hands folded in her lap.

"Well, now, Mrs. Mead, please tell me what you know about the young lady and the circumstances of her disappearance."

Detective Mack stood with his feet apart and his hands behind his back. He did not take notes during interviews; he thought scribbling on a pad made him look like a stenographer. Proud of his memory, he did not make a written record of his findings until he could do so in private.

"Around eight o'clock last night, one of our faculty discovered that Miss Mellish was not in her room. As far as we have been able to ascertain, Miss Mellish was not seen by any faculty or student yesterday, Friday that is. There was a sign on her door—a sign indicating that she did not wish to be disturbed—and so those passing the room naturally assumed that she was inside."

"But she was not?"

"We cannot know for certain. No one knocked."

"No one missed her at meals? Her friends didn't wonder where she was? Her teachers didn't question her absence from class?" Detective Mack was surprised. He thought such an institution for young ladies would be more careful in its supervision.

Mrs. Mead chose to evade the implications of his question. "Our students are mature young women. They are allowed a certain freedom in their movements and in their choice of activity."

"But, excuse me, Mrs. Mead. Isn't it odd that an entire day went by with no one asking after her?"

"Detective Mack, Miss Mellish is a well-loved member of the college family." Whatever her own suspicions, Mrs. Mead was not about to share them with a stranger. "She is an excellent scholar, the daughter of a respected minister. I have been told by her teachers that she is considered one of the most dedicated students here. She studies very hard, and her friends understand her desire to excel. They did not wish to disturb her when she was at her work and therefore respected the message of her sign." Mrs. Mead felt uncomfortably warm and hoped that her face wasn't flushed.

Shifting his weight onto his heels, Detective Mack folded his arms. "I see." The president was a little flustered, he noticed, a little too indignant in her tone. "And what about the day before? On Thursday? Was she seen at all on Thursday?"

"You must understand that Thursday was a very busy day at the college." Mrs. Mead seemed to have recovered herself and spoke evenly. Still, one of her hands, almost hidden in a fold of black silk, was clenched. "We celebrated our Founder's Day, you see, and so the usual schedule was disrupted. However"—and here her fingers opened –"she was seen on campus by several students. They will be here shortly," the lady glanced at the door, "and they can answer your question better than I."

"I would like to see the photograph now, if you don't mind. And the physical description."

The photograph was a bust-length picture of Miss Mellish taken on the day of her high school graduation, the only image found in the student's registration file. When Miss Cowles had shown it to her earlier that morning, Mrs. Mead recalled the young lady although she could not remember ever having spoken to her, not even on a receiving line at one of the president's receptions. In her photograph, Bertha Mellish was an ordinary looking girl, pleasant enough, with no particular mark of beauty or intellect. Elizabeth Mead, thirty years an educator of young women, knew how to recognize the dangerous ones, and she saw no danger there.

"This picture is two years old, but I'm afraid we have nothing more recent."

Detective Mack studied the photograph in silence. Over the years, he'd seen a girl about this age with her throat cut, another floating face-down in Holyoke's second-level canal, a third lying broken on the street beneath an open tenement window. He'd helped return a runaway farmer's daughter to a family who didn't want her, sent a shop-girl to jail for stealing from the till, delivered a mill-hand to life in prison for the murder of her husband. But the girl in the picture was bred in another world, the world of Sunday school picnics and piano lessons, and the detective could not imagine her in such company.

"How old is Miss Mellish?" he asked.

Mrs. Mead stood up and opened the bound volume on her desk to a place marked by a slip of paper. Eyeglasses low on her nose, she scanned the page that held Miss Mellish's anthropometric measurements, taken during her first term at the college.

"Miss Mellish is now twenty years old. She turned twenty in January. Would you like a description?"

Detective Mack reached across the desk. "If you don't mind, Mrs. Mead," he said and spun the ledger until it faced him. "Five feet five inches," he read aloud, "one hundred and twenty pounds. Medium build. Dark auburn hair. Brown eyes. Fair complexion. Small scar in middle of forehead." He looked up. "Anything you would like to add, Mrs. Mead?"

Before she could respond, a knock rattled the glass on the office door.

"One moment, Mr. Hill," Mrs. Mead called. She looked again at the detective. "No," she said, "I have nothing to add."

Earl Webster left Mary Lyon Hall and headed towards a cluster of brick buildings he thought must be some of the famous new dormitories. He felt conspicuously male in this outpost of feminine intellect and moral superiority. His only previous visit to the campus had been the night of the great fire and the following day when, protected by the general confusion, he'd been just one in an unusual crowd of men and boys. Now the place was orderly and neat and he was conscious of the curious looks and whispers that he excited among the passing young women. Not an altogether unpleasant feeling, he realized. His Chesterfield overcoat fit him well, but wished he had a walking stick.

As he strolled, nodding to those females who dared meet his gaze, he searched for a hint of uneasiness in the air, a touch of menace even, something anxious in the faces of the girls. Perhaps he did, but then he was already privy to an unfolding secret.

When he felt far enough away from the seat of power, Webster looked around for likely sources of information. Two girls, relaxing beneath a tree thirty feet or so to the left of the path, caught his eye. Changing course, he headed towards them, smiling in a familiar way that he hoped might fool them into thinking he was the other one's brother or cousin.

When the girls realized he was coming their way, they broke off their animated conversation. The prettier of the pair raised herself from her elbows and sat up straight, the plain one repositioned a carefully constructed ringlet to sit higher on her forehead.

"Good morning, ladies," Webster said with a bow, "I hope I'm not disturbing you."

They stared up at him in wide-eyed curiosity.

"If I may introduce myself. Earl Webster, correspondent for the *Holyoke Daily Transcript*." He searched the faces of his audience for signs of suitable appreciation. Good. Both seemed impressed.

"I wouldn't trouble you," he continued, "except that I'm here on important official business." His voice was serious now and tinged with regret. "Perhaps you have heard of the unfortunate situation now unfolding."

The pretty one spoke. "Do you mean the missing student?"

"Indeed. You've understood me, Miss. . . ." Webster tilted his head.

"Weller. Clara Weller."

Webster rewarded her with a grave smile. "Miss Weller, may I ask your cooperation in answering some questions about Miss Mellish?"

The girl shared an anxious look with her plain friend, who gave her a hint of a nod.

"All right," Miss Weller said, but her heart didn't seem in it.

"And me as well!," the plain one cried.

Webster lowered himself to the damp grass, reluctant to dirty his coat. The sacrifices I make, he thought, and readied his pad and pencil.

"Tell me, what do you know about Miss Mellish?" He looked to Clara Weller, but the plain girl answered.

""Without a doubt, she's the most peculiar girl in the entire college."

"Peculiar? In what way?"

"Well, she keeps to herself all the time, like she can't be bothered. I live in Porter Hall same as she does and I've seen her once or twice but she's never smiled or said hello." The girl frowned; a judgmental biddy in the making, Webster prophesied. "I don't believe she has a single friend and it's her own fault."

"Do you agree, Miss Weller? Is she a peculiar girl? Unfriendly?"

Miss Weller looked down, playing with a twig. "I don't like to gossip."

The plain one came to Webster's rescue. "But this isn't gossip, Clara, can't you see. We're helping!"

Miss Weller shrugged. "I suppose so," she sighed, as if forced to confess. "I have heard that she always keeps an engaged sign hanging on her door, to keep people away. And that she stays away from meals for days a time."

"I heard that, too," the plain girl said, "I swear I don't know what she eats."

"But she's a very good scholar," Clara Weller offered in Miss Mellish's defense. "Some people say she drove herself to exhaustion."

"A lot of the girls call her a grind." The plain one giggled, hid her mouth with her hand. "Some even say she's a freak."

"Indeed." Webster was a college man, familiar with both types, the colorless drones and the social pariahs. "And what does Miss Mellish look like?"

"Not very pretty, although she could be prettier if she tried. She pulls her hair back too tight and that makes her forehead look big." The plain one warmed to the topic. "And she's very pale which makes her eyebrows stand out dark. *And* she's got freckles." The girl wrinkled her nose.

You're one to talk, Webster thought.

"So," he turned to Miss Weller, "from what you tell me, Miss Mellish wasn't a very happy student here at the college."

Clara Weller hesitated before shaking her head. "It's a sad thing, so close to Thanksgiving," she said. "I hope they find her soon."

The detective was taken aback by the strapping young woman who settled herself into a chair in front of Mrs. Mead's desk. When standing, she nearly matched him in height and had offered her hand in introduction and given his a firm shake. Detective Mack composed himself into an informal but still masterful pose and cleared his throat. Although his gaze was directed at the girl, he could, with a shift of his eyes, see Mrs. Mead seated on her side of the desk.

"Miss Calder, I understand that you are one of the last people to have seen Miss Mellish."

Helen nodded. "Yes, sir, I guess so. I saw her on Thursday. On Founder's Day." She looked at Mrs. Mead while she spoke and not at the man leaning against the desk.

"Miss Calder!" Detective Mack said her name loudly and, a little startled, she shifted her attention to him. "Please describe when and where you saw Miss Mellish on Thursday."

"Well," she began slowly, still conscious of Mrs. Mead's scrutiny, "she came to the dining room in Porter Hall for the midday meal. I saw her there."

"Did you speak to her?"

"Yes, I did. That's why I'm so sure that I saw her, because she said hello."

"It was unusual for her to say hello to you in the dining room?"

Helen felt a little more relaxed under the detective's questioning. He was nicer now that he had seemed at first and nodded encouragingly when she spoke.

"Yes, sir. You see, Bertha. . . uh, Miss Mellish, didn't often come down to the dining room. She was assigned a seat at my table, she sat right next to me in fact, but even when she did come to meals, she hardly said a word. And then, I'd say in the last month or so, she stopped coming almost altogether. I guess she brought things to her room. I think she was studying too much and that made her strange."

Mrs. Mead rolled forward in her chair and both Helen and the detective turned at the sound. "Please, my dear, try to keep your answers succinct," she said, "Detective Mack is a busy man."

"Oh," Helen said, "I'm sorry." She thought she was being helpful--had felt quite proud of her contribution–and now wasn't sure what she'd done wrong. Puzzled, she looked at the detective who signaled his sympathy with a little shrug.

"That's all right, Miss Calder," he reassured her, "I'm interested in anything you can tell me about Miss Mellish."

Keeping her eyes on the detective, Helen felt rather than saw Mrs. Mead's displeasure. "Well," she continued, not quite as energetically as before, "I passed her in the dining room on Thursday but she didn't sit next to me. She smiled at me and said hello and wasn't it a pretty day–something like that–, but then she went to sit at the table where everyone speaks French. Kate, I mean Miss Sinclair, sat next to her at that table."

"Miss Sinclair is waiting outside, Detective Mack." Mrs. Mead stood up. "Perhaps you would like to question her now." She gave Helen a pointed look and glanced towards the door. Helen shifted forward, unsure if she'd been dismissed.

The detective turned and instinctively raised his left hand to silence the president. He noted with satisfaction that she sat down again without a word. "Not just yet, Mrs. Mead, thank you," he said , folding his arms across his chest.

"What kind of young lady is Miss Mellish?' he asked the student, who was now perched uncomfortably on the edge of her chair. She opened her mouth as if to speak and then abruptly closed it. He waited a moment before continuing. "For example, Miss Calder, is she of, shall we say, a romantic character?"

Helen's eyes widened at the question. She supposed the detective was trying to ask if Bertha had a young man. She and Harriet had discussed such a possibility just that morning. Together, they tried to imagine her as heroine of some passionate tale of the heart, the object of longing glances, soft kisses, ardent letters, roses.

"Oh no, I wouldn't say Miss Mellish is romantic." Behind her, Mrs. Mead exhaled and shifted in her seat. "She was always wrapped up in books. Someone said she spent a lot of time in the chemistry lab." Helen shook her head with renewed conviction. "No, she isn't romantic."

Kate Sinclair was a sophomore, easy with her friends but nervous around adults. An audience with Mrs. Mead alone would have been frightening; the addition of Detective Mack forced her to grip the arms of the chair in terror.

"Don't be anxious, Miss Sinclair." Detective Mack's voice was surprisingly soft for a big man. "We just have a question or two and then we'll be done."

Kate nodded. She wished she had a sip of water.

"Miss Calder tells us that you sat next to Miss Mellish at the French table on Thursday."

Again, Kate nodded silently.

"And did she say anything during the meal? Did she speak to you or to anyone else?"

Kate swallowed hard and licked her lips before speaking. "Yes. Yes she did say something."

"Please speak up, Miss Sinclair," Mrs. Mead said.

Kate took a deep breath. "Yes, she did say something."

"And what was that?" The detective's tone was not as patient as before.

"Well, everyone was talking about the exercises and then she said she wasn't going to go to them."

"The Founder's Day exercises?" Mrs. Mead's voice was louder than usual and she leaned so far forward that Kate shrank back in her chair. "But why not? Did she explain why not?"

Kate shook her head. She wanted to look away, but Mrs. Mead was staring and wouldn't let her.

"But surely someone must have asked her?" the president demanded.

"Yes, but she didn't really say. She just smiled and said she had other plans." Kate could see in Mrs. Mead's face just how stupid the president thought she was, and she realized now that a clever person would have pressed Miss Mellish for a more complete answer. Kate lowered her head and wished desperately that she could leave.

Detective Mack had moved away from the front of the desk to stand near the door, where Kate had to turn her back on Mrs. Mead to see him.

"And how did she seem at the table?" he asked, "Did she seem any different to you?"

Kate was confused and, for a minute, unable to respond. Different from what? Except for the encounter on Thursday, she didn't know Miss Mellish at all. She had seen her in passing only a few times before and they had no friends in common. She remembered Miss Mellish at the table that day, quiet but cordial, announcing her plans in a friendly voice.

"Her French accent was very good," Kate finally offered, "and she seemed quite cheerful."

Detective Mack was tired and leaned against the desk with his back to Mrs. Mead. The student in front of him now was of a different sort than the other two. She seemed older, not in looks but in her air of self-contained dignity. She reminded him of a nun from his grade school days whose black-clad holiness had both attracted and frightened him.

"You have been mentioned as a special friend of Miss Mellish," he said.

Mabel hesitated. She wanted to be truthful, and a few months ago she might have answered with untroubled sincerity: yes, I am her special friend. But Bertha hadn't been quite the same towards her since poor Eva Newton's death, and since the return to school in September had seemed deliberately distant. Mabel sometimes felt that Bertha was angry with her, might have even grown to dislike her.

"I do count myself as her friend," she said. "I have known Miss Mellish since she arrived at the college two years ago, although we're not as close as we once were." Mabel considered her words carefully. "I think it is because she is so engrossed in her studies. That has worried me, and I hoped. . . I hope to spend more time with her after the holiday."

"And when was the last time you saw or spoke with Miss Mellish?"

Mabel answered without hesitation; she remembered every detail of the encounter since recently she had seen so little of Bertha. "The last time I saw or spoke with Miss Mellish," she reported, "was on Thursday, sometime after two-thirty, maybe quarter to three. I didn't look at my watch, so I can't be positive of the hour. I was walking from Brigham Hall towards the chapel. I wanted to be on time for the exercises, which were to start at three. I noticed Miss Mellish on the path ahead of me and overtook her. I assumed that we were heading for the same place, but when she saw me she smiled and said that she was going for a walk.

And then she asked me"–the utter strangeness of Bertha's proposal suddenly struck her—"she asked me if I wanted to join her."

Mabel knew that Bertha often went for walks in the woods and the invitation, impossible as it was to accept, had surprised and pleased her. The first that Bertha had initiated in many months, it suggested to Mabel that she regretted her recent reserve, that she wanted to restore their friendship to its former warmth. At the time, Mabel figured that Bertha, perhaps distracted by her studies, had forgotten the exercises or, more likely, thought they started later in the day, despite the growing stream of people converging on the chapel. It did not occur to her until this moment that Bertha might have asked for her companionship in full expectation that the request would be declined.

Detective Mack cocked his head and frowned. "But she must have known you couldn't go."

"Are you all right, Miss Eaton?" Mrs. Mead leaned over her desk and studied the girl's face. Mabel Eaton was one of her favorites, a truly model young woman and a credit to Mount Holyoke. Mrs. Mead thought she saw tell-tale moisture in the young lady's eyes and wished to spare her embarrassment in front of the detective.

Mabel nodded. "Yes, thank you," she said and returned to the detective's question. "Maybe she forgot about the exercises or thought there was time for a walk before they began. But I did remind her and I said that I planned to attend."

"And what was her response?" Mrs. Mead asked.

It had been an odd little laugh, nothing that Mabel had ever heard from her before, and she didn't know how to describe it. "She laughed and said of course I was going to the exercises."

"And did you ask her why she didn't plan to attend?"

Such a question would have implied judgment and, at the time, Mabel had felt no desire to judge. "No, I didn't. It was a fine day and Miss Mellish likes to walk outdoors. I supposed she preferred that to an afternoon spent inside."

Detective Mack snorted. After a morning of speaking politely to a gaggle of sensitive girls, he had run out of patience. "Can you remember what she was wearing?"

Mabel was startled by the man's sharp tone. "Yes, I can," she said with a hint of hurt pride. "She wore her everyday clothes. She wore a black skirt and a black wool tam o'shanter. And a shaggy black jacket."

"Shaggy? What do you mean?"

"It was made of wool with a, a knobby texture, with little knots of wool. It must be new, because I don't remember that she wore it last year." Mabel glanced down at her lap. "I suspect that her underskirt is gray flannel."

Elizabeth Mead cleared her throat loudly to distract the man's attention from Miss Eaton. "Her clothes will be inscribed with her name. Our students are instructed to mark all items of clothing."

"I see," he said. "Anything else, Miss Eaton?"

Mabel concentrated on the image in her mind. She saw Bertha standing on the path with one arm hanging by her side. "Yes," she said after a moment, "She was holding a book."

"And when you left her, which way did she go?"

"I believe she went towards the gate, towards the village."

"And you haven't you seen her since?"

Mabel looked down at her lap and shook her head. "No," she whispered.

A knock on the door ended Mabel's interview. With silent permission from Mrs. Mead, she slipped away as Mr. Hill handed the president a small piece of paper, folded in half. Mrs. Mead read the note and refolded it before acknowledging Detective Mack's inquisitive look.

"It's a telegraphed message from the family," she explained, sliding open a drawer in the center of the desk. "Or rather, it's a message from a Dr. Henry Hammond, who informs us that Miss Mellish has not returned to her home." She stood up and leaned forward to support herself against the desk. "The young lady's father and sister are en route," she said, looking the detective full in the face, "and will be here before nightfall."

"I see." Detective Mack turned to Mr. Hill, standing sourly by the closed door. "I need to use your telephone," he ordered and with a nod to Mrs. Mead, followed the superintendent out of her office.

Elizabeth Mead was grateful for the solitude. There would be little enough peace for the rest of the day and probably for days to come; she refused to consider how many. She turned to face the window behind her desk and through it saw a crowd of men, villagers from what she could tell, farmers and tradesmen by dress, gathered just outside the college fence. Among them she recognized Mr. Lyman, away from his kitchen duties. Mrs. Mead watched as the group broke up and its members scattered.

She stared at the green lawn before her and at the road that led away from the college and raised one hand to her mouth. The lord had made her shepherd of these young women and she had lost one of her flock. She stifled a groan. What could she say to the girl's father? That we cared so little for the daughter you entrusted to us that she slipped away and was gone –Mrs. Mead closed her eyes in shame—was gone for almost two days before we missed her?

She remembered the parents of that poor girl who died of pneumonia last spring and did not know if she could bear such an ordeal again. Opening her eyes, she placed the palm of one hand against the windowpane. The sudden chill of the glass against her skin revived her and she regretted her weakness. It had not yet been two full days. There was no reason to believe Bertha Mellish dead. There were many other explanations for her absence although, she noted grimly, some of those explanations were as terrible as death.

Mrs. Mead lifted her hand from the glass, smoothed the bodice of her dress. Turning from the window, she noticed a pair of steam engines coming up the road from the south. Engines like those had taken the same route on the day of the fire, headed to the lake below Prospect Hill. But the water they pumped today would not be used to extinguish flames; it would soak uselessly into the ground until the lake-bed exposed its muddy surface to the air.

—ᴟ—

The detective knocked once and reentered the office without waiting, in time to see Mrs. Mead, whose back was to him, give a little start. She left her place by the window and sat again at her desk.

With careful dignity, Detective Mack lowered himself into the facing chair. "I have some news," he said. "The streetcar conductor on the South Hadley Line says that he saw a young lady answering to Miss Mellish's description on the car to Holyoke Thursday afternoon. And one of our officers saw her walking up Lyman Street about 5:30 that evening."

"She went to Holyoke?"

In her anger, Mrs. Mead forgot the terrible implications of the drained lake. What scandal had this selfish girl brought to the college? She stood up, sending her rolling chair backwards.

"If it really was Miss Mellish in Holyoke," the detective cautioned. "It could have been another girl. I'll have to show the photograph around to make sure."

"Of course," Mrs. Mead replied, but she seemed suddenly preoccupied. Detective Mack thought she was talking more to herself than to him. "It would be strange," she said, "if Miss Mellish went to Holyoke. She left her watch and her purse in her room. I saw them there last night."

"May I inspect the young lady's room?" Mack phrased his demand as a question; let the woman think she still had some measure of control.

Mrs. Mead stared at him coldly. It was repulsive, the idea of this man, this police officer familiar with the lowest order of human creatures, entering the innocent sanctuary of a young girl. Did he intend to search her belongings?

"Is that necessary?" she asked. "I have seen the room myself and just told you what was pertinent in it."

The detective, with a nod of ironic politeness, returned her stare. "Nevertheless," he said.

Without a word, Mrs. Mead found her shawl and the detective retrieved his overcoat and hat. He was scrupulously careful to carry the hat in his hand as they walked down the corridor towards the door of Mary Lyon Hall, the woman outpacing him with her relentless stride.

Mrs. Mead reached the outer door first but waited for the detective to open it. She stepped into the vaulted bay of the building's porch and raised one hand to shade her eyes—it was now almost noon on a cloudless day—and for a moment did not see the men lounging against the railings of its granite stairs.

"Excuse me, ma'am," said the one closest to the top "Aren't you President Mead?"

She nodded once, tersely. "I am."

"How do you do, Mrs. Mead? I'm Earl Spencer, correspondent for the Holyoke Daily Transcript. Would you care to comment on the unfortunate situation?"

His companions–in truth, his competitors, one from the *Daily Hampshire Gazette,* the other from the *Springfield Republican,* both recently arrived at the college–hurried up the steps and stood behind their spokesman. By now, all three had pencils at the ready.

Such an encounter with the press was inevitable, Mrs. Mead knew, although she had hoped to put it off a little longer. Detective Mack was now standing by her side with his arms folded and she was grateful for his imposing presence. She would be brief and answer no questions. She spoke slowly, measuring her words.

'Thank you, gentlemen, for your interest in our situation. We have little to report, except that our missing student has not yet returned. Miss Mellish is a very bright student, well-liked by faculty and students and a favorite of the residents of her dormitory. She is a happy girl in her connection with the college and, as far as we know, has had no trouble come to her. She is, however, an adventurous young lady and often goes for long walks in the woods and fields. Beyond that, I cannot speculate. Now, I must not detain the detective any longer." She indicated Detective Mack with an elegant extension of her hand. "Please excuse us."

With perfect composure, Mrs. Mead descended the stairs, nodding to the reporters in genial farewell but ignoring their pursuit and their insistent questions. Webster was the first to recognize the futility of the situation. Better to head back, he figured, stop by the station for another chat with the captain, and get his story to press while the two fools here chased after the old woman.

He caught the next car to Holyoke, the opening lines of his soon-to-be- written article forming in his head. "*Mount Holyoke College,*" he scribbled on his pad, "*has another sensation. They are getting mighty common these days and the latest is most pathetic.*" Webster imagined the lady president reading those sentences in the evening paper and he smiled.

"The young ladies are at dinner," Mrs. Mead explained in a voice just above a whisper as they passed through the entrance hall towards the staircase. "We shouldn't find many in the corridors." She hurried the detective up to the third floor and towards Miss Mellish's room with only one distressing encounter, an unfortunate girl who had opened the door to her room just as the detective walked by and then immediately slammed it shut.

"Here we are." Mrs. Mead stopped at Bertha's door. "You see, there is the sign I described. Things are just as I left them last night."

"Good." The detective waited; it wasn't his place to enter first. After a moment of silence he cleared his throat and, as if by signal, Mrs. Mead opened the door. The cardboard swung on its black ribbon, rattling against the wood. When she closed the door behind them, Mack hung his hat on the inside knob.

He surveyed the room, approximately ten by twelve feet. One window, closed, with simple curtains of unfigured cloth, pulled open. A bookcase and a table against the right wall, a chair pushed under the table, a bed against the wall to the left of the door, a bureau against the far wall, a small washstand with a mirror in the corner. A closet door in the wall. A shaded electric light over the center of the room. The room was strikingly neat; the bed was made, the top of the bureau was bare, the bookcase was filled with parallel volumes, only one carefully aligned pile of books and papers and a few small objects were visible on the surface of the table.

"Miss Mellish is a careful housekeeper, I see."

Detective Mack was not familiar with young girls' bedrooms (his sisters were dead or grown; he had no children), but this place was not what he expected. Young ladies appreciated soft things like frilly puffs of lace on the collars and cuffs of their shirts, and there was nothing frilly here.

When Elizabeth Mead, who *was* familiar with the interior of young ladies' dormitories, had visited the room the previous night, she too was struck by its utter starkness. There were no decorative pillows, no rugs, no figurines, no souvenirs, no plants, no comfortable rocking chair, no tea set. There were no pictures on the white walls, no framed prints or illustrated calendars. And, most surprising of all, there were no photographs, nothing stuck along the edges of the mirror, no little framed images of family and friends. In all her years, Mrs. Mead had never seen anything so ascetic.

Detective Mack began a circuit of the room with Mrs. Mead following behind, his chaperone. He stopped by the side of the bed, glanced down at its covering—the only item in the room that could be defined as decorative—a woolen paisley shawl in deep burgundy and black. Old-fashioned, Mrs. Mead noted, new perhaps forty years ago.

The detective moved to the bureau and opened its uppermost drawer, which smelled strangely of apples. He gingerly poked his right forefinger around the edges of a pile of white undergarments. Mrs. Mead, her face flushed, smoothed and straightened the pile, sliding the drawer closed as soon as his hand was clear. The second drawer contained more items of clothing—a belt, some stockings, a pair of mittens, a knit hat—as well as a bar of soap, a toothbrush and canister of powder, a comb, two pencils, a small box of pen points, another of paper clips, and a stack of writing paper. The bottom drawer was empty.

They investigated the closet and found a black wool skirt, one plaid silk and two white cotton shirtwaists hanging on hooks, and a pair of black leather boots, lightly scuffed. They stopped briefly at the window where Detective Mack affirmed that the sash was closed and, in fact, locked and then they went on to the desk. As Mrs. Mead reported, a small watch lay face up on a spotless sheet of green blotting paper, along with a black leather coin purse, a pen, a bottle of ink, and a neat pile of books and papers.

The detective picked up the watch, barely bigger than a quarter in his large hand. He felt rather than heard its ticking. Nickel, not silver, he noted, and put it back on the blotting paper. He opened the purse and emptied its contents. A modest pile of coins: five nickels, seven dimes, four half-dollars. He replaced the money, snapped the purse shut.

He opened the topmost book in the pile to a page filled with unfamiliar words and cryptic formulas. What kind of girl cared about chemistry, he wondered, much less understood it? He clapped the book shut and set it aside.

The volume underneath: *Freytag's Technique of the Drama.* A quick ruffle of its pages revealed nothing. Then a sheaf of handwritten pages held together with a paper clip. Detective Mack scanned the first page, flipped through the rest with his thumb. He could feel Mrs. Mead close behind him, reading over his shoulder. Insufferable woman. Some kind of theme, he noted, and dropped it on the desk.

In the bookcase: a collection of envelopes, tied with a bit of black ribbon and wedged between two volumes on the middle shelf of the bookcase. Detective Mack pulled them out, read them one by one. He checked their closing signatures, slipped each back in its envelope. "All from her family, father or sister," he announced, handing Mrs. Mead the letters and the black ribbon.

"As I expected," she said. She retied the bundle and set it down on the bookcase.

Detective Mack led the way to the door. With his back turned, Mrs. Mead slid the paper-clipped sheaf from the desktop and rolled its pages into a compact cylinder that she carried out of the room hidden in the folds of her black silk skirt.

The telegram had arrived that morning, delivered at nine o'clock by a boy on a bicycle. John Mellish had no pressing engagements and he'd answered the knock in his dressing gown and slippers. He felt an invigorating breeze on his face when he opened the door and he made the boy wait while he gathered a few loose coins for his trouble. Telegrams had brought their share of bad news in the past, but in recent years they were more often the bearer of pleasant tidings—the announcement of a visit from a friend, or an invitation extended by a former parishioner.

Mr. John Mellish, Dayville, Connecticut. The name and address were correct, he knew, but nothing else written on the piece of paper made sense. *Regret cannot locate your daughter. Please inform if returned home. Holyoke police notified. Trust God she is safe. Elizabeth Storrs Mead, President, Mount Holyoke College.* He stood in the tiny space behind the closed door, staring at the strange lines on the page. A tremendous buzzing in his head kept the words from settling in his mind and he staggered backward against the short, squat newel post at the bottom of the stairs.

It was Sarah who took the paper from his hands, read and grasped its meaning, supported him up the stairs and dressed him, sent him through the bright November morning to Henry Hammond's house, trusting that he would find his way by instinct.

He had been carried back home in Dr. Hammond's buggy and, all through the chaos of that day, while Henry Hammond was gone to send a telegram in reply and fetch Florence from her school and Sarah packed a carpet bag for both her husband and her daughter, while father and daughter boarded the train at the Dayville depot and then sat in wordless suspense with Florence gripping her father's hand throughout the interminable ride to Holyoke, and while, wrapped in blankets against the late afternoon chill, they were driven up to South Hadley in a carriage sent by the college, he silently repeated the same incomprehensible words: Bertha is missing.

Florence was not absolutely sure how she had come to be in this place. She felt dizzy and would have raised one hand to her temple, except that President Mead and the other lady—hadn't she been introduced as a doctor?—were staring at her, kindly but intently, and Florence did not want to answer any well-meaning questions about her condition. She glanced at her father, perched stiffly on the edge of an overstuffed chair to her left. His mouth was slightly open and he seemed confused, like a schoolboy left behind in a lesson. His cane was propped against an arm of the chair and his hat lay across his lap. He had refused to relinquish the hat or, rather, he had not heard the lady's offer to take it, and now he held it tightly, one hand gripping either side of its brim. He looked very old.

The moment she met the minister and his daughter, Elizabeth Mead knew they were good and decent people. Their age did not surprise her; she had learned something of the family's history from the bound volume of measurements. Although clearly upset—both had that drawn, harried look that often accompanied great shock– they were polite, understandably but not excessively agitated, and she was grateful to them for their composure. She had taken the old minister's arm with great solicitude and helped him down the path to Porter Hall, while Miss Florence Mellish—once a Mount Holyoke student herself, in seminary days– hovered with touching concern at his other side. Daniel Hill had followed behind, carrying the two small bags that constituted their luggage, and Dr. Mary Lowell met them in the building, appropriately equipped should either father or daughter be overcome.

President Mead had ushered them into the larger of Porter Hall's two parlors, closing its sliding doors against curious stares. She settled Reverend Mellish into a comfortable armchair, indulging his eccentric desire to keep his hat, and given Miss Mellish the chair by his side. After she positioned herself and Dr. Lowell on the settee opposite, she realized in horror that she had placed the Mellishes facing the room's bay window. She was able, thankfully, to signal Mr. Hill to draw the curtains and turn on the electric lamps, sparing those poor people the spectacle of rapidly fading daylight.

Mrs. Mead sent Mr. Hill for tea and placed cups of the beverage on tables within easy reach, but neither the Reverend nor Miss Mellish had touched theirs. They had listened silently while she explained the facts of the situation; how Bertha had apparently left the campus on Thursday afternoon rather than attend the college exercises, how she had asked a friend to accompany her on a walk that afternoon, how a young lady answering to her description had been seen in Holyoke on Thursday evening yet how Bertha had left her money and her watch behind although she carried a book; how the sign on her door seemed to explain her whereabouts on Friday; how she was discovered missing on Friday night, how the Holyoke police, the college and the village were all united in searching for her but how, as yet, she had not returned, sent word, or been found.

Mrs. Mead leaned forward, resting her clasped hands on her knees. "Do you understand?" she asked with patient concern, directing the question at Miss Mellish. "May I repeat or clarify anything?"

The information had come quickly, in disjointed snippets that Florence struggled to arrange. She thought, incongruously, of a puzzle, a scattering of jumbled pieces that formed no coherent picture. Only one thing made sense: Bertha had gone for a walk. Bertha was out there now, frightened, cold, hungry, perhaps hurt. Florence stood up.

"I need a lantern," she said, turning to Mr. Hill who stood guard with his back against the closed doors. He frowned and took a step forward.

Mrs. Mead and the doctor also rose. Reverend Mellish looked anxiously from one to the other. "Where is Florence going?" he asked. He dropped his head, covered his eyes with one hand, and began to cry.

His tears brought Florence to her senses. "It's all right, Father," she said, kneeling by his chair. "I won't leave."

"Of course not," Dr. Lowell said. She sat down; Mrs. Mead remained standing.

"Mr. Mellish, Miss Mellish," the president said, fixing each with a brief but fervent look, "I promise you that we are doing all that we can to find Bertha. The trustees of the college have posted a reward. Fifty men were out today, searching from dawn until sunset, and even more will be out tomorrow morning at first light. With their dedication and God's help, I know that we will find her."

John Mellish lifted his head. "With God's help, yes," he whispered, "but what about the hours between sunset and first light?"

The clock in the entrance hall struck. No one spoke or moved while it rang six times, as if action were impossible until the ringing stopped.

Florence returned to her seat. "Mrs. Mead," she said, "There is something I don't understand."

"Yes?" Mrs. Mead tilted her head, patiently expectant.

"I don't understand how Bertha could have been gone for so long without a friend or a teacher noticing her absence." Florence shifted her focus from Mrs. Mead's face—it was harder now, her eyes a little colder—to a point below the woman's chin where the flesh of her neck met the ruff of her high collar. "If her absence had been discovered sooner," –Florence heard her voice grow shrill—"if the search had begun yesterday morning, if someone had thought to look for her on Thursday night. . . ."

"Excuse me," the president murmured, and took her place beside Dr. Lowell on the settee. Florence caught a look pass between them; poor woman, the look said, she still does not see.

"President Mead explained about the sign." Dr. Lowell said. "Perhaps you don't understand the nature and purpose of such a sign."

Mrs. Mead raised her hand, a silencing gesture. "Thank you, Dr. Lowell," she said. "Let me try to make this clear to Miss Mellish." Mrs. Mead sighed, as if regretting what she was about to say. "The search was delayed because your sister misled the college family. Your sister was not missed because she chose not to be."

One forgotten sign, one afternoon's truancy—hardly evidence of a plot to deceive. Florence, too stunned to attempt an argument with President Mead, shook her head and defended her sister with a look of wounded disbelief.

Sunday, November 21, 1897

As the train rolled into the station, Reverend Mellish retrieved his hat and cane from the adjacent seat and stood up. The slow, chugging sway of the car made it hard for him to find his balance and he rode the last few minutes hunched over, gripping the top of the seat in front of him with his cane swinging useless from his arm. He was impatient to get off, but when the train came to a stop found that he could not release his hold. He thought of the unfamiliar streets that lay before him and wished he had allowed Florence to accompany him as she had begged to do. If he collapsed on the station platform or in the street on his way to the hospital, he did not know who would come to his aid.

He began the journey feeling stronger than he had since he first read the telegram. Now he had a task to perform away from the overbearing concern of the women, the president and the doctor, even his own daughter. But the hours spent alone on the train had given him too much time to think. One moment he was convinced that he would find her where the policemen said she might be, and he anticipated their reunion with such impatience that he could barely breath; the next moment he was certain that his mission was in vain and then he had to shut his eyes and clench his jaw to keep from crying out.

The telephone call from the Boston police department reached its counterpart in Holyoke early that morning and the message was relayed to the college soon afterward. Reverend Mellish heard it from Mr. Hill, who knocked on the door of his room at the village hotel and woke him from the sleep that, despite his wish to spend the entire night in prayer, had overtaken him. A girl, Mr. Hill reported, calling herself Bertha Miller and answering to Miss Mellish's description, had been received at the emergency ward of the Boston City Hospital shortly after midnight. Mr. Hill didn't know anything more; the Holyoke police captain who had called him with the news had not mentioned the young woman's condition.

Reverend Mellish struggled to master his panic. He watched a pair of gentlemen across the aisle and a single lady a few rows ahead gather their traveling bags and their packages and make their way through the car, and then he forced himself to calculate the date. He could not have said whether an hour or a week had gone by since the arrival of the telegram, and now he realized with a shock that it was Sunday. He shook his head and felt a weight settle in his stomach, a heaviness more of spirit than of body, unexpected but somehow familiar. Since his ordination, he recalled, he had not ridden a train on Sunday, except for one terrible journey to Washington twenty-three years earlier, during his brother's sudden, final illness.

The aisle was clear, but still he could not move. He felt as if every drop of will and vitality had been wrung from his limbs, and he wanted nothing more than to sit down again and close his eyes. Perhaps if he did, he thought, and if he waited long enough, the train would turn around and carry him back, not to Holyoke and the reality of his daughter's absence, but to a time before. Not back to the day of her birth—that would be too much to ask—not even to the last time he saw her face, glimpsed through a soot-covered window as her train left the Dayville depot, but to just one minute before a boy on a bicycle knocked on his door and offered him a telegram.

"Are you all right, sir?"

The man wore a blue uniform with bright buttons and for a moment Reverend Mellish thought he had been sent by the Boston police department, an officer like the one who had talked to him just before he boarded the train in Holyoke.

"Thank goodness," he said, his voice weak with relief, before he realized his mistake. The man was a conductor, of course, not a policeman. A small mistake, perhaps, but it frightened Reverend Mellish, showed him just how confused he had become. He released his hold on the seat and straightened. "Thank you, no," he said, refusing the man's arm.

He waited for the conductor to precede him down the aisle and, supported by his cane, walked alone through the empty car. When he reached the iron steps leading down to the platform, he hesitated before descending as slowly and deliberately as a mountain-climber. He paused again before negotiating the gap between the bottom step and the platform, cautiously setting first the tip of his cane, then one foot and the other on the solid pavement.

The eight-year-old daughter of Selectman Myron H. Judd was quite certain, when shown the two photographs, which one was the young lady who had walked by her just outside the schoolhouse this past Thursday at three o'clock, and which one was not. They looked nothing alike, and Liddie was insulted that the man who was asking her all these questions thought her stupid enough to confuse one with the other.

She squirmed in her chair, one of the fancy ones in the front parlor, and almost wished that she hadn't said anything to her father that morning at breakfast. It had scared her a bit when her father put down his fork and asked her, in the voice he used when he was angry, if she was telling the truth. But of course she was; she knew as plain as anything that she had seen a young lady dressed in black, just like the one she heard her father tell her mother about right before her mother went back into the kitchen.

Her father had jumped up from the table and run into the kitchen and then out of the house as fast as could be. Her mother came back into the dining room and fussed over her, said that after church she might have to talk to an important man and made her promise to tell everything she knew and not make anything up. Then Tommy got jealous and said he saw the lady too, and threw his cup to the floor.

At first, it had been exciting to sit in the parlor with the grown-ups listening to every word she said, but now Liddie was tired. She didn't like the detective anymore, the important man her mother said she would have to talk to, who asked her the same things again and again. How did she know what time it was when she saw the young lady? Because the clock in the tall tower across the street at the college said so, and Liddie knew how to tell time. Which way was the young lady going? She was going straight ahead, right past the school into the graveyard. Did the young lady say anything? How could she, when she was walking so fast and anyway, Liddie didn't know her and she didn't know Liddie.

Liddie kicked the heel of her left boot hard against a leg of the chair and sighed. She didn't care anymore about the stupid young lady who couldn't be found.

None of the men gathered on the banks of the pond where Stony Brook emptied into the river knew much about the proper use of grappling irons, and so the responsibility fell to Mr. Lyman, the only man from the college in the group. He wrapped the chain several times around his right hand before throwing it and its three-pronged hook into the water, aiming as near as he could to the bridge, where someone recalled seeing a young woman linger sometime on Thursday afternoon. The others—Hiram Bagg, whose farm lay a quarter- mile down the road, just below the place where Stony Brook met the river, one of the older Alvord boys, and two men who had come down from Moody Corners –stood nearby with their arms folded, watching.

The water was deeper than Mr. Lyman had expected and, as the chain slipped through his fingers, he felt but could not see the iron hook's slow, relentless descent beneath its sparkling surface. He didn't want to think about what the hook might find when it reached bottom, and he made himself consider, instead, the number of turkeys he needed to prepare for the college's holiday dinner. After a while, he felt a silent thump and the chain abruptly stopped. Suddenly nervous and feeling a little sick, Mr. Lyman took a few steps away from the muddy edge of the pond and then, with both hands, drew the chain towards him.

"Did it hit bottom?" Hiram Bagg asked.

Mr. Lyman nodded. The work was harder than it looked; the submerged iron resisted, reluctant as a hooked fish. He held his breath, hoping nothing heavy would get caught in its path.

"Pull it slow," Hiram said, "drag it slow."

Mr. Lyman pulled until the grappling iron, with a few ribbons and scraps of slick brown matter attached to each of its three prongs, skidded up the bank. He threw it again and pulled, several times over until he was too tired to continue, and then Hiram Bagg tried, and then the Alvord boy, and then both men from Moody Corners, until they were all exhausted and left the pond empty-handed.

Florence kept her eyes fixed on the back of Mabel Eaton's skirt as the young lady led her through the entrance hall and up the stairs to the third floor. Mercifully, few students were there to watch their progress. By now, Florence was conscious of the whispers that heralded her approach, and she knew that the girls, their eyes wide with curiosity and pity, drew back whenever she passed by. Their reaction made her feel like the carrier of some terrible disease, as if she were spreading germs of misfortune with every breath and, without realizing it, she wore a frozen half-smile of silent apology.

She had met Miss Eaton barely two hours before when, at Mrs. Mead's request, the young lady arrived at her hotel room to escort her to dinner and serve as her afternoon's companion. Florence recognized Mabel Eaton immediately, so clear were the descriptions she remembered from Bertha's earliest letters home. In the beginning, when Florence worried that Bertha might not settle easily into Mount Holyoke, nothing had given her greater peace of mind than the thought of kind Miss Eaton as her sister's friend, her guide through the intricacies of college life with its unspoken rules (broken, however innocently, at great cost) and its girlish but cruel rivalries. Florence had found no such guide during her own first weeks at the seminary and, she realized in hindsight, had suffered from the lack.

Mabel, on the other hand, had begun the day without a picture of Florence Mellish in her imagination. Although Bertha had spoken of her sister, she never displayed a photograph or offered a description of her appearance or character. Until Mrs. Mead told her, Mabel was unaware of just how many years separated the two. "Do remember that Miss Mellish is over forty," Mrs. Mead emphasized when giving Mabel her instructions, and Mabel took those words as a warning to treat her charge with particular care.

She was a surprised then, by the woman who met her with unexpected warmth at the hotel door. Miss Mellish wasn't the severe spinster Mabel had conjured, but a youthful figure in a simple, well-cut dress. The only marks of age that Mabel noticed were a few lines etched on her forehead and around her mouth. Her slightly swollen, red-rimmed eyes, Mabel guessed, were evidence of her current ordeal. Miss Mellish bore some resemblance to her sister –Mabel saw that most clearly in the shape of the forehead and the eyes—but she had a different set to her features than Bertha. There was something pliant in the way she held her mouth, Mabel thought, a mobility of expression that Bertha didn't share.

"Here we are." Mabel stopped in front of the last door at the end of the hallway. Bertha's engaged sign still hung by its ribbon from the knob, and Mabel worried that its presence might disturb Miss Mellish. She considered removing the sign before the lady noticed it, perhaps slipping it under her belt, but she knew it was not her place to meddle. Reluctantly, she stepped aside.

Florence had been to Bertha's room once before, the previous night with her father and Mrs. Mead. After a slow and labored ascent, they hadn't stayed long. The sign, written in Bertha's familiar hand, and the empty room, harshly lit yet full of shadows, agitated her father, and afterwards the visit seemed to Florence as strange and insubstantial as a dream. Grateful as she was for Miss Eaton's concern, she now wished she were alone. She wanted to knock once on the door, just loudly enough for Bertha to hear. Florence inhaled sharply and she felt the touch of Miss Eaton's hand on her shoulder.

"Are you all right, Miss Mellish?"

Florence knew that she should open the door, but the simple movement was beyond her power. She glanced at Miss Eaton and the girl seemed to understand.

"Excuse me, please," Miss Eaton said, and when she leaned forward to turn the knob, Florence smelled lavender.

Miss Eaton pushed the door ajar and withdrew. Florence forced herself to step over the threshold and walk without stopping to the center of the room. She heard Miss Eaton enter behind her and softly close the door.

The room was more insistently vacant in the afternoon sunlight than it had been the night before, when the electric lamp left its corners dark. Florence felt a stab of disappointment as intense as it was irrational.

Mabel hung back, careful of the lady's privacy. But she noticed a slackness in her posture, a small drooping of the shoulders, and, concerned that Miss Mellish might collapse, moved quickly to her side. Miss Mellish did not seem to notice her arrival. She scanned the space around her with her forehead drawn and her mouth tight. She seemed more puzzled than distraught, and Mabel followed her gaze.

During her walk from Mrs. Mead's office to Miss Mellish's hotel, Mabel tried to recall the last time she visited Bertha in her room. At first, she was certain it had been sometime this semester, very early in the term, before Bertha turned so cool towards her. She seemed to have a firm recollection—yes, they were sitting together on the bed, examining some pretty piece of needlework—but then she realized no, they were in Mabel's room, almost a year ago, when Bertha gave her that strange handkerchief. And, suddenly, Mabel could not remember what she'd done with the handkerchief. She resolved to find it the next time she went home, bring it back to school, take it out in front of Bertha to show how much she treasured it still.

Now, as she stared at the room's empty walls and bare floor and at the sparse still life arranged on its desk, Mabel was shocked to realize that, in all the years of their acquaintance, she had made only one visit to a room occupied by Bertha, in the old seminary building on the evening of Bertha's very first day at Mount Holyoke.

"But what did Bertha do with her pictures?"

Mabel, startled, looked at Miss Mellish. "Pardon me?" she asked.

"Where are Bertha's pictures?"

Mabel struggled to understand the question. "I'm terribly sorry," she had to admit, "but I'm afraid I don't know what pictures you mean."

Miss Mellish's eyes widened. "The pictures Bertha purchased, the ones she bought to replace those lost in the fire," she said, giving each word careful emphasis.

Mabel shook her head, regretful.

Florence tried again, more urgently. "Millet's *Angelus,* and the Colosseum. Bertha purchased them at a store in Holyoke. She wrote to us about them."

Again Miss Eaton shook her head, her cheeks flushed.

"But certainly you saw them, the last time you visited Bertha?" Florence let panic sharpen her voice. She wanted to grab Miss Eaton by the arm.

Mabel caught her breath and looked away. Through the window she saw oak branches spread like dark veins against the sky. A small, unfamiliar knot of resentment tightened in her chest. There had never been a need or an opportunity to go to Bertha's room, she argued in silent defense. She saw Bertha often enough in other places. She extended hospitality to Bertha in her own room. And Bertha had never invited her. Was she expected to impose herself without an invitation?

The branches moved in sudden agitation; Mabel wished that she were outside with the cold wind on her face. She turned back to Miss Mellish. Mabel would not insult the woman with the pitiful excuses she'd just rehearsed; she would offer no explanation but the honest one–a selfish immersion in her own affairs. "I must tell you," she said, "I must confess that I haven't visited Bertha in this room."

Florence saw in Miss Eaton's eyes a look so lacking in pride or guile or vanity, so mournfully contrite, that she forgave the girl and pitied her.

"I understand," Florence said, and raised her hand to touch Miss Eaton once, lightly, on the arm. "I understand about the sign." Miss Eaton looked strangely troubled, and Florence hoped the touch had not embarrassed her.

Mabel did not like to lie, and she would have corrected the poor woman if Miss Mellish hadn't seemed so comforted by her own mistake. If she preferred to imagine Bertha solitary by choice rather than neglected by a friend, it was simple kindness to allow her that small consolation.

"Bertha is very dedicated," Mabel said. "She needs a great deal of time to study. I . . . I haven't wished to disturb her."

"Perhaps too dedicated. I see that now." Miss Mellish pressed a hand to her mouth, closed her eyes. When she opened them again, Mabel noticed a tiny drop of moisture in the corner of each one. She waited for the drops to swell and fall, but Miss Mellish blinked and they disappeared.

Miss Mellish lowered her hand. "I should have seen it earlier," she said. "You know how hard Bertha worked this summer."

Mabel nodded. Miss Mellish was confiding in her and asking for her confidence in return; she was anxious to oblige. "And I think the loss of Eva Newton was very difficult," she said. "They seemed quite close, you know."

Miss Mellish stared at her blankly. Mabel was afraid she'd touched a subject too painful to address.

"Eva Newton?" Florence struggled to remember the names and histories of the girls who populated Bertha's letters and conversation. "Don't you mean Miss Cutts?" Phebe Cutts, the amusing little girl who had been Bertha's roommate and left college to be a teacher. Bertha had liked her well enough, but hadn't seemed particularly troubled by her absence.

"Well, yes, Phebe Cutts. But I don't believe her leaving bothered Bertha as much as Eva's death. Perhaps I'm wrong."

"Eva's death?"

Florence had to sit. Every law of God and nature that gave shape and pattern to her life shifted, melted, transformed and distorted. The world in which she now existed was no longer the one she had always known. The floor beneath her sagged, as if its wooden boards had turned to rubber. Somehow, she made her way to Bertha's bed.

Miss Eaton followed. Florence sensed the girl hovering above her bowed head.

"I'm so sorry, Miss Mellish . . . I didn't mean to upset you . . . I thought . . . I thought you . . . ."

Florence raised her head and forced a smile at the girl's stricken face. "Please. Please don't apologize," she said. "I know that. . . that Eva's passing was hard for Bertha. It's just. . . I had forgotten." She spoke as if she believed every word; from that moment on, she resolved, no one else would learn what Mabel had.

Miss Eaton smiled in return and gathered her skirt as if preparing to sit down. Florence shook her head. "Would you leave me for a moment. Please."

Miss Eaton hesitated, seemed about to speak. But she released her skirt and walked slowly to the door. "I'll be waiting just outside," she said, closing it behind her.

Florence had planned to make a careful inventory of the room. She was going to open bureau drawers with their linens and toiletries as familiar to her as they were to Bertha, inspect items on the desk—the watch she'd bought for Bertha in the store in Danielson, the purse that had once been hers–, review titles printed on the spines of the books lined up like soldiers in the case by the table.

But she could not force herself to rise. She looked down and, for the first time, recognized the dark fabric beneath her. Slowly, carefully, as if her bones were made of glass, she lowered herself onto the bed. She lay on her side with her knees drawn up to her bent elbows and her cheek flat against the woolen shawl. But she felt something in the quiet room that terrified her and she sat suddenly upright, heart pounding. It was the opposite of a haunting. It was as if this room had never sheltered her sister, as if Bertha had never breathed its air, as if not a single moment of her existence had been spent within its walls. Florence knew, but would not allow herself to admit, that Bertha was gone from this place.

Rebekah West hadn't left her house since going to church the previous Sunday, and both the soft-headed nonsense preached by the young minister and the silly pride that Clara Root had taken in a new hat made her vow not to return. She had kept her word and spent all morning mending by the stove. Rebekah was surprised and gratified that she felt no guilt over her truancy and, after eating her dinner, settled into the long, peaceful hours remaining in the day. But Clara had missed her at church and, busy-body that she was, came knocking at Rebekah's door in the afternoon, early enough that darkness was still more than an hour away but late enough that the sun shone thin and cold. Clara claimed to be drawn by concern, but Rebekah knew it was curiosity and the chance to gossip that had brought her.

"Goodness, Rebekah, isn't it just terrible about that poor girl from the college?"

"What girl?" Rebekah tried, holding out little hope that rudeness would drive her visitor away. Somehow, Clara had managed to make her way from the front door to the kitchen table and help herself to a cold biscuit that Rebekah had been saving for supper.

Clara swallowed and coughed daintily, but her hostess offered no beverage. She coughed again in deliberate reproach. "Goodness, Rebekah, you don't mean to say you haven't heard?" Clara cocked her head. "The girl that's gone missing—you didn't know? You poor dear, I guess your infirmities have kept you house-bound."

Rebekah stood tight-lipped in the middle of the kitchen, hands on hips, glaring at her guest. Clara, unfazed, smiled pityingly up at her and, for all her annoyance, Rebekah could not help but admire the woman's effrontery.

"Well, Rebekah, it's quite the topic. The town's in an uproar and I can only imagine the excitement and tears at the college." Clara stopped and surveyed the kitchen, sparse and shabby as its owner.

"Rebekah, dear, would you be so good as to give me drop or two of water. Even a little cider. Maybe tea, if it's no trouble."

Rebekah heaved a deep, exasperated sigh. She limped dramatically to a small sideboard, where she poured water from a pitcher into a glass that she had used at dinner and not washed. She returned just as painfully to the table and thrust the glass at Clara. "Here," she said.

"Thank you, my dear. Sorry to trouble you." Clara accepted the water and, without drinking, placed it on the table. "Anyway, she went missing on Thursday, but nobody knew she was gone until. . . until, let's see, until Friday night, I think. The last anyone saw of her was on Thursday afternoon. They say Liddie Judd saw her at three o'clock on Thursday, walking very fast by the school. They say that she was heading towards the cemetery. And then someone saw. . ."

Clara's lips moved, but Rebekah no longer listened to her words. It was just about three o'clock last Thursday, she realized, that she'd stood idling by her kitchen window, waiting for the kettle to boil. It wasn't like her to moon about, watching a pair of blue jays swoop from tree to tree, pecking and squawking at each other like an old married couple, but she wasn't feeling quite herself that day. Although the shooting pain in her left knee was barely tolerable, she'd used up the last of her Positive Rheumatic Cure and, with no money to spare for a new bottle, was forced to doctor herself with a foul-tasting cup of vinegar and honey tea. Her knee throbbed as the blue jays made one final lunge and then, in perfect tandem, flew straight towards the scrubby field that lay just beyond the oak tree marking the edge of her property.

Clara watched Rebekah's face carefully, but saw no sign of interest. She'd never known such a stubborn creature as Rebekah West, nasty as an old mule. Why she even bothered with her, Clara couldn't say. At that moment, she made up her mind. The way she was being treated today, this was the last she'd ever darken the woman's door. Clara stood up. "I'm sorry to have troubled you, Rebekah," she said in her iciest tone of impeccable politeness.

Rebekah did not say good-bye or follow Clara to the front door. She remained standing in the middle of the kitchen, staring out the window as she had on Thursday afternoon when she watched the blue jays fly away and when, just before she turned to take the whistling kettle from the stove, she caught sight of a small, dark figure, bent over in the sandy patch beyond the boundaries of her land and below the far end of the cemetery where old John Preston was buried. This was not the first visitor to that unpromising piece of ground that Rebekah had noticed over the years, and she herself had hobbled out there occasionally, looking for a serviceable button. She had seen the figure—a female from what she could tell of its shape—move slowly and methodically over the ground, like a plow horse, Rebekah thought, and at the time she had imagined the woman's fingers scraping, digging, turning up the dirt, searching in the sand for a few buttons to finish off a new dress.

Rebekah walked stiffly to the chair that Clara had occupied and eased herself into it. She took a sip from the untouched glass and snorted. No connection at all, she said to herself. Still, she felt a momentary sense of responsibility, a twinge of civic duty that irritated her. She flicked her hand dismissively. No business of mine, she thought. Rebekah smiled grimly, her resolve complete. She wouldn't give Clara Root the satisfaction.

The beds were lined up in two parallel rows facing each other across a wide center aisle, each bed separated from its neighbor by a tall window. The light, pouring onto the polished oak floor and onto the white sheets and the starched white aprons and caps of the nurses, made his eyes swim, and Reverend Mellish was forced to stop just inside the doorway to close them. He would have apologized to the nurse acting as his guide and asked her to wait, but could not find his voice. Helpless, he heard her efficient footsteps continue on ahead.

When he reopened his eyes and blinked hard against the light, he saw the nurse, her arms folded against her chest, standing at the foot of a bed halfway down the left-hand row. He could just discern the outline of a body lying motionless beneath its bedclothes, and for one awful moment he thought himself on the threshold of a morgue. But the restless stirrings of a patient a few feet to his right distracted and reassured him, and he began to make his way towards the stony-faced nurse.

The closer he drew, the more convinced he was that the figure in the bed could not be Bertha. He could assemble no congruence of events, could imagine no possible path that would have led her from the sheltered hallways of Mount Holyoke College to this place that smelled of antiseptic and echoed with the coughs and groans of the sick. Even so, by the time he reached the foot of the bed, the sound of his own heartbeat throbbed in his head and his legs were weak as water.

"She's asleep," the nurse observed. "It's the laudanum."

Although her words were muffled, as if spoken through a thickness of cotton, Reverend Mellish acknowledged them with a grave nod and slipped into the narrow space beside the bed. He crept towards its head with no desire but to see the girl's face, determine if she was his own dear Bertha or someone else's unfortunate daughter and, if she were, to leave her side without having shared a look or a word. The fact that she lay in a laudanum stupor seemed to him no guarantee against her waking up, and he was desperate to keep his cane from knocking against the bed's iron frame.

The girl was on her side, her face obscured by a tangle of dark brown hair. The hair was unbrushed and looked unclean, shiny as if slick with oil or sweat, and it glowed with a hint of copper. Bertha's hair sometimes shone like that, Reverend Mellish remembered, when caught in the direct light of the sun. He stood for a moment, resting both hands and all his weight on the curved head of his cane, and he noticed that beneath the sheet and a thin gray blanket, the girl's knees were drawn up to her chest. Since neither arm was visible, he imagined that her hands lay palm to palm beneath her head, as a child's might. As Bertha's had, one night when she was three and, careful not to awaken Florence, he had tiptoed to the little girl's bedside to watch her sleep by the light of a waning moon, so full of pride and gratitude that he shed silent tears.

Still leaning on his cane, he raised one hand, his index finger crooked and trembling. With it, he lifted a tissue of matted hair to reveal the girl's eye and cheek. Both lids were swollen, their translucent skin stretched taut as a balloon. The flesh on the bone below the eye was split and had been hastily sewn. The girl's upper lid was striated from red to purple to black; her lower lid was uniformly dark, as if covered with soot. Reverend Mellish felt the same involuntary disgust as when, on occasional woodland walks, he had dislodged a rock from the forest floor and sent fat beetles and centipedes scurrying in the unexpected light.

Before he could draw back, the girl's lids suddenly parted, revealing a sliver of white that glistened blank and cold against the bruised flesh. He thought of the flattened bodies of dead fish, lined up neatly on beds of ice in the shop on Danielson's Main Street, and he could not suppress a short, barely audible gasp.

"Well?" asked the nurse as sympathetically as she could manage. The old man was taking his time, and she had other duties to perform. He looked a little shaky, though, and she wondered if she had a vial of ammonium carbonate close at hand.

She watched as the old man withdrew his hand and let the dark tangle of hair fall back to cover the girl's face. He turned, his lips a grim line, and slowly shook his head in belated answer to her question. He took several halting steps forward and she left her post to meet him, ready to take his arm and help him to a chair. But he suddenly stopped and pivoted, retracing his path until he stood once again beside the patient. The nurse watched in surprise as he leaned forward, brushed the hair from the girl's eye and, gentle as a father, kissed her ragged cheek.

For comfort's sake, Mrs. Mead changed into her nightclothes before sitting down at the desk in her private study. It was past ten–in normal times she would have been asleep—and she would have read the essay earlier had she been allowed a single minute to herself the entire day. Every time she escaped to her office and shut the door, every time she settled in her chair and tried to take just one breath, someone—Miss Cowles, Mr. Hill, Miss Bradford, Doctor Lowell, Detective Mack, one distraught teacher after another—knocked on her door to deliver some urgent telephone message, to ask some impossible question or to report on the fruitless outcome of yet another clue. And in the evening there was poor Mr. Mellish, come back so distraught from his ill-advised trip to Boston, and all the arrangements to be made for his journey home.

At first, the tightly rolled pages would not stay unfurled, and she bent and twisted their edges until they yielded and lay approximately flat on the surface of her desk. She read them quickly by the light of a small lamp and when she was done she frowned and removed her eyeglasses.

If the world were as it should be, no unmarried minister's daughter would be aware of the things described in this strange story and if, somehow, she learned of their existence, she would not admit to that knowledge. But Mrs. Mead knew that the world was not perfect. She knew that young ladies–even a minister's daughter at a fine Christian college—could not always escape the ever-present onslaught of damaging influences. Bertha Mellish, in all innocence, could have come across such things in any number of places, in newspaper articles or modern novels, and then mimicked their content without truly understanding it. Mrs. Mead sighed and raised her head. Perhaps she should acquit Bertha Mellish, absolve her of willful prurience.

But no, she realized, she could not. She was too irritated—in truth, angry– at the girl's lack of consideration for the college and its reputation. That Miss Mellish felt free to express the figments of her overstimulated imagination in a class assignment, Mrs. Mead could not fathom. That Miss Mellish had written such a piece of sordid fiction only to wander off, leaving it in plain sight, waiting to be discovered, she could not forgive.

And there had to be a point, Mrs. Mead knew, there had to be a purpose in it. She stared at the pages, curled again into a loose cylinder, until, with a clarity of perception that sent her upright in her chair, she realized just how shrewdly staged, just how appallingly calculated, was the girl's disappearance. Her vulgar little story with its suggestive details and sacrilegious prattle ending in suicide–that tragic death so appealing to the self-pitying and undisciplined hearts of silly young women–was a ruse, a red herring, a clever bit of subterfuge.

Miss Bertha Mellish must be far away by now, perhaps sauntering down the crowded sidewalks of New York with whatever male companion had conspired in this deception, perhaps in Chicago, perhaps in Canada, perhaps on a boat to Europe, secure in the knowledge that she would not be followed, that people in their literal-mindedness would draw the only possible conclusion from her story: Bertha Mellish had flung herself into the river. Perhaps she was laughing to think of the fuss she'd left in her wake. Mrs. Mead could only hope that, even through her laughter, Bertha would begin to suffer the remorse she would inevitably have to endure for the pain she was causing her family, the embarrassment she was bringing to the college, and, above all, for the sins she was committing before God and man.

Mrs. Mead stood up, shaking with indignation, prepared to dress and summon Detective Mack from Holyoke, no matter how late the hour. But by the time she had walked to her bedroom, using her desk lamp to light the way, shed her nightgown and stood shivering in the dimly lit room, struggling to fasten her corset, she was no longer quite as angry, and she began to doubt what had seemed so logical and certain only minutes before. She admitted that she might have been a little hasty and uncharitable. She felt, had she cared to put a name to her discomfort, ashamed. Calm yourself, Elizabeth, she scolded. She's just a girl, showing off, playing with dangerous notions she doesn't understand.

Mrs. Mead slipped the nightgown back over her head and returned her corset to its bureau drawer. Despite the chill that raised the hair on her arms and legs, she moved with a deliberate dignity meant to compensate for her earlier show of temper. She lowered the wick in the lamp she had left on the night table and got into bed in absolute darkness, any glimmer of moonlight trapped behind heavy drapes. She pulled the sheet and coverlet up to her chin and lay beneath the bedclothes with her arms crossed tightly over her chest. She was desperately tired and began to drift. But in the first instant of sleep, a sound she could not identify woke her. She could describe it only as a thump, a thud, something heavy fallen, something dropped.

She lay on her back with her eyes open and, in the darkness, a terrible notion took root in her mind, a notion she had refused to give voice to before: perhaps the story was, after all, the pitiful last testament of an unhappy girl. But then she told herself that Bertha's story was just that—a fabrication, a fantasy, irrelevant to the girl's fate, no more indicative of her state of mind or her current whereabouts than if she had left a set of mathematical problems or chemical formulae sitting on her desk.

But she thanked God that Detective Mack had overlooked the essay in his search for clues, and that she'd had the foresight to secure it and keep it safe from public scrutiny. Whatever Bertha Mellish hoped to communicate through her story, Mrs. Mead was grateful that Providence had seen fit to make her guardian of that communication, to keep secret or to expose as the Lord guided her. With that comfort, she closed her eyes and drew the covers over her head.

Monday, November 22, 1897

"How long will you be away?"

Emma Hammond sat in the upholstered armchair by the side of their bed, watching Henry put the last of his clean shirts into a traveling bag. She tried not to sound accusatory, but found it hard to disguise her annoyance. Why on earth should Bertha Mellish's misadventures disturb their domestic peace, especially at this time of year? It was, she knew, a dreadful situation and she did not wish to be uncharitable. Henry's sense of duty was admirable and manly and he spoke so well about the obligations of friendship. But what about the obligations of family?

Emma almost said those words aloud, catching herself just before they passed her lips. She drummed the fingers of one hand against the knuckles of the other as they lay in her lap, delicately pink against the white lace of her dressing gown. What was that unpleasant young woman to Henry anyway? She was sorry if the search for his daughter had proved too much for Mr. Mellish, but didn't he or his wife have a relative who could more appropriately assume that responsibility? She tried to calm herself. It was her duty, she knew, to support her husband's worthy causes without complaint. If only he didn't have so many of them, she sighed, and forced her fingers to lie still.

"You know I can't say, Emma," she heard Henry answer, catching a note of exasperation in his voice. "I'll only be gone as long as necessary. You know that, my dear."

"But you must be back by Thanksgiving." Emma softened her voice and leaned forward. "Promise me, Henry, that you'll be home by Thanksgiving." This would be her first marking of the day as an orphan; he must realize that. Her eyes were moist and she blinked twice, sorry that he didn't see her struggle against tears.

Henry snapped the bag shut and sat down on the bed facing his wife, so close that their knees touched. He took both of her hands in his. Emma sensed victory but took care not to show it.

"I can't promise, Emma, but I will do my best," he said, and her first impulse was to snatch her hands away. But she resisted, signaling her irritation in one small twitch that Henry didn't seem to notice. "You do understand," he was saying, "the obligation I feel to the Mellishes—the long ties of friendship between my father and Reverend Mellish. And if all goes well, both Bertha and I will be home by Thanksgiving." He released her hands, stood up. "Now give me your blessing and see me to the door."

Emma forced a wan smile and followed her husband out of the room and down the stairs, the hem of her dressing gown gliding noiselessly over the carpet. She stood on the bottom step and watched as Henry took his overcoat from the hall tree and put it on without his typical attention to the smoothness of its lapels or the lay of its collar. He buttoned the coat, placed his hat without a glance at the mirror. Emma stepped down from her perch, lifted a woolen scarf from a hook on the tree and brought it to him.

"Wear this and think of me," she said, wrapping the scarf around his neck.

He kissed her forehead, just below the short fringe of curls that framed her face.

"Look in on Mr. and Mrs. Mellish while I'm away, will you, dear?" he asked. "Reverend Deans has been attentive, and so have Mrs. Darling and Mrs. Cogswell, but I'll feel better knowing that they're in your care as well."

Emma nodded gravely as he spoke, but her thoughts had wandered. Why not go directly to her sister's? Why wait here, rattling around the house with no idea when Henry would return? If he could not promise her Thanksgiving, he could not begrudge her that.

"Of course," Emma murmured and raised herself on her slippered toes to kiss Henry's cheek. His whiskers tickled her nose and she would have pretended to sneeze if the moment hadn't been so solemn. Emma waved farewell at the open door, then headed to the kitchen to find Bessie. As soon as the breakfast dishes were cleared and washed, she informed the girl, it would be time to pack madam's things.

Earl Webster had knocked twice already, waiting a decent interval between attempts. Still, he wasn't ready to give up. Someone had to be inside; it was inconceivable that the mother would be in any condition to go out and, thanks to a tip from his good friend Captain Murphy, he knew that the father, after suffering a fit at the college last night, had come home on a morning train. Some idler at the Dayville depot, the second or third that Webster had asked, remembered seeing the old minister get out of a car and into a carriage a few hours earlier, although the man hadn't checked his watch and couldn't vouch for the time.

Webster faced the door, picking absently at a blister of yellowed paint on its surface; a few tiny shards fluttered to the top of the wooden stoop. The place wasn't particularly down at heel—he'd seen worse—but it had a worn and tired air. You could tell old people lived there, he thought, and he wondered if it smelled anything like his grandmother's house, like rose sachets and the paper in old books. In his article, Webster decided, he would describe the Mellish house as a trim and cozy cottage, and he would have made a note of the phrase if it weren't too much trouble to pull out his pad.

He knocked again, took off his hat and pressed his ear to the door. No approaching footsteps or the faint shuffle of someone escaping further into the house. Hat back in place, he peered through one of the narrow sidelights that flanked the door. Even with his hands cupped around his eyes, all he could make out in the dim interior was a short, shadowy hallway and the silhouette of a newel post.

Maybe he'd been wrong, wasting his time shivering on the front stoop of this sorry little house. Maybe the old couple was somewhere else, keeping vigil in the home of a relative or friend. Webster turned to face the road, hoping that someone, anyone, man, woman, or child, would happen by. He crossed his arms, pressed them to his chest and hunched his shoulders, letting out a long breath into the chilly air. It wasn't raining here like it was when he left Holyoke, but he could tell from the heavy sky that rain was coming. He watched the vapor rise from his mouth and thought how good a cigarette would feel right then, warming him from the inside, and how sorry he was that he'd smoked his last one on the train.

"Who are you? What is it you want?"

The unexpected voice was female, hard and cold. The woman standing just inside the threshold of the open door was older than she sounded. Possibly the mother, he couldn't be sure. Webster imagined the mother overcome by grief; this woman stood straight as a rod with her arms folded tight across the bodice of her black dress, staring at him fiercely.

"Excuse me, ma'am," he said, fumbling in his pocket for a card. "I'm Earl Webster, correspondent for the *Holyoke Daily Transcript.*" He stepped forward with the card in his outstretched hand.

"We have no use for reporters," the old woman snapped. She uncrossed her arms and Webster knew he had precious little time before the door closed in his face.

"Please ma'am, I don't mean to trouble you. I'm here to help." He spoke quickly, with special emphasis on the last word.

She tilted her head and looked at him suspiciously. "To help?"

"Yes. I believe I can help."

Webster waited, but the woman didn't speak. She stood at the open door while the wind played with her skirt and sent a few wisps of hair across her face. He noticed the fine bones visible beneath her wrinkled skin and it crossed his mind that she might once have had some claim to beauty. Now a series of small spasms contracted her forehead and her mouth, and Webster realized she was trying not to cry.

"Do you know something about our daughter?" she asked.

For a moment, Webster considered answering with an outright lie, anything to get into the house. But, somehow, he lost his nerve. "Well, not exactly, Mrs. Mellish," he admitted, "But I . . . ."

"Then you have no business here."

The door slammed and Webster stood with his mouth open, astonished that he had come so far only to lose the game. He considered knocking again, more insistently than before; he considered grabbing the doorknob and letting himself in. But, given the old woman's mulishness, he figured an exploratory stroll through the village might prove more useful.

Webster started down the steps, stuffing the card back into his pocket. *The missing girl's elderly mother herself came to door,* he would write, *courageously struggling to hide her tears. She regretted that the family was too distressed to discuss the sad situation.*

He stopped at the edge of the road and pulled the collar of his coat tight around his neck. He was feeling bolder again and ashamed of his easy surrender; what would the city editor say if he went back to Holyoke empty-handed? Webster glanced over his shoulder, contemplating one last assault, and when he saw an old man standing at the open door, he congratulated himself on his persistence. A lesser journalist would have missed this opportunity.

Webster ran up the steps. "Mr. Mellish?" he asked, dipping his head. "I'm Earl Webster, correspondent for the *Holyoke Daily Transcript.*" He retrieved the business card that Mrs. Mellish had rejected and offered it to her husband.

Mr. Mellish held the card up to his eyes. Webster expected him to ask a question or demand an explanation, but the old man just stood there with the card in one hand and his cane in the other, vaguely startled, Webster thought, like someone used to darkness when the lights go on. He didn't look much like a minister; Webster could not imagine him in a pulpit, commanding attention.

"May I ask you and your wife a few questions, Mr. Mellish?" Webster enunciated every word as if the man were a foreigner or deaf. "I hope to write an article for my newspaper and bring the search for your daughter to a wider public."

Mr. Mellish gave no sign that he understood, but a movement in the dark hallway behind him caught the reporter's eye. Mrs. Mellish was there, listening. Webster raised his voice.

"There are many people out there, Mr. Mellish, whose hearts bleed for you and your family in your time of trouble." Webster had rehearsed this speech on the train to Dayville and he was pleased with his delivery, sincere but not unctuous. "They are very anxious to help you find your daughter, but they can only help if they know who they're searching for. The more you can tell them about Bertha, about her habits, what she looks like—with a photograph perhaps—the sooner someone will recognize her. And the sooner she is recognized, the sooner she'll be found. The sooner she'll come home." Webster held his breath; he could only hope Mr. Mellish was more lucid than he seemed and had some influence over his wife.

"It's cold, John," Mrs. Mellish said from the shadows. "Come in and shut the door."

The old man looked at Webster, as if suddenly aware of his presence. "Perhaps you're right," he murmured and, with a vague motion of his hand, invited the reporter in.

The house did not smell of roses and old paper, but of something moister, perhaps a hint of rotting wood, a tang of mildew. With the old man following, and Mrs. Mellish glaring from the end of the short hallway, Webster took the only path he could, passing to the right of the staircase and then turning sharply into what had to be the family's parlor. He stopped just inside its threshold, waiting for directions from the couple whose silent presence he felt behind his back.

The space was small—no surprise there, given the cramped entranceway and hall—but it wasn't stuffed with furniture and bric-a-brac the way his grandmother's parlor had been, where every horizontal surface supported vases and clocks, figurines of blushing ladies with piled-up hair and gallant little men bowing from the waist, arrangements of artificial flowers fading under glass–a widow's treasures.

The room's single window was covered by a half-drawn shade and the lamp on its central table was unlit. Still, Webster could see well enough to scan the pictures on the walls, neatly hung in sober wooden frames. Some were buildings, of that he was sure; others had figures, doing what he could not tell; two or three seemed to be single heads, probably portraits, maybe photographs. Perhaps Bertha was among them.

"Sit down. Please."

Webster turned to see Mrs. Mellish pointing towards a straight-backed chair near the table. How much effort, he wondered, had this grudging show of good manners cost her.

In a few steps he reached his assigned place and laid his hat and gloves on the polished tabletop. Better keep the coat on, he decided. If there was a fire in the parlor stove, he couldn't feel its heat.

The old couple settled themselves some five feet opposite, in a pair of armchairs flanking the ineffectual stove. They looked like ghosts in the dimness, soft around the edges and very pale.

"I can offer you no refreshment," Mrs. Mellish said.

She seemed less formidable now, almost harmless, a small gray figure encased in faded plush. "Of course not," Webster said. "I wouldn't presume to trouble you."

Under the old couple's silent scrutiny, Webster took his pencil and notepad from the inside pocket of his overcoat and held them in lap, as far under the table's edge as he could; experience taught him that note-taking distracted his subjects. He cleared his throat twice, a musician tuning up.

"Mr. and Mrs. Mellish," he said, "I am truly sorry if any of the questions I am about to ask cause you distress. I assure you that is not my wish, and it is not my intention to pry. I ask these questions only because I must."

Webster paused, expecting at least one of the pair to say something, show some appreciation. Not every one of his colleagues was so polite. But the old man just hunkered in his chair while the old woman glared at him.

Webster forgave them. "Mr. and Mrs. Mellish," he said, looking from one to the other, "clearly your daughter is a fine young lady, a fine scholar. And would you also say that she is comfortable at Mount Holyoke College?"

Mr. Mellish turned his head and craned it forward. Again, Webster thought of a deaf man. "Is Bertha comfortable?" the old man repeated.

"Yes, sir. That's my question. Is your daughter comfortable, is she doing well at the college?"

Still, the old man looked confused.

"What I mean to say, sir, is Bertha happy there?"

In the silence that followed, Webster could hear a clatter of icy raindrops on the roof above their heads. He imagined a slick skin forming on roads and railroad tracks and began to worry about his journey home.

For a moment, John Mellish forgot who the young man was, how he had come to be sitting in their parlor and why he was asking nonsensical questions whose answers were as self-evident as the unalterable facts of nature. The strange young man might as well ask if the sun was hot or the sky blue as to ask if Bertha was happy at college—the old minister would have looked at him with the same incredulity. Why would this person—who was he again?— ask such a thing, when all those letters, tied in neat packets and lying safe in the recesses of his desk, offered incontrovertible proof of Bertha's happiness.

"Of course Bertha was happy," John Mellish said.

But the young man didn't seem to believe him; John recognized doubt in the narrowing of his eyes.

"So then, Mr. Mellish, there was no indication, no sign at all that your daughter was not settled at school, that she was not. . . not friendly with her fellow students?"

The young man's words made no sense; they hurt his head. It was beyond him to answer. John turned to his wife.

"Of course not," she said. "How could there be such an indication? Our daughter was happy at school, just as she was happy at home, among her friends and her family."

Webster was tired of this game and his fingers were cold. The father was useless; he'd have to fight it out with the mother. "But I have been privy to confidential information," he said, meeting the woman's eyes, "evidence that suggests in recent weeks your daughter kept herself aloof from her fellow students. Evidence that suggests unhappiness on her part."

The old woman's response was swift and unflinching. "If our daughter did indeed keep aloof in any way, it was to concentrate on her studies and avoid idle distractions." She paused and lifted her chin. "As a journalist," she said, giving the word an unpleasant emphasis, "I am surprised to hear you traffic in such gossip."

"So you are saying, then, that your daughter left the college, that she left her friends, that she refused to participate in an important college ceremony, in order to take a respite from her studies?"

There might as well be bullets shooting from the old woman's eyes. "My daughter took a short walk, for exercise and recreation."

"Nothing more?"

She didn't answer. Get her good and mad, Webster decided, and see what comes of it.

"But how can you be sure. Couldn't there be a special friend," –he raised his eyebrows and cocked his head, flamboyantly rude—"a gentleman perhaps. . . ?"

She strained forward in her chair, ready to spring. "An elopement?" She spat the word. "Is that what you mean?"

Webster shrugged.

"Such a thing is inconceivable. It is an insult to our daughter, and anyone who knows her would never. . . ." The old woman broke off, pulled a crumpled handkerchief from her sleeve and held it to her mouth, breathing heavily.

Webster thought he might have gone too far; he considered apologizing.

"Bertha would never leave us like that."

Webster hadn't expected to hear anything more from the old man. Startled, he turned to face him.

"Bertha would never leave us," Mr. Mellish said. "She would never choose to leave us."

There was no hint of reproach in the old man's words, no sense that he was deflecting a challenge, or defending a position, just a calm certainty so complete, Webster realized, that nothing–no argument, no evidence, no proof plain as day or hard as nails–could ever shake it.

"I'm sorry," Webster said, "I never meant to suggest."

It was now so dark Webster could barely make out the old man's face. The effect was otherworldly, as if he were trapped in the murky waters of some cold lake, and a knot of panic tightened in his chest.

He rose, took a match safe from his pocket. With the old couple watching as if it were a magic trick, Webster lit the lamp on the table beside him. The glow of lamplight seemed to warm him and, buoyed, he decided to mend fences with the old woman.

Seated again, he gave her a contrite, sheepish look. "I'm sorry, Mrs. Mellish, I had no right to suggest such a thing in connection with your daughter."

No forgiveness in her glare, but, at least, no bullets.

Webster cleared his throat. The next question was the big one, the hard one. Better give it first to the father.

"I'm sorry, but I must ask you, Mr. Mellish. Do you have a theory, do you have any explanation that could account for your daughter's disappearance?"

The old man shook his head.

"Mrs. Mellish?"

She sat upright in her chair with her eyes closed and gave no sign that she had heard.

"Mrs. Mellish?" he repeated.

She opened her eyes and stared at him for a moment before speaking.

"I told you before. Bertha . . . our daughter went for a walk."

"Yes?" Webster kept his voice low, soft.

"There was an accident." Her voice was quiet too, almost a whisper.

Webster shook his head, the way people do to express the inexpressible, to acknowledge the terrible vagaries of fate, the tragic unpredictability of life.

"What sort of accident?" he asked.

The old woman covered her mouth with the crumpled handkerchief.

"What sort of accident?" Webster repeated gently.

He heard the rain's muffled hiss. It must be coming down harder now.

"Do you believe she is lost in the woods?"

Webster looked from one to the other. The father's head was down; the mother still held the handkerchief to her mouth.

"Did she walk along the river's edge?"

Again, no answer.

"Could she have met with foul play?" This last, so softly he wasn't sure they heard.

None of his police contacts had mentioned a crime, but why not? Young girls shouldn't go wandering off by themselves.

"Do you think she might have met a stranger in the woods?"

Webster no longer expected an answer. He rested his pencil on the notepad in his lap and listened to the old couple's stifled weeping. He felt a little guilty now, as if it were his fault they cried. Another minute or two and he would leave, just slip away.

Suddenly, the old man spoke. "You see," he said, "we thought so very much of Bertha. She was our hope and our pride."

The old man's beard and hair shone in the lamplight and for the first time Webster could imagine him a preacher.

"Pride is a terrible sin. That is a truth we must never forget."

"Yes," Webster said.

"God is just, and He punishes us for our sins."

The old man's eyes had the look of unshakable certainty that Webster noticed earlier, but now it seemed brighter, more sharply honed and finely tempered. "We have brought this tragedy upon ourselves," he said, "And I most of all."

Observed by neither her husband nor the young reporter, Sarah smiled. It was a wrenching grimace that came not from joy or pleasure, but from the bitter satisfaction of witnessing one's most terrible prophecy come to pass. She had been waiting years for this moment, not in happy anticipation, but with a dread so overwhelming that, on certain days, heavy as a rock on her chest, it had kept her in her bed. The dread began the moment that her younger daughter, so unexpected and so unearned a gift from God, came into this world. Sarah had understood, long before her gentle, trusting husband, just how conditional was that gift, and she had always suspected, as he had not, that Bertha was never theirs to keep.

"But why have you just now come forward with this information?"

The detective, the bigger of the two men standing over him, barked the question and Rufus, seated in one of the two chairs that furnished his dark, cramped cottage—more a cabin, really—flinched as if expecting a blow.

Rufus Hinckley, despite his protruding ears and a mouth that hung slightly open, was not as stupid as most people thought him to be, although it took him longer than most to figure out what words to use and in what order to use them. The two strangers stood not four feet away, watching him in the dimly lit room like cats ready to pounce, and he looked down at his hands, each one clutching a knee through the worn fabric of his trousers.

"Weren't back til now."

Rufus glanced at the short man with the whiskers before returning to the study of his hands. The bigger man scared him, made him think of a long-ago schoolmaster who had been too free with the cane, but the small one did not seem riled up.

The detective made a noise, some kind of grunt as far as Rufus could tell, but it was the whiskered man who spoke. "So, you were away, Mr. Hinckley, if I understand correctly."

Rufus, usually given to slow and careful movement, deliberate as an ox, looked up quickly. He was startled by the man's tone, natural and easy, just like one person talking to another.

"Yup," he said, hoping that would be enough, but the whiskered man, and the detective too, stared at him as if it was still his turn to talk. "My brother were poorly." The kindly man had a little smile on his face and bobbed his head up and down, clearly wanting more. "Went to set with him." Rufus had a moment of clarity. "But he ain't dying, so I come back," he explained.

"Yes, well, that's all fine." The detective took a step forward, jostling the whiskered man with his elbow. Rufus stiffened, but the victim of the insult seemed to pay it no mind. "So, you saw a young lady walking up the road towards Mount Holyoke near the Pass, you say, this past Thursday afternoon. And you're certain of the day?"

Rufus *was* certain of the day, no matter if this man believed him or not. Cousin Alma brought news of his brother along with the usual bread and pie she left with him every Wednesday, but his horse was lame and he had to wait until she was fit to walk again. And that, he knew, was not until late on Thursday afternoon, so close to sunset that he stowed an extra lantern to light him over the Notch.

"Yup." Rufus slid his chair back an inch or two. The extra distance gave him room to breathe, and he looked right up at the detective's face.

"And the time, you're also certain of the time?"

"It were near dark."

"A specific time, do you have a specific time?"

Rufus bit his lip. He had no clock in his house, never had need of a clock to tell him when it was time to get up, or milk, or eat his dinner. And he hadn't carried a watch in years, not since he lost the one handed down to him by his father.

The whiskered man stepped forward and put his hand on the policeman's arm. "If I may," he said. The detective shrugged and made another of his grunts.

"Mr. Hinckley," the kind man said, and Rufus felt better. "How long was it after you saw the girl that the sun set? Could you estimate, could you guess how many minutes it was after you saw her that it grew dark?"

Well, he saw the girl pass by heading north just as he turned south off the dirt path that led from his house to the main road. He was on his horse and she was on foot, but they had shared a glance, both startled and both anxious to look away. Now that he put his mind to the recollection, he had found it a little strange at the time, a lone girl walking so near to sunset, so far away from the village, so close to the

Pass that skirted Titan's Pier, but his thoughts were on his brother and on poor Betty's leg and he did not ponder the meeting for long. But now, as he reflected, he did remember stopping to light a lantern in Moody Corners, a mile or so down the road from where he had seen the girl. At Betty's plodding pace, that mile must have taken a quarter-hour or thereabouts to travel.

"A quarter-hour or such," he said.

"About four-fifteen, then," the detective said. "Sunset is near four-thirty. You must have seen her about four-fifteen."

Rufus nodded. If the man said he saw the girl at four-fifteen, then it must be so.

"And is this the young lady?"

Rufus took the photograph from the detective's hand and squinted as he studied it. The girl in the picture wore a white shirt with a frilly neck and looked young and sweet, like a round-faced angel. The girl he met on the road could have been her twin, although she was dressed in black, with a round black hat on her head. No, Rufus reconsidered as he remembered the pale face beneath that hat, she could have been this girl's ghost.

"Yup, that's her," Rufus said, and gave the detective back his picture.

Tuesday, November 23, 1897

Yesterday's rain and last night's bitter cold left the road's rutted surface slick and hard as iron. The men moved slowly along its path, hunched over and careful of where they stepped. Except for some sharp and fragile peaks, the ground did not yield under their boots, which left no tracks of their own. The Alvord boy saw it first, what looked to be the mark of a foot too small to be a man's, pressed into the road at the point where the fence ended and the land opened to the river.

The impression was shallow and indistinct, and anyone not deliberately looking for such things, anyone not aware of just how significant a small disturbance in nature's order could be–a broken branch, a ruffled patch of leaf cover, a stone rolled from its bed, an indentation in the dirt—would never have noticed it. But the Alvord boy was an expert by now, a veteran of three solid days of combing woods and dragging ponds, and, even early on a frigid morning, he attacked his charge with a single-mindedness that most of the older men, tired and anxious to get back to farms and families, could no longer match.

He dropped to one knee and touched the curved outline of the boot's toe and then the small square depression where its heel had struck the ground. His hand shook with excitement. The very path of the missing girl, he thought, this must be it. He forgot the seriousness of purpose that had led him this place and felt a flush of giddy pride. I found it, he exulted, *I* found it.

"Over here!" he shouted and waved his hands above his head. "Over here!" Satisfied that the other men were on their way, he looked again at the footprint, frozen as if for eternity in the dark brown soil, and then raised his head towards the river. The smell of coming snow hung in the air and, suddenly, he repented of his joy and was glad that no one had been there to see it on his face.

Mrs. Mead took refuge in her office. She leaned against a wall, hidden from the door's frosted window. For the better part of an hour, she had tried to dissuade Florence Mellish from following the men back to the Pass, those who had rushed down to report the discovery of footprints and collect a pair of the missing girl's boots to match for size. The folly of the woman, to think of such an expedition in her state of mental distress, not to mention her obvious physical exhaustion. But it was Dr. Hammond's entreaties alone that finally brought her to her senses. To Mrs. Mead's grateful relief, she was resting in her room, per doctor's orders. The doctor himself borrowed a pair of sturdy boots from one of the college men and was up there now, doing what he could to help, although Mrs. Mead thought that he looked a little fragile for such exertions.

A ragged line of footprints leading from the Pass to the river. That terrible discovery would, she knew, only confirm what by now was whispered everywhere at the college and hinted at in the newspapers. And, if the Hinckley man's testimony was to be trusted (she was bracing herself for its appearance in the afternoon paper) then those footprints marked a deliberate journey undertaken at dusk, a reckless walk over uneven ground in growing darkness, a half-blind scramble towards the rocky ledges above the river.

Mrs. Mead shuddered and found a chair. She sat down heavily, rested her chin on both fists. Whatever anger she had felt towards Bertha—and she no longer stood on ceremony in her own mind, but called the girl by her given name, as if they were now familiar—whatever indignation at Bertha's thoughtlessness she had once harbored was, she believed, finally, irretrievably gone. The whispers, the rumors, the uncle's sad story, the hard fact of the footprints—they all lead to one terrible, unavoidable conclusion. But she pitied Bertha now, as she might pity a condemned murderer, not forgetting the horror of his crime, but mindful of the suffering humanity he shared with his victim.

And by this time tomorrow, the whole world would know; that realization dried Mrs. Mead's tears before they had a chance to fall. They, all of them– parents, benefactors, loyal alumnae, perfect strangers, the scoffers, the cynical, those sinners who took delight in the stumbles of the righteous—each and every one would open their newspapers and learn that one of Mount Holyoke's own, one of her beloved, cherished daughters, had deemed life too miserable to be borne, that, though cradled in the arms of faith, she had found no hope or courage there.

And they—friends and enemies alike—would blame the college. What kind of academic family, they were sure to wonder, took so little care of its own? Too much had been expected of the poor girl, they would conclude. How terribly her teachers had burdened her with study, how thoughtlessly her fellow students had ignored her distress. What must the college have done, they would ask, to drive a healthy, happy clergyman's daughter to such an end?

But, of course, Mrs. Mead knew something they did not: Bertha Mellish was no healthy, happy clergyman's daughter, and whatever forces had compelled her towards the river were not of Mount Holyoke's making. Look instead to her family's dark past, the insanity it harbored, Mrs. Mead advised her imagined prosecutors. Look to the unwholesome places that the girl's own parents allowed her to frequent. She bent down to open the bottom right-hand drawer of her desk, and from its shadows retrieved the loosely rolled cylinder of Bertha's story. She placed it on her lap and stared at it long enough to conclude that, despite the regrettable embarrassment its publication was sure to cause the Mellishes, there was, indeed, nothing else to do.

Dr. Hammond found Florence alone that evening, pacing the floor of the parlor in Porter Hall.

"Those might not be her footprints," she said, before he had a chance to speak or remove his overcoat, soaked through with melted snow.

"That is possible," he said gently, "But think of the evidence."

He reached for her arm, intending to guide her to a chair, but she pulled away with a vehemence that surprised him.

"We. . . we found nothing, nothing in the water," he said, "That is reason for hope."

She turned towards him, with a look both plaintive and fierce. "I must go up there," she said, "I must see the footprints."

Dr. Hammond thought of the snow, the gaunt trees, the rocks and the icy river, and knew such a visit was impossible. "I understand," he said, as if he were soothing a fevered patient. "I understand."

She smiled and took a step forward, clearly mistaking his words for permission.

"Tomorrow, then," she said.

He unbuttoned his overcoat and, damp as it was, laid it over the arm of the parlor settee. He moved slowly, stalling for time.

"Well, yes," he said, and found he could not meet her eyes. "But if you are to be home for Thanksgiving you must leave first thing in the morning."

Florence was silent.

"Your mother and father need you," Dr. Hammond said and, after a moment, she nodded.

Wednesday, November 24, 1897

For a second day, the grappling irons that had been good enough for use in shallow ponds and brooks proved too light to withstand the current as it rushed by Titan's Pier. They could not plumb the depths of the upstream cove where the river curved slightly to the left or break through the ice that had formed along its banks. Until dusk put an end to their efforts, one team of men after another fruitlessly dragged the dark waters, while a light snow dusted their shoulders and their fingers grew too cold to manage the chains.

"You must agree, Mrs. Mead, that fifty dollars is not seen by many as a particularly generous sum." Dr. Hammond tried to keep his voice even; he would have used stronger language, but did not want to anger the president. What a small price to place on a girl's life, he thought.

Mrs. Mead nodded regretfully, and with a smile of apology refilled the cup sitting on the table by his knee.

"I'm afraid by now," he went on, "with so many days gone by, such an offer of reward will not continue to draw out many volunteers."

Mrs. Mead set the teapot on its stand. "I understand, Dr. Hammond," she said, "and I am sincerely sorry. I have conferred several times with our Treasurer, Mr. Williston, and he has spoken to the Trustees. The college just cannot afford to be more generous at this time."

"But. . . ." Dr. Hammond began.

Mrs. Mead offered the sugar bowl, which he declined.

"You realize, of course," she continued, as if he hadn't tried to speak, "You understand, of course, that the college is in serious debt. We have just rebuilt our entire campus. If we had not suffered the tragedy of the fire, why, things would be quite different."

"Well, yes, I do understand." Dr. Hammond had to stop for a moment, to keep control of his voice. "But surely there must be someone interested in the college's welfare, a trustee or an alumna with private means, someone who might appropriate to the college a more reasonable, a more attractive amount."

She looked at him with her brow furrowed, as if his suggestion were incomprehensible and, moreover, in bad taste. "Perhaps," she said.

He waited, thinking that, after the novelty wore off, she would see the logic of his plan and agree to take it to Mr. Williston. But she busied herself with straightening the tea things, almost, it seemed to his irritation, as if she were ending the interview. He felt his face grow warm.

"Mrs. Mead," he said, "I think you should consider more carefully what the present situation says about the college. A larger reward might not lead to Bertha's discovery, but it would say to the public"—he was angry now, and his voice rose—" it would say to the public that the college has a sincere interest in its missing student and it would show that the college is doing everything it can, everything in its power to find her."

"Are you suggesting that we do not have a sincere interest in Miss Mellish?" Mrs. Mead's tone was even, but hurt. "Are you suggesting that we are not doing everything in our power to find her?" She shook her head, mournfully. "Then you sadly misjudge us."

Dr. Hammond, still feeling the effects of his outburst, was struggling to regulate his breath and could not answer. Mrs. Mead pushed the tea table forward and stood up.

"Dr. Hammond," she said, looking down at him with her arms folded, "I suggest that it is those who know her best, those closest to her, those who love her who should convey that message to the public."

He stared at her, speechless, stung by the implication of her reproach.

"Now, if you'll excuse me," she said, "It's late."

He watched as she walked, ramrod straight, to the parlor door.

"But, Mrs. Mead, surely there's some way that, together, we can. . . ." He was calm now, reasonable.

She hesitated. When she turned, her face was livid.

"Find the money yourself," she hissed, and left the room.

Thanksgiving Day: Thursday, November 25, 1897

No one along the river had more experience pulling bodies from its water than Luke Day, and no one took more satisfaction in the job. He whistled as he rowed across from Northampton, told to bring his heavy irons and try his luck where others had failed. When they showed him the spot, he took the pipe from his mouth and spat on the ground by his feet. The current was too strong, he told them, and the bottom too deep and ragged. She's either a long way down river, or she's lying in the pool below Titan's Pier, snagged on the rocks. Either way, his grappling irons, heavy as they were, would do little good. But they insisted, and with his price met and nothing better to do, he went about his task with the vigor and spirit of a man half his age.

By mid-afternoon, both his strength and his interest flagging, he watched with satisfaction as the South Hadley men and the ones from the college struggled awkwardly to manage his irons. When, at last, they all gave up, he packed the gear in his flat-bottomed boat and, just before pushing off, volunteered some advice. "Tell the ferryman to keep an eye open," he said. "If the body's still around and it ain't caught, it'll pop to the surface pretty soon. They do that, you know, after a few days. It's the gas makes 'em float." He took a long draw on his pipe, savoring the men's shocked looks. "Oh, and if I was you," he added, "I'd poke around in the rubbish and brush alongside the river. She might be hiding there."

He pulled on his oars and left the men standing idly on the banks. "Thinking of their dinners," he snorted, as he saw them, one by one, turn and scramble up the rocky slope towards the Pass.

Saturday, November 27, 1897

The ocean was a field of gentle hillocks; Elizabeth Rogers could just make out a patch through the portholes on the other side of the Grand Saloon. Captive to its rhythm, she tried to relax into the comfort of her upholstered chair and ignore the churning in her stomach. Think of it as a sleigh ride, she told herself, just a smooth ride through the snow.

Yesterday—the first Elizabeth had ever spent on a transatlantic steamer– the water roiled and bucked, and she suffered through it in her narrow berth, sticky and pale, too queasy to do more than feed little Emily whenever George delivered the baby to her from its cradle. No more, she'd decided that morning, and dressed to join those lucky souls, George included, who could bear to eat breakfast and then sit upright in a public place.

Elizabeth turned her head from the windows, swallowed hard and decided she was feeling better. The tea and buttered toast would stay down.

And there he was, her own George, beside her in the next chair, spectacles high on his nose, reading a newspaper with that singularity of purpose that sometimes made her want to tear it from his hands. But she loved him still, more than when she'd pined for him those lonely days at the college. He'd rescued her, as she had rescued him. How fitting, then, the two of them and their little Emily, making a treacherous journey across the sea, bound for a new life in a new land.

"George," she said. A momentary wrinkle creased his forehead. "George!"

He looked up from his newspaper, confused, as if suddenly woken.

"Yes?" he said, lowering the paper to his lap. "Is there something you need, Lizzie? Would you like to go back to bed?" He leaned towards her, rested a hand on her arm. "I don't advise it though. Lying down can sometimes make it worse."

He had beautiful eyes, even through his lenses. They were blue, not ice-blue but darker, the blue of old china, cobalt.

"No," Elizabeth said, "I feel better."

"Are you worried about Emily? The nurse I left her with is well-trained, I'm sure of it. The ship wouldn't employ her otherwise."

"No," Elizabeth said, "I'm not worried." In truth, she was glad to leave her daughter in someone else's more competent care, at least for a little while. Motherhood frightened her, even two months on. How to know what was happening inside that tiny body? Every sneeze foretold a deadly fever. Diarrhea meant typhus, a rash signaled scarlet fever.

George straightened the newspaper, folding it neatly along its central crease and then again in half. "Take this, Lizzie." he said. "It's yesterday's *New York Times*, but its something to keep you occupied." He stood up, retrieved his hat from the arm of his chair. "I'll return with a book. In a bit, when it's warmer, we'll get some air."

Elizabeth accepted the paper, more to please George than herself. "Thank you," she said, smiling. But when he turned to leave, she felt a surge of panic, as if the hulking maze of the ship would swallow him forever. "Hurry back," she said, and he touched her lightly on the cheek before he left.

Just a glance at George's newspaper before she closed her eyes and tried to nap.

The first headline repulsed her: Boy Shot by Policeman. The next was hardly better, news of a riot in Vienna. The third was even worse, a report of cannibalism in the South Seas, nothing she wanted to read with her stomach so uncertain.

Elizabeth flipped the folded paper, hoping to find some small article that might entertain without disturbing her. A New Haven man drowns. Negroes riot at a football game. Another deadly streetcar crash. The search for Bertha Mellish yields nothing.

It couldn't be. She stared in disbelief. What an incredible coincidence, another person with that same odd name. She read the article twice, a hand pressed to her open mouth, barely breathing.

> "Springfield, Mass., November 24. The search, which was continued all day, for Bertha L. Mellish, the Mount Holyoke College girl missing since the eighteenth of this month, has been fruitless. It is believed that she is dead, and that her body lies in the Connecticut River. Small footprints, made by a woman, were found leading to a bluff beside the river, and beneath this bluff the river has been dragged. Suicide is suspected."

"Oh my God, oh my God . . ." Elizabeth whispered the words, a choked incantation against the horror.

She leaned forward, dropping the paper to the floor. I should never have left her. I should never have left any of them.

What secrets had Bertha kept locked in that cool and quiet mind, what unspoken sadness?

No. Elizabeth straightened, clenched her fists in her lap. Suicide was out of the question. True, Bertha was a private girl, but no unhappier than anyone else at her age. Whatever happened, it was an accident.

She saw them again, Bertha and that beautiful girl, Eva, the dancing one, standing too close to the edge of Titan's Pier, the swollen river roaring beneath them. If only she'd been firmer that day, ordered them off the dangerous rock. If only she had, Bertha might never have gone back.

So, finally, this was the punishment Elizabeth thought she had escaped. She bowed her head, covered her eyes, felt the floor, the walls, the world around her pitch and roll. Silent tears pooled in her cupped palm.

Phebe. Did she know? Had she heard? What news reached her, exiled as she was in that far-off hamlet?

Elizabeth had Phebe's last letter, unanswered for nearly two months. Since Emily's birth, there'd been so little time, so little energy, and then came the arrangements for George's new position and all the packing.

She should write to Phebe now, immediately, tell her terrible news, comfort her.

With what words?

Let it go, she told herself. This is not your burden to carry. You left the college to live your life. You had that right. You are not to blame.

Soon she'd be a professor's wife in a German city, a happy mother with a happy, healthy child, an ocean between who she was and would become and all the shame and loneliness of her past.

The sickness she'd fought all morning rose in her gut. With both hands clamped to her mouth, Elizabeth stumbled through the nearest door and across the slippery deck, leaning out over the dark and depthless water just in time.

Friday, December 3, 1897

Florence didn't wait for Dr. Hammond to descend before she started from the platform towards the terminal. She walked quickly, avoiding most of the obstacles in her path by luck and instinct. She brushed hard against a woman without apology, and when her elbow struck an iron column she was not conscious of the pain. It was enough to be in motion, pushing forward. The telegram lay safe in a small pocketbook clutched tightly to her side. *Girl answering Mellish description,* it read, *held by Jacksonville police.*

Before the telegram's arrival two days earlier, Florence had felt useless at home and desperate to get back to the college, as if the search could not continue without her. She would have returned to South Hadley immediately after Thanksgiving, but her mother clutched her hand and told her it would break her father's heart if she left.

Florence was not certain she slept during those restless nights at home. She lay awake, rehearsing her regrets. She should have insisted someone take her to Titan's Pier to see the footprints–she would have known immediately if they were Bertha's. She should have scouted out that rock-bound place before her sister was born, taken its measure, warned Bertha of its dangers.

But there must have been scattered hours of sleep; each morning Florence's eyes opened to a halo of light surrounding the drawn-down window shade and she knew another interminable night had somehow passed.

Bertha's letters were displayed on the parlor table. Florence and her mother spent most of the hours before dinner listening as her father read them aloud, one by one. When awkward well-wishers came to visit, unsure whether to offer condolences or express faith in a safe return, he read to them.

In the afternoons, Florence scanned the county newspaper, sadly noting each unflattering insinuation directed against her sister's character and state of mind. In the evenings, she shared with her parents only those sentences that did credit to their family.

Three days after Thanksgiving, the story of Uncle David Mellish appeared on the paper's front page. With sanctimonious sympathy, the report described how, in 1874, Congressman Mellish drove through the streets of Washington tossing coins to strangers, how he threw furniture through the windows of his house, how he was taken into custody against his will and spent his final hours raving in the national madhouse, tied to a bed. And, finally, how he died pitifully of acute mania, driven to it, people said, by single-minded attention to questions of national finance.

Staring blindly at the paper crumpled in her lap, Florence remembered the whispers, the surreptitious glances, the impertinent questions she endured when she entered Mount Holyoke Seminary just weeks after her uncle's death, bearing the newly-notorious Mellish name. And how had it been for her cousin, a decade later? Perhaps some of the faculty remembered the pathetic end of Alice's father and entertained their colleagues—maybe even their students– with its recounting. Perhaps they looked at Alice with that same mixture of curiosity and pity that Florence had seen on so many faces during her own recent visit to the college.

Poor Alice, Florence sighed, three years dead of a swift-acting fever, barely thirty years old. Our wretched family, Florence thought, and for one brief moment she wondered why God had cursed them so.

Florence remembered her uncle, kind like her father, brown-eyed and solid-jawed, but with a louder voice, a larger presence, a keen way of looking at a person that frightened her when she was small but admired as she grew older. Perhaps there *was* something of that look in Bertha's eyes. But there was no connection, Florence told herself, between her uncle's illness a lifetime ago and Bertha's disappearance. And what business was her family's tragedy to anyone, she thought, hot with resentment, what right had strangers to drag her uncle's sad story from its grave?

Florence tore the newspaper into ragged strips and burned them in the kitchen stove, late that night when her parents were in bed.

She did the same with the next day's edition. "The mother of the strange girl now missing," the paper observed, "has herself exhibited melancholic and reclusive tendencies."

Florence tried not to dwell on which neighbor had betrayed them to a curious reporter. She couldn't help considering Mrs. Cogswell, Dayville's worst gossip, although she tried not to accuse without evidence. Once, very briefly, the name of Emma Hammond crossed her mind.

When, like a miracle, the telegram appeared at their door, Florence opened it in the hall, her hands shaking, prepared for the worst. Her cry brought her mother to the head of the stairs and her father to the door of the parlor, and when she read it aloud, her voice was shrill with triumph and excitement. The old people stared at her dumbstruck, their mouths open.

"Praise God," her father gasped, then shook his head. "But how can it be?"

"We must not get our hopes up," her mother warned. "Remember Boston."

Burdened with a traveling bag in each hand—Florence had forgotten hers—Henry Hammond rushed down the steps of the train and tried to overtake her as she crossed the floor of the terminal. She seemed propelled by a kind of excessive energy, a mental and physical excitation that reminded him of cases he had seen in his younger days, of Bell's mania or traumatic neurasthenia, conditions often brought on by great shock to the body or mind.

She'd fidgeted constantly during the long trip, knotting and unknotting her fingers, tapping her foot, shifting in her seat. She'd toyed with her food in the dining car, been unable to concentrate on a book or conversation, displayed a curtness and inattention entirely foreign to her usual character. She refused a sleeping-draught and he believed that she had not slept at all; before he drifted off, he felt her restless movements in the berth below his own, and he felt them again when he awoke. He would have insisted they stop at a hotel before locating the police station, but he knew that, in her present state, she would never agree.

Henry did not expect to find Bertha waiting for them. Once, for a moment on Thanksgiving day while he stood shivering on the banks of the river watching the men drag the water again and again, he'd wondered if it were possible that she had planned it all, left her footprints to mislead the searchers, effected an elaborate escape. But he dismissed the thought as soon as it occurred and by the time he left South Hadley on Thursday, he was certain she was dead. He believed her a victim of her own carelessness or, rather, of the stubborn willfulness he had seen her display on more than one occasion. She had an independence from social niceties and other people's expectations that, except for the pain it caused Florence, he could not help but respect. It was, though, a trait more useful and better suited to a boy. But he refused to breath a word of his conviction to anyone; his first responsibility was to the Mellish family, not the truth. Until that moment when all three–father, mother, and sister—believed that Bertha was no longer among the living, he resolved to do whatever they required of him with all the dedication he could muster.

Still, Henry wanted the rest as much for himself as for Florence. It was nearly four in the afternoon and the train's incessant clatter echoed in his ears. He felt light-headed, with a tightness in his chest, and had to stop to catch his breath and wipe his face. Perhaps he should not have volunteered to serve as her escort; a younger, healthier man should be here, leading the way. When he lowered his handkerchief, Florence was already exiting the terminal through a set of double doors, and he had to run to keep her in sight.

Florence stepped into the unpaved road outside the station with no idea which way to turn. The air was not as moist or as warm as she might have expected this far south had she given any thought to the weather, but the sun was blinding and she had to shield her eyes. She wore a coat intended for northern winters, black and made of wool, but it did not occur to her to remove it although her face and body were damp with sweat.

Jacksonville lay across a river, its towers and steeples barely visible in the distance. Instinct told Florence to follow the path of the crowd, but the crowd was too sparse and scattered to sweep her up in its current. After walking a few yards in one direction, and then retracing her steps in the other she stopped, ready to cry in frustration. In her singleness of purpose she had forgotten Dr. Hammond until she heard his voice behind her.

"Miss Mellish, please wait."

Dr. Hammond stood with both bags at his feet, removing his overcoat. His face was flushed and his breathing labored, and she was sorry to have brought him to such a state. For one brief moment, she wished she had a husband of her own, a man for whom such acts were duties and not favors.

"That's better now," Dr. Hammond said. He leaned over to pick up the luggage, his overcoat slung in the crook of one arm.

Florence grabbed her bag. "Please," she said, "let me carry this myself." She straightened and looked around, squinting. "It can't be very far from here. Which way do you think we should we go?"

The reckless nature of her suggestion–that the two of them, exhausted and anxious, walk blindly through the streets of a strange town in the heat of a tropical afternoon –was a sign, Henry understood, of just how distraught Florence had become. Yet how like her too, he thought, to manifest her distress as resolve, however irrational. He watched for a moment as she stood with her traveling bag dangling from one hand and her pocketbook held tightly in the other, scanning the distance like a scout, pathetically courageous.

"We'll take a cab, my dear," he said and gently pulled the bag from her hand. She looked at him, startled, but did not protest.

"Please wait here while I find one." With a backward glance to reassure himself that Florence was not wandering off, Henry walked a short distance down the road to flag a passing carriage. "That lady and I," he instructed the driver, motioning towards Florence, "that lady and I would like to go to the Jacksonville Police Station."

Henry helped Florence up the step and into the back seat of the carriage while the driver, a large man with a dusky face, the darkest he had ever seen, watched over his shoulder.

"All right now," the driver said when they were settled, giving the reins a smart slap, "let's take Mister and Missus to the police."

They rode in silence across a bridge, down two or three narrow, unpaved streets, along a wide thoroughfare lined with solid frame and red brick buildings and rows of rough-hewn telephone poles.

Henry monitored Florence from the corner of his eye. She sat forward in the seat, bent slightly at the waist, gripping her pocketbook with both hands. She vibrated in a way unrelated to the jolting of the cab and he knew that her legs jittered beneath her skirts.

The warning came back to her as it had, uninvited and unwelcome, throughout the journey. We must not get our hopes up. Florence acknowledged the wisdom of those words, but she wished her mother had kept that wisdom to herself. There is nothing left but hope, she thought in silent reproach. I won't let you take it from me.

Yet even now she could not imagine what desperate circumstance, what folly or fear, could have driven her sister to a jail in Florida. But what did it matter, why she had gone? All that mattered was to see Bertha again and bring her home.

"Here we are, folks. City Hall."

The carriage rolled to a stop in front of a large brick building, the most imposing on the thoroughfare. Attached to its side was a tall square tower and, next to that, a shorter round one like a castle's keep. The driver gathered his reins in one hand and with the other pointed towards the round tower. "The police is in there," he said.

By the time Henry paid the fare and collected their belongings, Florence was already up the flight of stairs leading to the tower's entrance. He hoped she would wait until he joined her but, without a backward glance in his direction, she opened the door and went in.

The interior was dark as a closet after the brilliant glare of the afternoon sun and Florence had to stop just inside the door, nearly blind and breathless with anticipation. The silence, too, was shocking, as if the whole busy world outside its walls had vanished.

Dr. Hammond joined her, and they stood side by side in a small, windowless half-circle of a room with dull gray walls. A single unlit electric lamp hung above their heads, but neither one thought to pull its cord.

"This is strange," Dr. Hammond finally said, and picked up the traveling bags resting by his feet.

Florence followed him through a wide doorway into a larger room and up to a high desk that ran parallel to its far wall. From what she could see, no one stood behind that desk; if someone sat behind it, she couldn't tell. Brown paper shades were drawn over both of the room's windows, with an inch or two left open at the bottom. The only sound to ruffle the close air was the lazy spinning of a small electric fan perched on the near end of the desk. The scene was so different from what she had expected, so unlike anything she had imagined that, if Dr. Hammond hadn't been there to guide her, she might have thought it a dream.

"Excuse me!" Henry called. "Is anyone here?"

The coat he carried over his shoulder slipped and his arms ached from the weight of the bags. He dropped all three in a heap on the floor and knocked several times against the desk, which was topped with a railing like a miniature fence. "Is anyone here?" he called again, making no effort to hide his irritation. He was about to knock once more, when he heard what sounded like the scrape of a chair and then approaching footsteps.

Clearly, the officer who appeared through a door in the wall behind the desk had been interrupted at a meal; his jaws still worked as he ambled forward and he gave his mouth a swipe with the sleeve of his uniform. "Yes?"

Henry refused to be flustered; he'd had enough experience with policeman to recognize the bullying type, more bluster than bite, too proud of his blue uniform and brass buttons.

"I am Dr. Henry Hammond of Dayville, Connecticut," he said with careful dignity, "This lady is Miss Florence Mellish, Bertha Mellish's sister." He paused, thinking the name explanation enough of their mission.

The policeman, mouth drawn in an exaggerated frown, looked from one to the other. He lingered, Henry noticed with disgust, on Florence, pale and wilted in her winter coat. "And what might be your business?"

Florence opened her pocketbook and drew out the folded telegram. She hated to relinquish it; once it left her protection the fragile promise of its message could easily be broken. But she was too tired to form the words necessary for an explanation and too impatient to wait for Dr. Hammond to speak. "Read this," she said, and dropped the pocketbook, empty of its only precious cargo, on the pile of luggage.

With greasy fingers, the policeman took the telegram, unfolded it. He gave a hard yank to smooth its creases.

"I remember something about this," he said when he was done, fanning the paper near his face as if to jog his memory. "But I have to get the captain."

He strolled away with the paper in his hand. Henry knew that he was taking pleasure in their torment–whether from boredom or natural meanness, he couldn't tell—and the thought infuriated him. "Hurry up, sir!" he shouted at the man's back, although he knew the command was pointless. He felt sheepish when the officer merely shrugged and sauntered out of the room, and he kept his eyes fixed on the door as if his impatient glare had some power.

Florence, waiting silently behind Dr. Hammond, felt the weight of her woolen coat and shifted slightly to the left. The faint breath of the electric fan touched her cheek. She closed her eyes until she heard footsteps again, firm and brisk.

"I'm very sorry to have kept you in such suspense!" The captain strode forward, bypassing the desk, with his right hand outstretched. His trim figure and energetic manner cheered Henry. So did his strong handshake.

"Dr. Hammond," he said, "Captain Rutherford, at your service." He turned to Florence. "And Miss Mellish," he said, dipping his head. "I'm sure you're anxious to meet the young lady in question. Let's see what we can do."

Henry stepped aside and let the captain take hold of Florence's elbow. With some chagrin, he realized he was glad to share temporary responsibility for Florence's well-being, and he walked a half-step behind the pair as they moved in slow procession across the room.

The captain bent solicitously towards Florence's ear. He slowed their already ponderous pace to a crawl. She would have broken free if she knew where they were headed.

"You must be wondering," he said, "how this mysterious young lady came to our attention and how we associated her with your sister's case."

The only thing I care about, Florence thought, is to see if that young lady is Bertha, but she answered yes because there was nothing else to do.

"Well, Miss Mellish, we have Mrs. Hatch to thank for that." They were now back in the curved anteroom in front of a closed door that Florence had not noticed before. The captain released her elbow and rested his hand on the doorknob. "Mrs. Hatch is the proprietress of a respectable boarding house here in our city," he continued, while Florence stared at his hand and prayed for it to turn. "She hails from your part of the country. She is"—and he let out a little laugh, as if amused by a private joke—"she is a Yankee, if you will."

Florence's arm moved with a slight upward twitch and, as if responding to her impatient signal, the captain opened the door. She felt a rush of subterranean air and began to shiver in the clammy chill of her sweat-soaked clothes.

"Allow me to go first, Miss Mellish," the captain said.

There was no sound except the clatter of their feet against the rungs of the narrow iron staircase. The stairwell was brighter than the rooms above—the electric bulbs, dim as they were, were lit—and the scabs and scars where fresh paint had been laid over peeling walls were more visible. Florence recognized the sour smell of mildew and the faint odor of unwashed chamber- pots. She held one hand to her mouth and nose, and gripped the iron railing with the other. Now she shivered violently and felt a strange tingling in her hands and feet.

Henry followed Florence. He was no stranger to city jails and prisons; as a young man he'd served time as a police surgeon and that job took him into stinking cells and airless tenements. He treated drunkards raving in delirium, prostitutes infected with the diseases of their trade, young women hemorrhaging from bungled abortions, men bleeding from ragged knife wounds.

He did not imagine such horrors awaited them at the bottom of these stairs, but he knew that their influence hung in the air of every prison, however small. Crime and sin were the lifeblood of such places; no veneer of efficiency, or respectability, or of law could hide that fact. Florence, with her sensitive nature, would feel it too. He experienced a mounting discomfort, a kind of claustrophobic pressure in his chest that, if he were to follow its advice, would send him running.

The captain paused at the bottom of the stairs, facing them like a showman addressing his audience. He nodded towards an iron-barred cell and smiled apologetically. "This isn't the most pleasant of reception rooms," he said, "but it is necessary for the safety of our visitors."

He opened the cell door with a large key and gestured towards a plain wooden bench located in the center of the cell. "I have sent a man to fetch the young lady, if you'll wait here."

Florence hesitated. Although she held her arms across her chest she could not stop shaking, and she knew that when she crossed the threshold of that terrible room, her blood would turn to ice.

Dr. Hammond guided her through the open door and towards the bench, and sat next to her on its hard surface. He took her hand in his. She looked down and saw that his arm now vibrated in concert with her own.

"As I was explaining," the captain said, placing himself in front of his seated visitors with his back to the door. He blocked Florence's view of anything outside the room and, at that moment, she hated him more than she had ever allowed herself to hate another person. "This Mrs. Hatch—your fellow New Englander—keeps abreast of the news from home and so, through correspondence with a friend, learned of your sister's unfortunate situation. I believe, in fact, she was supplied with several newspaper clippings, some of which contained quite detailed physical descriptions of your sister."

Florence thought she heard voices and strained to see around the captain. Any words spoken were unintelligible, but the rhythm of distant conversation was unmistakable. Low tones, loud but slow, followed by higher and faster notes. And then a hollow clang, perhaps the echo of an iron bar struck by a hand or a foot.

"Shortly after Thanksgiving, it seems, a mysterious young woman presented herself at Mrs. Hatch's door, asking for accommodations. According to Mrs. Hatch, the girl seemed unaccountably nervous and would not give reasonable answers to reasonable questions. And"—the captain lowered his voice—"she was visited every night by a man, somewhat older than herself."

Again, the sound of voices, louder, high and low mingling, an argument. More hollow clangs and thuds and then scuffling, reluctant feet dragging on stone. Florence pushed herself a few inches off the bench with her right hand, but Dr. Hammond still held her left in his.

"Mrs. Hatch, naturally concerned, noticed a striking resemblance between the girl in her house and the description of your sister published in the newspapers. And, intelligent woman that she is, she alerted us to the connection rather than confront the girl and scare her off."

The scuffling was closer but the voices had grown silent. Florence stood up, bringing Dr. Hammond with her. The captain continued unperturbed. "The man, it sadly turns out, was a married scoundrel. And the young lady, well, we shall see. . ."

The girl in the doorway was of medium height and medium build and her hair, which she wore pulled straight back, was dark auburn, but Florence couldn't tell if she bore a faint scar on her forehead. She was certain, however, just before the room began to spin and everything went black, that the girl in the doorway wasn't Bertha.

Saturday, December 4, 1897

Mile after flat mile, patches of yellow sand, clusters of spiky-leaved palmettos, stands of skinny pine trees hung with moss like old men's beards, dark green swamps filled with thick-rooted cypress. Florence kept her face to the window with her forehead resting on the glass and surrendered to the movement of the train.

Henry—she called him Henry now, both to herself and when she spoke to him (the polite ceremony she had observed until yesterday seemed suddenly pointless)—Henry slept beside her. He had been asleep for three hours, almost as long as they had been traveling, and she wanted to give him his privacy. She knew he would be embarrassed when he awoke, if he thought she had been watching him with his head lolling and his face slack.

She felt surprisingly calm, yet wasn't drowsy. Yesterday, every muscle and nerve in her body had been taut, stretched to breaking, but now it seemed as if she had no muscles and no nerves, no physical or mental volition. She was like a basin drained of water, waiting to be filled.

Perhaps it was relief, she finally roused herself to think, this feeling of exquisite exhaustion. After the initial shock came bitter tears, but she had taken the sleeping-draught Henry pressed on her last night and awoke this morning with a sense that maybe it was better, after all, that Bertha hadn't been the girl in the jail cell who ran off with a married man. A homecoming under such circumstances would have been a terrible blow to their parents, grateful as they would be for her safe return. Perhaps it was better to wait just a little longer, for Bertha to come back to them more . . . more herself.

But where was she *now*, this very moment? Florence squeezed her eyes shut. Perhaps it would come to her like a vision, Bertha's place in this strange new world. But all Florence could see was a patternless web of railroad tracks and roads scarring the surface of the earth, a crazy quilt of cities, each filled with crowds so dense that no one person was distinguishable from any other. She saw forests and mountains too many to number, lakes and rivers feeding into oceans, oceans stretching to infinity.

Bertha could be anywhere, it was true, but she must be somewhere. Florence shook off her discouragement and sat up, her back barely touching the cushioned seat. She no longer held her sister entirely responsible for her disappearance. Some larger force, some divine compulsion, some mysterious turn of fate, had a hand in this drama and no puny show of human impatience, no arguing or stamping of feet, would hasten its resolution. Florence raised her head and looked over the passing landscape into the sky. She saw that the sun was hidden behind a thick white haze, but that the haze glowed with a bright and shadowless light. She smiled, a small signal of understanding. It was only a question of time and faith and will.

A sudden rightward sway of the train sent her off-balance and into Henry's side. She glanced over to see if the movement had disturbed him, secretly hoping that it had. Except for a twitch of his head and a barely audible murmur, he did not react. Florence knew she should shift her weight but found herself reluctant to break contact. She liked the feeling of his arm against hers and she remembered the pressure of his hand, warm and comforting in the bone-chilling air of the jail. She looked down at his lap where both hands now rested, the left tucked under the right, pale against the dark wool of his trousers, the fingers delicate as a woman's but the back of each swollen with blue veins branching like tiny rivers below the surface of his skin. She wanted to trace the course of those rivers, follow them with her fingertips, feel the pulse of blood they carried.

Henry's head pitched forward and she drew back, guilty as a thief.

He woke abruptly and for a moment could not recollect where he was. He might have been napping on the couch in his parlor except that the room vibrated and the incessant racket in his ears sounded like a train. Of course, he thought, and ran his hand over his disheveled hair and adjusted his collar before looking at Florence, whose attention was, thankfully, fixed on the passing scenery.

"I must have dozed off," he said, trying to sound alert. He was able to stifle a yawn before Florence turned. "I hope I didn't disturb you."

"Oh no, not at all. You were quiet as a mouse."

He was pleased to see the hint of a smile on her lips, although she dropped her eyes after meeting his. Perhaps lingering embarrassment at her behavior yesterday, he thought, although she had no reason to be ashamed. There were strong men who could not have withstood what she had been forced to bear; Henry was not sure that he could have. Still, he was glad to see her looking so much better; last night's restorative sleep had done her a world of good.

"Would you like something to drink? Some tea or coffee? A bite to eat?" He leaned into the aisle, looking down its length for a porter.

"No, thank you," Florence said. "Maybe in a while."

Henry righted himself and considered whether it would be better to allow Florence a respite from the subject so naturally on her mind or to encourage her talk about it. He was relieved when she spoke first.

"I'm not discouraged, Henry" she said. "In fact, I'm more certain now than I was before that Bertha is alive and that we'll find her. God is merciful. We . . . I mean I—you've done so much for us already—I'll just have to work harder, search more diligently. I have to be patient. I have to do everything required of me and not expect too much too soon."

She gazed at him with such untroubled confidence, such unblemished trust in the inevitable resolution of a benevolent plan, that he wanted to take her by the shoulders, look her in the eye as he might look at a dying patient were he a different kind of doctor, and tell her the truth. You have no hand in this, he wanted to say, you can struggle and you can sacrifice, you can do your duty until it wears you out and kills you, or you can do nothing. Either way, the outcome will be the same.

"I will continue to help," he said, "until we find her."

He had set the wheels in motion while still in South Hadley, on the day after Thanksgiving, with telephone calls and telegraph messages to the leading citizens of Dayville. His goal from the start was to raise ten times the paltry sum so grudgingly offered by the college, to meet the president's angry challenge and show her and the world how precious Bertha was to her family and true friends. He had planned to wait until all the money was secured before surprising the Mellishes, but now Florence smiled at him so bravely.

"I've managed to collect some funds," Henry said, "a reward for information leading to Bertha's safe return—not the fifty dollars offered by the college, but something substantial, an amount to catch people's attention. Five hundred dollars." He stopped, unselfconsciously proud, anticipating Florence's grateful surprise.

"Five hundred dollars?" she gasped.

The amount must be staggering, he realized, probably near to what she earned in a year's hard work as a teacher. "And most of it is already promised, gifts from your friends and neighbors."

Congressman Russell—a wealthy man, not ungenerous, and a shrewd politician always looking to win voter's hearts—had been the first solicited and had guaranteed a full hundred. The Sayles family, communicating through an agent, pledged an amount yet to be designated. Reverend Deans, the soul of kindness, contributed what little he could and vowed that his parishioners would open their purses to the suffering family in the spirit of Christian charity.

Florence held one hand to her cheek, overcome more by Henry's efforts than by the generosity of her neighbors, which, in her heart of hearts, she thought only right and natural. But Henry—shouldering without invitation the onerous task of begging, sparing her and, more importantly, her father, that humiliation. There never was a man as good as Henry Hammond.

'Thank you," she said, her voice breaking, "I . . . my family. . . we're very grateful."

He shrugged, not rudely or dismissively, but with genuine humility. "It's no trouble," he said, "and I think it will be useful. With your father's permission, of course, we'll send notices to all the newspapers in New England, in New York and Philadelphia, in Washington, even Chicago. And we'll print handbills, too, with Bertha's photograph and description on them, and distribute them for display in public places in Connecticut, Massachusetts, Rhode Island, as far as we can send them."

"Public places?" Florence echoed. Bertha's picture reproduced in countless newspapers, hung on post office and police station walls, tacked to train station schedule boards, propped in store windows next to piles of soap and bolts of cloth. And Bertha's life priced for all the world to see at five hundred dollars.

Henry must have recognized the hesitation in her voice. "I know," he said softly, "but think of all the people out there who might be able to help. If just one of those people knows anything at all, has just one clue, it will all have been worthwhile."

Of course he was right, but she felt the sudden sting of resentment. Who were these people, these curious strangers, these gawkers at their private suffering, whose help they had to buy? She looked down and spoke more to herself than to Henry. "People shouldn't need a reward. They should want to help because it's the right thing to do."

Dear, sweet Florence, Henry thought, steeped in selfless duty, effortlessly moral. How to explain to her the venality of the world outside her experience. He smiled ruefully. "I'm afraid that's just the way things are. Most people aren't like you, Florence. They need something outside themselves—if not the promise of reward, then the threat of punishment– to do good."

She gave him a strange look, sadder than he would have expected, given the compliment he had just offered. "I suppose so," she said, and turned her face to the window.

One day when she was five, Florence stole an apple from a neighbor lady's kitchen. She was on an errand for her mother and when the lady turned to mind the stove, Florence saw the apple, shiny, red and irresistible, sitting on a nearby table and, without thinking, she grabbed it and ran away. Her mother found her crouched behind a chair in the parlor with the half-eaten fruit in her hand and when she asked Florence where it came from, Florence said the lady gave it to me, she told me I could have it. Her mother took her by the arm and marched her to the lady's house to find out if, indeed, the apple was a gift and when the lady said no, it wasn't, Florence was exposed as both a liar and a thief. The shame that burned her soul at that moment and the pain in her cheek where her mother slapped her were nothing compared to the heart-freezing desolation she felt that evening when her father learned of her crimes and looked down at her in sorrow and disappointment and she believed his love was gone forever.

No, Henry, she thought, you're wrong. I've done nothing good in my life without the hope and expectation of reward; I've resisted temptation only because I fear the loss of that reward. And now, she realized with sickening clarity, the gift that God had given her in exchange for the uncomplaining sacrifice of her youth and her freedom– the child that was hers by right if not by nature–was slipping from her grasp.

Friday, December 10, 1897

Will Cogswell managed to break off a piece of biscuit and sneak it into his mouth before his mother finished saying grace. He was, as usual, ravenously hungry, and supper was now more than half an hour overdue, thanks to one of Charlotte's piano students, late to her lesson.

There was something odd, Will noticed as he waited for the boiled potatoes to pass from his mother to his sister, something strange about the look they shared. He'd seen that look before, although less frequently as he got older, and it told him that there was a subject they wanted to discuss but wished he wasn't there to hear.

"What's going on?" he asked his mother—by far the easier of the two to break but now studiously avoiding his eyes—and then at Charlotte, who stared him down. He felt a momentary pang of unspecific guilt until he remembered there wasn't anything in the recent past that he'd done wrong. He turned back to his mother, "I know something's up," he said, a little insulted that at fourteen they were still treating him like a child.

"I have no idea what you're talking about," she said as she handed him the potatoes, but he saw her glance at Charlotte. And Charlotte, he noticed, answered with one tiny shake of her head, like a warning.

Will sat with the bowl in one hand and the serving spoon in the other, his curiosity stronger than his appetite. The best strategy, he decided, was to wait until his mother's irresistible need to say whatever was on her mind overpowered her effort to heed Charlotte's silent command. Will scooped a healthy portion of potatoes onto his plate, speared a slice of ham from the nearby platter and bided his time.

The silence around the table lasted longer than he expected and made him uncomfortable and a little bored. He was about to wonder aloud if it would snow anytime soon—he was anxious to try out the family's new sleigh– when his mother asked Charlotte, in an unconvincingly off-hand way, whether she had read that afternoon's edition of the newspaper.

"Mother!" Charlotte cried and put down her fork.

"What? What? What's in the paper?" Will swallowed a barely chewed mouthful and looked wildly from his sister to his mother. He pushed back from the table and would have rushed from the dining room to the parlor if Charlotte had not given him a dangerous look.

"Don't you dare leave this table," she said.

Will, fuming, appealed to his mother for support.

She gave him a commiserating smile but did not override Charlotte's order. "Eat your supper, Will," she said absently, and turned to his sister. Will folded his arms and set his jaw, determined to maintain an injured silence until both of them apologized.

"He's going to hear about it soon enough," his mother said to Charlotte, "Don't you know that all of Dayville's already talking about it?"

"Talking about what?!" Will shouted, forgetting his recent vow.

"Bertha Mellish's story," his mother said. "Don't yell." She laid both forearms on the table, one on either side of her plate, and leaned towards her son. "Bertha Mellish wrote a story while she was at the college and it was published in today's newspaper."

So, Will thought, more about that mystery. Everyone in town had been buzzing about it for weeks and he followed it in the papers, although he'd missed that day's installment. The fact that he knew Bertha Mellish, that she was a friend of his sister's, that he'd seen her—talked to her, in fact—this past summer, at a picnic he remembered, only a few months before she disappeared, all that made the situation seem more personal than any other report he'd ever read about people missing from places he'd never heard of or seen.

No wonder, then, that Charlotte was acting so high and mighty. She didn't like to speculate about Bertha's disappearance and, he noticed, she never said anything bad about Bertha even when other people did. He'd even heard Charlotte snap at Hattie Darling, when Hattie said that Bertha was a little strange just like her mother and that Roy Spaulding told her Bertha borrowed a book from him and never gave it back. Will had to admit he respected Charlotte; she never used her connection with the missing girl to make herself important.

"Can I read it?" Will asked. "Can I get the paper?"

"After you've finished your supper." His mother straightened and took her arms off the table. She looked at Charlotte, who was sawing her meat with short, quick strokes.

Will considered leaving without permission until it dawned on him that he'd do better to lay low. He'd learn more if he concentrated on his food and showed no undue interest in the women's conversation.

"Bertha worked in the mill here, didn't she?" his mother asked Charlotte.

"You know she did."

Will thought it rude, the way Charlotte answered, and wondered why their mother allowed it.

"Like the girl in the story," his mother persisted.

"I suppose so. But it was a different mill in the story, a made-up mill."

Will imagined a trial might sound like this—the prosecutor attacking, the defense, well, defending.

"And a girl in the story deliberately throws herself into a river," his mother continued.

"Yes," Charlotte said, "in the story."

"And didn't they find Bertha's footprints near a river?"

"They found somebody's footprints."

"And do you really think that's all just coincidence—the mill, the river?"

"Just what are you trying to say, Mother?"

Will heard an exasperated sigh. "Charlotte, you know perfectly well what I mean. The story can only be poor Bertha's confession—her farewell."

His mother sniffed and Will looked up from his plate, wondering if she was going to cry. "It's rather touching and pathetic, if you think about it," she said, dry-eyed.

"It's a story, mother. Fiction. From Bertha's imagination."

His mother snorted. "It doesn't sound so imaginary to me."

Will sat with his fork in his hand and his mouth open, no longer feigning indifference. He had rarely seen his mother and his sister set so stubbornly against each other. It was exciting to watch, at least from from a safe distance.

"And do you think, Charlotte, that the"— his mother glanced in Will's direction and he took a renewed interest in his food—"that the"—she lowered her voice—"that the inclusion of an *infant* is imaginary, too?"

Charlotte rose from her seat and dropped her napkin on the table by her plate. "I'm surprised at you, Mother."

"Don't be naïve, Charlotte," his mother answered.

They watched in silence as Charlotte left the room. When she was gone, his mother exhaled sharply, shook her head, and picked up her fork.

Something scandalous had been exposed, Will knew, but he didn't quite understand the nature of that scandal. "What was that all about?" he asked.

"Never mind," his mother said. "Finish your supper."

Friday, December 17, 1897

Someone came into the kitchen through the back door, slamming it shut. Even with her head down, Phebe knew it was Sam by the clomping of his boots against the floor she'd scrubbed that morning. Sam had the biggest feet of all the Cutts men and the dirtiest boots. She sighed and kept at the potato with her paring knife; no sense telling him to wipe his feet. The Cutts men did whatever they wanted without a thought for her and everything she did to keep them and the place clean.

"Just come from town," Sam said.

"Hmm," Phebe answered. Sam wasn't much of a talker; no sense asking him who or what he'd seen there. She finished with the potato, dropped it in a bowl of cold water, picked up another.

"Letter for you," he said as he passed the table on his way to the pie safe.

The envelope fell face down in a mess of peelings, but Phebe was too excited to care. She'd been expecting it for weeks, ever since she'd sent off her own letter to Mrs. Rogers saying how happy she was about the baby. And a tiny part of her thought that maybe, finally, after all this time, it might even be from Bertha.

Phebe wiped her hands on her apron and, fingers clumsy with anticipation, managed to slit the envelope open with the paring knife.

A single page from Mrs. Rogers, written on a piece of paper with the picture of a ship at the top. Phebe didn't stop to study the picture or look at the date.

Dear Phebe,

This is a difficult letter for me to write. I'm not sure if I send you sad news that you already know—I expect you do—or if I am breaking that terrible news to you. Perhaps you have come across it the newspapers as I did, or perhaps someone from the college or her family has sent you word.

Our friend Bertha is missing; that much I know. Perhaps you know more. If you do, please tell me.

This is all I have learned: she left the college on the eighteenth of November and did not return. As of the date I write this, she has not been found. And there is a clue that frightens me. It seems small footprints were found at the edge of a bluff above the Connecticut River, and I can only think that bluff is the one we visited last year.

There is something else, but I hesitate to write the words. I only do so because you may have read the newspapers yourself and so already know the ugly rumor.

I do not believe, and I am sure you do not believe, that our friend would destroy herself. I saw no indications of despair in Bertha, none of the hopelessness that is necessary for such an act. Reserve, yes, a slowness to open herself to others, but as you and I know perhaps better than any but her family, when she did open herself, as she did for us last winter, Bertha was a true and loyal friend. We should remember, you and I, that we left Bertha. She did not leave us.

This is all I can write for now. Emily is crying. I will write again with an address when I reach our destination.

You and I must pray for Bertha's safe return.
Elizabeth Rogers

"What's the matter with you? You look like you seen a ghost."

Phebe gaped at her brother, leaning against the pie safe with a chunk of bread in his hand. She did not understand his words because the ones on the paper she gripped in her shaking hands still skittered and raced in her head.

A rush of cold air at her back and the kitchen filled with the smell of hay and wet wool and with the lumbering bodies of Caleb, Ben, and Pa.

Before the door closed behind them, Phebe was through it, running across the crusted, snow-slicked ground towards the barn, skirt and apron flapping, no shawl, no hat, no gloves, the letter clutched tight against her chest above her thudding heart.

When Phebe stumbled into the barn, Mollie turned to look, no alarm in her placid, patient eyes, and she lowed a soft greeting when Phebe pressed herself to Mollie's side and cried into the warm velvet of her coat.

After a time Phebe could no longer cry and she sat down on the milking stool with the back of her head leaning against the generous curve of Mollie's belly. The hand holding the letter rested in her lap. Although she knew it wasn't there, Phebe felt for the button that used to hang beneath her clothes, that small, hard fragment of faith and courage she'd found buried in the sand.

She hoped that now it hung from Bertha's neck, wherever she might be.

She would have written to Bertha, but she wanted Bertha to write to her.

She would have written to Bertha, if she'd had anything to say.

I am not a teacher. I keep house for my father and my brothers now that my mother is dead. I cook, I clean, I milk, I wash, I scrub.

None of that was good enough.

But sometimes I take out my schoolbooks—you remember them, Bertha, you helped me with them, the Geometry and the Latin, the History and the Greek—I take them out and read them so I won't forget everything, so I can remember the time when I was part of something bigger, something finer, something, Bertha, I owe to you. Without you there to guide me, Bertha, I would have been lost. Without you there to save me, I would have died.

Mollie shifted her weight and Phebe sat up. A letter to Bertha's family. That, at least, she could do. A letter, telling them how much Bertha meant to her. A letter, saying how sorry she was.

Using a corner of her apron, Phebe wiped the tears from her face and, with a kiss to Mollie's flank, left to boil the potatoes for dinner.

Saturday, December 18, 1897

Hank Robinson stopped in a bar-room down by the New London docks, one of those places where the whiskey was cheap and the company didn't look at him funny. A quick glass or two and he felt better, right as rain. With a couple of pickled eggs in his belly, he was a new man, too good for a joint like that.

With no more money in his pocket, Hank picked up his hat, set it firmly in place and pushed away from the table. One last drop from the glass and he headed for the door, past the clots and clusters of broken-down men wasting their days in darkness, stinking of failure and stale beer.

He stopped at the threshold, stunned for a moment by the brilliance of the sun. He pulled his hat brim lower, screwed his eyes against the light. Might as well go home. There was that piece of beef, a good-size bone with plenty of meat, just enough fat. To hell with his wife; dead drunk or wide-awake, he'd just pretend she wasn't there.

Hank passed the hulk of an old whale-ship and a row of derelict warehouses and turned right towards Bank Street, his attention fixed on the ground. Two years ago he'd found a dollar winking at him from a smear of mud right in the middle of the Bank Street sidewalk. If he kept close enough watch, he figured, something like that could happen again.

A glint of silver; he stopped short, covered it quickly with his foot. No one else was going to claim this prize. Hank bent over, pretended to fuss with his lace, slid his boot to the side, fingers itching for that dollar.

Glass. A goddamn piece of glass.

He could tell they were staring at him, laughing under their breath—the old man behind him, the two boys on his left, the woman on his right. The whole street was suddenly alive with the sound, a muffled hum of contempt.

Just get up and keep going. Don't let them think you care. Hank straightened, brushed the knee of his trousers, sauntered to the window of a nearby shop like he'd meant to do that all along.

At first all he saw his own reflection in the glass and he recognized it with some satisfaction. Given all he'd been through, not a bad-looking man. Then he noticed the display set up on a table just inside the window, a pyramid of canned fish, cracker boxes stacked neat as lumber, honey jars like soldiers in a row. Damn. With that dollar, he could have had a feast.

He took a step back, ready to leave, and as he turned his head, he noticed a poster stuck to the inside of the window, not two feet from his face.

$500 REWARD.

Five hundred dollars; what he wouldn't do with that. He'd quit his job, that much was certain. He'd go straight to old widow Weldin, tell her to find some other fool to work her farm for the pitiful wages she paid. He imagined the shocked look on her high-and-mighty face and the way the Weldin boy—a sicklier pup he never saw—would beg him to stay.

Hank pressed his hand against the glass, leaned closer.

Just below those big, black letters, some lines of smaller print.

Not much of a reader, but good enough when there was something worth reading. Lips moving, he sounded out each word to himself.

Miss Bertha Mellish, missing from Mount Holyoke College since Thursday, the 18th of November. No trace of her found since that day. Five feet five inches tall. Medium build. Dark auburn hair, pale complexion, brown eyes, round cheeks, full lips.

Five hundred dollars paid for the girl alive; one hundred dollars for her body. Amount to be paid by Rev. John H. Mellish of Dayville, Connecticut.

Five hundred goddamn dollars. What a pile of silver that would make.

At the bottom of the poster, a photograph of the girl's head and shoulders.

It hit him like a punch in the stomach and he staggered backward.

The strange girl at the Weldin farm who wouldn't give him the time of day, the girl who came out of nowhere, just showed up out of the blue on . . .on . . . He couldn't calculate the exact date he first saw her in the Weldin kitchen washing dishes, but he knew it wasn't very long ago. He squinted at the girl in the photograph and tried to remember what the other one looked like. This one—this Bertha Lane Mellish—maybe looked a little younger, maybe her face was rounder, but the longer he studied it the more certain he was that the girl on the poster and the girl at the farm were one and the same.

They had to be—a girl disappears one day, another one who looks like her shows up somewhere else a few days later.

Soon he'd scrounge together a few sheets of paper, find a pen, some ink, a pencil if need be, then he'd carry a letter to be mailed, hand over whatever postage they asked for, a small price to pay.

I know where she is, he'd write to the missing girl's father. But he wouldn't say exactly where—he knew how to play it smart, hold his cards close to the vest. Meet me in New London, he'd tell this Reverend Mellish, meet me at the depot and I'll take you to her.

Sunday, December 19, 1897

Although the engaged sign was gone, nothing within had been touched and everything, according to rumor, lay just as Bertha had left it a month before. Mary Bradford gripped the key in her shaking hand, reluctant to enter. For some of the students, the locked room, now a secret and forbidden place, held a certain romantic fascination, like the madwoman's attic in *Jane Eyre* or the banquet hall where Miss Havisham's wedding cake moldered. But Miss Bradford was too old for such imaginings, and she knew the room contained only the silent trappings of an abandoned life.

Perhaps it was too soon, she thought as she brought the key slowly towards the door, although she was certain Bertha was dead, and everyone she talked to—the teachers, that is, for she refused to speculate or gossip with the students—was certain as well. She wished Mrs. Mead had given this assignment to someone else. Bertha's trunk, brought up from the basement early that morning, sat next to her in the hall like a small black coffin.

But she knew that Mrs. Mead was right; the empty room was a constant and upsetting reminder to the students that one of their own was gone. And, as Mrs. Mead explained, it was unlikely Bertha would ever return to the college even if, God willing, she were still alive. Miss Bradford, despite her tender heart, realized like Mrs. Mead that sentiment must, at last, give way to stern reality. But her eyes filled as she turned the key in the lock, thinking how the poor family would feel, when the black trunk came home and their daughter did not.

February 20, 1915

That morning Florence could not manage the state of bland equilibrium she accepted as contentment. She moved restlessly from one chore to another until just after lunch, when she forced herself to sit at her writing desk. In the even gray light she picked up her pen.

Dear Miss Crewell,

You will pardon my delay in answering your kind note. I think, as you suggest, it might be best to omit my sister's name from the address book and later to place after her name in the general catalogue—'died in 1897'. I have had that date engraved on the family monument under her name.

I have no knowledge of my dear sister except what I could gather at the college soon after her disappearance, but I always think of her as dead. Her loss, as you can imagine, was a terrible tragedy in our family life and is to me a perpetual sorrow.

Yours very sincerely,
Florence Mellish

She had not meant to write anything as confessional as that final sentence, and considered crumpling the paper and starting again. Having never met Miss Crewell, she imagined her a youngish woman whose eyes would mist as she read these words. Florence was sure she would show it to her colleagues with a few sad shakes of her head.

It was this imagined sympathy that kept Florence from destroying the note. Since the death of her mother, who followed her father to the grave two years ago, she hadn't spoken to anyone about Bertha. She did, as she had written in her letter, think of her sister as dead. But she had not always thought so, as she claimed, and it had taken years of mental effort for her to believe what many others quickly accepted as fact. (Except, of course, those people who never would let go, that terrible Robinson man, still tormenting her with news of Bertha's whereabouts, claiming the reward he said was rightly his, or the woman who insisted she'd glimpsed Bertha in a Canadian madhouse, or the one who said she'd seen her in a jail in Illinois.)

Miss Crewell's gestures would be an acknowledgment of Florence's victory over pointless hope as well as a small tribute to Bertha's memory.

On the desk to Florence's left was a photograph, placed there when her sister left home for college. Although she never considered removing the picture, a few weeks after her mother's funeral, Florence quietly turned it so that Bertha faced the dark pockets of the desk. Dust had long since coated the glass and muted the color of the frame's dark wood. Bertha, impassive and serene, was barely visible beneath its soft blur.

Florence sealed her note to Miss Crewell and placed it on the desk. Moved by an impulse faster than thought, she picked up the photograph and wiped away its cottony film with her fingertips. In the ancient photograph, Bertha's face was turned to the side and her eyes were averted and heavily shadowed. Her lips curved in the slightest of smiles and her cheeks were full and smooth.

Florence thought of the small black trunk, resting as it had for nearly eighteen years, upstairs by the foot of Bertha's bed. Then she saw the gravestone, forever scarred with the date of her sister's vanishing. The walk to the cemetery would be cold, Florence knew, but she rose to get her coat.

The gravestone is solid granite, light gray speckled with black and pink, a heavy rectangular slab with a curved top. Danielson's New Westfield Cemetery is a flat, scrubby place filled with similar monuments. The picturesque old cemetery across the street, with its ancient oaks and its slate stones, its sweetly mournful angels and its elegant urns, was already full when Florence chose the plot, the day it became clear her father's illness would be his last. She bought room enough for four, though reason told her only three would lie there.

MELLISH is carved in low relief in graceless block letters along the top edge of the monument; even the S is angular. The dates of Reverend Mellish's birth and death and those of his wife are incised in the same stiff letters on the side of the stone facing the graves. Florence's name and the date of her birth, and the name and dates of her sister are on the other side.

The location of each parent's body in the ground below the monument is marked by a small square of granite, carved with initials and embedded in the snow-specked grass. John Mellish lies in the far right of the family plot, beyond the edge of the gravestone, and Sarah Mellish rests to his left, under its protection. They are a pair, husband and wife, and Florence thinks of the day when she and her marker she will complete this small, sad family.

She looks a little to the left, at the undisturbed ground beside her mother's stone. Someday I will lie there, she thinks, until she sees the unbroken field stretching outward from her future grave.

Florence recognizes the terrible asymmetry she has just decreed: three small blocks of granite, one beside the other, grouped forever in loving proximity. No, she shakes her head, I give the place beside our mother to Bertha. I will lie beyond, at the outer edge where I can stand guard over the empty ground between my mother and myself.

And when I'm gone, she thinks, every soul, living or dead, who sees that sheltered space will know: my sister has a home, whether she sleeps in it or not. And maybe, she hopes, more years from now than I can count, some fisherman, some hunter, some walker in the woods, will find Bertha and then she'll rest among us.

Florence kneels on the frozen ground; she does not feel its hardness or its chill. She closes her eyes, covers them with a black-gloved hand.

—ꟺ—

Bertha stands on the rocky outcropping of Titan's Pier, a safe distance from the edge. She faces the river. The wind plays with her hair and ruffles the hem of her skirt. It is chilly and almost dark, but she isn't cold. She wears gloves and a hat, and holds a book in one hand that hangs loosely at her side. The book might be a chemistry text or a Latin grammar. No—it contains poetry.

Her progress from the college to this place has been slow, rambling through fields and along the river. She is tired, but not fatigued, and happier than she has been for many weeks. The Founder's Day speeches would be over by then and the college would be eating, and she thinks of the tedium she has escaped. Bertha likes it there, alone, with no one to judge her, no one to scrutinize what she says or how she looks, no need to make awkward conversation. All the work she has to do is back in her room, and that room seems very far way.

The growing darkness does not frighten her, although perhaps it should. She feels brave to be in this high place with the broad river below and the mountains at her back. She thinks of her story, of Hilda and Marie, and feels a sudden recklessness. She takes a few steps forward, and then a few more, until she stands close enough to the edge to feel its pull. She wants to turn back, but is ashamed. Hilda followed Marie; what kind of coward is she to stop there?

The book in her hand disturbs her balance, but Bertha doesn't want to leave it on the ground. She inches forward, with her arms outstretched until there is nothing in front of her but air.

In that moment she feels as if gravity no longer holds her down, as if her body has shed all heaviness of bone and flesh, and she believes that if she steps forward she will float, a feathery seed released from its husk. The wind will catch her and take her, and she will surrender to its whim until it gently lays her down, somewhere she cannot anticipate or imagine, far from that place or any place she has ever known.

But the moment passes, and Bertha looks down towards the dark water that she can barely see. She has stayed too long, she realizes, and wonders if there will be a moon to light her way home. She wonders if she has been missed, and begins to shiver. It is colder now, and the wind is stronger.

Bertha turns to leave. Perhaps she turns too quickly. Perhaps her foot slips on a fragment of loose stone. Perhaps the wind catches her skirt and pushes her back. Florence sees the look on her face, more surprised than afraid, and then Bertha is gone. Beyond that, Florence has taught herself not to go.

A lthough based on a true story and extensive research, *The Button Field* is a work of fiction. Even those characters whose names are taken from real people—including Bertha Mellish– are figments of the author's imagination.

Before Bertha Lane Mellish left the campus of Mount Holyoke College on November 18, 1897, and was never heard from again, she wrote the story "La Petite" excerpted in these pages; the story was published in full in the *Willimantic (CT) Weekly Journal* on December 17, 1897. The letter addressed to Miss Crewell from Bertha's sister Florence is in the collection of the Mount Holyoke College Archives, South Hadley, Massachusetts, as is the photograph of the Class of 1899.

I am very grateful to Gerri Hutner and Amy Wallen for their careful reading of earlier versions of these pages and for their insightful comments. And I owe more thanks than I can express to Madison Smartt Bell for his inspirational teaching and his unflagging support.

To learn more about the actual Bertha Lane Mellish, her family and her story, please visit www.gailhusch.com.

Made in the USA
Charleston, SC
28 September 2014